D1178506

A MOTHER'S WAR

HELEN PARUSEL

Boldwood

First published in Great Britain in 2023 by Boldwood Books Ltd.

Copyright © Helen Parusel, 2023

Cover Design by Becky Glibbery

Cover Photography: Alamy and Shutterstock

Every effort has been made to obtain the necessary permissions with reference to copyright material, both illustrative and quoted. We apologise for any omissions in this respect and will be pleased to make the appropriate acknowledgements in any future edition.

A CIP catalogue record for this book is available from the British Library.

Paperback ISBN 978-1-83751-532-5

Large Print ISBN 978-1-83751-528-8

Hardback ISBN 978-1-83751-527-1

Ebook ISBN 978-1-83751-525-7

Kindle ISBN 978-1-83751-526-4

Audio CD ISBN 978-1-83751-533-2

MP3 CD ISBN 978-1-83751-530-1

Digital audio download ISBN 978-1-83751-524-0

Boldwood Books Ltd
23 Bowerdean Street
London SW6 3TN
www.boldwoodbooks.com

To Mum, who always believed I would someday write a book.

PART I

1

NARVIK, NORWAY, 9 APRIL 1940

220 km inside the Arctic Circle

The sounds of the fjord were different that night. Laila lay in bed, listening: a faint drone beneath the whine of the wind, a low hum from the churning sea. She heard a shout. Her body stiffened. More shouts. She kicked back her eiderdown and swung her feet onto the wooden floor. Her long, white nightdress twisted around her ankles as she darted to the window. Ice and snow covered the glass. She pulled at the window but the old frame jammed. A jiggle and a yank; she forced it open. Raw air gushed in and covered her face in a cold mist.

Through the swirl of snowflakes, she saw a mass of grey-black silhouettes hulking across the fjord. People with torches and binoculars were gathered along the shore. A man pointed and the crowd ran from the water's edge.

Laila gripped the windowsill, digging her nails into the splintered paint. Her eyes searched the darkness. A deep roar erupted and echoed across the fjord; a shape on the water exploded and flames split open the night sky, illuminating the scene.

Battle ships. Rows of them.

Battle ships looming over the fishing boats that leaped and rolled in the storm beneath the snow-tipped mountains.

She watched transfixed, unable to move or think until her bedroom door flew open. Mama, small and grey, stood in the doorway, the neck of her nightdress clutched in her hands. Her voice shook. 'My God, what's happening?'

As Laila reached for her, a blast shook the house; vibrations shuddered through her body. She swung back to the window; nearby houses crackled orange, dense black smoke spiralled above. Horrified, she saw the Andersen family topple out the front door of their burning home.

Laila froze.

Heartbeats passed.

Something inside her shifted and adrenalin ignited.

Papa wasn't here. She must act. Get the family to safety.

She strode over to her mother and grabbed her shoulders. 'Mama, we have to leave. Now.'

Light, swift footsteps. Olaf, in his red pyjamas. 'Is it the Germans? Are they here? Or have the British come?'

'I don't know. We must get out of here.'

Hanna ran in with their baby sister cradled in her arms.

'Get dressed, everyone,' Laila said. 'Quickly, your warmest clothes. We'll meet in the kitchen. Hurry.'

Laila took baby Inge from Hanna and propelled the family down the hall. She tore off her nightdress, climbed into ski pants, and swathed the baby in blankets, hugging her against her chest. She rushed down the narrow stairs. With the family now dressed and gathered in the kitchen, Hanna glared at Laila.

'We can't just leave,' she said. 'That's crazy. Where should we go?'

'We'll go to Aunt Kirsten. It'll be safer away from the coast.'

'But Papa took the car.'

'We'll walk.'

'No. It's too far. We should go to the cellar and wait for Papa.'

'And wait till the house collapses on top of us?'

Laila turned to her mother and clasped her hands. 'Are you strong enough to walk, Mama? Could you—'

'Of course she's not,' snapped Hanna. 'She's still recovering from—'

A flash of light, the earth trembled, the window shattered, and their six blue coffee mugs tumbled from the shelf and smashed onto the floor. The family stumbled into the hall, plucking coats and scarves from hooks on the wall, and Laila took her father's torch. Then she grabbed some paper and a pen from the commode and scribbled a note.

The lamp with the beige, fringed shade lay on the floor. Mama gazed at it a moment, picked it up, and placed it back on top of the commode.

Moments later, they stepped out into a blizzard of snow and ash. Laila's throat burned from the smoke; her eyes watered. A blur of images swirled around her: people ploughing through the freshly fallen snow, small children in their arms, or pulling sledges bearing elderly and infirm relatives; the timber houses aflame, the wind flinging snowflakes and burning embers into tornados of black speckled with white.

Worst of all was the noise. The boom of the explosions and the staccato of gunfire that bounced between the mountains. But the most terrifying sound was the wail of men, which the wind tossed through the air from the sea.

The caravan of bundled figures trudged through the snow, stooped against the storm. Ahead of Laila, a small child flung over a man's shoulder dropped a doll which had been dangling from one mittened hand. The child wailed as the father, busy shouting instructions to the rest of his family, strode on. Laila, clutching Inge tight, bent down and scooped the doll from the snow, and stomped as fast as she could after the child. Laila's breaths came in short, painful smoke-filled gasps. Coming up behind the father, she held up the doll to the child's outstretched arms. The child choked back a last sob, clutched the doll with both hands, and gazed at Laila as she and her father headed on. Laila turned back to her own family.

At a crossroads outside of town, the caravan split up in different directions. Laila and her family departed along a narrow, winding country road. They were on their own.

Away from the blaze of the port, the path darkened, and Laila flicked on the torch. The note she had left said they were on their way to Aunt Kirsten. Maybe Papa had already seen it and was on his way with the car; headlights would appear behind them, and they would all pile in with relief at being with Papa again. Safe.

But they heard no engine. They saw no lights.

Laila led the way, baby Inge in the crook of her left arm and the torch in her right hand, swaying the beam from side to side, keeping them on the snow-entrenched road that wound between the trees. They followed the small circle of light, a pinprick amid the towering pines that massed like implacable guards alongside them.

'Stop.'

Laila turned at her sister's shout. Mama had dropped to her knees in the snow, her arms still linked to Hanna on one side and Olaf on the other. Laila stamped back, treading through her own footprints, watching her siblings try to hoist Mama back to her feet, but her limp body sagged between them. Fear twisted in

Laila's belly. Fear as cold as the Arctic wind that whipped around them in circles. Had she made a terrible mistake leading her sick mother into the freezing night? Her impulse had been for the family to flee the flames. What if her mother died here?

'Mama, Mama.' Laila balanced Inge on her hip, and with her free hand helped to hoist Mama, then dragged her to a fallen tree trunk beside the road. With a sweep of her arm, Hanna cleared the snow, and they lowered their mother onto the log. Laila shone the torch on Mama's face; her skin was translucent, her frosted lips purple-blue. Snowflakes clung to her closed eyelashes. The children called her name again and again, but she didn't reply. They rubbed her hands, her arms, her face. Olaf screamed his mother was dead. But no. They could see her wisps of breath.

'Mama, please,' Laila said through numb lips. She massaged her mother's chest. They couldn't lose Mama. Mama, who knitted Selbu rose pullovers, baked *pannekaken* with blueberries and spoke of mystical folktales; trolls and *huldra*.

Mama moaned, her eyes fluttering open. 'Please. A short rest. Please.'

In the sallow torch light, Laila saw Hanna's hard, accusing stare. Laila looked away and upwards; the sky had cleared, and a half moon cast a watery, silver glow on the shifting snow. It was Anton who should have been here to make the decisions. Pain jabbed at her heart. How she missed her elder brother.

When Mama could stand again, they continued their journey. Laila focused on counting her steps, her boots scrunching hollows in the snow. She liked the soothing rhythm of counting. One step, then another. She and Hanna, their arms under Mama's shoulders. Olaf carrying Inge, who cried and whimpered and slept.

'Nearly there,' repeated Laila over and over. 'Nearly there.'

The torch light dimmed and flickered. It flickered again. And was gone. Laila halted and shook the torch, beat it against the palm of her hand, then flung it to the ground.

Darkness.

Hanna cried out.

Laila strained her eyes, making out the jagged outlines of mountains, backlit by the palest glow. 'We'll make it. The sun is rising.'

* * *

Aunt Kirsten flew out the door in her dressing gown, her slippers disappearing into the soft snow. 'Thank God you're here! Uncle has been listening to the BBC.' Then reaching for her sister, 'Astrid, let's get you inside. Where is Ivar?'

'Papa drove to see Grandpa yesterday, but we haven't heard from them,' answered Laila.

Aunt Kirsten ushered them into the sitting room, lit the fire, and served steaming fish soup whilst Uncle twirled the dials of his radio searching for the latest news.

Late morning, Laila heard the rumble of a car motor and the crunch of snow. Everyone rushed to the front door and there stood Papa with Grandpa. Screams of delight followed, then hugs and tears. Laila was weak with relief to have the family reunited.

No one left the farmhouse for five days. What started as a hum soon became a roar as each day, planes flew overhead. The family huddled around Uncle's radio, desperate for news; BBC London announced that Norway, a neutral country, had been invaded by Germany. Local radio, now under German control, instructed Norwegians to carry on their *normal* lives and continue working. They had nothing to fear if the German rules were obeyed.

Our normal lives? Laila was bewildered. Nothing about their lives was normal now.

Papa decided to drive into Narvik to see what was going on, praying their house was still standing. He was also anxious to see if the sardine factory he managed had been hit. Laila and Hanna begged to accompany him, desperate to know what had happened to their home, their friends, and neighbours. At first, he said it was too dangerous, but then relented. The three of them set off on a sunny, cool morning, waving limply to the rest of the family gathered on the doorstep.

They saw the first soldiers at a roadblock to the town. They wore long, grey-green, belted coats and round helmets, and carried rifles strung over their shoulders on brown leather straps. A soldier raised his arm in a gesture for them to stop. He approached the car and Laila watched his rifle swing as Papa wound down the window.

'*Ausweis, bitte.*' The soldier held out his hand.

Laila's father rummaged around in his coat pocket for his papers. The soldier studied the documents and peered into the car, his gaze flitting between the sisters. Did his glance at Hanna linger a moment too long? Laila's chest tightened. He was young, about the same age Anton had been.

The soldier waved them through. He *allowed* them to pass. How dare this invader order them around in their own land. What right did he have?

As they drove through Narvik, Laila gaped out the window: smouldering buildings, houses turned to charcoal, and rubbles of stone piled along the roadside. The air was laden with grey-black ash. Soldiers stood on patrol or marched the streets, their stiff legs encased in long black boots. Laila's eyes swam with tears. She didn't recognise this place.

They passed the town hall where above the entrance, a blood-red flag cracked in the wind, the black swastika leering out at her. Bile rose in her throat.

Her world tilted. Everything she'd known and understood had crumbled, the ruins of a life reflected in the debris that surrounded her.

As they approached the harbour, the carnage spread before them: burned-out boats and debris from supply ships littered the water; a partly submerged destroyer lay flipped on its side like the dead pilot whale Laila had seen last winter. They rounded the Ofotfjord and headed towards home.

The mountains soared from the navy sea, crags of bare rock jutting through the snow. These mountains that Grandpa said were trolls that had turned to stone. These mountains, Laila's mountains, now brooded at the destruction below.

The trolls were watching.

Papa slowed the car. Close to the water, the ruins of their neighbours' houses stood like blackened skeletons, their disjointed limbs naked in bizarre poses. Laila could hardly bear to look out the window.

Then she saw a house still standing.

And another.

She held her breath.

And there stood their two-story, green, wooden home.

'Thank God,' Laila murmured to herself.

The house was blackened, the windows shattered, but the structure appeared intact. It looked tired but defiant. Worn but strong. Laila was overcome by the pull of the emotional bond she felt with her home as if it were the core of her existence.

Her father parked and they all climbed out.

Laila took a deep breath but instead of tasting sea salt on her tongue, it was ash. She looked at the rowan tree that stood guard over their home, its bark and branches singed. The rowan tree they always danced around on Midsummer's Eve, the girls wearing garlands of flowers in their hair. Would the branches sprout feathery leaves this spring? Would they bear blood-red berries in autumn?

Papa pushed open the front door and they entered, taking in the chaos: splintered glass and ash-smeared walls.

Laila hauled out the cleaning supplies and they set to work.

2

MAY–JULY 1940

Laila and her father pulled up in his black Volvo outside the Hotel Nordic where Laila worked. Over the entrance, the German flag whipped back and forth in the wind. Laila wondered what fate had met the Norwegian flag that had flown outside the building for the last thirty years. She turned to face Papa as he switched off the engine. As always, he wore a hat and a three-piece suit with matching waistcoat, today with a white shirt that Laila had ironed that morning.

'Take care, Laila. If the sirens sound, go to the hotel cellar immediately.'

'Papa, I don't want to work for the Germans. Maybe I'll quit and find work elsewhere.'

'You can't leave without serious repercussions. And where would you find a job? The Germans are controlling all businesses now. Keep your head down and try to carry on as normal.'

Normal. That absurd word again.

She kissed him on his cheek. 'Have a good day, Papa.'

She climbed out and hurried up the steps, rummaging for her pass in her handbag. It was an outrage to have to show the soldier on duty identity papers. In her country. She determined not to look at him. When he said, '*Guten Morgen*', far too politely, she stared at a point above his round helmet; it looked like her mother's cake mixing bowl. Her fingers trembled as she held out her pass and a gust of wind whipped it from her grasp. The soldier sprang after it and returned it to her. She was forced to look at him.

Dark eyes. Thick lashes.

He gave her a gentle smile. Did he expect a thank you? She said nothing and, shoving her pass back in her bag, she swept past him.

There was a lot to do today. She had to ensure that the thirty rooms were clean and ready for the German officers arriving that afternoon. All the other guests had been ordered to leave; the hotel had been requisitioned as quarters for the German *Wehrmacht*.

Laila and the housekeeper, Sigrid, surveyed each room, checking under the beds for dust and the bathroom for clean towels. Sigrid muttered and shook her head. She had worked there for twenty years. How could such a thing happen, here, in Norway? Everyone had heard what had happened in Poland, of course. But here? And to think that the king and the royal family were forced to flee the palace in Oslo.

Laila straightened the curtains, looked towards the bedroom door, and lowered her voice.

'It won't last. Our troops are gathering, and people are joining the resistance. And the British will help.'

'Help? From the British? How does it help bombing Narvik to smithereens and killing us all off?'

Laila had no answer.

Her stomach had been churning all morning in anticipation of the arriving officers. She had one final task to perform: organising the staff to fit blackout blinds on all the windows. The German command had been specific about this regulation.

At lunch time, she took a short break and walked around the

block. The air was so thick with grime, she could taste it. Rubble littered what remained of the pavement. A woman and a young boy were heaving debris with their bare hands into a wheelbarrow. Laila stopped beside them and giving them a weak smile, lifted some stones too. They worked in silence for a short while before Laila nodded goodbye and headed back towards the hotel.

As she turned the street corner, she saw a German soldier addressing three children. A girl was wiping tears from her eyes and the two older boys stood solemnly staring at their shoes. Laila gritted her teeth. A German harassing children. Despicable. Striding towards the group, she saw it was the same soldier who had retrieved her pass that morning.

In her best school German, she said, 'What are you doing to these children?' She hated the tremor in her voice. That she was afraid.

He looked surprised. 'Nothing. I—'

'What's the problem here?' said Laila, addressing the children in Norwegian.

The girl spoke up. 'The boys were trying to take the sweets a German soldier gave me earlier. They got some too, but they want mine as well and that's not fair because they're mine.'

'Yeah, but you got more than us,' the taller boy said.

'I did not.' The girl stamped her foot. 'Anyway, this soldier saw the boys pushing me around and stopped them.'

Laila looked at the soldier whose bewildered expression told her he didn't speak Norwegian. Surprise took the place of her anger.

'So, you are trying to help out here?' said Laila in German.

'Yes,' he said, digging out a handful of sweets from his trouser pocket. 'I have enough for everyone.'

He divided the sweets, placed them in the children's upturned palms, and waved them off. Laila watched them scamper away with mixed emotions. Buying favour with a few sweets didn't seem right somehow. But at least he hadn't been threatening the children.

'Let me introduce myself. My name is Private Josef Schultz. We met this morning.'

She was speechless. He spoke as if they were meeting at a dinner party. Not as an aggressor she had to show her papers to.

In the absence of knowing what else to say, she replied, 'I'm Miss Laila Olson, the reception manager.' To her horror, she felt a flush creep up her throat.

'Pleased to meet you,' he said, formally.

This was too ridiculous. Laila nodded, saying she must get back to work, and then walked on.

Later that afternoon, Laila heard a commotion outside the hotel: a rumble of car engines, orders barked in German, the opening and closing of car doors, and the trample of boots on the hotel steps.

The manager ran out of his office, buttoning up his jacket. 'Call the staff, Laila. Quick. Everyone has been ordered to welcome the officers.'

Welcome? Laila chewed the inside of her cheek. She snatched a couple of breaths to calm herself and rang the small brass bell on the reception desk. Staff bustled into the entrance hall and the manager ushered them into two lines on each side of the entrance. Laila stood with the manager and the housekeeper at the top of the steps outside.

The officers were wearing crisp, new uniforms: jackets adorned with coloured stripes and metal pins, and riding pants ballooning over tops of boots polished to an impossible shine. Laila was not sure if the nausea she felt was fear or revulsion.

An officer shook the manager's hand, and the Germans were led inside past the waiting employees. The soldiers nodded in greeting. Some even smiled. For a wild moment, Laila had the urge to turn her back on the soldiers. She had heard stories of villagers in the south of Norway lining the streets, their backs to the incoming army. But she did not turn. She would find other ways of defiance. Her cheeks flamed as they passed by, but she met their eye.

The manager called Laila to his office where he introduced her to Herr Major Haas. The officer was broad, from his chest to his forehead.

'This is my assistant, Miss Laila Olson,' the manager said. 'She will make sure you and the other officers have everything you require.'

'*Guten Tag*, Fräulein Olson,' said Major Haas.

Fräulein? How she hated the sound of her name from his thick lips. She gave a curt reply. The manager glowered at her, willing her to offer more than a *good afternoon*, but she remained silent. The major's smile dropped and he gave a sharp nod as dismissal. As she left the office, she noticed sweat had pooled under her armpits, dampening her grey wool dress.

At five o'clock, she collected her coat and left the hotel. Josef Schultz stood at the entrance. In spite of herself, she glanced at him. He wished her a good evening. Bizarre under the circumstances. She didn't reply. Why did he have to be so damn polite?

Her father was parked outside. They would pick up Hanna from where she worked at the tailor's shop and drive back to the countryside where they were still living with Aunt Kirsten.

'Papa, when can we return home? It's been a month now,' she said as they drove off.

'It's not safe yet, with the continual air raids from the British. It terrifies me enough that the Germans insist you work. At least you're safe at night.'

'How long will it take to drive the Germans out? What will happen to us all if they stay?'

But Papa just shook his head, murmuring he didn't know.

They drove in silence. Traffic had increased in Narvik. Laila watched military trucks trundle by, motorbikes speed past, those with ridiculous sidecars that the Germans were so fond of. Soldiers patrolled on huge, intimidating horses that had been brought by ship.

After a while, Papa said, 'What's the matter with you and Hanna? You barely speak to each other any more.'

'Hanna's angry that I made us leave the house. She says I risked Mama's life when she is so fragile. Did I make the right decision?'

'You did fine, Laila. You're a sensible girl. Reliable. You always were...' His voice trailed off as he became distracted by the sight of a tank, which dwarfed them as it passed by.

Eventually, they pulled up outside the tailor's shop and waited for Hanna. She appeared, nudging the door open with her foot as she struggled with a large, white box. The dresses. Laila felt a wave of affection for her sister and determined to try to get on better with her.

* * *

After a supper of fish dumplings, swedes, and carrots, the family retired to the sitting room whilst Hanna stayed in the kitchen, working at her aunt's sewing machine. Laila watched her from the doorway. She was intent on her work, feeding the fabric expertly under the needle. Her hair, dark and wavy like their father's, had fallen forward over the left side of her face. She was a pretty girl, as everyone said, and at the age of sixteen had a fuller, rounder figure than Laila. She looked like a woman, thought Laila, wincing at the thought of her own flat chest.

Hanna didn't hear her approach over the clack-clack of the machine.

'It's beautiful,' said Laila, appraising the *bunad* Hanna was working on.

'I promised you it would be finished for the National Day celebrations,' said Hanna, looking up. 'Of course, when I started, we couldn't imagine how life would change. I'm going to finish it anyway.' She slipped the material out of the machine and handed it to Laila, who held the dress against her. It was royal-blue wool, buttoned to a fitted waist and had a full, pleated skirt. She would wear it with a white puffed sleeve blouse and the apron embroidered by her grandmother.

'They may forbid the celebrations, but they can't forbid me from wearing my new dress. You're so talented, Hanna, thank you.' Laila leaned down and placed a kiss on her sister's cheek. Seeing her surprise, Laila said, 'I'm sorry things have been so difficult between us. We're all under such strain. Can we try to get on better? We need to stick together. As a family.'

Hanna smiled and stood up, opening her arms. 'You're right. Family is important.'

'Family is everything,' said Laila.

As they embraced, the tightness in Laila's chest softened. Perhaps things would improve between them.

* * *

When Laila and Hanna left the house the next morning, their father had just finished washing and polishing the car. He stood back proudly, inviting comment.

'How grand we will look arriving in Narvik, Papa,' said Hanna.

'You must've been up early,' said Laila.

'I couldn't sleep. Hop in, my princesses.'

The three drove off in a brief lightness of mood.

First, Papa dropped Hanna off at the tailor's shop, and then drove Laila to the hotel. 'Papa, what is happening with the resistance? Surely, we must do something too?'

'There is a movement growing,' he replied. 'Be patient. But your priority is to keep safe. Don't antagonise the Germans. Leave resistance to others. Obey the rules.'

Her jaw tightened. *Obey the rules.* She would follow Papa's advice. On the surface. But she could not remain passive. She would find out more about this resistance movement.

As she climbed out of the car, she saw Major Haas at the top of the stairs, his brown briefcase clutched under his arm, talking to Josef Schultz. Haas studied her as she climbed the steps and then stared after her father as he drove off.

'Who brought you to work, Fräulein Olson?' he asked.

'My father,' she said as politely as she could.

'Nice *auto*.' His thick lips attempted a smile, but the result was a bizarre grimace.

* * *

When they got home, Uncle was twirling dials on his radio.

'Is there news?' Laila asked.

'King Haakon has sent out an appeal from hiding, telling Norwegians to join their local forces and retaliate. Our young men are gathering in the mountains, preparing for battle.'

'Can we win? We must win. It can't go on like this.' Laila looked at her father.

He sighed. 'We don't have the military equipment the Germans have. But we know these mountains and the Germans underestimate us. I pray we have a chance.'

'You won't fight, will you? Please don't think about fighting.'

Laila grabbed his hand. He gave her a smile that didn't reach his eyes but said nothing.

That night, Laila lay awake for hours. How could this be happening? Norway was a peace-loving nation; it had remained neutral in World War One. They didn't want to be involved. In any of it. It was so unfair.

She cringed at her own childishness; she sounded like Olaf. The king had called on the people to fight. Would her father join up? She felt a chill. What if he never came back?

Much later, she drifted into a sleep where blackened buildings were silhouetted against the dust sky shrouding the fjord, where soldiers marched and hung their alien flags on buildings that didn't belong to them, and people were told where they could stand. Families stared at piles of rubble that were once their homes.

* * *

The sun shone through the windows on National Day. Laila entered the bright kitchen in the new *bunad* Hanna had sewn for her. Papa looked up from his newspaper and gave the broadest smile she had seen from him since the invasion. 'My beautiful girl.'

She was surprised. Her father's unfamiliar words stirred a rare joy. Warmth enveloped her and for a moment there was no world outside, just her and Papa. She twirled around for him, spreading the pleats of the skirt. He reached out his arms and she skipped over to hug him, wishing this moment would last forever.

The rest of the family gathered, dressed in their best clothes. It was National Day and they would celebrate in spite of the occupation. Hanna arrived last, sweeping in, dressed in an emerald-green *bunad*, the bodice trimmed in velvet. Her hips swayed and her skirt swirled. Everyone exclaimed: she was stunning, she looked like a film star. What needlework. So skilful.

Laila busied herself with the coffee pot.

The women tied aprons over their dresses and prepared the celebration brunch. Officially, National Day had been cancelled, but some Norwegians were still able to take a day off work and honour the day at home with their families.

The table was spread with traditional food: smoked salmon, scrambled eggs, and cured ham. Olaf and his cousins rummaged around in wooden boxes, digging out small Norwegian flags on sticks and a string of bunting in national colours. Hanna stood the flags in a stone jug on the table, and Laila and her mother hung the bunting on the kitchen wall. Grandpa was there too, playing folk tunes on his harmonica. Despite his memory lapses, he didn't miss a note.

Aunt Kirsten had invited a local family who Laila had known since her childhood. They arrived with a basket of gifts: home-made jams, freshly baked biscuits, and bread. Aunt Kirsten was particularly pleased with the latter, commenting that flour was becoming scarce. Laila wondered what they would eat when their supply of bread ran out.

The eldest son of the visiting family was Karl, whom Laila hadn't seen since he had left to study in Oslo. In the three years since she had seen him last, he had grown tall, broad, and hand-some. A memory came of a hot summer day, of Karl chasing her and Hanna through long grass to the water's edge. The girls, in matching red swimsuits, had jumped into the cold, clear water, shrieking. Karl had torn off his shirt and, still wearing his trousers, plunged in after them. In a few swift strokes, he had caught up with Laila and wrapped his arms around her. She had noticed that the blond hair on his forearms had gone dark in the water. He was fifteen.

Now they sat next to each other. He told her about how the Germans had met little resistance when they sailed into Oslo, enabling them to take swift control. There had been little damage to the capital and under the new regime daily life had more or less resumed. He was shocked to hear Laila's eyewitness account of the invasion of Narvik and the fierce battle that had ensued.

She inquired about his life at university. There had been a time when she'd hoped to study literature, she told him. Or languages. She'd enjoyed English and German at school.

'I would've liked to become a teacher,' she said.

'Really? Most of the teachers I know are men.'

'Exactly. But times are changing.'

'Why didn't you go on to study?'

'I couldn't leave the family. After Anton.'

Laila had decided at an early age that she wanted to be a teacher. She liked children. She'd planned to study at Tromso Teachers Training College. But after that devastating midsummer's night, her plans had been sucked into a chasm of grief as if they'd never existed.

'I'm sorry about Anton,' said Karl. 'It's been nearly two years, hasn't it?'

Laila gave a nod, suddenly aware that Hanna was watching them from across the table.

There was a rumble outside. Everyone stopped talking and looked at each other. The switching off of a car engine. The clunk of car doors.

'Germans,' said Uncle, peering out the window. Aunt Kirsten snatched the flags from the jug and threw them into the cupboard under the sink.

Three thumps on the door.

Laila looked up at the red and blue bunting strung along the wall and half rose to pull it down, but Uncle was already saying good afternoon and stepping aside to allow two soldiers to enter the room. Laila's heart jumped. The one with more stripes and metal pinned on his jacket was Major Haas. Two steps behind him stood Josef, looking solemn.

Haas, a slight smirk on his face, spoke. 'Please excuse the intrusion. This is a brief visit.' He surveyed the room and studied the food-laden table. 'It appears I have disturbed a celebration.'

'No,' said Aunt Kirsten, 'a normal family meal.'

'Then you have a large family. And an abundance of food in these difficult times.'

'We grow our own vegetables. And we have a cow, four pigs, and twelve chickens.'

'How enterprising. That is good to know.'

He turned to the bunting.

'It appears you have made a mistake. The colours displayed on your wall are incorrect.'

Silence.

Laila's breaths sounded loud in her ears.

No one spoke.

Major Haas continued to stare at the bunting. Laila cleared her throat.

'Herr Major Haas. What a coincidence to see you here. Can I offer you something to drink?'

He ignored her, took three swift strides towards the bunting, and tore it down, knocking over a vase as he did so, which broke apart as it hit the floor.

'How dare you?' Uncle's voice shook. 'This is my house. I must ask you to leave.'

'Leave?' Haas gave a mock smile, shaking his head. 'You don't seem to understand the situation. I am the one who gives the orders here.' He stood in front of Uncle, his heavy frame twice the size.

'Not in my home,' said Uncle.

Papa moved to stand by his brother-in-law. 'Nazis are not welcome here.'

Haas's arm catapulted forward, his fist thumping into Papa's stomach.

Laila cried out as she watched her father fall to his knees. Haas looked down at him, and with a casual flick of his boot sent him sprawling onto his back. A terrible commotion followed. Mama screamed. Josef, his face shocked, stepped forward, and Karl sprang from the table, charging at Haas, and struck him on the shoulder.

Haas drew his pistol and aimed at Karl's head.

Everyone froze. The room fell silent.

'You are under arrest for attacking an officer of the *Wehrmacht*.' He held the gun steady at Karl, giving a swift glance at Josef. 'Private Schultz. Take this man into custody.'

Laila caught Josef's eye. His hesitation was minimal, but Laila saw it, before Josef stepped forward and took Karl by the arm. Karl offered no resistance as Josef led him to the door.

Haas announced he had merely wanted to deliver a letter to a certain Ivar Olson. He dropped the envelope on the floor beside Papa. Then he wished them all an enjoyable afternoon and left.

Anger and hate pulsed through Laila. It was an ugly, powerful emotion she'd never felt before. But at that moment, it made her strong. She made a decision. She would fight back. Whatever the cost.

When Papa had recovered enough, he opened the envelope and slid the letter out, his hand shaking. He read the few lines and looked around the table. 'My Volvo has been requisitioned by the Third Reich. But that's hardly important now.' He looked across at Karl's sobbing mother. 'All that matters is getting Karl back.'

* * *

Laila finished work and made her way to the bus stop to meet Papa and Hanna, her mind whirling with the events that had occurred on National Day. It had been a week and there had been no news of Karl. It was terrifying to think what may have happened to him. And over and over again, she thought of Papa on his knees, gasping for breath.

Suddenly, an ear-piercing shriek split the air: the air raid siren. All around her, people were running for cover. Her best protection would be to go back to the hotel, to the cellar, but what about Papa and Hanna? They might be already waiting for her. If she ran to meet them, they could all duck down behind the bus station, but that was nowhere near as safe as a cellar. Or they could run to the tailor's shop where Hanna worked and shelter there in the basement, but for Laila that was further than heading back to the hotel.

Bombs fell. Precious moments slipped past. The drone of aircraft approached.

A high-pitched whistle.

Artillery fire cracked through the air. The noise was behind her and in front of her, and to her left. Something knocked her off her feet and she dropped to the ground, scraping her hands on loose stones. She was pushed down the grass verge dipping off to her right and rolled down the wet slope. She lay on her side as someone rolled next to her, and then over her.

She couldn't hear what he was saying, but she knew his voice.

Josef.

'Please God, make this stop,' she prayed.

He held her tight as explosions shook the ground.

She didn't know how long they lay there.

And then all went quiet.

Josef took his arms from her and sat up. 'Are you hurt, Fräulein Olson?'

For a moment, she was too dazed to reply and struggled to sit up.

'Are you all right, Laila?' he asked, his voice full of concern.

He had called her Laila. She looked at him. 'Where did you come from? What happened?'

'I was on my way back to the barracks when the air raid started. You were just standing there. I'm sorry if I hurt you when I pushed you to the ground.' She looked at her grass-smeared knees and felt the sting of her grazed palms.

'I'm fine. I must get to the shop.'

Her initial relief that the bombing had stopped turned to fear as she noted the silence. What would she find? Had Papa and Hanna been hurt? Or worse? Josef stood and reached out a hand in an offer of help, but she shook her head and scrambled to stand up. Her legs felt weak.

As they climbed back up the ditch, she gulped in deep breaths, but the acrid smoke choked her lungs, causing her to cough till her throat was raw. Josef, his voice hoarse, said he would accompany her to meet up with her family.

'After what happened on National Day, I shouldn't think for one moment that they would want to see you.' She strode down the street, yet he continued to walk along beside her.

'I must sincerely apologise about what happened at your uncle's home. Major Haas's behaviour was inexcusable. I'm so sorry about your father. We have been instructed to treat Norwegians with consideration and respect and to maintain good relations.'

She gave a hard laugh. 'Haas beat and humiliated my father! And what's happened to Karl? You marched him out of the house.'

'I'm hoping he'll be released. I think I may have been able to persuade Major Haas not to press charges, to prevent any further unrest. Especially as the event took place in a private home with so many witnesses. It's not an image we want to portray.'

'Really? And what sort of image does Germany want to portray when it invades a country?'

Josef did not reply, and they hurried on in silence.

The town centre had been badly hit but the small row of buildings with the tailor's shop still stood. Once they were outside the shop, Josef departed. Laila pushed open the door and was met by a stream of people leaving the cellar. The last to come up were Papa and Hanna. They rushed towards her, hugging and crying, and thanking God.

That evening, the family gathered around Uncle's radio. Germany announced a victorious battle in Narvik and advances in France.

Uncle shook his head. 'The situation has escalated. Narvik is a battle zone.'

'We are all to stay here for the next few days. No one is going to work,' said Papa.

'But the British Navy will beat the Germans, won't they Papa?' said Olaf.

'I hope so, but they have their own problems in France.'

'There is one piece of good news at least,' said Uncle. 'Karl was released unharmed today.'

'Thank God,' said Papa and patted his stomach, 'and my bruises are fading. But he sure packs a punch, the major.' He gave a wry smile.

As Laila drifted off to sleep that night, she thought of Josef's body pressed against hers as the bombs rained down around them.

She thought of his deep voice and the musk of his sweat mixed with the faintest hint of citrus cologne.

Five days later, Laila listened as a BBC newscaster announced that the British had pulled out of Norway and were deploying all troops to Dunkirk.

Norway was on its own.

3

JULY–AUGUST 1940

Laila cycled past another poster proclaiming 'The New Order' under which the Norwegians were instructed to live. She had counted seven so far. Every tree and lamp post, it seemed, had a board strapped to it dictating a list of rules and regulations to be followed. Orders of how many people were allowed to gather in one place, and for how long. Orders on when people must return home in the evening and when they could leave the house in the morning. Orders dictating which radio station to listen to, what food they could buy, and how much.

It was surreal.

Turning from the harbour, she cycled down a narrow street between the warehouses. The usual wind tunnel greeted her and she picked up her pace, her long legs pumping furiously to keep warm in the chill of the early morning.

They had been back home in Narvik for two weeks following Norway's capitulation; the fighting had stopped, more troops had poured into town, patrolling the streets, and the locals carried on with their lives with pale, stunned faces.

The Germans liked to march and sing. Their favourite tune

was, 'When we go, when we go, when we go to England.' Laila liked to imagine them marching into the North Sea and disappearing beneath the waves. Something biblical in that.

Their home had survived but they'd found it in a terrible state. Ash smothered the furniture, floors, and walls. Broken glass lay scattered around, shards embedded in cushions and carpets. Mama was terrified to put baby Inge down anywhere. The whole family toiled to restore order. They swept, washed, and scrubbed. Papa, with help from his friends from the factory, replaced the windows. The next job, planned for the weekend, was to paint the outside of the house. Uncle would bring spare paint he had at the farmhouse.

Laila parked her bicycle in the shed at the side of the Hotel Nordic and headed to the entrance. Josef was on duty. She felt suddenly too warm in her wool jacket as she hurried past him remembering what she'd dreamed last night.

Seated at reception, she saw the comings and goings of the officers, heard their German voices, saw their rifles on their shoulders and pistols at their waists.

She had enjoyed her job at the busy hotel, greeting the guests, many of whom were merchants involved in shipping fish or iron ore. It was satisfying to keep everything in order, and she liked the staff. But now the sound of boots stomping past jarred her nerves and she was grateful when it was time to do her rounds with the housekeeper and hand over the reception to another member of staff.

The housekeeper, Sigrid, had plenty to say as they walked down the hallway on the first floor, past the chambermaids unloading fresh towels from a trolley.

'How could the king surrender our country? They say he escaped to London.'

'I think he had no choice but to surrender,' Laila replied. 'Our young men were outnumbered and being slaughtered. But King Haakon and the British are supporting the resistance. Help will come. It must.'

Sigrid opened a room with her master key and cast a glance around. The room was tidy and sparse of belongings. On the narrow desk lay a pack of cigarettes next to a small radio. Laila and Sigrid entered the neighbouring room. Again, there was little of note, except a small picture frame on the bedside table. A black and white photograph of a young woman wearing a large, brimmed hat, slightly tilted, and on her arm a small fair-haired boy displaying a gap-toothed grin. The sight of the picture made Laila's stomach churn, but she couldn't identify why.

Most of the staff ate in the kitchen but Laila, the manager, and Sigrid had been allocated a small table in the corner of the restaurant where the officers ate. Laila liked to eat alone whilst looking at a book that she lay open in front of her. She occasionally turned a page as if reading, but in reality, she was straining to hear the officers' conversations, eager to hear anything that might be useful. Hopefully they would underestimate her knowledge of German, and sooner or later let something important slip.

If she gleaned any information, she would speak to her best friend Oda who'd said her brother Finn wanted to get involved in resistance. The picture of Papa on his knees haunted her. But also made her determined. She would use her position at the hotel to do something meaningful for her country. Although she'd heard nothing of interest from the officers that day, she decided to visit Oda anyway.

As she walked to see Oda after work, she spotted a giant iron ore freighter at the harbour being loaded with a supply that had just arrived from Kiruna, Sweden. Laila perched on a low wall to watch and sighed. More ore heading for Germany for weapon manufacture. But it would be a perilous journey for the freighter;

the British had mined the North Sea. That's why Hitler was planning to extend the rail network. Was there no stopping the man? There must be a way.

A group of loud, young men who had been milling around began to jeer. Laila turned to see what they were angry at and saw two familiar faces approaching. Josef and another guard from the hotel who she had heard Josef call Heinz. The gathered men threw out taunts in Norwegian. Josef's face remained calm, but Heinz set his jaw, his eyes narrowed. One of the men, who looked to be aged around sixteen years old, pushed himself forward, swayed for a moment, and then pulled firmly on his cap.

'Looks like trouble's coming,' said Heinz, in a sing-song voice.

'He's just a boy who's had too much to drink,' said Josef. 'Let's avoid a confrontation.' At that moment, he noticed Laila. He gave her a concerned look and she instinctively moved a few steps away from the impending brawl.

The boy staggered up to the soldiers.

Josef smiled and nodded. '*Guten Tag.*'

Heinz, at Josef's side stood rigid, his fists clenched.

The boy slurred some more Norwegian abuse and then spat out, '*Deutsche Schweine.*'

Heinz shot at him like a cannonball, smashing him in the face with astonishing fury. Laila gasped. Josef sprang forward trying to restrain Heinz as he pummelled the young boy to the ground. The boy screamed, blood spurting from his nose. Josef wrestled with Heinz, shouting at him to stop, and managed to drag the two apart.

Within moments, other soldiers appeared with raised guns and surrounded the group. Josef hoisted up the semi-conscious, blood-covered boy and with an arm under his shoulders, led him away from the pier. As he passed Laila, their eyes locked. She saw him acknowledge her horror. And she saw how he hated this moment. And how he hated the uniform he wore.

* * *

Oda and Laila had been best friends at school. In summertime, they would spend afternoons lying amongst the wildflowers, talking about family, teachers, and books. They both loved to read. On dark, winter days, they would huddle in blankets on Oda's bed and talk for hours about the changes in their bodies, their friends, and boys. Oda was always more knowledgeable than Laila about boys. She often said Laila was too *prim*.

Today, in the bookshop, the friends chatted, catching up on news as Oda removed books from shelves and set up a new display on a small round table.

'We've had a rush on everything Norwegian, history, culture, and folklore, so I'm presenting a selection near the front of the shop.'

'Great idea,' said Laila picking up a book about the artist Edvard Munch. 'Hopefully, you won't be forbidden from selling them.'

'Who knows what will come next, but for now it's business as usual.' Oda stood back to appraise her display.

Laila looked around her and lowered her voice.

'Oda, you mentioned something about Finn being involved...' she said, her pulse quickening. 'My position at the hotel could help.'

'Not now. Come to my house on Thursday evening and we can talk.'

Laila felt a shiver of anticipation.

* * *

The townsfolk called them the white nights, when the long cold gloom of winter succumbed to the endless days, and people were beset with insomnia and agitation. Each night, Laila lay frenzied by thoughts of ways to fight back against the German occupiers.

But there was something else that the white nights weaved into Laila's consciousness.

Yearning.

At night, when she was hot and her skin damp, she tore off her nightdress and lay naked on her bed, spinning dreams. Images of Josef rose unbeckoned and swirled in her head. Guilt gnawed at her when she thought of him, and she tried to blank him out with plans of revenge against the Germans. But still he stirred something in her that she fought to ignore.

And behind her blackout blind, the silver white light strayed till dawn.

* * *

One evening in August, after a dinner of salted herring and potatoes, Laila and Hanna walked down to the harbour to enjoy the light summer evening. At least curfew was later this time of year, and the blackout blinds could stay open longer.

The sisters looked out across the harbour, a brisk wind tugging at their skirts. The fjord was littered with wrecks of ships and boats from the recent battles. A German destroyer lay flipped on its side, half submerged like a dead whale. The debris of supply ships and iron ore transporters was scattered around the port, masts and funnels protruding from the waves, macabre shapes against a navy-blue sky. Fishing boats negotiated their way through slicks of cloying oil, heading for home ahead of curfew.

Laila turned away from the devastation. 'Let's walk further out from town.'

They stopped again further down the coast at an outcrop of large, flat rocks, where they sat on the sun-warmed stone, their legs straight out in front of them, their skirts clamped between their knees. They watched in silence as orange-billed oystercatchers shrieked and dived for mussels and tiny crabs amongst the rocks. The sky dimmed to a deep purple, releasing a copper sun into the waves.

Laila sighed. She couldn't imagine living anywhere else other than Norway. Papa's older brother had emigrated to America twenty years ago. America. So far, strange, and different. The idea had never appealed to her.

In the lull of the wind, snatches of voices floated through the air.

Laila and Hanna edged forward on the boulder and peered down. Some way beneath them, a couple sat, holding hands. Laila recognised the girl, Marion. She had been in her class at school. Marion was leaning on the man's shoulder. He wore the uniform of a German soldier.

Fascinated, Laila and Hanna watched the couple as they chatted and then embraced, their kisses becoming increasingly passionate. Laila began to feel uncomfortable and nudged Hanna. 'Let's go.'

'It's just not right,' said Laila as they headed for home. 'How could Marion start something with a German?'

She thought of Josef and claws of guilt tore at her insides.

'Marion has always been a bit of a flirt,' said Hanna, laughing. 'And the soldiers have only been here three months.'

'Flirting is one thing. But with a German? We've enough young Norwegian men in this town.'

'But maybe Marion thinks they're not as attractive as those clean-cut, well-built young soldiers in their smart new uniforms.'

Laila gave Hanna a sharp look. 'I don't know how you can say that. I think they look exactly what they are, in their military uniforms and wielding guns. The enemy.' Her own words left a sour taste on her tongue as she thought of her recent fantasies. But of course, they were not real.

'Of course, you're right. I'm just saying that Marion obviously feels differently.'

'Obviously,' said Laila, ending the conversation.

On entering the hallway, Laila saw her father's box radio standing on the floor next to the shoes he wore for work. She and Hanna went into the sitting room where he was sitting in his armchair smoking his pipe, staring at the sideboard where his radio normally stood. He looked up at his daughters. 'I have to hand it in tomorrow. All radios have been requisitioned. A German official came by to tell us, and there'll be severe repercussions for anyone harbouring one.'

Laila swallowed hard. Papa loved his radio. Listening to music every evening after dinner, tapping his feet along to the Glenn Miller band. Or keeping up to date with the BBC news, even though that was *verboten*. She squeezed back the tears. After his car and radio, what would they take next?

It was raining, so Laila left her bicycle at home and took the bus to work. She climbed on, paid the driver, and looked around for a seat. The only available place was next to a German soldier. She hesitated. He glanced at her and nodded at the space. She felt the heat rush to her cheeks. Turning her back on him, she remained standing and held on to the bar. An elderly woman with a basket on her lap smiled at her. Laila smiled back, enjoying her small triumphant gesture.

Laila continued her small acts of defiance. If she was already seated on a bus and a German came to sit next to her, she got up and either sat somewhere else or remained standing. She noticed other Norwegians started to do the same. They would cross to the other side of the street when soldiers approached. And if a soldier greeted Laila when passing, she'd turn her face and not reply. The fact that they were often polite or even friendly infuriated her. Papa said the soldiers had been instructed to win the population over. The Germans called them their 'Nordic cousins' who they were protecting from the French and British.

The idea was absurd.

But she wasn't satisfied with just these small acts and was excited when the evening that she was due to meet Oda and Finn finally arrived. However, first she had to help Olaf with his homework and then came supper.

Their meal of stockfish and mashed swede was smaller than usual. Laila ate quickly, eager to finish and get over to Oda's.

Hanna asked her about news from the Hotel Nordic.

'Any more handsome officers arrive this week to tempt our local girls?'

'Handsome? I really don't notice their faces. All I see are uniforms, metal eagles pinned on collars, armbands with swastikas. All I see is our enemy.'

'I know. I know. It's awful. But at least they are polite.'

'Polite?' The word shot from Laila's lips. 'How do you invade a country *politely*? How do you occupy a land and suppress its people *politely*? Do you know how ridiculous that sounds?'

There was a choked sob. Laila turned to see her mother twisting her cardigan around her fingers.

'That's enough,' said her father.

Laila bowed her head. 'I'm sorry.'

Her father fixed his eyes on Hanna. 'The soldiers have been ordered to be courteous to prevent unrest. Hitler sees us as a simple, gullible folk who'll believe his propaganda. He underestimates us.'

'But, Papa, we must do something,' said Laila.

'I tell you what you must do. You must keep yourself safe. Keep the family safe. Do not antagonise the Germans. Do not befriend them. There are rumours about some girls and the soldiers. These girls are betraying their land.' He looked again at Hanna. 'Do I make myself clear?'

There was nodding around the table.

* * *

Laila followed Oda up the steep staircase that led to the attic where her brother was waiting for them. Finn greeted Laila with a firm hug and gestured to two small wooden stools. The girls sat down, and Finn pulled up an upturned crate for himself. Laila looked around the low-ceilinged room. A screen separated the space from the family's storage area. There was an unmade bed, a cupboard, and numerous crates scattered around, including one that served as a table. Propped up against a wall were a pair of skis and poles. A once white camouflage suit dangled from a hook on the wall, the uniform enabling a Norwegian soldier to blend into the snow.

'How was it in the mountains?' she asked, softly.

'A short and brutal battle,' he said. 'We didn't stand a chance. Not enough men. Not enough weapons.' He turned to stare out of the dirty attic window.

Laila hadn't seen him since he had returned from fighting the invasion and she noticed the change in him; he was thinner, his face more angular, his eyes duller.

He leaned forward, placing his forearms on his thighs. 'Oda tells me the Hotel Nordic now houses German officers.'

Laila nodded, expectant as to what would come next.

Finn got up and began to pace around the room. 'Listen, Laila. I don't want to put you in danger, and I don't want to push you into something you don't want to do. But your position at the hotel could provide us with valuable information.'

'Us?' she asked.

'It's safer for you that you know as little as possible. Suffice to say there's a growing movement of resistance; it's expanding and becoming better organised. We're collecting guns, radios, and information. And information is something you may have access to. Anything you hear, see, or read could be of vital importance. Information is also useful for the resistance newsletter we're planning.' Finn's words came fast, his eyes recovering their shine.

Laila nodded eagerly as he spoke. This was the opportunity she had been waiting for. She thought about the brown briefcase that Major Haas kept by his side.

'I can help,' she said.

After the talk with Finn, the girls went down to Oda's bedroom. Sitting on Oda's bed, Laila looked at the familiar things around her. Oda's old schoolbooks stacked on a shelf beside tatty boxes of puzzles with missing pieces. At the end of the shelf stood a birthday card Laila had painted for Oda's thirteenth birthday. On the windowsill, a row of wooden dolls in traditional Norwegian dresses stood next to a vase that held a poppy made of red tissue paper, covered in dust. And a small, framed photo of Laila and Oda when they were eight years old, in their matching dresses on National Day.

The friends fell back on the bed, shoulder to shoulder.

'It's hard to believe we're an occupied country,' said Oda.

'Occupied?' said Laila, her tone thoughtful. '*Occupied* is such a harmless word. Our bathroom is occupied when Hanna takes a bath. Papa is occupied when he is reading the newspaper. Calling Norway occupied imparts none of the horror we're experiencing. Our loss of liberty. The assault on our pride and identity.' The girls fell silent, pondering what the future might hold.

As she cycled home, the surge of adrenalin she'd had from her meeting with Finn started to fade. Her desire to fight the occupation was as strong as ever, but her father's words echoed around her head. *You must keep yourself safe. Keep the family safe. Do not antagonise the Germans.*

She would have to be extremely careful. She mustn't do anything to endanger her family.

* * *

The queue outside the shop stretched the length of the street. Laila took her place at the back. People around her, mostly women, nodded at each other or spoke in hushed voices. Sometimes they checked over their shoulder whilst they exchanged news. Others stood with bowed heads.

Laila stood in the queue, shuffling forward two steps each time it moved.

She tapped the woman in front on the shoulder and said, 'Red is a nice colour for a hat, don't you think?'

The woman looked at her confused, then up at the beret she wore.

'Norwegian elves wear red hats, our national flag is red, red is a signal,' Laila continued. 'But in the end, it's just a colour.' She winked.

The woman grinned and nudged the woman in front of her.

Laila watched the message pass down the queue.

Women exited the grocery shop with baskets of meagre provisions. A stout woman in a purple headscarf bustled towards her.

Borghild, the town gossip.

Laila lowered her gaze and studied her sturdy brown boots. 'Laila, is that you?' The voice shrieked. She flinched.

'Hello, Borghild. How are you?' She readied herself for the onslaught.

Borghild began to recount all of her woes, her bunions, the mice in her kitchen, and her son's intolerable fiancée, and then she lowered her voice. 'Awful about these hussies, isn't it? The German girls, as they're called. Our local girls *fraternising* with soldiers. They should be ashamed of themselves.'

Laila found herself, on this rare occasion, agreeing with her.

'It's certainly hard to understand their behaviour.'

'I saw that girl, Marion, hanging all over a German, down by the docks. It's disgusting. Treason. That's what it is.' Borghild shuddered.

Laila thought treason a bit extreme. Or was it?

Borghild pressed her face closer. She had a long black hair protruding from her chin. 'She'll be wearing silk stockings next. They're selling themselves, those loose women.'

Laila thought of Hanna's interest in the young Germans, how she'd said she thought them good looking, well built and polite. Laila could not bear to imagine a scene where Borghild was whispering about Hanna. No, that mustn't happen. She would keep an eye on her sister.

But what about her own feelings for Josef? No. She had that under control.

'Well. I must be off,' said Borghild, adjusting her headscarf.

Laila watched with relief as the woman pounded away down the street. She had not enquired once about Laila and her family.

Two days later, Laila joined the food queue and grinned at what she saw before her. An array of new headwear. Wool hats, berets, headscarves, felt hats, boaters tied with ribbons. All red.

But the most striking thing was the lift of spirits. Heads raised and lively chatter.

A nearby patrolling soldier looked bewildered, uncertain

whether a transgression had taken place or not, but after watching for a short while, he moved on.

* * *

Laila's opportunity came sooner than expected. Major Haas blustered out of his office checking his watch and barked at her that he would be at the town hall for the rest of the afternoon.

As the major swept past her at reception and out the door, her breath caught. He did not have his precious brown briefcase under his arm. She had never seen him without it. As she watched him climb into the waiting car, her head started to spin. This was what she'd been waiting for. Now was her chance.

But maybe he would realise he had forgotten it and return. Excitement and fear bubbled inside her. Watching the clock, she forced herself to wait ten excruciating minutes before she ambled nonchalantly towards his office, checking around her. There was no one in reception or on the stairs that led to the first floor. The soldiers on guard had their backs to her.

The major had shut his office door. She turned the brass knob and pushed the door open just wide enough for her to slip through. Another quick glance over her shoulder and she was inside. The brown briefcase lay on the desk.

Her breath caught in her throat. This was crazy. She was crazy.

Three swift steps. A glance back at the door.

With shaking hands, she placed her fingers on the smooth, polished leather.

The case had a single lock. No key. It was bound to be locked.

She pressed the sides and heard the satisfying click. Heavens, it was open. How careless. How lucky. What would she find? Secret Nazi documents, plans, maps, names... She could make a difference. Now was her chance.

'Fräulein Olson.'

Laila jumped, clicking the case closed. 'Oh, Major Haas. Good that you have returned. I've just seen your briefcase is still here. I thought I'd organise for it to be brought to you at the town hall.' Her cheeks burned. She held the briefcase out in front of her like an offering.

'How thoughtful of you, Fräulein Olson.' His voice was taut. He closed the door behind him, stood against it, and studied her a few moments before extending his hand. 'You can hand it to me personally.'

She hesitated.

'I'm waiting.'

She stepped towards him. His look was a challenge. As she neared him, pungent aftershave and cigar smoke filled her nose. She was so close she could see the hairs protruding from his nostrils.

He took the case from her, his fingers brushing hers as he held her gaze. She stepped back.

'What were you actually doing in here, Fräulein Olson?' His eyes narrowed.

'What was I doing in here?'

'That was the question.'

'Well, I was checking if the window was closed.'

'I see. Very responsible.'

'Well, I won't keep you any longer from your meeting, Major Haas.'

She went to step around him, but he blocked her way. Again, he stood too close. 'Norwegian women are really remarkable. Strong, tall, bold. Not all, of course. But many, like yourself.'

Laila said nothing.

He cast his eyes over her.

'As you know, our Führer admires the Aryan blood that flows

through your veins, your blonde hair, blue eyes, athletic bodies.' He moistened his lips. 'It has come to his attention that some Norwegian women are having relations with our occupying forces.'

Laila stiffened.

'In fact,' said Major Haas laying a hand on her arm, 'our Führer encourages such, how should I say, liaisons. There are advantages for such women. Privileges, if you understand my meaning.'

'I really must be getting on with my typing, if you allow me, Major,' said Laila, sweat dampening the back of her neck.

He gripped her arm and lunged at her, his fat, wet lips pressing against the side of her neck.

She recoiled, twisting her arm to free herself. 'Let go of me at once. Or I'll scream.'

He squeezed her arm harder, digging strong fingers into her flesh.

'Oh, I don't think that's a good idea. I caught you snooping, spying. Could be unpleasant for you.' He gave a menacing smile.

She struggled in his grasp. Suddenly he released her, laughing. 'Another time, then.' She rushed from the room.

In reception, an officer was addressing Josef. They both glanced at her as she sped past to the ladies' cloakroom, where she vomited into the toilet. At the sink, she splashed her face with cold water. She knew she was in trouble now. Her first task for the resistance and she had completely messed it up. This disgusting, vulgar man could have her arrested. What on earth could she do? It was clear what he wanted.

When she'd stopped trembling, she returned to reception. The officer was gone but Josef was still there, standing at her desk.

'Is everything all right? Did he do anything to you?' Josef studied her closely, his head tilted to one side.

'No,' she said, trying to calm her breathing. She could hardly tell him Haas had caught her with her hands inside his briefcase.

'It's my break. I'm on my way to the kitchen to get a coffee,' he said. 'Can I bring you something? A glass of water?'

'No, really. Thank you.' She sat behind the desk and started to fumble with the post.

As he walked away, she tried to lick her lips. Her mouth was parched.

* * *

It was a wet, blustery, day and a car had just drawn up outside the hotel. Laila looked up from her typewriter. Two dark figures appeared at the entrance.

Long, black, leather coats. Black hats, brims tilted forwards over their eyes. The men didn't move like the soldiers or officers. They slid their way towards her, languid strides, soft steps. Their leather coats creaked as they moved.

The door of the manager's office flew open and Major Haas strode out, with the hotel manager scuttling behind him. Haas made a big show of greeting the arrivals, introduced the manager briefly, and waving Laila aside, took the room keys she held ready in her hand. He would show the guests personally to their rooms.

The three men climbed the narrow, carpeted staircase.

Gestapo.

Laila pulled her cardigan across her chest. She felt chilled.

Oda had told her of rumours she'd heard in the bookshop about the Gestapo converting an old warehouse on the edge of town. She told Laila they were some type of secret police, but no one knew much about them.

Back at her typewriter, she picked up a letter printed on official German government paper and studied the contents.

The letter to be translated from German to Norwegian was a reiteration of regulations ordered by the Reich:

Gatherings of more than five people in public are prohibited.
All political parties other than the Nazi Party are prohibited.
The tradition of the church prayer for the Norwegian royal family
has been abolished.

Laila massaged her temples, trying to ward off a headache that had been threatening. What sort of punishments could be expected for those breaking the rules? It seemed the friendliness with which the *Wehrmacht* had first greeted the Norwegians was diminishing as they discovered that not all were as compliant as first expected. Some of the more vocal citizens had disappeared, and the patrol soldiers were increasingly vigilant in their stop and search routine.

Major Haas returned to reception, his face redder than usual, his upper lip moist. He looked over her shoulder at her translation; a pointless exercise since his Norwegian was limited. He leaned forward as if to study the document closer. His uniform brushed against her hair.

They were alone in the reception area.

He placed a hand on her shoulder. Her hands froze over the keys of her typewriter. His thumb pressed the skin at the base of her neck.

'You are tense, Fräulein Olson.'

Tell him: get your hands off me. But the words wouldn't come. He had caught her with his briefcase. The Gestapo were one floor above her. He started to massage his thumb into her flesh. He spoke into her ear, his voice thick.

'A drink perhaps in my room? You know the number, of course.'

Her skin crawled.

4

SEPTEMBER 1940

The following day, in the soft morning light, Laila cycled along the rugged coast, leaving the noise of the harbour and town behind her. She could hear only the sounds of nature here. The slap of the sea against the rocks and the shriek of the oystercatchers gathering above for breakfast: tiny crabs, mussels, and worms on the mudflats below.

She turned from the water and headed through wispy birch trees and bushes bearing blackberries, redcurrants, and gooseberries. She and her family would harvest here at the end of the week to preserve fruit and make jam for the winter.

She was bringing provisions to Gudrun, an old schoolfriend of her grandmother. Gudrun had lost her son and daughter-in-law in the attack on Narvik. But her two-year-old grandson, Tore, had survived. Now Gudrun took care of Tore. He was all she had left of her family.

Laila knocked on the door and waited. There was no movement or sound from inside. No sound of Tore's chatter or footsteps. She knocked again, more firmly this time. Had they gone out? They couldn't have gone far. Gudrun had a bad hip. Puzzled, Laila shouted out her name. The floor creaked on the other side of the door. There was a shuffle of footsteps and Gudrun appeared with a somewhat sheepish expression.

'Sorry, Laila. I didn't hear you. Come on in.'

'Is everything all right?' she asked, placing the groceries on the kitchen table. 'Where's Tore?'

'He's sleeping. I was... actually... I was listening to Radio London.'

'You still have a radio?'

'Yes, hidden in my storeroom. I sit on a stool and write everything down in my notebook. It's a comfort to know that the fight against the Nazis is going on out there. I get to hear the real news, not just the propaganda that now fills our newspapers.'

'You can speak English?'

'My father was a Scottish fisherman. He made his life here when he met my mother.'

Laila was impressed by her bravery but also concerned. 'You're taking a big risk harbouring a radio.'

Gudrun laughed. 'The Germans won't bother with an old grandma. They are more concerned watching our young men. Do you want to see my notebook?' She sounded proud.

Laila felt a surge of excitement. Gudrun's notes could prove invaluable for the resistance newsletter Finn was planning.

* * *

After work, Laila stopped by her house and took out the notes from her wardrobe, hidden between her pullovers. She folded the paper into four and stuffed it under her bra, then headed for the bookshop.

Oda was locking up as she arrived. The friends hugged each other and went up to join Finn in the attic.

'I've been on the lookout for anything interesting at the hotel whilst I do my routine check on the rooms. But I haven't found anything. Just a lot of socks. The Germans seem very fond of their socks.'

'Be patient. These things take time,' said Finn, setting the kettle on the small stove in the corner. He reached for a tin of fake coffee. 'Something that at first glance may seem insignificant might prove valuable. We're not expecting you to find an envelope stuffed full of Hitler's battle plans hiding beneath a mattress.'

Laila laughed. 'But I do have the notes I made from Gudrun's notebook.' Copying the notes meant there would be no link back to Gudrun. She pulled them out from the top of her blouse and handed them to Finn. 'Gudrun is eager to help.'

He smiled and nodded appreciatively. 'This is good stuff, Laila. Well done. I'll hand the notes to my editor friend. I hope our first newsletter will be ready before Christmas. By then we should have a printing press available. Any news of the outside war effort will boost morale and drum up support for our cause. We'll have to think of a way to distribute the letters. Our fascist police are on the lookout.'

Laila stood up from the crate and took the whistling kettle off the stove. As she made the coffee, Finn paced up and down, rubbing his hands through his hair.

'I could do it,' said Laila. 'They're not looking for young women. They think we're compliant and are too busy flirting with soldiers to be a problem.'

'Me too,' said Oda, piping up.

Laila handed her a mug of coffee. They locked eyes with each other. She saw her own determination reflected in her friend's eyes.

'You'd have to do it anonymously or you'd be arrested straight away,' said Finn.

'We could go unnoticed, slipping them into letter boxes, and we could pop them into empty prams outside shops, in the playground...' Laila's mind was whirling now. 'Slip them into boots left outside doors, leave them in bicycle baskets.'

'It's very risky.' Finn frowned.

'We'll be careful... we'll work in quiet parts of town, early morning when everyone's sleeping, avoiding the main streets, working our way round the backs of buildings...'

Finn nodded, his brow creased. 'It might work. The Germans have been instructed to behave *correctly* towards women here. Luckily. Unlike elsewhere in Europe.'

They sat in silence for a while sipping their coffee. Laila pondered on Major Haas's behaviour towards her. That was anything but correct. He was always too close. Too touchy.

After a few moments, Laila said, 'Two members of the Gestapo arrived today.'

Oda's eyes widened. 'So, it's true that they are setting up in Narvik.'

'In an abandoned warehouse, I've heard,' said Finn.

They fell silent again, each conjuring up their own images of horror.

* * *

Laila's problem with Major Haas was keeping her awake at night. But Finn's comment about how the Germans had been instructed to treat their 'Aryan cousins' prompted an idea, a solution. She had never been very good at playacting, useless in the school nativity play. But now the time had come to sharpen up her skills. And be less *prim*.

The next week, Major Haas summoned Laila to his office and signalled her to take a seat opposite him. She sat and crossed her legs, pulling her skirt over her knees. She saw him register the gesture.

She and Oda had practised conversations and scenarios, Oda playing Haas in various moods ranging from overbearing to comically inept. Laila had attempted a version of a seductive but elusive Marlene Dietrich which had left the girls in hysterics, clutching their stomachs. But now, sitting with him here in reality, the mood was far from humorous. He was a dangerous man and Laila fought to control her fear.

'I wanted to ask you how you feel you are settling in with the new routines here and...' Haas smiled. '...with the new management.'

He stood up, came around, and leaned against the front of his desk, his arms folded. She didn't like that he was looking down at her and that they no longer had the desk between them. But now was her chance to utter the sentences she'd practised. She spoke in a calm, even voice. 'I think I've adapted well to the new circumstances, and I must add I have been pleasantly surprised by the integrity of the German military.'

'Really? In what way?' He sounded amused.

'I understand that orders from the high command are to treat Norwegian women with respect, in a manner befitting the correct behaviour Germans are renowned for.'

He gave a slight frown.

'Of course, there is nothing wrong with those of us who are willing to indulge in relations with Germans. Some of us, though,' Laila lowered her eyes and gave a shy smile, exactly as practised, 'need to take our time. Especially, when it's someone we admire and respect.'

She forced herself to look up at him with wide eyes.

He was silent. His expression pensive.

She had gone too far. He had not fallen for her bad acting and would be angry to be taken as a fool.

'I see, Fräulein Olson.' He stroked his chin, his expression softening. 'I may have been too hasty in my attentions. I look forward to a *mutual* growth in our fondness.'

* * *

Later in Oda's bedroom, Oda squealed with laughter when Laila told her about the conversation. 'Men and their egos!'

'Can he really believe I like him?' Laila shook her head. 'It's bought me some time, at least. I just have to keep up a constant expression of admiration.'

Oda clapped her on the shoulder. 'And you thought you couldn't act.'

In the weeks that followed, Haas worked mostly at the town hall. A rumour had started stating that he'd met an extremely accommodating telephonist who worked there. Laila breathed a sigh of relief and wondered how long her respite would last. Though his absence from the hotel brought with it an unexpected frustration. He had also taken Josef with him to work at the town hall and Laila found herself missing the sight of him.

5

'Do you want to hear a joke?' said Olaf as he followed Laila down the cellar stairs into the washroom.

'Only if it's funny.' Laila handed the armful of lace curtains to her mother who plunged them into the sink of water.

'We'll let them soak all day. It will save on the soap,' said Mama, nodding towards the small bar of green soap on the draining board. 'We still need to wash the Christmas tablecloth and runners.'

The whole month of December would be spent cleaning the house and preparing for *juletid*. Laila had always loved this time of year when daylight seeped in at eleven in the morning and faded by two in the afternoon and Mama would light candles and the house would smell of baked cinnamon. This year would be different. Candles and flour were scarce and there was no cinnamon. But they would improvise. Nothing would hinder a traditional family Christmas.

'I want to tell you my joke,' said Olaf tugging on Mama's apron.

'Go on then. Make me laugh.' She dried her hands on the small towel that hung on a hook above the sink.

'What's the difference between a swine and a German soldier?'

The women raised their eyebrows.

'None. They both can't ski,' said Olaf proudly.

Mama laughed and Laila gave a half smile. Everyone was telling jokes about the Germans. It helped somehow. Most soldiers were standing on a pair of skis for the first time, and this provided much entertainment for the locals.

On the first Advent at the beginning of December, Laila, Hanna, and Mama started to bake biscuits. Laila reminisced how Anton used to hang around, scooping up dough from bowls with his finger, and Mama would laugh and scold him. Anton would tease Laila and Hanna about their reindeer-shaped biscuits saying they looked more like goats or pigs, or nothing at all. And Mama would tell Anton to do something useful like fetch the huge, dried cod from the cellar.

Laila smiled at the memory.

This year they weren't able to bake the seven varieties of special biscuits, but they got creative with oats and barley. Whilst the biscuits were in the oven, Laila and Mama sat at the kitchen table with Olaf and made tree decorations from shiny paper: baskets and hearts attached to red string. Papa worked at his wood bench in the cellar where he crafted shapes and figures: bells, elks, and elves.

All the while, Laila planned how she would distribute the newsletters that had now been printed.

* * *

For once, Laila was grateful for the long winter days as it allowed her and Oda to distribute their newsletters under cover of darkness. Even the days were dim, and Laila slipped like a shadow through the town, clasping her wicker shopping basket. Inside, in full view, lay a pile of knitting and a copy of Jane Austen's *Northanger Abbey*, which she was reading to improve her English. The newsletters were hidden beneath the lining of the basket, inside pockets which she and Oda had sewn with scraps of fabric. Afterwards, they'd practised slipping the pieces of paper in and out of the pockets until they were confident they could do it effortlessly.

The newsletters were well received. She heard women talking about them as she queued for food:

'I found one in an empty flowerpot in my front garden. Apparently, our Princess Martha is in exile in America trying to get support from President Roosevelt.'

'Who could be leaving us these letters?'

'Some very brave souls. I hear the Germans are getting a bit uppity about it.'

At last Laila was doing something meaningful.

* * *

It was a frigid morning close to Christmas, nearly dawn, and Laila was finishing up distributing her letters before it would be time to start work at the hotel. She was considering where to place the last few when a familiar voice came from across the street. It was Sigrid, the hotel housekeeper.

'Hello, Laila. You're up early too.' She crossed over. 'I wanted to be first in the bread queue. Have you got the early shift?'

'Yes, I'm on my way now.' Laila placed a gloved hand on the knitting in her basket. She had to get rid of the last letters first. Even if she just left them lying in the street.

At that moment, two soldiers approached them. One was Josef. The other, who was tall with an angular face, spoke. 'Good morning, *Die Damen*. You're up and about early. Where are you going?'

'I'm off to get my ration of bread,' Sigrid answered, 'and my friend here is on her way to work.'

'May we look in your baskets?'

'I beg your pardon?' Sigrid said, incensed.

Laila's stomach turned.

'We have new orders, I'm afraid.' Josef sounded apologetic.

Sigrid stiffened and grasped her basket, holding it firmly against her ample bosom. 'This is an outrage. Are you accusing me of carrying contraband?'

'It's just routine stop and search,' said the angular soldier, reaching out for her basket.

'I'll check here,' said Josef, as he moved towards Laila.

She looked at him. Could he see the fear in her face? Despite the cold, droplets of sweat were forming along her hairline under her hat.

He tipped his head to one side. 'May I?'

She had no choice but to hold out her basket and try to steady her shaking arm. Beside her, Sigrid was babbling angrily. Humiliation. Disgrace. Intrusion to privacy.

Laila said nothing as Josef pushed her knitting and book from one side to the other. She felt sick as he ran his hand along the inside of the basket. She could see that a piece of paper was sticking out of the lining. Josef prodded it with his forefinger.

This was it. She was finished.

She could smell the leather of the Gestapo coats. She could hear cries from an abandoned warehouse. Her cries. How long would she hold out before naming Finn and Oda? Black lines danced before her eyes.

'Thank you, Fräulein Olson. You can carry on.' Josef turned away and nodded at the other soldier. 'Everything is fine here.'

And then they were gone.

Laila leaned against a garden fence, waiting for her heart rate to slow and to catch her breath. Surely, Josef had seen the letters. He had his fingers on them. He had only needed to tug them out. But he hadn't betrayed her. Why ever not? He was German.

The next day was quiet. Major Haas was thankfully at the town hall all day but he'd left Josef at the hotel. Laila sat at reception filing index cards, trying to keep her mind on the next delivery of newsletters from the printer, but was worrying about Josef. Had he told someone about what he'd seen, or was he about to?

A motorbike roared up to the entrance and Laila watched Josef spring down to receive the parcel from the rider. He walked past her towards Haas's office.

'I'll pop the post on the major's desk, Fräulein Olson.'

He opened the office door a fraction and slipped through. It seemed a strange way to enter the room.

Moments passed and Josef did not reappear. Puzzled, Laila got up and crept to the door to listen. All was quiet. Or did she hear the shuffling of paper? Holding her breath, she peered around the door. Josef was shifting through some papers in a manila folder. He pulled out a letter and studied it carefully. As he replaced it, he turned his head towards the door. Laila jumped back and sped over to her desk. But he had seen her.

He left the major's office and, without looking in her direction, went back to his post. What had she just witnessed? A German soldier sorting the post of his major? Harmless enough. However, an ordinary, low-ranking soldier didn't usually do such a thing. Was he searching for something? Snooping, maybe? Laila stared at Josef's straight back, wondering.

When it was time for his break, he approached her, and after a quick glance around, said, 'Would you mind joining me for a few moments in the back yard?' He sounded nervous.

Laila waited a short while, put a *Back Soon* sign on the desk, and went outside to where Josef was drawing heavily on a cigarette. He looked at her, uncertainty in his eyes.

'I'm not sure what you thought you saw, but please can I ask you not to mention it to anyone?'

'Then may I ask exactly what I saw?' Her tone was wary. She sensed danger.

'Please, Laila, believe me. Lives are at stake. Norwegian lives.'

'What do you mean?'

'You shouldn't get involved. It's not safe. Please. Forget the incident.'

Laila's heart started to race. 'But I am involved now. Tell me what's going on.'

He exhaled deeply, his shoulders sinking.

'Major Haas received copies of documents for the chief of police. Some arrests are due to take place at dawn, tomorrow.'

Laila had heard snatches of conversation from the officers at breakfast. Something about a crackdown and examples being made of.

'I want to warn those in danger of arrest,' he said, his voice suddenly determined.

'But why you?' she said in disbelief.

He swallowed hard. 'I watched once. Did nothing. Just stood there...' His voice trailed off for a moment but then he spoke again, telling her the five names on the list, two of which she knew personally: two communists, an activist, a Jewish furrier, and a teacher. Laila insisted that she help and so they agreed that, as soon as it was dark, Josef would leave anonymous notes under the doors of three of them, and Laila would inform the two she knew, by way of a friendly visit.

When the fascist police banged on doors the following daybreak, yelling to open up, they were met by silence. They broke down the doors and ransacked the empty houses, helping themselves to what they could find.

Laila was confused about her feelings for Josef. Yes, he had kept the secret of the letters in her basket, but he was still the enemy. Yet he had saved Norwegian lives, risking his own. If he was caught, he would be shot as a traitor. The thought made her feel sick. When she saw him day after day, noticed his face brighten when she arrived for work, heard his warm voice greeting her good morning, she felt a tug in her chest. They shared a secret. One they didn't speak of.

* * *

Josef was on duty the day before Christmas Eve. Laila could see his back from reception where she sat at her typewriter. He stood outside the entrance, occasionally stamping his feet. He must be cold, she thought, even in his full-length coat.

As she left work, it was snowing softly.

'*God jul*, Fräulein Olson.' He smiled. Her heart swelled at his attempt at a Norwegian accent. There was so much she would have liked to say to him; about him overlooking her newsletters, about his own resistance efforts. But staff and officers were milling around. They never had a chance to speak alone.

'*God jul*, Private Josef Schultz,' she said, trying to convey more in her expression than the few words could.

He looked so pleased that she couldn't help but smile. Catching herself as an officer came up behind her, she turned up her collar, hurried down the steps, and headed for the bus stop. The streetlamps had been covered with blackout tape except for a thin strip that allowed only a sliver of light, which lit the way enough for her to see the path. The night was cloudy and dark, and all she could really make out were the fluorescent badges on people's coats that bobbed around her.

The bus was crowded when it arrived, and she had to stand. The journey took longer now that the buses had no petrol to run on. Instead, each vehicle was fitted with an external wood burning box, producing energy from carbon monoxide. But the power was insufficient to get the full bus up the hill. Twice, passengers had to get out and walk alongside whilst Laila and the stronger passengers pushed the bus from behind.

As she settled back in her seat, she thought about Josef; how he saved those people from being arrested. She relived every moment of how they had worked together as a team. She wondered how he would be spending Christmas. A festive meal in the soldiers' canteen, probably. Perhaps with cured pork. No doubt with more food than Norwegian families. Would he miss his own family? Maybe he was married or had a fiancée. It must be miserable to be separated from your loved ones this time of year.

Laila stepped off the bus, anticipating the comfort and warmth of a family Christmas. They would make the most of it. Despite the occupation.

On Christmas Eve, Laila had to rummage in drawers for old stubs of candles to add to the four she had managed to get with her ration coupons. As there were no candles for the tree that year, she'd suggested they could take it in turns to hold one in front of the tree whilst they sang carols.

As was tradition, the tree Papa had felled was waiting in the yard to be brought in and decorated by Mama and Papa later, whilst everyone else was at the church's children's service. Laila and Hanna, although technically too old for the service, would accompany Olaf to church.

Everyone helped set the table: the Christmas tablecloth, the best porcelain plates, and the silver cutlery that Papa had polished that morning. Laila laid twines of spruce on the starched white napkins. Mama served the lutefisk, dried cod which had soaked in water and lye for days and was now flaky and soft. It was a smaller fish than normal, but Mama stretched out the meal with boiled potatoes and mashed dried peas. There was no butter, so they ate the fish dry.

'Next Christmas, the war will be over,' said Papa, 'and we'll have a giant lutefisk drenched in butter.' Everyone cheered.

During the meal, Mama turned the jovial tone more serious. 'I'm not one to gossip, but I've heard a rumour.'

They all looked up with interest. 'Apparently, Marion is pregnant, and the father is a German soldier.'

'Well, that's no surprise.' Hanna smirked.

'How terrible,' said Laila.

'Her father never had any control over the girl,' said Papa, shaking his head. 'Women of shame, these girls are. Bringing dishonour to their families.'

Everyone nodded in agreement.

* * *

Laila smiled at the typical winter scene. Skis and poles leaned against the wall of the house and snow-covered boots were piled up at the front door. It was these pictures of normal life that she found comforting in a world that was anything but normal. She strapped on her skis and set off, but when she arrived at the ski slope, the illusion was shattered; the *Wehrmacht* were having their ski lessons.

'Trust the *svina*, swine, to spoil our Sunday,' Oda said when Laila had skied over to her.

The lesson appeared to be finishing up as Laila could hear the Norwegian instructor saying a few final words to the soldiers.

'What a bunch of oafs.' Oda sniggered.

Laila studied the group. Josef was there with that awful Heinz who had beaten that teenage boy down by the port. They were chatting to two girls.

Hanna and her friend Petra.

Laila's chest tightened.

Oda followed Laila's gaze.

'Seems like your baby sister is having fun.'

'She is anything but a baby. That's what worries me.' Laila frowned. 'And that Petra has always been a bad influence on her.'

'Drink and boys?'

'Exactly. And she started young.'

Hanna was standing close to Heinz, laughing, her head tilted to one side whilst Petra chatted to Josef. No doubt, Petra was flirting. Laila felt a pang in her chest. After a few moments, the four seemed to come to some agreement and set off down the slope.

'Seems ski school isn't finished,' said Oda.

'Obviously not,' said Laila.

Petra probably had her eyes on Josef. And if Hanna decided to mess around with Heinz, who was not only German but violent, that would be bad news.

It was nearly dark when Hanna arrived home, her cheeks glowing. She hummed as she hung up her coat and flounced into the sitting room. Laila looked up from her book that she hadn't been able to concentrate on. She'd been agitated the whole day, waiting to know what had happened. Especially any news about Josef. Papa lowered his newspaper.

'Where have you been, young lady?'

'Skiing with Petra. I told you, Papa.'

'All afternoon?'

Laila shot Hanna a glance.

'The air was so wonderful today, and the snow perfect. We had so much fun.' Hanna plopped herself down on the sofa. Laila didn't like the way she looked.

Radiant.

Two days later, at noon, Hanna turned up unexpectedly at the hotel. Laila saw her stop at the entrance to speak to Heinz. What were they talking about? Before she entered the lobby, she pulled off her felt beret and shook her hair around her shoulders. '*Auf Wiedersehen,*' she called out as she walked away from him.

She spoke as if to a friend. A German friend. Laila clenched her teeth.

'What a surprise,' she said as Hanna approached the reception desk.

'A nice one, I hope. I thought we could spend our lunch hour together.'

This was a first.

They ate their sardine sandwiches in the hotel kitchen and then went for a walk down to the harbour. Everything about the day was grey: the sky, the sea, and Laila's mood. She tried to wait for the right moment to voice her concerns, but in the end just blurted it out.

'Why are you getting friendly with the soldiers? You know that people gossip.'

'Petra and I have only offered the poor lads some ski lessons. What's the harm in that?'

An image of Petra and Josef alone in the snow-covered pine forest popped into Laila's head.

'Be careful. I've heard bad things about that soldier, Heinz. And think what Papa would say.'

'Then you'd better not tell him. Anyway, you *work* for the Germans. That's far worse.'

Hanna's words stung.

'I work for a Norwegian hotel.'

'Run by Germans.'

Laila bit her lip. She turned around. 'I have to get back.'

She began to walk, her sister struggling to keep up with her fast stride.

'Don't you sometimes think our life here is small?' Hanna's voice had a wistful tone to it.

'Small?' She had no idea what her sister was talking about.

'Countries like Germany seem more sophisticated somehow. Their fashion and nightlife, for example. I'd prefer to live in a lively city than stuck in the canning factory gutting fish.'

When they reached the hotel, Laila said a curt goodbye and Hanna hurried back to work. But not before flashing a quick smile at Heinz at the top of the stairs.

'Is that your sister, Fräulein Olson?' Major Haas was on his way out the door.

'Yes, Major. She was on her lunch break.'

'Where does she work?'

'She is a seamstress at a tailor's shop.'

'Tailors? Jews most likely. Well, I must be off. I have an appointment at the town hall.'

As she watched his bulky frame descend the stairs, Laila felt uneasy.

* * *

Over the next few days, Laila tried several unsuccessful attempts to broach the subject of Heinz with Hanna. Laila started to panic. She thought of her conversation with Borghild that day in the food queue. There was no doubt that Hanna was playing with fire, risked being labelled a German girl. Look what happened to

Marion. She was pregnant and now she had disappeared. No one knew where she had gone. Or they weren't talking about it. And something else gnawed at Laila. Whilst Hanna was with Heinz, they made a cosy foursome with Josef and Petra.

The following Sunday at breakfast, Hanna announced that she would be spending the day skiing with Petra. Laila tried to catch her eye, but her sister avoided her glance.

An hour later, Laila went to the ski slopes to see what was going on. There was only a handful of soldiers flailing about in the snow, without an instructor this time. It appeared that the lesson had been cancelled. Laila searched around but there was no sign of Hanna, Petra, Josef, or Heinz.

Laila imagined Heinz taking Hanna into his arms. Or worse, him harming her. She shook her head to free herself of such thoughts and skied away from the slopes along a path through the conifers. Breathing in the scent of the pine calmed her. She made a decision. It was time to intervene, something she needed to do before it was too late. She would speak to Josef about the situation.

Hanna came home that evening just in time for dinner, a smile playing on her lips, which made Laila all the more resolute.

The next morning, on the bus on her way to work, she rehearsed what she would say to Josef. Maybe he wouldn't like to get involved but she had to try. Finding a moment alone with him though, to talk unobserved, was the difficult part. Outside on the steps or in front of the reception was out of the question. The chance came when during his break, he stepped out to the back yard to have a cigarette. Laila took her full wastepaper basket to the bins that stood in the yard.

He was leaning against the wall, smoking, and he greeted her as she passed him by. She tipped the rubbish into the container and approached him, swinging the empty wire basket as if to high-light her reason for being there.

Her mouth went dry as she stood before him, and she struggled to find the right words.

'Did you enjoy your Sunday?' she asked.

He looked surprised. She felt uncomfortable.

'Yes, thank you. And you?'

'Did you have ski school?' she said, ignoring his question.

'Actually, it was cancelled. But I practised anyway. Your sister and her friend were kind enough to give us instruction.'

Instruction. An interesting term.

'Private Schultz do you know what people say about the girls who befriend Germans? Do you know what harm it does to their families? The pain it causes? Naturally, I'm concerned about my sister. Especially as I've witnessed how violent Heinz is.'

He frowned, stubbing out his cigarette on the icy ground.

'The last thing I want to do is cause trouble. I know what you mean... I will keep Heinz away from Hanna. I've no intention other than friendship with her and Petra.'

'Friendship can lead to other things.' Laila's pulse was racing.

'Not in this case.' He fixed his dark eyes on hers.

She swallowed. 'Even friendship is frowned upon,' she said.

'Really? I thought you and I had a friendship. An understanding between us.' His expression was intense, his lips parted slightly. Alarmed, she felt her insides grow soft and warm. Like when she thought about him at night. They shared a massive secret. One that could put both their lives in jeopardy. But if anyone, such as her father, suspected a friendship between them...

'Well, you thought wrong. I could never be friends with a German.'

His head whipped back as if she'd slapped him. In a tight voice, he said, 'I've got your message. You have no need to worry further. I shall deal with Heinz. I wish you a good day.' With that, he turned on his heel and marched back inside.

Laila's hand shook as she carried the basket to reception.

For the rest of the day, she watched Josef's back from her desk, utterly miserable.

And the following Sunday, her stomach was flipping somersaults when Hanna left the house with her skis. She returned an hour later, frowning, her lips pursed.

She took Laila to one side. 'This is your doing,' she hissed.

'What do you mean?'

'Heinz and Josef didn't turn up.'

The relief on Laila's face gave her away.

'Why did you interfere?'

'It's for your own good, Hanna.'

'Rubbish. You're just jealous,' she snarled. 'Jealous because no man is interested in you. I bet you've never even been kissed, let alone anything else.'

Hanna shoved past her and ran upstairs, leaving her words ringing in Laila's ears.

6

JUNE 1941

Laila was gazing over the fjord when suddenly Josef appeared beside her, holding out a packet of cigarettes. She shook her head.

Josef pulled one from the pack. His fingers were long and slim. Not fisherman's fingers. Laila watched as he placed the cigarette between his lips, held it there, struck a match, and cupped the flame. He exhaled and looked out across the fjord, not to the east where the burned-out wrecks of the recent battles scarred the view, but to the west where today the water was jade green, and high above, flashes of black and white chequered the sky; the terns were screeching and diving.

'What a beautiful land this is,' he said, his voice so quiet she could hardly hear his words above the wind. They stood shoulder to shoulder. She was as tall as he was.

'Is that why you are all here? Because you like our beautiful land?' she said, her tone weary.

He turned to look at her, his eyes sad. Or guilty? She held his gaze. He turned away. Said nothing. This time, he looked towards the shipwrecks, towards the waters where so many men had lost their lives. She thought she saw him give the slightest nod.

They stood in silence for a while. She had hardly seen him the last few months. He'd been posted elsewhere in Narvik. She'd often wondered if he was carrying on with his own resistance attempts. But over the last few days, he'd been back at the hotel, and she had felt guilty at her joy at seeing him again.

Josef looked up at the mountains. 'The landscape here is really as romantic as a Hans Dahl painting.'

'You know his paintings?' Laila was surprised he knew a Norwegian artist.

'His landscapes are always in bright sunshine, and often in the foreground is a beautiful Norwegian girl.'

'Not always too realistic,' she said.

'Oh, I don't know.' He gave her a soft smile.

Her cheeks flushed.

'I prefer Munch,' she said. 'There is more depth to his work.'

'He's too melancholy for me. So much angst of the human condition.'

'Well, life isn't always sunshine and pretty girls,' she said, indicating the carnage in the fjord. 'Are you interested in art?'

'My mother is an artist and owns a small gallery in our hometown. I paint too, but nowhere as good as she.'

'What's it like where you come from?' Why was she even interested?

'My home is Dresden. It's a beautiful town. Very different to here of course.'

'I haven't seen many towns. I visited Oslo once. I liked it there because it was by the sea.' God, how naïve she sounded.

'Dresden doesn't have the sea, but it's on the River Elbe.'

Laila fell silent. There was so much she wanted to say to him. But his closeness made her uneasy, so she turned to leave.

'I'm lucky you learned German at school,' he said, stopping her in her tracks. 'Maybe, you could teach me to speak Norwegian.'

She hesitated a moment, wrestling with herself. It was dangerous to get too close to him. She shrugged and walked away.

* * *

The next day, there were no customers in the bookshop when Laila entered. Oda was swishing a feather duster half-heartedly along the shelves, and her tired face brightened when she saw Laila. She ran over and the friends hugged.

How thin Oda had become.

'How are you?' Laila asked, unable to hide the concern in her voice.

'I'm worried about Finn. We haven't seen him for days. Mama is beside herself. And we keep hearing about people disappearing. I can't stop thinking about that warehouse where the Gestapo moved in.'

'Finn is clever. He won't get caught.' Even to Laila, her words sounded lame. The thought that something could happen to Finn was too hard to bear.

Oda looked over her shoulder at the door. There was still no one around but she lowered her voice anyway. 'Any news your end?'

'I'll bring the notes I made from Gudrun this evening.' She and Gudrun made a good team supplying the newsletters with up-to-date information from London. 'Not much in the hotel rooms. Just lots of socks still, and letters from home.'

'Letters can contain useful information about the situation in Germany.'

'I think they're censored. The ones I've read are only about how little Fritz won't eat his sauerkraut and *Tante* Helga has been at the schnapps again.'

'Finn says the Germans love eating sauerkraut and running around naked.'

'Both at the same time? What a horrible thought.'

Oda burst out laughing. A deep belly laugh. It was good to hear it again.

Laila was eager to get to what she really came for.

'Do you have any books on German cities?'

'Of course. They're not on the latest banned list. Unlike the books on Munch. And so many others that we've had to hand over to the Nazis. Why are you interested in German cities?'

Laila gave a fake laugh. 'An officer at the hotel is feeling homesick.' She wondered whether she should tell Oda how Josef had risked his life to save Norwegians. But here wasn't the right place.

Oda led her to shelves now stacked with German titles, ran her finger along the spines, and pulled out a book. Laila took it and turned to the contents page where she saw what she was looking for. 'How much is it?'

She only had a few kroner in her purse, which had to last to the end of the month.

'Plenty for an officer.'

'I'm not sure if this is what he's looking for. Can I show him and bring you the money tomorrow?'

'Of course.'

Laila's chest tightened. This was the first time ever she had lied to her best friend. Oda took the book to the cash desk and slid it into a brown paper bag.

That evening, when everyone had gone to sleep, Laila sat crosslegged on her bed, hugging the small, pale-pink cushion that Oda had crocheted for her one Christmas. She stared at the brown bag in front of her for several minutes before removing the book and turning to the chapter on Dresden. The town was rich in culture and architecture. She gazed in awe at photographs of the cathedral, the churches, the ornate palace, and the stone bridges that crossed the River Elbe. The town had a fairy-tale quality.

It was late when she closed the book and returned it to the brown bag. She would return it tomorrow saying the officer changed his mind. A flicker of guilt. She wouldn't lie to Oda again.

* * *

The white nights were back again. At four o'clock in the morning, Laila was awake and restless. She thought how it was nearly a year ago that she and Hanna had sat on the sun-warmed rocks overlooking the fjord. When they'd spied Marion, down by the water's edge holding hands with a German soldier. Laila remembered her outrage at Marion's betrayal to her country and the shame that her family would suffer. Perhaps she had been a bit harsh. Perhaps not.

Marion was still missing. Other pregnant women too. They had all had affairs with Germans and had left Narvik to have their babies. But where? Enquiries were met by a wall of silence.

She climbed off her bed and went to the window to open the blackout blind.

Silver-white light flooded the room.

Infused with nervous energy, she dressed in an old pinafore dress and bounced down the stairs barefoot, grabbed the large wooden broom, and started to sweep the kitchen floor, despite her mother already having swept it the previous night after dinner. Her heart pounded, not from the exertion, but from the tempest in her head.

Josef wanted to learn Norwegian. Maybe that could help him in other acts of resistance. Maybe they could all work together: Josef, Finn, Oda, and her. The idea made her heart swell. Where would it be safe to meet Josef? Maybe down by the row of disused and burned-out boat houses. They could sit with their feet in the cold water whilst she taught him the basics of her language. His voice soft and low, nothing like the harsh tones her father employed when mimicking Germans barking out orders.

She filled a metal bucket with water, fetched a handheld stiff bristle brush, and on her hands and knees, scrubbed the floor in short powerful strokes. The boat houses were too near the town. They might be seen by those young lovers who sometimes wandered there to be alone.

Of course, she and Josef weren't lovers. She wouldn't allow that to happen. They weren't even friends. A few exchanged words and looks. But he had ignored the newsletters in her basket. And he had warned her about the arrests. Had she seen regret in his eyes that day when she demanded to know why Germany invaded? Was there a softness about him? A conscience she could reach? Maybe he could aid the resistance. But would Finn trust him? And what would Finn and Oda think if they discovered there was something going on between her and Josef? Heavens, what was she thinking? There was nothing going on.

She emptied the bucket and opened the front door to allow the floor to dry. She looked at the mahogany clock on the sideboard. Papa would be awake soon. She set about making coffee.

Of course, there was the summer cabin, the *hytte* belonging to Grandpa that lay in a clearing deep in the forest, surrounded by spruce trees. Flowers would be blooming now, sweet scented and — no. That was a stupid idea. What sort of girl would he think she was, leading him to an isolated cabin, alone, just the two of them?

A flash of a thrill. She quashed it.

No, she wasn't that sort of girl.

Papa appeared in the kitchen. Even on a Saturday, he rose

early. He looked at her in surprise. 'What are you doing up at this hour?'

'I can't seem to sleep at the moment, even though I go to bed tired.'

'Me neither. This time of year makes us all feel strange.'

Laila wasn't sure if he was referring to the white nights or the upcoming anniversary of Anton's disappearance. How she wanted to hear her brother's name from Papa's lips. A comment. A sigh. Something. But a silence filled with unspeakable pain massed between them.

She poured him a mug of *Ersatz* coffee and set it on the kitchen table next to yesterday's neatly folded newspaper which no one had read yet. He took a sip, grimaced, and pushed the cup of insipid brown liquid away. He grabbed the newspaper, snapping it open, and scanned the pages.

Laila poured herself a mug of coffee and sat down opposite him, watching him read. A few moments later, he slapped the paper down on the table.

'God, these pictures are sickening.'

Laila could see an upside-down Adolf Hitler strolling down a street with two wide-eyed, fair-haired children. Crowds lined the kerb, hands waving, arms saluted in a silent cheer. Another photograph showed Hitler with his dog.

'Why do the local papers keep printing such photos, Papa?'

'Because the Nazis think we are stupid and gullible. They believe that showing us some pictures of Hitler with animals and children will make us relate to him. Make him seem humane.'

'That's ridiculous. We all know what happened in Poland. And now there are all these rumours about the Jews.'

'I fear they aren't rumours.'

'How then can the people in these photos cheer him?'

'I really don't know, Laila. Probably, some of the photos are staged. Propaganda. But what terrifies me is that many may be real. We must get the bastards out of our country. And we will. The resistance movement is getting stronger.' Laila wondered whether her father was involved in *Milorg*, the organised resistance group. She dared not ask. Too risky. He may suspect her own involvement which he had warned her against in the sternest tones. On the other hand, maybe he would be proud of her?

Laila turned away to wash out her mug. Her father sighed and scraped back his chair. 'I'm going to the factory,' he said.

'But it's Saturday.'

'There's a problem.'

She didn't believe him.

After the discussion with Papa, and seeing the Hitler photos, all romantic images she had of her and Josef dissolved, only to be replaced with those she had been trying to block out: the arrival of Russian prisoners a few days ago, barefoot, emancipated in tattered striped clothing, herded along by soldiers who had jeered and laughed and prodded with their rifles. A woman standing near Laila at the side of the road had handed a piece of bread to a prisoner. His sunken eyes gazed at the woman with wonder as he took the bread, only a heartbeat before the butt of a rifle struck the side of his head and he pitched forward onto gravel, blood trailing down his cheek bone. The crust of bread rolled into the dirt and stopped by the feet of another prisoner who glanced at it with wild eyes but kept walking. The wounded man lay sprawled on the ground as the convoy moved on.

Laila had turned away and sped in the direction of home. When the shot came, she hadn't turned round.

Now, anger pressed tears against the back of her eyes. Anger at herself. A soldier had shot the prisoner dead. She had known it. And blocked it. Probably just a warning shot or... the man with eyes of wonder at a piece of bread had been murdered. *We must get the bastards out of our country.*

Laila rushed to the toilet and vomited coffee and bile.

* * *

Five days after Josef had stopped to talk to her beside the fjord, she arrived at work to find him on duty again.

'*God morgen,*' he said with a shy smile. His attempts at a Norwegian accent were really terrible. She wanted to laugh but managed to reply, enunciating the words for his benefit. She was nearly through the door when he whispered, 'I'm off duty this evening at seven.'

She stopped and looked around before replying. 'So?'

'So, I thought maybe you could help me improve my Norwegian.'

'Why would I want to do that?'

His eyes glinted as he smiled. He didn't answer. She went to take another step and hesitated. Perhaps he really wanted to help their cause.

'Down by the disused boat houses, the last one,' she said. 'At the back, on the water's edge. At eight. But only if no one is around.'

She swept through the double doors, her heart beating double time. What had she done? Was she mad?

That evening, she considered the three dresses that hung in her wardrobe. A pink button through, a navy dress, and the beautiful one that Hanna had sewn for Mama's fortieth birthday party. Laila took out the latter and held it against her, splaying out the full skirt. The fitted, red and white, floral dress with the white lace collar really suited her. It was a dress she kept for special events.

Too obvious, of course. She lay it on her bed and reached for the navy dress.

Fifteen minutes later, she hurried out the back door, calling out to Mama that she was off to see Oda. As she strode down to the harbour into the white night, she had a swing to her hips, the red and white dress fluttering in the breeze.

7

Inge gurgled and kicked, showing no signs of tiredness as she lay on her nappy-changing table.

'She's such a happy child,' said Mama. 'How wonderful not to be aware of what's happening to our country.'

Laila struggled to pull Inge's arms through her pyjama top. 'All she needs right now is our love.'

'That's what we all need.' Mama picked up the baby and placed her in her cot where she promptly pulled herself up on the bars and bounced up and down on the mattress.

Mama placed a hand on Laila's wrist. 'And you have shown me so much love these past three years, and I have offered you none.' Mama's eyes filled with tears.

'That's not true, Mama,' said Laila gently.

'But it is. I have been engulfed in my own grief over Anton. I was broken. Your father thought a new addition to the family would help. But the conflict I felt over Inge's birth overwhelmed me. I know it's a terrible thing to say, but I felt having Inge was a mistake. I had nothing left to give. To Inge. To your father. To anyone. I'm getting better, I think. I'm really trying.'

'I understand, Mama.' Laila took her frail hand. 'We all understand.'

'Thank God I have you, Laila. I know I can rely on you.'

When Laila went to bed that night, it was still light. She closed the blackout blind against the silver whiteness and lay on top of her eiderdown, her thoughts a storm of emotions. Her mother had finally opened up to her. It was the first time since Anton's disappearance that she had spoken of her feelings. A rush of warmth and love for her mother clutched her heart. But also, something else. The weight of responsibility.

Her mother said she could rely on her. Of course, there was Hanna too, who adored Mama. But Hanna had a restless spirit, and Laila felt her sister was pulling away from the family, finding her own way. She had started dating Karl and was spending more time with him on the farm. She was well over Heinz, thank goodness, having mumbled something about him and Josef staying away from the ski slopes and how rude that was.

Papa had always told Laila how she was such a sensible girl. He had been so angry over the local girls' affairs with Germans.

Yesterday evening, she had been bursting with expectation as she raced down to the waterfront. Young couples had milled around, arm in arm, gazing at each other and at the silver-blue sky, and Laila had watched as they kissed and smiled.

She passed the boat houses one by one, rounding the curve – and halted by a pile of fishing equipment. She crouched down and peered over a fish barrel.

He had stood there, smoking a cigarette, looking around him. He looked so handsome. Expectant and nervous. He paced a few steps. Two fishermen passed him by. He stubbed out his cigarette and waited till no one was in sight before ambling to the dilapidated boat house standing last in the row and disappeared behind it.

The coast was clear. If Laila hurried, no one would see her. Her heart pounded up into her throat. A few steps and she would be there.

With him.

Alone.

And then... what? What had she actually been contemplating? To teach him Norwegian? Perhaps. But what else had he wanted? What else had *she* wanted? She had felt something powerful stir within her. She had thought of his deep, dark eyes, his lips, his long slim fingers stroking her neck...

Women of shame, her father had spat the words. *They bring dishonour on their families!*

Despite Josef's good deeds, guilt had spread out its tendrils and her yearning had withered. What had she been thinking? Betraying her family? Betraying her own integrity? No. She would not do that. She had turned away and run home, her vision hazed by the tears in her eyes, her beautiful dress flapping around her knees, as she tried not to think of him standing there by the shore, watching the sun lower in the sky as he waited and waited for her to come.

Now she tossed around her bed, unable to settle. How long had Josef waited at the boat house before he had realised she wasn't going to show up? She couldn't bear to think about it. But she had done the right thing; her conversation with Mama confirmed it. The last thing her family could do with was a scandal.

Laila sighed and readied herself for another long, sleepless night.

The next day, Laila's stomach churned as she cycled to work. How should she behave when she saw him at the hotel? Cool and distant? Polite? Friendly? But more importantly, how would he react to her? He was bound to be at the least disappointed or at the worst, angry that she had made a fool of him. By the time she was climbing the hotel steps, she was a bunch of nerves.

She looked up to meet his gaze and found herself staring directly into the eyes of a stranger. Her eyes darted to the soldier on the other side of the door; he was the regular guard that she knew. But Josef was not on duty. Flustered, she mumbled a hello and sped through the door. Maybe Josef would be here later. But at the end of the day, he still wasn't there.

It was the same the next day. And the day after that. No sign of him. She thought about casually asking the guards if he had been transferred to another post, but she didn't trust herself not to blush or appear over-interested. She became unsettled. Disappointed each time she didn't see his face.

On the third day that he did not appear for duty, she had an idea. After work, she walked to the point on the fjord where he'd stopped to talk to her the previous week. Where he'd talked about the landscape and artists and Dresden. She knew this spot lay on the route from town to the barracks where he returned each evening. She sat on a rock in the exact spot as last time, withdrew her sketch pad and pencil from her bag and half-faced the sea whilst also keeping an eye on the road.

Of course, she had sketched the mountains many times, but not from this spot. Even the slightest change of angle revealed different ridges and crevices. The sun's rays were broken by protruding crags of rock throwing alternate shadows of light and dark. The time of day influenced the number of seagulls that circled above, or how many fishing boats bobbed on the waves. Laila became absorbed in her drawing. Sometimes an army truck rumbled by, but when she looked up, he wasn't inside. A group of off-duty soldiers strolled past laughing and smoking. Josef wasn't one of them.

She finished the outlines of her sketch and started to shade it in. Another military truck drove past. Glancing up, her heart leaped. She saw the distinct profile of Josef as he drove by, his eyes fixed on the road.

He didn't stop.

He didn't even look at her.

Surely, he'd seen her sitting on the rock. Of course he had. He was angry with her and had ignored her. What did she expect? She had made her feelings quite clear by not showing up. And he had made his feelings quite clear by passing without a second glance.

Losing interest in her sketch, she shoved the pad and pencil back in her bag and made her way home. It had been her decision not to meet him. So why then did she feel so miserable?

* * *

The front door was wide open. Tore's pushchair stood out front, a teddy bear with a red knitted scarf in the grass nearby. Laila held her basket with the provisions she'd prepared over her arm. Gudrun was expecting her.

'Hello,' she called through the open door, expecting to see Gudrun playing with her grandson in the kitchen. There was no answer. 'Gudrun, are you there?'

Laila walked into the small hallway and entered the kitchen. On the table was a basket filled with reels of sewing thread and various sized needles. A cloth, half embroidered, lay on the table. She put her hand around a full cup of tea that stood to one side. It was cold.

As she rushed from room to room, panic swelled in her chest. Breathless, she called, 'Gudrun, Tore, where are you?' But there was no answer. She checked the storeroom. The radio and note-book were still hidden behind a packet of toilet paper and a bundle of towels. Bewildered, she ran back outside and into the woods that surrounded the house.

She fought back the feeling of dread. They had merely gone for a walk. Leaving the door wide open? It was possible. Gudrun was sometimes forgetful. Locals didn't need to lock their doors. Why make a full mug of tea and go out? Maybe Tore had been restless and needed to play outside. Gudrun couldn't walk far because of her hip. Laila yelled her name. Where was she?

A light summer rain had started to fall and Laila sped through brambles and darted around ash trees, not sure which direction to take. They wouldn't have come this far, surely? Tore could only manage a few steps before he plumped to the ground. And Gudrun wouldn't be able to carry him far. Perhaps she had become ill and collapsed with the toddler at her side. 'Tore! It's Laila, can you hear me?'

She circled back to the house. The trees were denser now, the tall conifers blocking the light, the ground uneven and rocky. She heard it on the waft of a breeze. A low-pitched whine like a wounded animal. She held her breath and listened. To her right.

She ran lightly, straining to hear. Louder now, an agonised sound.

Gudrun lay on the ground on her side, her frail body trembling. Laila kneeled by her side, swept back her matted silver hair, and stared at her face which was smeared with tears and dirt.

Gudrun gazed at her with desperate eyes and let out a visceral cry.

'He's gone. My Tore is gone.'

* * *

An intense search for Tore began; police, townsfolk, and German soldiers scoured the forests and searched the warehouses around the harbour. House-to-house enquiries were conducted. Laila and Hanna joined the police early one morning on the beach looking for clues: maybe a shoe or an item of clothing. Maybe he had been brought here to the beach. But why would someone do that? Terrifying images assaulted Laila as she stared at the sea. She felt dizzy.

She heard the squelch of wet sand beside her. Turning, she looked into the searching eyes of Josef. She felt herself sway. His strong arm encircled her waist, holding her upright, his breath warm on her cool cheek as he spoke. 'Laila, are you unwell? I'll help you off the beach. Come, lean on me.'

'I'm all right. It's the shock of little Tore.'

'A terrible thing to happen. We're doing everything we can to find him. I'll take you to my truck. It's parked just ahead and you can rest there a while.'

As he guided her, she was engulfed in his presence: her shoulder tucked under his arm, his touch around her waist, his fingers against her stomach, caressing her skin through the thin fabric of her sundress. And the smell of him: the lingering of soap or hair shampoo mingled with the musk of his sweat. He supported her, their bodies half entwined, almost wrapped around each other as if—

'Laila, what's wrong?' Hanna rushed towards them, the concern on her face turning in a flash to something uglier when she saw it was Josef who had come to Laila's aid.

Josef settled her in the back of the truck, gave her water from his flask, and said that she and Hanna could rest there till she felt better. He returned to the search party on the beach.

'What was *that* all about?' said Hanna.

'I felt faint all of a sudden.'

'I don't mean your dizzy spell. I mean *him*.'

'Josef? He helped me, that's all.' Laila realised her mistake.

'You're on first name terms now?'

'He was helping me, that's all.'

'That's not all that was happening. You're such a hypocrite, Laila. All the time telling me to keep away from Heinz.'

'It's not like that.' Laila rose from the bench at the back of the truck and began to clamber out.

But Hanna continued. 'You're no better than Marion. Some meaningless sex, no doubt. Up against a wall behind a canning factory. Very romantic.'

Laila dropped out the back of the truck and fled, shocked to her core at Hanna's words. What had Laila done to make her sister despise her so?

The mood that evening at dinner was subdued. Mama said that Gudrun was being taken care of at the small senior home run by the church. The family again discussed Gudrun's account of events. How she'd left Tore sleeping in his pushchair outside to enjoy the fresh air and have a nap; she had strapped him in, left the front door open, and peeked out regularly at him. She'd put a kettle on the stove and waited till the water bubbled and the whistle blew, made herself a mug of tea, set it on the table, and went to check on her grandson. The straps on the chair had been unbuckled and flung open. The child was gone. She had heard nothing over the noise of the kettle.

Papa shook his head. 'Tore couldn't have undone the safety strap.'

The family ate in silence. Laila and Hanna avoided eye contact with each other. Laila looked down at her meagre plate of food. She had no appetite but leaving food in wartime was almost considered a crime. She nudged Olaf who was sitting next to her and gestured to her food. He nodded eagerly and swopped his already finished plate with hers. Papa glanced over in disapproval but said nothing.

Excusing herself with a headache, Laila went upstairs and

flopped on her bed. Poor Gudrun. She adored her grandchild. He was everything to her and now he was gone.

She paced to the window and looked out over the fjord. The sky and the sea were a shimmer of purple. It would not get dark tonight, a few days before Midsummer's Eve. She heaved a deep breath. What on earth was happening between her and her sister? As young children, they had got on well. Hanna, always cheerful, happy, and mischievous. For ever prompting Laila to do something impetuous, and then Hanna's delight on the odd occasion Laila succumbed to her sister's whims.

She walked to her wardrobe and looked at herself in the mirror on the door. Hanna's words had been vile that afternoon: *some meaningless sex, no doubt. Up against the wall behind the canning factory.*

Where did Hanna get such ideas from? Hanna had been dating Karl since he'd comeback from Oslo. Were they having sex? Hanna had just turned seventeen; still so young. But probably she had more experience than Laila, who had none. She felt so naïve. When she was fourteen, there had been a school dance, and a boy with stubble and pimples on his chin forced his tongue between her lips. Disgusting. That was the sum of her experience of intimacy.

Her bedroom was hot and stuffy. She started to undress, and she watched herself in the mirror as she did so. Slowly, she undid the buttons of her pink dress, one pearly button by one pearly button, slowly, slowly, enjoying the sensation of the air on her skin as her dress fell open. She slipped it off her shoulders and watched it float like a huge rose petal to the floor.

She stood in her white brassiere and underpants. Her feet were bare. Her breaths quickened. She removed her undergarments and stood naked, looking at herself in the mirror, appraising her appearance, her small breasts, the fair hair between her legs, allowing longing to swell within her. And when she could bear it no longer, she lay on her bed and circled her nipple with her fingers, and with her other hand she stroked her stomach, her pelvis, and lower.

But now the hands touching her were not her own but Josef's, his long slim fingers caressing her. She could smell his cologne, shampoo, and musk. She could feel his strong grip around her waist, his breath on her cheek. And she heard his voice, thick and urgent: *I want you, Laila.*

* * *

The next morning, Laila woke so early, she decided to leave her bicycle at home and walk to work, take her time, and collect her thoughts. She went over and over the various possibilities of what might have happened to Tore, but nothing made sense and inevitably her thoughts led to a dark place.

There was the honk of a horn and a military truck pulled up beside her. Her heart jumped. Josef smiled at her through the open window.

'What a lovely coincidence seeing you, Fräulein Olson. I'm on duty today at Hotel Nordic. Hop aboard.'

Laila flushed. 'Actually, I'm enjoying the walk. The weather is lovely. But thank you.'

'I'd like to talk to you. How are you feeling today? On the beach yesterday, I was worried about you.'

'I'm absolutely fine, really.'

Josef glanced at his watch. 'You're a bit pressed for time. You don't want to be late.'

'I'll make it. Just need to pick up my pace a bit.'

Frustration crossed his face. 'Are you always so exasperating, Fräulein Olson?'

'Often, Private Schultz.'

'Please. Laila. Please.'

The plea in his voice made her stomach flip so she climbed aboard. She saw him studying her. She was wearing the same pink dress as yesterday. The one his hands had clasped around as she had leaned on him. The same dress she'd let fall to the bedroom floor yesterday evening before she fantasised about him loving her. Her cheeks burned at the memory. It was as if he could read her thoughts, as if he knew what she'd done last night.

He leaned close to her. She could feel his warm breaths as he glanced at her lips. She felt the pulse in her throat. Then he turned back to the steering wheel, thrust the gear forwards, and drove off.

After a few moments, his voice light again, he said, 'Shame my language teacher didn't turn up the other evening.'

Laila wanted to explain. But she said nothing.

He continued, 'But it was such a beautiful evening, I hung around the boat house anyway. It's quiet down there. Then I walked back towards the harbour, and do you know what I saw?'

Laila shook her head.

'I saw couples walking hand in hand. German soldiers in uniform with local women.'

Laila sighed. 'And do you know what we think of these women? They are betraying our country. They are befriending our enemy.'

Josef drove into the hotel car park, switched off the engine, and turned to face her.

'When we were sent here, our instructions were to protect Norway from the British. Adolf Hitler admires the Nordic race. Our troops were instructed to treat the Norwegian people with respect and politeness as far as possible.'

'And when it's not possible? We are lined up and shot or whisked away by the Gestapo. You yourself saved some from that fate. I still don't know why.'

When he didn't reply, she continued. 'Hitler marches his troops in, dictating how our country is to be run, throwing New Order regulations all over the place, forbidding free speech, banning political parties, and smothering our nationality, our culture. How on earth is that protecting us?'

Josef blinked. Remained silent.

'How could you imagine we could be friends, Private Schultz let alone anything else?'

'Some of your countrymen are trying to come to terms with the situation we all find ourselves in. To try to live alongside each other. I hoped that you and I could do the same. Especially after what we did together. But I see I was wrong. I let my emotions get in the way of common sense.' His tone had turned hard. Josef jumped down from the truck and walked around to Laila's door, opened it, and stood back to let her out. 'Please forgive me if I have offended you in any way. Good day Fräulein Olson.'

Laila stepped out, avoiding his gaze, and hurried to the back entrance of the hotel. Her eyes stung.

8

The twenty-third of June was the commemoration of Midsummer's Eve, *Sankthans*. It was also the anniversary of Anton's disappearance – or death, depending on one's point of view. The family rose at five o'clock and, as in previous years, visited the spot where his skiff had been found washed up on the shore. Papa said a prayer, Mama and Hanna cried, and Olaf hung his head, studying the tiny sand crabs below. Laila had dreaded this moment for the last three weeks, but now standing here, she felt strangely numb; dry eyed, she was aware of Hanna watching her, judging her, no doubt thinking Laila cold hearted not to shed a tear.

Afterwards, Laila cycled to work. The weather was perfect for Midsummer's Eve, the sky cobalt blue, the sea a crystal mirror of the mountains, the air already a warm kiss. Official celebrations, bonfires, and gatherings were banned of course, but families and couples would find spots along the shore to marvel at the sun's defiance to set. As an exception, curfew was to be extended to midnight that evening. People spoke of love being in the air on this mystical day. Longing swelled within Laila, but with a sense of hopelessness too.

As she settled herself behind the reception desk, she thought about what Finn had said about needing radios, and the radio she had seen in the officer's room. She could see a chambermaid climbing the stairs and suddenly, an idea started to form in her mind.

After sorting the post and checking the register for new arrivals, she went up to the first floor. The maid had piled linen onto a trolley and was delving around in a store cupboard on the landing. She emerged with a handful of toilet rolls which she stacked on the trolley before disappearing into one of the bedrooms. Laila went to check the store cupboard. The shelves were stacked with soaps, towels, bed linen, and toilet rolls. But no boxes. She needed a box big enough to hide a small radio in. All items had been unpacked and the boxes disposed of, probably in the rubbish bins in the back yard. Laila's heart sank. She couldn't be seen rummaging in the bins outside.

She returned downstairs to her typewriter and opened the drawer where she kept the writing paper. There were only two sheets left. She stared into the drawer. Paper. Paper for writing letters.

A spark of an idea.

Two officers came down and headed for the breakfast room. A few moments later, Major Haas arrived, his brown leather briefcase clutched under his arm. He honoured Laila with a grumpy, 'Good morning' and hid himself away in his office, slamming the door.

Laila mulled things over. She took a piece of carbon paper, slipped it between two sheets of writing paper and fed them into the typewriter roll. Her drawer was now empty. She shut it and went to the library. No one was around. In the corner stood a heavy, wooden cupboard. She paused and took a breath. *Please.* When she opened the door, she smiled. Brown boxes of writing paper. Big boxes, but not too big. She hauled one out and carried it back to reception, refilled her drawer, and left the box with the remaining paper on the floor next to her.

As the hands of the clock lingered over every passing second, Laila fidgeted at her desk. It was risky. Very risky. If she got caught… she wouldn't think about it. This was an opportunity to help the resistance that she couldn't ignore.

Her shift ended at six o'clock. The porter, Johan Elstad, kept an eye on the reception in the evenings after Laila went home. She could see him outside next to Major Haas's car. A few moments later, Major Haas left his office looking more morose than he had that morning, bid Laila a curt farewell, and hurried out. Johan opened the car door for him and after the major had departed, he approached Laila at reception.

'You can get yourself off home, Miss Olson. I'll keep my eye on things.'

Laila was fond of Johan, who had worked for the hotel since it opened. 'Old school type', her father called him, 'a man of integrity'. She'd told him many times to call her Laila, but he didn't feel comfortable doing so.

'Thanks, Johan, but I still have something to do.' She picked up the box of paper. 'I need to distribute writing paper to the officers' rooms. They send so many letters home, I can't keep up with the paper supply.'

'They should get used to writing shorter letters. Word is that paper will be rationed next. Shall I help you with the box?'

'No, I can manage, thanks. It's not heavy.' She withdrew the master key from her desk and went up to the first floor.

Each room had a small writing desk with a black leather folder containing paper and envelopes. Some contained an ample supply, but she added more anyway. She had to empty the box. With the last few sheets, she hurried towards the officer's room where the radio was. She had to be quick. From her evening shifts, she knew that the officer in question worked late at the town hall; she had noticed he returned to the hotel around seven thirty.

Walking down the hall with the box, she felt conspicuous. No, she told herself. She was an employee carrying out her normal duties. The box stated that it contained writing paper from a Norwegian supplier. An officer exited his room and walked towards her. She straightened, met his eyes, and in spite of a dry mouth, wished him 'Good evening'. He seemed preoccupied and showed no interest in what she was holding. Why should he?

She stopped outside room twenty-eight, took a sharp breath, and knocked.

She listened.

No reply.

She knocked again. Nothing.

She stuck the key in the lock and entered. The room was one of the larger ones and had the extra luxury of an armchair with an embroidered cushion. There were no personal effects around except a framed photograph on the bedside table: an elegant woman in a fitted jacket and pencil skirt stood behind three grinning young boys with varying degrees of missing teeth. It felt strange seeing glimpses of the enemy's family lives. She didn't want to know there were people who loved them.

The radio stood on the writing table. It looked larger than she remembered.

Oh, God, it wouldn't fit in the box. Or would it?

It must.

She slid the remaining paper into the black folder and placed the empty box on the table. Hands trembling, she lifted the radio into it.

The box bulged; the metal handle across the top poked out. The flaps of the box wouldn't close.

Sweat dampened her forehead.

Voices and footsteps in the hall outside. She stared at the door. It would open. And she would be standing there, caught stealing a radio from a German officer. She'd be arrested, sent to a camp or... shot. Shot dead like the Russian prisoner who'd accepted a crust of bread. But her crime was far worse.

She couldn't breathe. She couldn't move. The voices were outside the door.

Then the voices and footsteps faded as they passed away down the hallway. All went quiet. Laila turned back to her task. She must hurry. Adrenalin focused her as she wrenched the radio back out of the box. The metal handle was adjustable. She slid it down. Then she wound the cable into a tight loop and tucked the plug inside. Everything was more compact now. Stuffing the radio back in the box, she sighed with relief. It fitted. She closed the top, tiptoed to the door, and listened intently before slipping out of the room and locking the door behind her.

This was the most dangerous part. Crazy, actually. Waltzing through the hotel with stolen German property. She half expected to meet the officer on the way back to his room. But the corridors were empty. She heard talk and laughter from the restaurant downstairs where some officers were having dinner.

She descended the staircase, trying to make a heavy box look light. Empty.

At reception, Johan smiled at her. 'All done?'

'Yes. I'll put the box outside in the rubbish and go straight home. Good night, Johan.'

She forced herself not to rush. Slow her step. Look casual. Just a few more paces, past the restaurant and towards the backdoor.

Three officers stood chatting in the hall, in front of the restaurant. One stepped forward in front of her.

'*Guten Abend.*'

She forced herself to reply. She felt as if she was standing before him clutching a bomb.

Her knees started to shake.

He nodded at the box. 'What's in there? A bunch of secret files?' He gave a crooked smile.

She managed a nervous smile. 'Just an empty box I'm disposing of.'

His hand reached out.

The room swam before her eyes. This was it. The end.

And then, Josef appeared patting his pocket for his cigarettes. He looked at the box and then at Laila, a look of recognition in his eyes.

'I can dispose of the rubbish with Fräulein Olson, sir. The restaurant is about to close.'

'Come on, Wolfgang, I'm starving,' one of the other officers called out.

Wolfgang studied Laila a moment, then gave an exaggerated laugh and strode off for his dinner.

Josef opened the back door and allowed Laila to exit first. There was a metal table with an ashtray outside and Josef went to it and lit up a cigarette. He watched Laila with a curious expression as she stood rooted to the spot.

'You look pale, Laila. Is everything all right?'

'Yes. I'm just clearing the rubbish, then I'm off home.'

'So you said.' He blew a smoke ring into the air. 'The bins are behind the hedge.'

'Yes.' She didn't move.

He stared at her, his lips twitching slightly. He knew of course. Laila breathed easier.

He didn't know what she had, but he knew she had something. Another secret between them.

'You must be very careful, Laila. If you want to talk to me, I'm here for you. Tonight is Midsummer's Eve. I'll be down by the derelict boat house again. I'm not asking you to come. I don't want to pressure you, but I just want you to know, I'll be there.' He stubbed out his cigarette. 'I'd best be getting back to work. Remember what I said. If you want to talk.'

After he left, she put the box in the basket on the front of her bicycle and pedalled off.

Every part of her body was pumping, her legs, her heart, pulse, and breath. She had never experienced this mix of terror and exhilaration. Flying through the haze of static in her head, she was a wild thing unleashed by a summer madness. She could prove her worth to Finn and the resistance.

Drenched in sweat, she arrived at the bookshop. Oda had already locked up for the day. The family lived above the shop, their entrance around the back. Laila leaned her bicycle against the fence, and clutching her prize, she banged on the door.

Oda looked at Laila surprised. 'What—'

'Is Finn here?'

'He's upstairs. He turned up safe and sound mumbling about a secret mission. Is everything—'

Laila charged past and up the stairs to Finn's attic room, Oda running behind her.

Both of them stared at her. She could imagine how she looked. Face burning and dress soaked in perspiration, clinging to her legs.

'What on earth do you have there?' asked Oda.

Laila placed the box on the floor and lifted out the radio as if it were a sacred offering, savouring her pride at the admiration on the faces of her friends.

'How did you manage that?' Finn was stunned.

'My crazy, clever friend.' Oda smiled.

* * *

They sat in silence over their tiny portions of food that evening. Laila wished that they could talk about Anton. Not about his death, but his life. Rejoice at the time they had spent with him. But Mama would sob, and Papa would remain stiff and silent. Hanna always became agitated and tearful. Olaf was able to talk about Anton, but at eight years old, his memories were patchy, and he knew better than to raise the subject. Laila hoped that with time, it would become easier.

Hanna announced she was meeting Karl after dinner, and Olaf was meeting some friends down by the harbour. Papa told him to be home by eight-thirty. Mama and Papa retired to the sitting room, she, picking up her knitting, he, his pipe.

Laila couldn't bear the suffocating silence so she went to her room and picked up a book but put it down again. Staring out at the window, she felt very alone. Midsummer's Eve, even during the occupation, was a special time and here she was stuck in her room like a sad spinster aunt. But there was someone who consumed her thoughts.

She decided to go for a walk along the waterfront, get out of the house, but first she needed to change out of the clothes she had been wearing all day. She undressed, freshened up in the bathroom, and returned to her wardrobe. She put on her red and white dress. After all, Midsummer's Eve was a special occasion. She unplaited her hair, brushed it out, and left it loose.

As she strolled down to the harbour, she breathed in the sea salt, tilted back her head, and felt the breeze in her hair. She relived the excitement of taking the radio. Success against the enemy felt good. What would her next assignment be?

She found herself walking along the harbour front. She couldn't help herself as her feet led her on. Ahead she saw the fish barrels which she had crouched behind as she watched Josef before she'd turned back home.

'*I just want you to know, I'll be there,*' he'd said. '*If you want to talk to me, I'm here for you.*' What could she possibly talk to him about? Could she tell him about the radio?

She stopped by the barrels. There were more people milling around than usual: soldiers and locals taking advantage of the extended curfew. Josef would be just ahead, behind the ramshackle boat house, sitting on the water's edge, admiring the view, absorbing the magic of *the* white night of summer. And she wanted to be there with him. She realised she'd decided that when she'd changed into her red and white dress.

The fog of doubt cleared, and she marched past the barrels, past the crumbling, splintered wooden sheds, until she came to the last one.

She waited. Two oncoming soldiers passed her by. A family had stopped to look at the fjord, a small boy on the father's shoulders. She waited. After a while, the mother said it was past the child's bedtime and the family ambled off.

Laila looked about. There was no one to see her, so taking a deep breath, she slipped round the side of the boat house.

He sat facing the water, stretched out on the ground, leaning back on his elbows. He was in full uniform but had taken off his cap and jacket and placed them next to him. The noises of the fjord hid her approach: the shriek of the gulls, the motors of returning fishing boats, and the slap of waves on the rocks. She stood motionless behind him, studying the back of his neck where his dark hair met his skin in a precise razored line. There, his skin was reddened by the sun. She could back quietly away, and he would never know she had been there.

'Hello, Josef.'

He spun round and his whole face was a smile.

'You came.' There was wonder in his tone.

'Obviously.' She spread her hands and smiled at his pleasure as her heart beat double time.

He jumped up and spread his jacket on the grass next to him. His shirt sleeves were rolled up, revealing the toned muscles of his forearms.

'Please, sit down.' He indicated his jacket.

She sat, kneeling her legs to one side, and tucked her dress beneath her. He sat down too, leaving a respectable distance between them, his legs stretched out, crossed at the ankles.

Now that Laila was here, she didn't know what to say to him.

After a few moments of silence, Josef glanced at Laila's handbag and said, 'Have you brought your sketch pad with you?'

When she shook her head, he said, 'Shame, I'd like to watch you draw.'

'You had the chance recently when I was sitting near the road. But you ignored me and drove straight past.' Why was she being argumentative when he was trying to be friendly? She'd managed to kill the mood in the first two minutes.

'After you didn't turn up that evening, it was clear that you didn't want anything to do with me. And I understood how you felt. I wanted to respect that and didn't want to impose on you, so I drove past. Should I have stopped?'

So reasonable, she thought.

'Sketching on a night like this doesn't do the view justice. You need colour, the nuances of light. My brother Anton always used to paint on *Sankthans*. His friends would drink and dance around bonfires, and he would paint.' She shrugged and gave a small laugh.

'Doesn't he paint any more?'

And there it was: what she wanted to talk about.

As they both gazed out at the sea, she told him the story. How Anton had gone out to paint, intending to join friends later that evening. Hanna had left to spend the night with Petra, and Laila had joined Oda, Finn, and some others on the beach. Finn started the fire the traditional way using flint stones. The girls, wearing wreaths of flowers, danced and sang. The boys watched and drank beer until the girls pulled them to their feet to dance before they all collapsed to the ground and watched a sun that refused to die.

When Laila had returned home, her brother was not there. He didn't return the next day. She found his newest painting, his brushes, and colour palette back in his room, so he must have returned home at some point. She spoke to his friends who said he hadn't joined them as planned on Midsummer's Eve. But where did he go next? And what happened to him?

Days later, his empty skiff was found washed ashore. Anton had never been seen again.

She finished her story, fell silent, and stared out at the silver-blue sky which was streaked with orange. She heard Josef say he was sorry, and they sat for a long time in silence watching the colour and shadow shift across the mountains.

Laila looked at Josef as he gazed out. She felt the pull of a bond between them. She felt like she could trust him. He had of course saved the people on the list. And helped her today when, holding the box, she was questioned by an officer. She longed to share her work with the resistance with him. To tell him about the radio. But again, she thought of Oda and Finn and how she mustn't implicate them in any way. To confide in him was to betray them.

He started to rummage in a duffel bag he had brought with him. 'Are you hungry? I've brought a picnic.' He withdrew a tin box, opened the lid, and showed her the contents.

'What is it?' she said, not recognising the thin slabs of black bread.

'Pumpernickel.'

'That sounds like a dwarf from a German fairy tale.' She grinned.

'It's German bread. Try it. Would you like ham or sardine?'

'Ham, please. My father is the manager at the sardine factory, so we have that quite often. Ham is something special.'

He handed her the ham sandwich and took the other. The smell of it made her realise how hungry she was. She studied the bread and frowned. 'I've never eaten black bread,' she said, biting into the dense, heavy mass, so unlike the light, soft bread her mother baked. She chewed and chewed, but the volume seemed to increase in her mouth. He laughed, and when she managed to finish her mouthful, she laughed too. She wasn't sure she liked the slight sour taste, but she was starving, so she ate it all.

He produced two bottles of Pils from his bag and handed one to her.

'You seem to have brought two of everything this evening. Were you expecting company?' she said, her tone teasing.

'I hoped.' He gave a shy smile.

They ate and watched as the sun transformed the view before them. The mountains grew dark, prominent formations etched against a fluid painting of orange, yellow, and fierce pink. The fjord was quieter now; the boats had returned to the harbour, followed by the gulls scrounging for scraps of fish.

'I need to ask you something,' she said. 'When you warned those people about to be arrested, you said that once you'd just watched something. Something that seemed to distress you.'

He was silent. She waited.

Just when she thought he wouldn't answer her, he turned to her with tears in his eyes. He told her about his best friend Isaac who'd lived three houses away. How he'd watched in horror as Isaac and his parents were driven from their home at gunpoint and shunted into the back of a truck. People stood on the kerb, watching. Josef had wanted to scream and run and haul them out. But then he looked at his own mother standing by his side and swallowed the bitter bile in his mouth. How would it help if he was arrested or shot? They would accuse him of being a friend of Jews, and his mother would be implicated by association. So, he had looked away. Like so many others; the worst possible crime.

'Shame burns in the pit of my stomach,' he said. 'Every day. So now I help where I can. It's not much. But it's something. Haas likes me for some reason, and I use that.'

Laila could see the agony in his face. She was moved by his words and had to again fight the urge to confide in him about her acts of resistance. However, she could maybe learn some things from him that would be useful. She fidgeted with her skirt.

After they had eaten, he asked her to teach him some Norwegian. She started with some basic expressions, enjoying hearing his thick accent as he repeated after her. For some reason, she found his inexperience endearing whilst fully aware she should find his accent threatening. But there was nothing threatening about Josef's voice.

'How do you say beautiful sky?'

She told him.

'How do you say beautiful night?'

She told him.

'How do you say beautiful girl?'

She lowered her eyes for a few heartbeats, then met his gaze.

She told him.

He leaned across and brushed a kiss over her lips. A kiss as soft as the breeze.

He pulled back. 'I don't want you to get hurt.'

'That sounds funny coming from a soldier,' she said with a soft smile.

He looked back over the fjord. The sun hovered low, teasing

the horizon, impatient to start the dawn; the sky flamed copper and the sea rippled gold-black. An eagle soared above.

Soon it would be curfew.

As they prepared to leave, Josef told Laila to set off first and he would follow some minutes later. 'I'll watch from a distance, check you're safe.'

She peeked around the corner of the boat house to make sure that no one was around and then returned along the harbour; she didn't turn to look back. But she had a warm feeling in the knowledge Josef was there, taking care. Her mind in a haze, a piece of prose came to her from a book she had read by Knut Hamsun:

> Night was coming on again; the sun just dipped into the sea and rose again, red, refreshed, as if it had been down to drink. I could feel more strangely on those nights than anyone would believe.

And that was how she felt. A strangeness she had not known before. A magical, midsummer strangeness. Or was it madness?

In bed that night, she replayed the evening over and over again in her head. Beneath the midnight sun, on a warm white night, something magical had happened: she had been kissed by a German soldier.

No. Kissed by a man. A good man.

Josef.

* * *

The hotel staff were questioned by the fascist Norwegian police force. A missing radio was taken seriously. Laila fought down her fear as the main suspects were interviewed in the manager's office. Chambermaids, maintenance workers, the housekeeper, and Laila all had access to the rooms. She knew nothing, she told the police officers. No, she suspected none of the staff. She saw the frustration on the officers' faces. Everyone was then lined up in the entrance hall whilst Major Haas paced up and down, his hands clasped behind his back.

'Somebody knows something,' he growled. 'We will take the main suspects to police headquarters for further questioning.'

He glanced around the room, his eyes settling on Laila fleetingly. The fear in the room was thick. Stifling. What would be the price of Laila's actions? She could hardly breathe.

The officer whose radio she'd taken stepped forward. 'I don't think that is necessary, Major. It's possible I didn't lock my door. In which case the culprit could have come from outside. Let's keep the incident contained and keep the hotel's good reputation.'

Laila glanced at the officer. His eyes were troubled. The man with the photo of his wife in the wide-brimmed hat and his sons with the gap-toothed smiles.

Major Haas pursed his lips, weighing up the options. 'Very well. We will dismiss the issue. But as a warning, overtime will be unpaid for a month.'

As the staff dispersed, the porter Johan whispered to Laila, 'The radio is worth the unpaid work,' and gave her a wink.

9

JULY 1941

The church bell was gone. They had taken it. Wrenched from where it had hung for over two hundred years and melted down to make cannons. Laila stood before the church and looked up at the void in the bell tower. Bronze was a valuable metal and the Germans had been taking the church bells down around the country and replacing them with replicas made from cheap metal. 'Lord knows how that will sound,' her father had said. 'And He won't like it.' However, the new bell for Narvik had not yet arrived so the empty tower gaped in a silent scream over the town. But worse was the recent arrest of the pastor for continuing to recite the King's Prayer at the church service. The exiled Norwegian king was no longer recognised by the Nazis and the prayer was now forbidden. The pastor had been sent to the prison camp at Grini near Oslo.

Laila felt low today as she walked over to a one-storey, wooden building next to the church. How could a Christian nation cause such sacrilege? Was this the behaviour of a civilised country?

She knew this building well; it was where a home had been set up for elderly people who were without family to care for them.

Whilst she had been at school, she'd helped out here in the school holidays.

Clutching the posy of wildflowers she had picked that morning, she went to look for Gudrun.

She entered the communal room where she found her friend sitting by the window. On her lap was a crochet needle and a ball of wool, but she had not begun anything. Pain squeezed Laila's heart.

She pulled up a chair and took Gudrun's hands in hers. The old woman blinked and turned to look at her.

'My dear girl, thank you for visiting me. I'm sure you have better things to do.'

'Not at all,' said Laila. 'I'm happy to see you.'

'Is there any news? Any news at all? Have the police found something? They must have found something. My darling Tore hasn't vanished into thin air.' She clasped Laila's hands with surprising strength. 'Some of the others here, they talk nonsense. They rave on about trolls and evil spirits and such like. Well, I don't believe in any of that. He's alive and he'll come back, of that I'm sure.'

'The police and army are still searching, and I'm sure you're right. You must believe in it for it to be true. We *will* find him, I promise.'

Gudrun pushed herself out of her chair. 'I've made a decision. I must get out of here. They act like I have one foot in the grave. Well, I'm not finished yet! I'm going back home, and I'll carry on making radio reports. We must fight on.' Her voice was strong and clear.

Laila was proud of Gudrun and relieved they would be able to carry on using her radio reports for the newsletters.

Laila and Oda continued with their deliveries, but the endless daylight made their work difficult and more dangerous.

10

JULY 1941

He had brought pumpernickel again, this time layered with ham and cheese.

She thanked him and popped it in her bag. She would give it to Olaf later. He was so skinny. Gazing out over the fjord, Josef said, 'I wish I had my painting things with me. It's certainly different here to the motifs in Dresden.'

Laila thought about how Anton had loved to go to her grandfather's cabin in the forest to paint. There were still some of his paints and paper there.

'What do you do when you're not being a soldier?' she asked, drawing her knees to her chest and resting her chin on her hands.

'I trained as an architect, which I suppose is not surprising considering the inspiration I get from my hometown. I'd just started a good job when the war broke out.'

'Not much inspiration here, for an architect.'

'I don't know. I think it's possible for buildings to reflect the nature that surrounds them.'

'Has your family always lived in Dresden?'

'No. I moved there with my mother and sister in 1921. My father was killed a few weeks before the end of World War One. He never met me, and only saw my older sister once whilst he was on leave.' He spoke without self-pity.

'That's so sad. Your poor mother.' She reached out to his hand on the grass and lay her fingers over his.

'She can't believe that only twenty-three years later, it's all happening again. Neither can I. I hate this war. I keep telling my mother that here, in Norway, I'm away from the action which is some relief for her.'

'Might you be posted elsewhere?'

'It's possible.'

They were quiet after that, Laila dwelling on what he had told her. At one point, loud voices came from the road, a group of three or four men engaged in a heated discussion. It sounded as if they had stopped on the other side of the boat house just a few feet away from where Laila and Josef sat. The men were shouting about collaborators and Nazi spies. Laila froze. This was not a good time to be caught having a picnic and a beer with a German soldier. They both looked at each other, remaining motionless until the voices drifted away.

Josef turned to her, his face troubled. 'We shouldn't be doing this. *I* shouldn't be doing this. It's dangerous for you.'

'Here's not such a good place to meet. There are too many people around,' she said.

'The irony is our army is actively encouraged to have relationships with Norwegian women. In contrast, these same young women are being persecuted by their own people. I don't want you to get hurt, Laila.'

Her throat was dry, and she took a sip of beer from the bottle. She should agree and finish this now, before their actions caused pain for everyone. But...

Her voice was hoarse when she spoke. 'My grandfather has a cabin in the woods. It's secluded there.'

The words were out. She couldn't meet his eyes.

Silence.

He moved closer and brushed her cheek. 'Is that a good idea, Laila? Really?'

His voice held a pleading tone. For her to agree or disagree? She turned to him and pressed her lips firmly against his. She sensed his surprise and heard his sigh as he gave in to himself – and her – and returned the kiss. She understood in that moment that she had made her choice; she had crossed a line and now the course was set.

11

The first thing that Laila did when she stepped out from the trees into the clearing was slip off her shoes and socks and walk barefoot through the white and fuchsia willow herbs that led to the *hytte*. She warmed with nostalgia as she stood before the red wooden cabin that Grandpa had built with his own hands. He wouldn't be able to make it here this summer because of his arthritis. And her parents had bought their own cabin a few years ago. No one would come here.

The *hytte* had one window at the front and one at the back, and a turf roof covered in velvet green grass, daisies, and buttercups. Grandpa had told the story many times of how family and friends had helped to hoist up the sod onto the roof and pack it firmly down; this kept the house warm in winter and cool in summer. When the job had been completed, Grandpa held a roofing party, providing food and drink for everyone. He had taken Grandma's hand and the two newlyweds had danced late into the light Arctic night. There had obviously been more than dancing that night; nine months later, Papa had been born.

The key was under the large boulder by the door as always. Laila let herself in.

Although the one-roomed house was simply furnished – a table, two chairs, an armchair, and a bed – Grandma's handiwork lent a warm and cosy atmosphere. She had embroidered cushions with animals such as reindeer and moose, and on the wooden walls hung tapestries with mystical motifs, tree spirits, and elves. Laila hadn't thought much about her grandmother lately, and the realisation made her feel sad. She remembered how when Grandma had laughed her whole body had shaken and her eyes had streamed with tears.

On the floor lay two sheepskin rugs. There was a small kitchen and woodstove on one side of the room, and along the back wall was the narrow double bed that Grandpa had made from spruce pine. In a corner stood Anton's easel, covered up by an old table-cloth. On the floor beneath were a tin of paints and brushes. She removed the tablecloth and folded it away.

Laila opened the windows, swept the floor, and shook out the sheepskins. Then she went to collect wood from the shed outside and filled up the stove so she would be able to heat water. The bed was unmade, the eiderdown folded with two pillows perched on top. Thinking this made the place look unlived in, she found some clean linen and made the bed.

There was no running water or electricity so she checked that there were candles and a bucket in the cupboard under the sink. Grandpa had chosen to build close to a nearby stream so that water could be fetched easily. Finally, she went to check the outhouse, a grey wooden hut with the traditional heart shaped peephole in the door that let in light.

Satisfied that everything was in order, she took the bucket and strolled to the stream where, as a child, on warm summer days, she would paddle with Hanna and Anton.

Today, the banks of the stream were scarlet with lupins, shocked by the random arctic poppy in bright orange. Laila picked a bunch of flowers, dipped her bucket into the stream and, back at the cabin, put the flowers in a vase of water and set it on the table. Stepping back, she surveyed the room, pleased with what she saw. She couldn't wait to see Josef's expression when he came tomorrow.

She had taken her time drawing the map. Sitting cross-legged on her bed, she had indulged in each stroke of the pencil. A winding road. A crossroads. An old hut near the bus stop. The first few conifers followed by denser forest. Then the cross where she would meet him, about two hundred metres from the bus stop. She wrote the time, ten fifteen; half an hour after the bus had left and half an hour before the next would arrive. There would be no one around.

At the hotel, when Josef had come to reception to ask for a pen and paper, she had handed the map over to him. Their eyes smiled at each other.

Now, on the eve of their meeting, unable to believe her own actions, she felt as if she were a protagonist in a movie. It was nearly dinner time when Laila skipped back through the woods to retrieve her bicycle at the side of the road. Guilt and excitement coursed through her as she sped home.

* * *

She peeked out between the trees. Looked left. Right. No one. Stepping out, she saw him cycling over the hill. When he returned her wave, she retreated into the trees, waiting. She heard the creak of pedals and the rattle of the bicycle chain.

Josef appeared, pushed his bicycle off the road, and propped it against a tree. Laila was relieved to see him without a helmet, rifle, or a pistol at his hip. The top buttons of his shirt were undone. She realised she had never seen him in civilian clothes, never mind in the more casual style he now wore his uniform.

They stood opposite each other. The awkwardness she felt was reflected in his face. He moved to kiss her hello, but then didn't. He was freshly shaven. She had the urge to reach out and touch his soft cheek.

Grabbing his hand, she said, 'I can't wait to show you the *hytte*.'

He laughed as she pulled him along through the trees, the scent of pine whispering around them. They stopped before the clearing and she watched his face as he saw the *hytte* for the first time.

'Oh, Laila. It's wonderful.'

She kicked off her sandals and pointed at his shoes.

'You must take off your shoes. It's a family tradition. We always cross the meadow barefoot.'

'Really? I'm not used to showing my feet in public.' He grinned.

'It might seem improper to you Germans. Against regulations and all that.'

'Definitely against regulations. That's why I'm going to do it.'

He kneeled and untied his laces, folded his socks carefully, and tucked one in each shoe. She had the urge to fling his socks through the air. It was funny to see him in uniform with bare feet. She had never seen his toes before. The thought made her smile from the inside out.

Shoes in hand, they walked across spongy moss and into the sunlight, through the flowers, sidestepping the bees.

Laila retrieved the key from under the rock and opened the door, aware he was watching her every movement. She felt expectation in the air.

'It's idyllic here,' he said as he took in his surroundings.

'It's my special place.'

He glanced at the freshly made bed. Laila grew hot. She bustled over to the easel.

'I thought you could paint.'

His face became earnest. 'Thank you. I know how precious Anton's things are to you.'

There was an awkward pause.

She headed back towards the door. 'Let's go for a walk.'

Laila loved the way you could hear the sound of the water long before you broke from the trees. They reached the waterfall just after noon. A drape of white lace cascading down, fringed with silver light.

They sat in silence at the rock pool's edge, watching the prisms of rainbow hues in the halo of mist.

Josef took off his jacket and rolled up his sleeves.

She tried not to stare.

Then the dam of tension and uncertainty broke within her, and she turned to him, lifting her face.

They kissed. Long and deep.

They watched a group of white wagtails playing on the rocks, flapping their tails in the water spray.

They kissed again.

They cupped their hands and drank water from the pool.

'Do you ever swim here?' he said.

Laila pointed to a large boulder at the edge of the pool. 'What do you see there?'

'A rock. Jagged and covered in slimy moss.'

'Look more closely.'

He squinted against the sun and shook his head.

'Look at the form,' she said.

'It looks like a person. Hunched over. With a bulbous nose.' He grinned.

'It's a troll,' said Laila. 'He guards the waterfall. Those that have trespassed in the rock pool have disappeared without trace. Legend says they get eaten by the troll and he grows taller with each meal. I swear it was much smaller when I was a child.'

He laughed. 'Do you believe in trolls?'

'I believe in the importance of our legends.'

'I admire the way you love your country. Admire your pride.'

'Doesn't everyone love their country?'

'What makes a country? Its heritage? Its culture? Or the things it does?'

Laila didn't answer.

Josef sighed. 'I'm sickened of what is being done in my country's name. How could our people bring Hitler into power? I didn't vote for him, but too many did, hoping for the better life he promised out of the depression. And then the terrible propaganda of hate that followed. I feel so helpless. So insignificant. The few things I do are not enough. I want to do more.'

Was that a questioning look he gave her? She wanted to say that he could do more. She could ask him to help her and her friends. But would Finn trust him? She would have to speak to him first.

They were silent for a while.

'My favourite place to swim is in the stream by the *hytte*,' she said.

'I would like to swim there too. With you.' His face brightened.

Laila led Josef back through the forest. They hunted for trolls – in the gnarled bark of trees, amongst piles of rocks, and etched in boulders.

When they reached the stream, he rolled up his trousers, and she lifted the hem of her pink dress. They waded in, gasped, paddled, and splashed. He grabbed her waist and pulled her to him. They kissed and she could feel every contour of his body through his wet clothes.

After they had clambered out of the water, they lay on their backs on the grass, eyes closed, faces towards the sun. She felt him move beside her. Above her. His lips on hers. Deep, urgent kisses. He pulled back, his breath heavy on her neck, undoing the top buttons of her dress. His lips brushed her skin. His tongue on her breast. He paused and looked up at her.

'Is this all right? I'll stop if you tell me to.' His voice thick.

'Don't stop,' she whispered.

He took her nipple in his mouth. He slid his hand under the hem of her dress and grazed his fingers along her inner thigh. Her body tensed, her breaths quickening as his tender fingers stroked, explored.

It was finally happening. The moment she had imagined for so long. The moment she knew would come when she told him about the *hytte*. Part of her thought how unreal everything was. Yet, another part of her was rooted to the here and now of every sensation. Every nerve alert and exposed craving for more. And there was no outside world, war, soldiers, oppression. No guilt. No shame. Just her and Josef and this moment of honesty.

'I love you, Laila,' he said.

* * *

They left their wet clothes stretched out on the grass to dry. Laila fetched towels from the linen cupboard and wrapped hers under her arms. Josef tied his at his waist and unpacked the bread and *wurst* he had brought. She washed the wild blueberries she had picked that morning and they sat outside by the stream to eat their picnic.

When they took their plates back to the *hytte*, Josef studied the easel.

'Would you like to paint?' she said.

He tugged at her towel, and it fell to the floor.

'Obviously not...' She smiled.

This time they made love in bed, taking their time. She was in awe of how her body responded to his touch, and his to hers. But there was more; their souls were entwining like ivy. Lying in each other's arms, they talked for hours about their lives. Laila had never shared herself like this before. She could tell him almost anything. Except of course her involvement with Oda and Finn in the resistance.

At six o'clock, Josef had to leave to return to his barracks. The wrench she felt when he left was a physical pain. But sweet too.

She tidied up the *hytte* before setting off for home, preparing a story about how she had spent her day: sketching, picking berries, and a walk with Oda.

'Your day out has certainly agreed with you,' remarked her mother. 'You look very well.'

Laila had never felt such joy.

12

JULY 1941

The intense smell of the *Leberwurst* was overwhelming. Laila dabbed a finger on the smeared knife and licked her fingertip, amazed at the elation she could feel from taste. The Hotel Nordic cook had invited her to the kitchen to help herself to the leftovers from the officers' breakfast meeting that morning. Supper had been meagre last night, and she'd had no breakfast, so her stomach ached with hunger as she spread a crusty slice of bread thickly with the smooth, creamy meat paste and clapped another piece of bread on top. It took all her willpower not to eat it there and then. Then she made another sandwich, for Hanna.

They were meeting in their lunch break, the date suggested by Hanna, an unexpected but welcome surprise. Hanna's stance had softened in recent days and although Laila had struggled to come to terms with her sister's harsh words that day by the beach, she also struggled with the chasm between them.

Laila popped the sandwiches in a tin and, leaving by the hotel's back entrance, set off to meet Hanna.

'Do you remember how obsessed we were with hopscotch?' said Hanna swinging her legs as they sat on a wall looking down on the port. She nibbled her sandwich slowly, savouring each bite.

'Every afternoon we played after school.' Laila smiled. 'It was fun,' she said, tilting her face up to the sun.

'And you were so pedantic that the rock we threw had to be smooth and flat, and the squares we made from sticks all had to be equal size.'

'Was I really such a pain?'

'Oh, yes. Particularly as you always won. Anything sporty we played, like tag, I didn't stand a chance against those long legs of yours.'

'But you were much better at hide and seek, and more creative when we played dressing up. Remember those amazing hairstyles you gave me?'

Hanna reached out and fondled Laila's long single plait of hair. 'Why don't you have your hair cut? A modern style?'

Laila surveyed Hanna's new short hairdo: soft curls that bounced above her shoulders. She looked very sophisticated compared to Laila.

'I'm not sure it would suit me.'

'Of course it would. I can ask my friend Elinor to cut it for you. She did mine very well.'

'I'll think about it.' She would ask Josef's opinion.

'I have some spare fabric at the shop, by the way. I made a dress for an officer's wife. He sent it to Germany for her birthday. I'll make a dress for you with the rest of the material.'

'But how about a dress for yourself?'

'I have pretty dresses.'

'And I don't?' Laila laughed, linking her arm in hers. 'What's all this about, little sister? Are you trying to make me look presentable?'

Two soldiers passed by and smiled at them.

'You need a boyfriend, Laila.'

Laila thought of her and Josef making love on sheepskin rugs in the *hytte*.

'You need to have some fun,' Hanna continued.

She and Josef swimming naked in the stream.

Decadent. Risky. Delicious as chocolate melting on her tongue.

'Do you have anyone in mind?' Laila asked.

'Karl has a friend you might like.'

It would be four days before Josef had time off again. She tingled with anticipation.

When Laila didn't reply, Hanna said, 'Unless you have your eye on anyone else...'

'No, no one.'

'And that German soldier?'

'There never was anything.'

Josef was everything. She could think of nothing else.

'You're sweet to worry about me. Thank you,' she said, and quickly changed the subject. 'And I'd love a new dress.'

Laila felt a swell of affection for her sister. She was as changeable as the colour of the sea, yet the times when she was like this were worth all the times she wasn't.

'You remember the carpenter's sons?' Laila's voice held that soft tone of reminiscence. When Hanna didn't answer, Laila added, 'Mikal and Rolf. They were older than us, but when you were about fourteen, Mikal was quite taken with you.'

Laila turned to look at Hanna's profile. Her face was rigid.

'Are you okay?' she asked, upset that the mood of moments ago had gone, as if flicked off like a light.

Hanna jumped down from the wall. 'I have to get back to work.'

Laila followed, bewildered.

A large ship had arrived whilst they were talking, and a group of SS soldiers had gathered on the quay.

'I wonder what's going on,' said Laila.

A stream of prisoners disembarked, dazed and slow, stumbling along in ragged striped clothes resembling pyjamas.

'They're Yugoslavian, poor souls.' An old port worker standing beside them spoke. 'Around 900 of them, I've heard. The Nazis have built a new camp, ten kilometres from here. I bet the swine make them march the whole way by foot.'

The prisoners, exhausted and starving, were spurred along with long sticks and bayonets on rifles. By Norwegian SS guards.

'It's sickening to see our own people behaving that way,' said Laila.

'A Nazi is a Nazi, whatever his nationality,' said the port worker and ambled away, shaking his head.

Over the next few days, the prisoners were seen in small groups working around Narvik, hauling cargo, repairing the pier, and building armaments. The whole coast was being fortified against the British, and slave labour was used to erect lookout towers and build cannons. When a worker was no longer able to stand, he was hauled onto a truck and taken away; either pushed into the sea or taken back to the camp to be shot. The townsfolk tried to help as much as possible, passing on food when the guards weren't looking, and occasionally, a *Wehrmacht* soldier would look in the opposite direction on purpose. Josef was one of them.

One evening, Papa said there were rumours that typhoid had broken out at the camp and that an eight-metre-high barbed fence had been erected, splitting the camp into two parts: a sick area and a healthy area. He warned the family to keep their distance from the prisoners because of the danger of infection. After that, Laila and Hanna had to throw pieces of their bread ration along the ground to the starving men.

Two weeks later, Laila and Oda were waiting for Finn in his attic when he burst into the room, angry and breathless.

'That new prison camp is a huge fireball. The Germans have set fire to the sick enclosure and the prisoners in there are burning alive. Apparently, the fire has got out of control and some of the healthy prisoners have managed to escape.'

'But that's mass murder,' whispered Laila.

'Things are getting worse now that the SS is involved. They have the say over the *Wehrmacht*.' Finn slumped down onto a crate. 'And the Gestapo has also increased its presence in the town. We're all going to have to be extra careful.'

When Laila cycled to work the next day, she felt a stillness, heavy and sinister hanging over the town. The air was thick with smoke and the pungent smell of burned wood and human flesh.

* * *

Something shuffled. A scrunch of stones underfoot. Laila froze, listening. An elk? Maybe a reindeer? She had seen many in these woods over the years. She held her breath. The figure appeared between the birch trees, crouched low, moving erratically. A child. A boy. He caught sight of her and stared in shock. Wide, sunken eyes in a face of bone, his head shorn. Clad in threadbare, black-and-white striped clothing; each foot was wrapped in a bundle of rags.

Laila remained motionless, her mind racing. Any sudden move would send him scuttling away. She gave a warm smile and then, gently, set the basket she was carrying on the ground. Placing both hands over her heart she mouthed the word, '*venn*'. Friend.

He glanced over his shoulder, then at her, and then to the trees to his left. She repeated the word, '*venn*', soft, reassuring. She nodded at him, pressing her hands against her chest. She could see now he was not a child, but an emaciated young man.

Alone and terrified.

She pointed up at the way she had come from the *hytte*. Then she pointed at him and beckoned him to her. He stood, transfixed staring at her. She took a step backwards and waved for him to follow. Picking up her basket, she half-turned and continued to walk back up the path, keeping her eyes on him. Again, he looked into the forest to his left and right.

He would bolt away. He didn't trust her.

She kept smiling, repeating over and over, '*venn, venn*'. Haltingly, he took a step towards her and paused. Then another step, his oversized trousers flapping around his thin legs.

He followed her. Laila's pulse quickened.

She walked into the clearing and pointed towards the *hytte*. He hesitated on the edge of the woods. She crossed over and opened the door wide, turning to him smiling, beckoning him to her. Then she went inside, put a jug of water on the table, and fetched a glass. Would he come? She sat down at the table and waited.

There was no sign of him. He didn't trust her. Why should he?

There were so many Norwegians who collaborated with the Germans for favours. In a way, she was a collaborator herself for she loved a German.

The sound of a footstep. His grey face appeared around the door post. Smiling, she pointed at the water jug and the chair opposite her. He surveyed the cabin, looked over his shoulder, then entered, shutting the door behind him.

Sitting opposite, he drank the water down in one gulp. She poured him another glass and unpacked the basket she had been carrying. The contents had been brought by Josef that morning and she had intended to take them home with her, but now they had a new purpose. She took out the quarter loaf of bread, a small piece of cheese, and two apples and put them in front of the young man. He stared at her and mumbled something she didn't understand as he pulled chunks of the bread with dirt encrusted fingers and shoved them into his mouth.

Laila watched him eat, his angular jaw working, his restless eyes darting from her to the food and then back towards the door. He left a piece of bread and an apple which he pocketed. How ironic that Josef's food went to an escaped prisoner. A tiny piece of justice.

He said something, nodding, which she thought might be thank you. She didn't think he was Russian. Most likely he was one of the Yugoslavian prisoners who had fled the fire. Pointing to herself, she said, 'Laila.'

Then she pointed at him.

'Mislav,' he said.

'Mislav,' she repeated.

'Laila,' he said.

She fetched a notepad and pencil from a small commode. She sat back down, wrote her name and the number nineteen, her age. She pushed the notepad towards him and offered him the pencil. He wrote his name and the number twenty. Younger than Josef. Taking the pencil, she wrote down the word: friend, *venn*, repeating it several times and gesturing between the two of them.

Returning to the commode, she searched another drawer where her grandfather hoarded yellowed newspapers and some crumpled maps. She laid out a map of Europe on the table then raised her shoulders and spread her hands as if mimicking a question. The man studied the map and ran a bony finger along the Swedish border. That was not where he was from, but where he wanted to get to. A neutral country. The border was about sixty kilometres away through rough terrain and patrolled by German troops. They would be on the lookout for the escaped prisoners.

If Mislav was to have any chance of making it to Sweden, he

would need a guide, someone who knew the hidden routes; one of Finn's Sami friends.

Laila made a decision. First, she opened the trunk of Grandpa's old clothes and indicated to Mislav to look inside. Then she mimed washing herself under her arms and picked up an empty bucket. He smiled at her for the first time, and it warmed her heart. She ran to the stream, filled the bucket with water, returned and placed it by the sink. She found a clean cloth and placed it by the bucket. There was no soap to offer him, but water was better than nothing. Now came the hardest part. To make him understand what she intended.

She led him back to the table and sketch pad. Her hands flew over the paper. Time was short. She sketched a figure and wrote Mislav beside it. Then she sketched another figure and wrote the word Sami and *venn*. She drew arrows, rough outlines of mountains and trees, and then at the edge of the paper a wavy line where she wrote the word Sweden. It was a crude map, but he seemed to understand.

Gesticulating and miming, she explained that she would fetch the guide and that Mislav should wash and change out of his prison clothes. He chewed his lip, watching her face. She knew he was deciding whether he could trust her or not. She pointed to her watch, indicating she would be back in an hour.

Before she departed, she placed her hand on his chest and fixed her gaze on him, willing him to understand her.

'Mislav, you can trust me. Laila. Mislav. Friends.' She smiled and pressed her hand against his heart.

And then she left him. Fear twisted her stomach. She was now concealing an enemy to the Reich. In her grandfather's *hytte*. She was endangering her whole family. And if Mislav was now caught, he would be shot.

Her legs pumping with adrenalin, she raced down the hill

through the trees, grabbed her bicycle that was hidden from the road, and sped to the bookshop, praying that Finn would be home.

She was in luck. Finn and Oda were in the back yard cleaning their bicycles. Breathless, she jumped down, 'Thank goodness you're here. I need your help.'

She explained about Mislav.

'We have to act quickly,' said Finn as he mounted his bicycle. 'They'll be searching for him. I'll find a guide. You get back to the *hytte*, so he doesn't get nervous and run; he won't get far on his own. I'll meet you there as soon as I can.'

When she arrived back at the hut, the door was open. Her heart sank. Fearing the worst, she ran inside.

Empty. He had fled. Or worse still, he had been captured.

Tears pricked her eyes. She had wanted to help him. Maybe he hadn't trusted her and ran. Maybe the Nazis had shot him. The empty water jug and glass stood on the table; a few breadcrumbs lay scattered. The lid of the clothes chest was open. With heavy legs she went to the chest. Hopefully he had changed clothes.

If he'd been captured, the Nazis would be after her. And her grandfather. And—

A floorboard creaked behind her.

She froze. They had come for her.

Her blood pulsed in her ears.

She turned and cried out.

Mislav stood there, clean faced, wearing Grandpa's old clothes: baggy brown trousers tied at the waist with some string he had found, and the navy fisherman's jumper that Grandma had knitted. On his head, he wore a navy cap.

Thank God. She took a step towards him in joy but stopped short when she saw the penknife in his hand.

Surely not. He wouldn't hurt her. Would he? She backed up against the wall, holding up her hands in surrender.

He saw her fear and shook his head, dropping Grandpa's penknife onto the table. He stretched out an arm, opening the palm of his left hand, offering her to look. Cautiously, she approached him as he spoke words that sounded earnest and kind. She took the object from his hand. It was a flat smooth stone, probably collected by the stream. She rubbed her thumb over the surface and read what was engraved there. Two words: Laila and, underneath, *venn*. She turned the grey-white stone over, and there on the other side, she read the initial M and again, underneath, *venn*.

She looked up at him, swallowing hard. Briefly, she wondered why he had engraved only his initial, but of course he was protecting her. If she were to be found with a keepsake bearing a Yugoslavian name that would be difficult to explain. She thanked him, knowing that she would treasure this memento of the briefest of friendships.

They sat at the table to wait. He took the notepad and drew, not very well, a childlike drawing with matchstick figures: two larger figures, and three smaller ones with long hair. His parents and three sisters. He wrote their names above their heads. Then he drew a house next to a large tree. His family. His home. A tear ran down Laila's cheek. He must survive. He simply must.

There was a sharp rap on the door and Mislav jumped up, grabbing the penknife, which he held out in front of him.

Finn entered the room with another man, and Laila put a reassuring hand on Mislav's arm.

'*Venn*,' she told him.

He lowered the penknife but kept it in his hand.

The Sami guide was broad-shouldered and bearded. He wore a brown tunic tied with a leather belt from which hung a leather pouch and two knives. His loose pants were tucked into short, reindeer-skin boots, stitched in red, which curled upwards at the front.

He had come well prepared; in a large skin bag, he had brought water, food, and blankets. He introduced himself as Saba.

'It's about ten hours' march across mountains to the border. I use paths unknown to the Germans.' He looked at Mislav as he spoke, although he knew he would not understand. 'There's a mountain cabin where we can rest, but we should reach Sweden in about two days. On the one hand the summer weather makes the going easier, but on the other hand there's no darkness to hide us.'

The shoes that Mislav had taken from the clothes chest were too big for him, but after Laila had stuffed some old newspaper in the toes, they fitted better. When it was time to say goodbye, Mislav spoke to Laila, his hands steepled as if in prayer. She liked to think he was saying he would tell his family about her and that he would always remember her. She wished him well with all her heart and watched him and Saba disappear into the forest.

Laila went to visit Finn every evening for the next few days to enquire if he had heard any news. And each morning, when she woke, she took the engraved stone from her bedside table and turned it over in her hand.

Please God, keep him safe. She had wanted to keep the drawings they had done together. But Finn had been adamant and had burned them.

Five days later, Finn was beaming as Laila entered his attic room. Saba had returned with the news that Mislav had crossed safely into neutral Sweden. Hearing this was one of the sweetest moments of Laila's life.

She kept Mislav's escape a secret. It saddened her that Josef was the one person she could not share her story with. But she still would not risk betraying Oda and Finn.

13

AUGUST–SEPTEMBER 1941

The time Laila spent with Josef was the most joyful. She was amazed at how their love had transformed her; how even during the terrors of war, she could feel such happiness. She had become someone else: daring, carefree. A sensual woman. She didn't feel sensible at all. And that was wonderful.

One afternoon, they wandered to the waterfall where they sat by the plunge pool and dared to cool their feet whilst the troll was looking the other way.

Josef cupped his hands in the water and brought it up to Laila's décolleté, where he released it, drop by cold drop. She shivered as the water trickled beneath her dress and between her breasts.

Kissing her wet skin, he undid the buttons, unhurried, pausing, teasing. With a sigh, she lay back on the grass and gazed into the bluest of skies and heard water splashing on rocks. If only this purest of moments could last for ever. If only there was nothing and no one outside this pinpoint of time.

After they had made love, she lay in the crook of his arm. There was so much she would have liked to share with him: her fear and exhilaration when she distributed the newsletters. She wanted to ask if he'd known that time when he stopped her with her basket. But then he would ask where the newsletters came from. He must have suspected something when he caught her with the box that hid the radio. If only she could talk about Oda and Finn. And Mislav. In another world, there would have been no secrets between them.

When she had tentatively suggested to Finn that there may be a sympathetic German, he had ranted with fury that the evil bastards could not be trusted, that they would betray them to the Gestapo. Laila hadn't mentioned it again.

'How I wish we weren't at war,' she said. 'We wouldn't have to hide our love. We would go to dances, take a boat across the fjord, sit by the harbour. You would come to lunch with my family and play with Olaf. My parents would love you and treat you like a son.'

'A perfect dream, *Liebling*. But without the war, we would never have met. Fate has our joy and misery entwined; one cannot exist without the other.' He turned on his side to face her and traced a finger along her cheek. 'I love you, Laila, and I can't imagine a life without you. We'll work it out, somehow. The war must be over soon. Then we can marry, have a family, a normal life.' His voice was thick with emotion.

Her heart swelled. She felt light and dizzy at the realisation this was the happiest moment of her life.

'I love you too,' she whispered.

14

MARCH 1942

Everyone was looking forward to spring, but none more than Laila. Finding places to meet Josef in secret was nearly impossible in winter. Her father had locked up the *hytte* in October, bringing their summer dream to an abrupt end. They sought alternative venues. The *Wehrmacht* used the ski club to put on dances for the soldiers, and local girls that dared to attend despite public opinion. Laila would not contemplate going public with her relationship to Josef. So, they were confined to meet in an icy, derelict boat house and in the back of army trucks where they had hurried sex fully clothed. This lacked the romance of their languid, summer months, but those snatched moments only heightened their passion for each other. Sometimes on a frosty, clear night, they watched the northern lights; bolts of fluorescent-green silk unrolling from the heavens. And Laila continued her deceit. To her family, Oda, and Finn.

* * *

After the town picture house had been bombed, an improvised movie house had been set up in a disused warehouse to entertain the troops, and also in an attempt to encourage acceptance of the new regime. The Norwegians had not easily been bought; they boycotted the German *Kino* at first. But eventually, weary and needing escapism, they started to line up outside to buy tickets.

The news reel flickered to an end and Laila let out a sigh of relief. A tight knot always formed in her chest when she watched the German propaganda films.

She had come alone to see one of the increasingly shown German musicals. Since America had joined the war, Hollywood pictures had been banned. No more Errol Flynn movies. She sat amongst the soldiers and townsfolk, eager for the film to start. Her handbag and coat sat on the seat beside her, a way for her to ensure nobody sat down next to her. An elderly woman had tutted at the offending articles but luckily had not asked for them to be removed and chose to sit elsewhere.

As the film titles appeared on the screen, the familiar scent of his aftershave could be detected in the air. She kept her eyes fixed on the screen.

'Excuse me. Is this seat taken?' he asked.

She looked up at him as she removed her things and placed them on her lap. Even in the dark she could see the mischievous gleam in his eye.

Everything had gone according to plan.

So close to him. In the dark. Small, rapid breaths.

Not daring to look at him, she watched the dancers on screen as they marched and sang along to a brass band.

She let her hand slip from her lap and rest on the edge of the seat. Within moments, his fingers brushed against her skin and he linked his little finger around hers and gave a gentle squeeze. She squeezed in return. Then he slipped his whole hand in hers.

In public.

This was bold. Dangerous. Thrilling.

He stroked the inside of her palm, just whispers of a touch. And on the screen the hero and heroine embraced in a classic pose.

Josef pressed his thumb into her palm, making small rhythmic circles.

Laila swallowed. Goosebumps on her arms.

An image of her and Josef in the freezing boat shed, her pressed up against the wall.

It was hot in the cinema.

Perspiration between her breasts. Her heart frantic in her chest.

Finally, the movie came to an end.

His hand withdrew and she clasped her bag in front of her, rearranging her features as the lights went on.

Josef rose and left, whilst Laila waited till her heart had calmed before affecting a nonchalant exit from the cinema.

One day, in late March, Josef stepped out from behind a tree, causing Laila to nearly fall off her bike. It was midday and she was on her way to her late shift at the hotel. The brakes screeched as she came to a stop. Instinctively, she checked over her shoulder, but Josef had chosen a quiet spot to wait for her and there was no one around.

'What a lovely surprise,' she said, as she got down from her bike.' Her smile faded when she saw his grim expression.

'I've just come off duty. Major Haas was talking with the chief of police a short while ago. They've had orders to arrest all Jews. They mentioned a tailor's wife. Hanna works for a tailor. Is he

Jewish?'

'No. But his wife, Vera, is.'

'I must warn them,' he said. 'Is their shop the one opposite the old schoolhouse? Give me your bike. I'll go straight there.'

Laila fought back her terror. They must think straight.

'No, Josef, I'll go. You're in uniform and someone will report that you visited.'

She mounted her bike and sped off. She wasn't going to risk Josef being executed as a traitor. She glanced over her shoulder and saw him running after her. She pedalled faster.

It only took five minutes to reach the shop. A police car stood outside. Laila pulled up beside it, her heart ramming against her ribs. The front door flew open, and two policemen hauled Vera through the doorway.

'I haven't done anything,' she screamed.

Her husband ran behind. 'Please. Don't take her. She's a good woman. Please!'

'Stand back, Jew lover, or you'll be next,' one of the policemen snarled.

Within seconds, Vera was bundled away. A shocked Hanna appeared at the doorway. At the same time, Laila saw Josef running up the street, and gave him a shake of her head. His shoulders slumped as he turned back the way he'd come. They had been too late.

* * *

When Laila came home from her late shift, the family were sitting solemnly around the kitchen table, the dinner plates not yet cleared away. Hanna's eyes were swollen from crying. Mama was distraught. She had not been close friends with Vera at school, but they'd got on well at social gatherings and Vera's son had been in the same class as Anton.

Laila fell heavily into a chair. The terrible scene of Vera being dragged away had spun around her brain all day.

'Why were you at the shop?' Hanna asked.

'I had extra time before my shift. I just thought I'd stop by and say hello. Maybe look at some fabric,' she said, stumbling over her lame explanation.

Hanna was too distressed to notice.

* * *

The hope that Vera would be returned home faded over the next few days. Her husband's enquiries as to her whereabouts fell on deaf ears. Rumours circulated that she had been sent to a work camp in Poland, but no one knew for sure. There was a renewed surge of hate against the Germans.

When Laila saw Josef on duty at the hotel, they looked at each other with sad eyes. The excitement of anticipation at seeing him every day was tainted with a swell of guilt. Yes, he had tried to help. But he was still their country's enemy.

Everyone was talking about Vera. Her family at dinner, the staff at the hotel. They knew of course that Jews were being rounded up in Europe and being relocated. But now terrible rumours were circulating about work camps. She had seen how the Russian and Yugoslavian prisoners were treated like slaves. Surely, they wouldn't treat a middle-aged Norwegian woman the same way. Would they?

Ten days passed before she was able to meet Josef again. It was a grey, windy Sunday. Sleet whipped through the air. A quick check around her, and she slipped into the derelict boat house from the back. Half the structure had collapsed, but at least it was sheltered from the wind. Josef was waiting with a flask of mushroom soup and crusty bread.

They wrapped their arms around each other and kissed. But she was the first to pull away.

'I'm so sorry about Vera,' said Josef. He cupped her cheek with his hand.

'You're sorry? That's it? Sorry?' Her voice went up an octave.

'I know how you must feel. It's terrible—'

'You don't know how I feel, Josef. I've been cocooning myself in our love. Trying to hide from the real world, lying to my family, betraying my own people. I thought our love was pure. But how can it be when it's tainted with blood and suffering?'

'Our love is pure. It has nothing to do with the war.' He stepped towards her, but she held up her hand, hot anger rising.

'How long can we carry on pretending we don't know what the Nazis are doing? What *your* people are doing? What's happening in these work camps? What's happened to Vera?' She thumped her fist on his chest and screamed, 'What's happened to Vera?'

'Please, Laila. Calm down. I'll try to—'

'Calm down?! I can't do this any more. I love you but it's killing me.'

'Oh, Laila.' She watched his dark, beautiful eyes brim with tears as he reached for her.

'No,' she said with a racking sob, turned and bolted out of the boat house.

Back home, she slipped up to her room without being seen and cried into her pillow, soaking it with her tears. When her sobs subsided, she turned on her back and stared through swollen eyes at the ceiling. She had vented all her anger and frustration over the Nazis on Josef. Because she could. He would not report her, arrest her, or harm her. She had flung the full force of her emotions at him, and it had been freeing. In that moment, she knew she'd been right to end it.

For her family. For Norway. For her self-respect.

Yet the thought of living without him left her hollowed out like a gutted salmon.

That night, she dreamed about Vera being dragged into the black car. About the prisoner being shot for accepting bread. And the prisoner became Vera. And the man holding the gun was Josef.

And then things got worse.

The next day, they took Vera's son.

* * *

Josef averted Laila's gaze as she passed him each morning. He had stopped greeting her too. He was angry with her, of course. But surely, he understood how she felt. Or did he? Maybe he hadn't really loved her at all. Perhaps he took her to bed because there were no German women around. No, that was ridiculous. Josef wasn't like that. Then why didn't he try to reconcile with her? There were no notes passed over her desk. No whispers of his next time off. He had moved on. It was what she wanted. Then why did she feel so sad?

Then one morning, he wasn't there any more.

* * *

A week later, Uncle came to visit with provisions. Laila's stomach growled with hunger as Mama unpacked the box in the kitchen.

'It's not much, I'm afraid. The *Wehrmacht* are taking virtually everything from the farm that I have. They're sending it all to their troops in Russia.'

Laila looked up from the kitchen table where she was helping

Olaf with his homework. 'Do you still have your hidden radio, Uncle? Any news?'

'The BBC reckon Hitler has bitten off more than he can chew invading Russia. He's piling his troops in there. He's sent a load from here in Narvik.'

Laila felt a chill. Josef.

'Hitler's sending his fresh men who haven't seen much action. Like those here in Norway. But they've no real fighting experience.' Uncle gave a bitter laugh. 'They've been living a soft war. Drop like flies, they will.'

Olaf jumped up from the table and then quickly dropped to the floor playfully. 'I'm a German fly, Uncle.'

Laila bowed her head over Olaf's maths book. His pencilled sums danced before her eyes. Josef hadn't even said goodbye. He'd simply left as if nothing had ever happened between them. He hadn't tried to reach out to her after their argument. Her stomach twisted at the thought of him in battle.

Outside Hotel Nordic, only one guard stood now. Soldiers had been plucked from their soft war and tossed onto the front line. Fresh, healthy fodder for the war machine. Laila looked across from her desk at the empty space where Josef used to stand, yearning for the sight of his back. Wishing that their last conversation had been different. That she had acted differently. That she had let him speak.

* * *

That night, Laila opened the drawer where she kept the strips of cloth she had cut to size, ready for use tucked beneath her underwear. She slipped some pieces into her panties under her nightdress, sure her period would come that night. But the next day the cloths were dry.

Every night she positioned her cloths, and every morning there was no blood to be seen.

Don't panic, she told herself. They had been careful. Most of the time.

People didn't talk about their monthlies much, but Oda had mentioned that some girls had stopped menstruating due to lack of food. Laila realised how thin she had become and thought that was probably the reason. But one morning, she rushed to the toilet and was sick.

Then she knew.

15

JUNE–OCTOBER 1942

They called her the Nanny. Laila thought what a sick irony that was and wondered how the name originated. The path she was following became littered with boulders, forcing her to dismount and push her bicycle as she meandered through dark flickering shadow under the dense spruce trees. The air was chilled.

The shack appeared, shrouded in a blanket of brown, brittle, pine needles. This wasn't the Nanny's home. It was where she worked. Apparently, business was booming since the occupation.

Laila propped her bicycle against a tree and approached the door; the paint, once red, now faded to rust and peeling. There was a sign made from a plank of wood. It hung from a piece of wire on a nail in the door. It read:

Please Wait

Opposite the shack was an old tree stump. Laila sat down and stared at the closed door. Why had she come here? Could she really go through with it? First, she would learn about the possibilities. What the process entailed. To speak to this woman, the Nanny.

Laila had heard the rumours and gossip. Many young women had trodden this path. And for different reasons. Their lovers had abandoned them, or died, or were married. Or their lovers stood by them, but their families would not. The women were shamed and ridiculed. Shunned. Hated.

And that was why Laila was here. She was terrified of being hated by her family. The family she loved so much. But she also loved Josef with an intensity that thrilled and scared her. She had lost control of her world. The control she'd lost with Josef was exquisite, but the control she'd lost to protect and support her family was excruciating. If only she could talk to him, hold him. But that wasn't possible, so she must make this decision alone.

She chewed on a piece of loose skin around her thumb nail. She chewed till the first drop of blood oozed out, then stood up and walked back to the cabin door. Pressing her ear against the faded wood, she held her breath.

An old woman's voice, mumbled words.

A clang of metal.

Silence. A young voice, a moan. The older woman's voice. Harsh.

Shuffling sounds. The scraping of chair legs. Footsteps.

Laila jumped back from the door as it swung open. A young girl, maybe fifteen years old, appeared, her hair stuck to her face with sweat, her skin as ashen as birch wood. She leaned on the door frame, her gaze vacant. Laila stared at the bright red stain on the front of the girl's skirt, blooming outwards like an opening rose.

'You're bleeding,' Laila said.

'That's normal,' came a voice from inside. A putrid smell wafted out and a face threaded with red veins appeared. 'Have you come to take her home? Make sure she lies down for two days and she'll be fine. I've given her padding for her underpants.'

The girl looked down at her skirt. Her voice shook. 'I can't go home like this.'

'Get along, now,' said the Nanny, shoving the girl out the door. 'I have to clear up in here.' The door closed.

The girl stared at Laila with desolate eyes.

'What's your name? Where do you live?' Laila asked.

'I'm Lilly. Not far. Fifteen minutes' walk from here.'

Laila looked around her and indicated a patch of deep green moss. 'Lilly, go and sit there. Wait for me. I'll fetch you a skirt of mine and then take you home.'

Lilly whispered her thanks as Laila helped her to sit down on the ground.

Laila marched back to the cabin and thumped on the door.

'What now?' said the Nanny, snatching the door open, her hands on her hips. That awful smell punched out again. Did it come from the old woman or the room?

'Lilly will rest over there till I come back for her. Keep an eye on her.'

'That's not my job. I've done my part.'

Laila lowered her voice and hissed, 'If that young girl bleeds to death, I'll report you to my father.'

'So?'

'So, he is the police chief in town and an SS sympathiser,' she lied. 'And as I'm sure you're aware, carrying out abortions is illegal and, under Nazi law, is punishable by a firing squad.'

'All right, I get the message. Just be quick.'

'And bring her out something to drink,' called Laila as she ran down the path, pushing her bicycle until the ground flattened. Then she leaped on the saddle and pedalled home furiously.

Twenty minutes later, she returned with a navy skirt and some underpants. And a paper bag containing the last granules of sugar her family had left.

Laila's heart missed a beat when she saw her. Lilly lay motionless on the ground, her eyes closed. She ran and kneeled beside her, shook the young girl's shoulder.

'Lilly, wake up. Are you all right? Lilly, please wake up.'

The girl mumbled something and Laila lifted her head onto her lap gently. 'Open your mouth. I've brought you sugar.'

She dipped her finger into the bag and tapped some grains onto the girl's lips. Lilly licked her bottom lip and parted her mouth as Laila tipped the remaining sugar onto her tongue. The sweetness worked its magic. Lilly opened her eyes and after a few moments sat up.

'Thank you,' she said, 'for coming back.'

Laila helped her out of her soiled skirt and into the clean one.

'I'll walk you home and come back to fetch my bike later.' She put her arm around Lilly's waist and supported her weight.

The shack door opened.

'Good. You're back.' The Nanny leaned her head to one side and gave Laila a sly look. 'Is there anything else I can help with?'

'No,' said Laila. 'Definitely not.'

Lying in the bath, Laila stared at the swell of her stomach as it broke the surface of the water. She estimated she was about four months pregnant. Seeing a doctor was out of the question but she had witnessed her mother's pregnancies with Olaf and Inge so had some idea what to expect. How long before someone noticed? Mama was bound to be the first. A burgeoning stomach could not be explained by overeating on food rations.

And then the most amazing thing happened. A flutter in her

stomach as light as a butterfly wing. She lay her hand on the tiny bump, holding her breath, waiting. Again, she felt it. No, not it. Him or her. Their child. Thank God she hadn't let the Nanny do her evil work, let her destroy a part of Josef.

Over the next three weeks, it was impossible to concentrate on work. Her mind was a constant stream of potential conversations with her parents. How to break the news and make them understand? And how would others react? Hanna? Oda? People at the hotel? She was so nervous, she dropped things constantly: keys, pens, coins would slip through her fingers. Time was running out. Her stomach was beginning to show.

The opportunity came one morning when Laila had a late shift at the hotel. She was alone with Mama as they stripped the bedclothes in Olaf's room. Laila dropped the pillowcase on the floor and took a deep breath.

'Mama, let's sit down a moment.'

'Sit down? Whatever for? We need to get the washing done.'

Laila sat on Olaf's bed and patted the mattress next to her. 'Please, Mama. I need to talk to you.'

Mama gave her a quizzical look and after a moment's hesitation sat next to her.

Laila felt sick knowing she was about to shatter her mother's world. As if Mama didn't have enough to contend with.

'Mama, there is no easy way to say this. I'm expecting a baby.'

Mama's whole body jolted; her eyes popped. 'You're pregnant?'

Laila nodded.

'But with whom did you... I mean who is the father? I didn't know you were seeing anyone.'

'No one knew. The father is called Josef.'

'Josef? Who's Josef? That's not a Norwegian name.'

'No. It's German.'

Mama slumped and shook her head. 'It can't be true. A German. He raped you.'

'He didn't rape me. We were – are – in love.'

Mama sprang to her feet and with a fury in her eyes that Laila had never witnessed before, spat, 'How could you?'

'Mama, I—'

'How could you do this to us? A German! What will your father say? My God, Laila. What have you done?' Her mother was shaking. Laila stood and reached out to her, but she turned and ran from the room. Laila sank her head into her hands; she had let her family down in the worst way possible.

At ten o'clock that evening, Laila returned home from her shift to find Mama and Hanna sitting side by side on the sofa, darning socks. Papa was dozing in his armchair. Laila noticed her mother's expression was no longer angry. It held something else. Fear.

'Ivar,' she said, her eyes fixed on Laila. 'Your daughter has something to tell you.'

Laila's father rubbed his eyes and sat up. 'What's so important at this time in the evening?' He sounded weary.

Laila tried to swallow but her mouth was too dry. She had been rehearsing this all day.

'Sit down, then,' he said.

Laila remained standing. 'I have some news. I've fallen in love.'

Papa blinked and gave a slow smile. 'At last. I was wondering when you would finally find a young man. I was worried you'd end up an old maid.' He chuckled. 'Do I know the lucky fellow?'

'There's something else, Papa. We're expecting a baby.'

Papa's jaw dropped.

Laila heard Hanna gasp.

Shock turned to confusion as Papa struggled to speak. 'But who... when? I didn't think you were that kind of girl. Who's the father? I presume you're getting married. It will have to be quick.'

'There's a complication.'

'A complication?'

'The father is...' Her voice broke. 'German.'

There was a heartbeat when nothing happened. Then Hanna shouted, 'No', and Papa leaped from his chair.

'I'll kill the bastard for forcing himself on you.'

'He didn't force himself on me. I wanted to. We are in love.' Hot tears ran down her cheeks.

Her father struck her face. Hard.

'Ivar!' shouted Mama.

Laila fought the urge to step back or hold her cheek.

'I'm sorry, Papa. I love him. Like you love Mama.'

'How dare you taint your parents' love with such a comparison.' Spittle shot from his mouth.

'I didn't mean—'

'My own daughter. Of all people. A German whore.'

His words were a thousand times worse than the slap. They took her breath away. Papa's face contorted. The force of his rage overwhelmed her. She fled from the room, up the stairs, and into the bathroom. She locked the door, dropped down, and hugged her knees.

An hour later, exhausted from sobbing, she sneaked to her bed and waited for dawn.

Disgusted looks and silence met Laila the next day, and the day after, and the next. Hanna made a show of comforting Mama whenever Laila appeared. She would sit beside her, drape an arm around her shoulders or hold her hand.

The only member of the family who spoke to her was Olaf. 'Why's everyone so cross with you? Hanna called you a hypocrite. What's that?'

She hugged him to her. 'I have a German boyfriend. People think that's wrong.'

'Oh,' he said, pressing his head just above her stomach. 'Does he give you chocolate? Is that why you're fat now?'

Laila gave a small laugh.

'That's not fat. That's a baby.'

Olaf pulled back and looked at the swelling beneath Laila's dress.

'Is it a German baby?'

She took his hand and placed it on her stomach. 'It's just a baby. A baby made from love.'

'Oh,' he said.

For the first time in her life, Laila had no idea what to do. When Anton disappeared, she knew to grieve. When Inge was born and Mama was silent and sad, she knew to support her. But now she didn't know anything. Should she leave home to save her family from the shame? Did they want her to leave? Where would she go? Where would she have the baby? And what about Josef?

Laila's head spun with unanswered questions. She avoided seeing Oda. At work, she wore her loosest clothes. And to make matters worse, Major Haas was showing renewed interest in her again. Imagine when he found out she was pregnant and the father was Josef.

Then one afternoon, she had an idea. She went to see Marion's mother.

'I'm sorry to intrude,' she said as Marion's mother opened the door. 'But I need help.'

Surprise fluttered across the older woman's face, but she invited Laila into the sitting room and brought her a cup of coffee. They spent a few stilted moments enquiring about each other's families, before Marion's mother said, 'You said you needed help. What can I do for you?'

Laila took a deep breath. 'I'm in the same situation as Marion was. I know Marion left town to have a baby and I wondered where she went.' Laila registered the shock in the woman's eyes before she answered.

'Marion went to have her baby at a maternity home somewhere near Oslo. It's run by Germans.'

'Where's Marion now?'

'With the father's parents. In Germany. I have a grandson I will never see, but I'm left with the gossip and the sneers. I've lost friends. People either pity me or blame me.' Her voice was full of bitterness.

'I'm sorry,' whispered Laila.

'Save your sorrow for your family. My advice is to disappear before people notice. I'll give you a contact at the town hall.'

'Thank you. What's the name of the home?'

'Lebensborn.'

PART II

16

NOVEMBER 1942

The Lebensborn Home, Norway

The woman opposite had a moustache. She wore a hat and a frown. She leaned towards the elderly man next to her and whispered in his ear; his gaze darted around the railway carriage as he lowered his newspaper, taking care not to look at Laila. She felt his distaste pulsating at her. She lowered her hands from her rounded belly and turned to the window.

Two years ago, when she had spied Marion with her German lover, outrage and incomprehension had burned through her. The woman was a traitor. A woman of shame. Now Laila was in the same situation and being judged by the people opposite her. Of course, they didn't understand. They didn't know Josef.

She watched the scenery chug by. The gentle hills gave way to steeper slopes and the bare branches of the birch trees were replaced by rich green conifers. Bleak and grey, the November sky matched Laila's mood. She had no idea what lay ahead of her, what to expect at the Lebensborn home. Everyone knew unmarried mothers were unrespectable. She imagined she would be treated accordingly. As unworthy.

The sadness of leaving her family was bad enough, but their hostility and outrage were shards of glass embedded in her heart. She had only ever wanted Papa to be proud of her. Now he despised her. If only she could tell Josef how she felt, to feel his arms around her. She'd written him a letter with her precious news and had handed it to an official at the town hall in charge of the field post for Josef's regiment. Sometime later, a letter arrived describing his joy at becoming a father and his hopes for their future as a family. The argument from their last time together was forgotten. But that letter had come three months ago, and she was desperate to hear from him again, to hear he was safe. Her gaze drifted back into the carriage. The woman with the moustache jabbed around in her carpet bag before pulling out her knitting. The needles clacked as the train rattled on.

Two other pregnant women exited the station with Laila. They exchanged nods, a shy hello, and walked uncertainly to the waiting bus with the sign, 'Lebensborn Transport', stuck to the windscreen. As Laila approached the bus, she noticed the difference in the air. There was no smell of salt. No shrieks of gulls.

She chose to sit alone on the bus. The thought of speaking to anyone exhausted her.

The bus trundled through the small village and out along a narrow country road, thick forest on both sides. Laila felt closed in. She already missed the vastness of her fjord, that exhilaration of the endless sea and horizon blended into one.

It rained and stopped just as quickly. A watery sun appeared. Mid-afternoon, the light began to fade as they drove past a cluster of white wood houses and a post office. Laila prayed they would soon be there; the baby was pressing on her bladder. She shuffled in her seat.

The bus passed through a wrought-iron gate, wound up a drive, and stopped outside a white mansion house fronted by two pillars and wide steps. The driver announced they had arrived. Laila heaved herself out of her seat and followed the two other women out of the bus.

A grey-haired woman in a nurse's uniform bustled towards them, a clipboard in her hand.

'Welcome to Lebensborn, ladies. I am Matron Schwarz, and I am in charge of looking after you during your stay here.' She spoke in German. 'Let's get you ticked off my list and out of the cold. Tea will be served in the library and then you will be shown to your rooms. Follow me, please.'

One of the pregnant women looked at Laila, confused. Laila whispered her a translation.

Above the entrance hung the Nazi flag, and on the door was a bronze plaque engraved with the word 'Lebensborn', Fountain of Life, and the logo: a Y-shaped chalice.

Laila asked for the cloakroom and the other girls nodded with relief.

Matron Schwarz led them down a thickly carpeted hallway, her sturdy calves straining against black nylons.

Mint tea was served in a library that smelled of old wood and polish. Laila noticed the floor to ceiling bookshelves were sparsely filled. A portrait of Hitler hung over the fireplace.

Matron Schwarz ushered for Laila and the two other arrivals to sit down in the deep, brown leather armchairs that sat in the middle of the room, and then left promptly.

'What a lovely house,' said the woman who'd needed the translation, 'I was expecting something more basic. Harsher. My name is Marit, by the way.' In low voices, names were exchanged, and questions asked. 'Where are you from? When is the baby due? What do you know about Lebensborn?' This last question revealed little.

After tea, a young Norwegian maid in a white apron and white cap took Laila's suitcase and led her up the sweeping, oak-panelled staircase.

'You have an attic room. It's small, but you only have to share with one other.'

Laila took in her surroundings, stunned. Such luxury for unwed mothers?

'This house is beautiful.' She gazed at the oil paintings of fjords and mountains which lined the walls. 'Who lived here before?'

'No one knows.'

They stopped outside a door. The maid knocked and then led her inside.

The room was small with velvet curtains in deep pink, and wallpaper covered in tiny lilac, arctic poppies. Two beds were arranged on opposite walls, each with a varnished wood bedside table. It was a pretty room. A young girl's room.

A pregnant woman holding a mirror and a pair of tweezers sat on a bed, the skin under her eyebrows red. She glanced up and pursed her lips. 'Oh, I thought it wouldn't last that I'd have the place to myself. I'm Greta. Welcome to the farm.'

The maid set the suitcase on the other bed, winked at Laila, and left. Greta continued to pluck her eyebrows as Laila unpacked her few clothes and put them in the wardrobe. In her suitcase lay the brown package tied with white ribbon that Mama had thrust into her hands before she'd left: 'for the baby', she'd said. Laila stored it on the top shelf of the wardrobe. Her sketch pad and pencils, she placed in the drawer of her bedside table. The last thing was the pink crochet cushion that Oda had made for her all those years ago. She hadn't been able to face Oda and had left

Narvik without saying goodbye. What would Oda think of her now?

'What did you mean by "welcome to the farm"?' Laila asked.

'It's what they say in the village.' Greta shrugged. 'Farm as in stud farm.'

'What on earth do you mean?'

'They call us the German whores. Here to breed.' She appeared to be enjoying Laila's discomfort.

'That's unjust.'

'Is it, I wonder? Here we are, unmarried and pregnant.' The amusement left her voice. 'And the fathers nowhere to be seen.'

'That's because they're away on duty. They haven't abandoned us.'

'How can you be so sure? Maybe your lover is already married.'

'Of course he's not.' Laila opened her handbag, removed a framed photograph of Josef, and put it on top of her bedside table. It was a picture of him at an easel in his mother's art studio. There was no photograph next to Greta's bed.

'That's him, is it?' Greta said, narrowing her eyes at the picture. 'He doesn't look like a soldier.'

'That's what I like about him.'

Greta snorted.

Laila chewed her cheek. Best not to retort. She would be living with Greta a while.

* * *

At six o'clock, a deep chime echoed through the house.

'That's the dinner gong,' said Greta, swinging her legs off the bed and slipping her feet into a pair of black patent shoes. 'It's feeding time.'

Laila followed her down to the dining room, marvelling at how she could walk in high heels at eight months pregnant. God knows how she dressed before her pregnancy.

They joined a queue of expectant mothers, which shifted forward slowly. Laila picked up a tray. A savoury aroma emanated from a huge terrine. She breathed in the rich scent. Chicken soup. A red-cheeked woman in an apron ladled a bowl full and held it out. Such large chunks of meat. Thickly sliced carrots and potatoes, enough for two. Laila put her soup on the tray and gaped at the buffet; there were different types of homemade breads, and dishes of creamy yellow butter. When was the last time she had eaten butter? Tasted that rich smoothness? And there were plates of thickly sliced ham, and cheese, a bowl of apples, and a glass dish of compote, deep-red, plump berries. It was like Christmas. Before the war.

Now holding her loaded tray, Laila surveyed the room.

'We sit over there,' Greta said, indicating a long table by the window. 'The round table in the middle is for the nursing mothers.'

Laila looked over to a group of women who appeared to have already finished eating.

'They dine earlier,' Greta continued. 'That way, we are kept apart.'

Before Laila could form a question, Greta had moved away.

A woman next to a vacant seat gave her a wide smile punctuated by two dimples and Laila sat down next to her. She was called Dagny, came from Oslo, and had been at the home for four weeks. 'I'm getting nervous, now,' she told Laila, 'about the birth.'

'My mother always says you forget the pain once your baby is in your arms.' She thought of her mother cradling Olaf as he sucked greedily from her breast.

'Oh, I'm not nervous of the pain. I'm nervous I might scream.' Dagny leaned closer. 'They don't like screaming. It's unseemly. And it might frighten the others. If you scream, it goes on your report card.'

'We have report cards?'

'Everything is recorded. How we behave in—'

'May I have your attention, ladies.' Matron Schwarz's voice boomed over the chatter. Women stopped talking mid-sentence, put down their cutlery, and turned to face her.

'It is my pleasure to welcome our new guests. Please could the three ladies pick up their itineraries from the information desk in the hall after they leave the dining room. Also, please could Frau Dagny Larsson come to my office after dinner.'

Glances were exchanged around the table. Dagny started to chew her nails. She stared at her uneaten compote in silence for the rest of the meal.

After dinner, Laila picked up her itinerary and slipped it into her dress pocket to read later. She saw Dagny heading towards the matron's office. Laila watched as she knocked on the door at the end of the hall and went inside. The other women whispered as they meandered away to the library or up the central staircase. She caught the words '...bad news from the front.' Laila hesitated, then sat in an armchair nearby. She would wait for Dagny.

The enticing aromas of an hour ago had vanished, the air now stuffy with the smell of stale cooking. The taste of soup lingered in her mouth, sour on her tongue.

A maid passed with a bundle of towels.

Baby cries echoed from the nursery upstairs.

Opposite Laila, a painting hung on the wall: a winter scene with families skating on a frozen lake. She started to count the people in the picture.

Try not to think the worst for Dagny. Try not to think. Count the figures. Start with the child in the red hat, and work around the lake. There were twenty. Laila's age.

Dagny emerged, her face white with shock, a letter clutched in her hand. She staggered a few steps and then crumpled against the wall. Laila rushed to this woman whom she barely knew and hugged her awkwardly, positioning her baby belly next to Dagny's. Their unborn children, pressed side by side united by the tremors of their mothers' grief and the beating of four hearts.

Later, as Laila lay in bed, studying the lilac poppies on the wallpaper, impressions of the day jumbled around her head: the unexpected luxury of the home, the formidable Matron Schwarz. They were served tea in sumptuous leather armchairs. And the food. How could she have been so lucky to have been given a place here?

But then sadness enveloped her as she thought about her family and her own home. Her own bed. Her thoughts jumped to Dagny, their meeting at dinner. Then afterwards, as Dagny clutched the letter bearing the news: the father of her child, the man she loved, had been killed in action. Poor Dagny. The thought of receiving such tragic news about Josef was too awful to contemplate. She started to count the poppies to soothe herself. She wondered who else had lain here looking at this wallpaper.

'Can't you turn the damn light off?' called Greta. 'I want to sleep.'

Laila clicked off her bedside lamp and counted poppies in her head until she drifted off.

* * *

The next morning in the dining room, Laila stood in the queue and smiled with delight as she received a generous helping of porridge for breakfast. She heard a chuckle behind her. 'Better get used to that. We get porridge every morning.'

Laila turned to see a highly pregnant woman grinning at her.

'I like porridge. Don't you?' said Laila.

'Well, I did when I first came here. But I can't seem to get anything down any more. No room.' She patted her stomach. 'But I'll do my best. Big trouble if you don't eat your oats.'

When most people were hungry at the moment, like her family, Laila thought that sounded ungrateful. She moved along to the boiled eggs. The sign said: one only please. Next came bread. There was no sign here, so Laila watched the woman in front of her, who took two thick slices. Laila only cut herself one slice; two seemed greedy. Then she popped some butter and blackberry jam on her plate and headed to the table for expectant mothers. The table for nursing mothers was empty and from the way the chairs were half pulled out, she judged that they had already finished breakfast. She found a place to sit and helped herself to the coffee pot that stood on the table.

She looked at the faces around the table, searching for Dagny's. She wasn't there. She soon learned that Dagny had been given 'something to calm her down' and was resting in bed. Laila determined to visit her as soon as she had the chance but first, she had an appointment. On the itinerary, it stated:

Herzlich Willkommen – Matron Schwarz 08.25. Please be punctual.

Four chairs stood in a row outside the matron's office. Laila took a seat. Moments later, she was joined by the other girls she had arrived with, Marit and Anna. After a nervous hello, they sat in silence. She glanced at the grandfather clock opposite and as the hand clicked to 08.24, Matron Schwarz charged towards them with an impressive arm full of documents, a fob watch bouncing off her bosom. They followed her into her office.

'Discipline and hygiene, ladies, are the golden rules here at Lebensborn. Discipline and hygiene.' The matron studied each one of them in turn across her desk. 'We expect our house guests to follow the rules. We have thirty-three mothers here, twenty babies, and five kindergarten children, one of which belongs to Frau Hanson.' Matron Schwarz nodded at Anna. Laila was surprised to hear that Anna already had a child. The matron held up a sheet of paper full of dense text. 'The only way to avoid chaos is through regulations.'

Seeing Marit's confused expression, Matron Schwarz flipped the list over and stabbed the paper with her finger. 'On the back, in Norwegian. German classes will start this afternoon.' She leaned back, smiled, and in a warmer tone, continued, 'We are delighted to have you here. Women like you have been blessed with a special charge, and rest assured, both mothers and children will receive the best possible care, from nutrition and exercise to the finest medical provisions. Now, ladies, I'll show you the nursery.'

They followed the matron up the central staircase, where a maid was kneeling on a deep red carpeted step, polishing the wood at the edges of the carpet. Laila swept her fingers along the engraved banister. This was not the care home she had been expecting. She had heard distressing stories of homes for unwed mothers, run by the church or charities. Here, the surroundings and care were exceptional. Matron Schwarz seemed strict, but she had a job to do which she obviously took seriously. Why would the Germans treat them so well?

They arrived at the nursery. Arched windows ran the length of the room allowing the milky light to bathe the rows of white painted cots. Babies gurgled, cried, slept, or played with their feet. The sheets were pristine white, the blankets soft. Nurses in starched uniforms were performing various tasks, taking children to and from the nappy-changing station, changing bedding, or rearranging knitted caps and tucking in blankets.

Matron Schwarz spread her arms and puffed out her chest.

'Here they are, ladies. Each perfect being is a wonder. A gift. A prize that will ensure the next generation.'

Laila exchanged glances with Marit and Anna.

Matron strode along, inspecting the cots and peering at each child. 'Nurse,' she called out. 'This child is wet.' She emphasised the word *wet* with distaste. A young nurse scuttled over and swept the child away. Matron Schwarz shook her head. 'Discipline and hygiene. Discipline and hygiene.'

After their tour, the women retired to the library to read through the regulations. Laila read how unwed mothers were not to be discriminated against, compared to those who had recently married their German partner. Hence, the term *Frau* would be used to address all women. A community atmosphere was encouraged and everyone was to participate in all classes, including the evening gatherings in which they listened to radio broadcasts from the Führer. That seemed to be the worst rule.

An exercise hour followed with a walk in the grounds, then lunch, followed by a rest period: Laila's first opportunity to visit Dagny. A list on the noticeboard displayed the room numbers of each guest along with their arrival date. Goodness, the Germans really were the paragons of organisation.

Dagny was alone in the four-bedded room. She lay awake on her side, staring at a photo on the pillow next to her.

'Can I sit with you?' asked Laila.

Dagny nodded. Laila sat on the edge of the bed and tried to think what to say. What words of comfort could she offer? Nothing came to her. She could tell Dagny that she wasn't alone, or that her baby would bring comfort, or that the love she'd lost would live on in the child. But that all sounded so trite and inadequate. So, Laila just sat quietly next to her and held her hand. When the other roommates returned, Laila whispered she would come back later and left.

* * *

The following day, Laila stood in the entrance hall studying one of the portraits that had been hung. The man had small eyes behind round glasses. In fact, much about his features was small; his ears, his mouth – but not the power he exuded. Laila felt a shiver.

'Ah, there you are, Frau Olson,' said Matron Schwarz, striding towards her. 'I see you are admiring our Reichsführer Heinrich Himmler.'

Admiring? Like one admires a toad. *Hitler's henchman*, her father had called him.

'It's him you have to thank for being here,' Matron Schwarz continued. 'He values a mother's service to the Third Reich. Even those unwed. What an honour has been bestowed upon you.'

I'm just bearing the child of the man I love, thought Laila.

'I'm glad I've found you, Frau Olson. You have a medical examination at two o'clock this afternoon.'

'But I had one this morning. Everything is well with both me and the baby.'

Matron Schwarz placed a broad, muscled hand around Laila's wrist.

'And how happy I am to hear that. Here at Lebensborn, we are duty bound to take the utmost care of you and the child.'

Laila looked down at the matron's heavy hand. How different it was to her mother's: fine boned with delicate fingers. Laila dropped her arm to her side, and the matron's touch fell away.

'The test is just a formality,' Matron went on, 'to fill in some gaps in your doctor's notes from Narvik. Nothing of concern. Be punctual.'

* * *

Everything was white: the walls, the floor, the strip lighting, the doctors' coats. Laila felt exposed, more so than this morning when she had lain half naked in front of the midwife and gynaecologist. This room was cold. She drew her cardigan across her breast but was unable to cover the bump that housed her unborn child. Her skin puckered with goose bumps.

A doctor approached, tall and stoop-shouldered. He peered at her through colourless eyes. On his white coat pocket there was a black pin with the swastika emblem and a name badge that read Dr Klinger. He consulted his clipboard and tutted. 'These tests should have been done before you arrived, Frau Olson. I will have to compile the report myself. Take a seat.' He gestured to a metal stool.

Laila eased herself down and entwined her fingers to stop her hands from shaking. Another doctor, younger, rolled up with a trolley laden with instruments. He checked and straightened the utensils. Dr Klinger handed the young man the clipboard and pen.

What was this all about? What did they want? She should ask. Open her mouth and speak. Not such a difficult task, surely? But her mouth was dry, her tongue large and cumbersome and all she could do was sit there, vulnerable and afraid.

Dr Klinger bent over the trolley and picked up a steel instrument; it looked like the steel plyers her father used to repair the car. The doctor pressed the handles together and they opened like scissors. He held them up to Laila's face. She drew back, startled, and cried out.

'Now, now, don't make a fuss. Nothing to worry about. Hold still please.'

Her whole body trembled.

She smelled the coffee and cigarettes on his breath. Her stomach churned.

He placed the open instrument so that one of the arms lay on her left temple and the other on her right, the cold hard metal pressing against her skin.

If he squeezed now, he would crush her skull.

There was a click.

He withdrew the gadget and held it against a chart held up by his assistant. 'Thirty-nine centimetres, grade B.'

The assistant nodded and wrote the measurement down.

Laila sucked in a breath. Again, came the instrument; this time it was placed on either side of her jaw. Another click. Another measurement and grade. Then from her forehead to the back of her skull. Her chin to her crown.

When the procedure was finished, the doctor chose a slim narrow chart, the size of a bookmark. Round glass-coloured buttons were attached in a vertical line, each with a description next to it. He held the chart level with her left eye. 'Blue-grey 2b,' he said.

His assistant noted this on his clipboard.

Dr Klinger produced a new chart. Laila was astounded to see drawings of noses. What did this all have to do with her pregnancy, her baby? What did any of this mean? The bizarre chart was held alongside her nose. The examination continued: the length of her arms, the width of her hands, even the length of her toes. She was no longer a young woman, but a specimen in a laboratory. The stool she sat on became harder and smaller. At times, she thought she would faint.

An hour later, back in her room, she lay on her bed, exhausted by her ordeal. She tried to sleep, but her baby was wide awake, turning somersaults. Laila placed a hand on her stomach and a tiny foot kicked under her skin. Or was it an elbow? She marvelled at the tiny being that shifted within her; a rush of emotion over-whelmed her, forcing tears from her eyes.

The door swung open, and Greta entered. 'Goodness, what's the matter with you?' she said, flopping down on her bed.

Laila picked a handkerchief from her pocket, wiped her nose, and sat up. She told Greta about the examination.

'I had one of those in Oslo. I think I did quite well.' Greta studied her long fingers.

'In what way did you do well?' Laila asked, intrigued.

Greta laughed. 'You don't know much, do you?'

'Then tell me.'

'I'm tired. You'll find out anyway.' She curled up on her bed, her back to Laila, and promptly fell asleep.

Laila took her sketch pad and pencil from her bedside table and lay the pad on her drawn-up knees. She sketched swift, firm strokes, not pausing to consider, but letting the image burst onto the page, her breaths calming as she drew. Only when she had drawn the outline of the doctor's close-set eyes, did she stop to think. How to portray eyes that had no colour?

She left his eyes blank; soulless.

Greta had accused her of not knowing much. But today she had learned there was much more going on here than met the eye. Maybe even here, pregnant, shunned, and labelled a traitor, she could still make a difference for her country.

17

NOVEMBER 1942

The procession of identical white prams, each embossed with the Lebensborn logo, left the house. Laila watched from the bench where she sat with Dagny: close, hip to hip, bonded in silence. Laila didn't intrude into Dagny's grief, speaking only when Dagny needed to talk, which was seldom since she'd learned her beloved Georg was dead. She sat slump-shouldered, staring at the wet pebbles on the ground.

A mixture of mothers and nurses took the babies for their allotted mid-morning dose of fresh air; the nurses straight backed, black wool capes fluttering behind them, the mothers in a jumble of coloured coats, struggling to keep up the brisk pace.

As always, Laila counted the prams: her morning meditation. There would be eleven, just like this time yesterday – the second round of mothers out for their stroll. There had been no births the past few days. The procession passed by; the pram wheels rumbling over the gravel drive. Nine, ten, eleven... twelve. Twelve? Laila had miscounted. She stood up and counted again before the prams disappeared around the curve and headed towards the gardens.

Twelve.

Laila turned to Dagny. 'Do you know if there were any new arrivals yesterday?'

'I haven't noticed anyone,' said Dagny.

'Me neither. Then who is baby number twelve?'

* * *

The Motherhood Preparation class started every day at two in the afternoon.

Laila and Dagny each stood behind a small table. In front of them lay a doll, white cloths, safety pins, and a selection of tiny clothes.

'Hygiene, hygiene, hygiene, ladies,' announced Matron Schwarz from the front of the room. She paused and looked at each mother standing before her. 'You are blessed with the charge of our next generation. Hygiene and discipline are the foundation stones of their upbringing. Nappies must be changed six times a day.'

Matron Schwarz, after giving precise instructions on the art of nappy changing, instructed the women to commence their practice. Laila smiled to herself. How ludicrous this was. She knew how to care for a baby. She had learned from watching and helping her mother with Olaf and Inge. And her decree that one should change a nappy six times a day was obsessive. Imagine a woman with four children. Laila folded the white cloth into a kite shape, slapped the doll on top, folded in the ends and punched the safety pin through the cloth. She finished first, stood back from the table and gazed at the clock. Matron Schwarz swept to her side and contemplated Laila's performance.

'Rather slapdash, Frau Olson.' Laila fought the urge to roll her eyes.

The matron unclipped the safety pin, repositioned the nappy flaps, and replaced it in a perfect horizontal position, then stepped back with a satisfied nod.

Laila took this opportunity to ask about baby twelve. 'Matron Schwarz, I noticed a new baby has arrived. But there doesn't appear to be a mother.'

'How very observant you are.'

'I've been wondering about the mother.'

'That is really none of your concern. I suggest you pay more attention to your classes and learn how to change a nappy properly.'

Laila suppressed her grin. How pompous the woman sounded. Laila didn't need these absurd classes on how to care for a newborn. All these rules had no relevance to being a loving and caring mother. She could look after her child as she saw fit. She took a breath, her thoughts returning to baby twelve.

'But where is the baby's mother?'

'How persistent you are, Frau Olson.' The matron's tone was sharp.

Some women had looked up and were listening to the conversation. The room went quiet. Matron Schwarz clasped her hands in front of her, pressing her thumbs against each other until they turned white. She locked her stare on Laila and with clipped words, said, 'The mother is in hospital. Unwell, I'm afraid. We will be looking after the child, temporarily.'

But what was wrong with the mother? Laila wanted to ask. And why was the child at Lebensborn? Surely the child had some family or friends to care for it. But she knew she had already gone too far. She must be careful. Nodding, she turned back to the doll.

As the matron walked away, Laila pulled the safety pin out of the nappy and it flapped open. Some mothers sniggered and smiled at her. She returned their smiles and in a rush of childish joy, behind Matron's back, she grabbed the stupid doll by the foot and dangled it in the air; the nappy slid off. She scooped it up and wrapped it around her head like a scarf. Stifled giggles rippled around the room. Laila watched the broad back of Matron Schwarz bristle as she stopped in her tracks. The room went silent. Matron Schwarz allowed several heartbeats to pass before turning around. When she surveyed the room, all the women were bent industriously over their charges.

After the class, a group of five women gathered around Laila in the sitting room, laughing at her antics with the doll. Laila said she didn't need such lessons because she had younger siblings. Marit, who had arrived with Laila, asked her about her family, which ended with the group breaking out into lively chatter, exchanging stories of noisy younger brothers, irritating older sisters, and adorable toddlers. The maid came in and lit the fire, drew the brocade curtains, and plumped the cushions. A few moments later, she rolled in with the tea trolley.

With a plate of... no... were they biscuits?

Laila leaned back in the deep armchair and gazed around at her new-found friends, taking in their animated faces and pregnant stomachs. In spite of everything, they were smiling and laughing, leaning towards one another, nodding in agreement. Bonding. Maybe the class this afternoon hadn't been a waste of time at all.

* * *

Later, after dinner, Laila sat again opposite the painting of the skaters on the frozen lake as she waited for Dagny who'd been summoned to see the head of the home, Dr Albers. Laila counted the deep green conifers tipped with snow. There were twenty-seven.

She looked down the corridor. No sign of Dagny. What did they want from her now? Had she not been through enough?

She counted the wooden kiosks around the lake that served *glögg*. Five. She could almost taste the hot spiced wine prickle her tongue.

She shifted in the armchair. Heartburn. She stood up and paced a few steps. Waddled, really, like the geese on her aunt's farm. She wondered what her aunt and uncle thought of her now. So many fond memories of the family around the kitchen table, pancakes, and blueberry jam. Everyone huddled around the radio listening to plays or dancing to folk music.

Dagny appeared, red-faced and angry. She marched towards Laila with an energy she hadn't possessed since Georg's death. Laila followed her to the library where they sat alone in a far corner of the room.

'They want me to give up my baby. *Our* baby; a living part of Georg. I won't do it.' She clutched her stomach. 'They say I could nurse the child for eight weeks and then hand it over for adoption in Germany. To some Nazi family, no doubt.'

'They can't make you do that. You have rights as a mother.'

'What's all the drama about?' Greta arrived and plonked herself down next to Dagny on the two-seater sofa.

'Nothing,' said Laila, folding her arms across her chest.

But Dagny needed to vent her anger. Even if it meant confiding in Greta. She explained what Dr Albers had suggested.

'Sounds the perfect solution,' said Greta. She smiled at the astonished faces. 'I'll give up the child as soon as possible after the birth and get on with my life. The Germans have offered to find me a job and apartment in exchange; I get a second chance, and the child will be well cared for.'

'Well cared for?' said Laila. 'Sure, if being shipped to Germany to live with an SS family is well cared for.'

'My God, you girls are so naïve,' said Greta. 'The Germans will win the war. We will all be part of the Third Reich anyway.' She turned to Dagny. 'Where will you take your fatherless child? To your family in Oslo? They threw you out! Who will give you a job? A job to the mother of a German bastard?'

'That's enough,' snapped Laila, seeing Dagny's eyes glaze with tears.

Greta shrugged and, looking bored with the conversation, got up and left. Laila watched her freshly washed and curled hair swing around her shoulders and marvelled at her elegant, self-assured walk. She was a good-looking woman. She wondered who had been her lover and where he was now?

Laila took Dagny's hand. 'Take no notice of Greta. I'm sure there will be a way for you to find somewhere to live and bring up your child yourself.'

But she had no ideas to suggest.

At seven o'clock, everyone left the library to attend a talk on 'Political Orientation' in the large entrance hall. It being the end of the day, the women were tired and the talk was dreary; Laila grinned at Dagny as they heard the occasional soft snore floating through the air.

Finally, the official day was over, and everyone made their way to their bedrooms. Laila, still angry from Greta's callous words and not in the mood to face her, decided to take a short wander around the house. There was still time before lights out at nine o'clock.

Instead of taking the main staircase, she ambled down the hallway to the back of the house until she came to a closed door. With a quick check over her shoulder, she turned the doorknob and walked into a small hall with a spiral staircase. Her heart quickened. She had not been in this part of the house before. With the softest of footsteps that her added weight allowed, she sneaked up the wooden stairs. A stair groaned. She stopped. Her ears buzzed in the silence. What was she actually doing here? What was she looking for? She didn't know, but she liked how she felt. Adventurous.

Hanging on the wall alongside the staircase was a series of three small oil paintings in gilt oval frames. The first depicted a stag surrounded by fir trees; the second, a doe and her two fawns drinking from a stream. And the third was of two reindeer ploughing through snow, drawing a sleigh in which a girl sat with a sheepskin draped over her knees. Something about this painting made Laila stop and study the girl. She looked to be about ten years old, her cheeks flushed from the cold. Long, dark hair protruded from a blue and red knitted hat. Her head was tilted back, her tongue stretched out as fat snowflakes melted on her tongue.

Laila wasn't sure how long she stood mesmerised in front of the painting, but at some point, voices from below shook her from her reverie, and she hurried up to the landing above. It was dark there, so she began to make her way back to the front of the house, following a soft glow of light in the distance. She passed several closed doors to her right. On impulse, she tried a doorknob. Locked. She looked over her shoulder and tried another. Locked.

As the light ahead grew brighter, she heard baby cries and the soothing tones of a woman. Laila recognised where she was now; she had arrived at the nursery. She had approached from a staircase at the back of the house that she hadn't known existed.

The nursery door was ajar, and Laila peered in to see the night nurse beside the rows of babies tucked up in their cots. The nurse picked up the crying baby and held him against her shoulder, patting the child's back. She looked at Laila in surprise.

'Can I help you?'

'I've had awful heartburn since dinner, so I'm taking a stroll before lights out,' she said. She looked along the row of cots. Now was the chance. 'Could I take a peek at the children?'

The nurse hesitated and then nodded. 'Just for a moment then.'

Laila smiled at the sleeping faces peeping out from the lace-trimmed sheets. She stopped at a cot and, her tone casual, said, 'A new baby has just arrived, I heard. Is this the one?'

'No. Our new arrival is the little boy at the end.'

Laila approached the last cot.

Baby twelve.

The name plate said, *Gunther Schmidt*.

All the other babies had Norwegian names.

'Do you require some assistance, Frau Olson?'

Laila started, turned, and met the narrowed grey eyes of Matron Schwarz.

'Visitors to the nursery are not permitted at this hour.'

'My apologies. I needed a short walk before bedtime, and thought I'd take a look in the nursery. I can't wait to hold my own child in my arms.' Laila surprised herself with her quick response.

'It is indeed a blessing to bear a gift for the future generation of pure blood. The highest honour for a woman. A gift for the Führer. Not all of us, in spite of our devotion to the cause, are bestowed with this prize.'

Laila saw the briefest softness in Matron Schwarz's eyes but in a blink, it was gone, making her wonder whether she'd imagined it.

On the way back to her room, two questions gnawed at her. Who was the girl in the painting with snowflakes on her tongue? And who was baby Gunther Schmidt?

18

The post van crunched over the icy gravel. The women huddled around the entrance but were waved aside by Matron Schwarz who stepped out into a flutter of snow to receive the small brown sack. She bustled back past the crowd and into her office. The women waited outside her door: anxious, hopeful faces. A letter from their loved one, please. Please.

The door opened and Matron Schwarz handed letters to outstretched hands: crumpled envelopes, some smeared with dirt, others in colours of lilac and blue, or thick brown paper. The letters would be censored, inappropriate or negative comments blotted out in black ink. Laila's heart sank as the pile of letters depleted and no envelope was offered to her. Another week had gone by without hearing from Josef.

The women clasped their letters to their chests, or placed them in their dress pockets, hurrying away to read in some quiet, private corner.

Laila fetched her coat and hat and went outside; she needed fresh air. Was post getting through to where Josef was stationed? Were her letters being withheld from him? Unlikely. She was careful not to write anything inflammatory; just that she missed him and that their child was healthy and growing, kicking, and somersaulting inside her.

Large, lazy snowflakes drifted on the wind, circling slowly before dusting the ground. As she headed down the drive to the main gate, in her mind she wrote Josef an alternative letter. She told him about the bizarre examinations, the political orientation classes that scared and confused her, the strict regime, how mothers' time with their children was controlled; how everything was controlled. But then she felt guilty for being ungrateful. She and her unborn child were being cared for; in many respects her life was easier than that of her family's.

She had brought her family so much pain. If she could see, touch Josef, then perhaps it would all make sense. If she would receive a letter from him... what if he could no longer write? What if...? No. She refused to think it.

She stepped up to the wrought-iron gates and pulled at the two rings. Locked. Of course. She clenched her fingers around the bars and peered out onto the narrow road lined with dense conifers, tipped white. Even in the brisk air, she couldn't breathe. She had to get out, just for a while. Church bells rang from the direction of the village. She would ask Matron for permission to go to the village; short outings were sometimes sanctioned. The distraction would be good for her. Maybe she could talk to some of the locals, find out something. She had many questions and the village seemed like a good place to start.

* * *

Laila and Dagny, bundled up in hats and coats, stepped into the sharp, cold air. Matron Schwarz had granted them permission to visit the village, saying it might lift Dagny's spirits. The bus driver was the one who'd collected Laila from the station when she'd arrived. His name was Einar and he sported a bushy grey beard. His voice was gruff but his eyes were kind. The women climbed aboard and the bus headed down the drive to the main gate.

The bus halted in front of the locked gates; Einar tutted. 'Where is the old guy, then?'

An elderly man in a long, khaki parka and heavy boots hurried towards them. In his hand swung a metal ring dangling with keys. The groundskeeper raised an arm in apology and unlocked the padlock on the gate before heaving open the iron doors.

Today was the first day that Laila had been outside the Lebensborn home since she had arrived; the tension in her shoulders eased at the thought.

It was a short drive of about ten minutes. Einar stopped outside the post office and swivelled round in his seat.

'Here we are, ladies. I'll pick you up in an hour on my way back from the station with the new houseguest.' He gave a knowing nod. 'An important guest, I've been told,' he said with a wry smile. As the two friends climbed out, he added, 'There's not much to see here. You can kill time by taking a walk to the lake.' He pointed down the high street. 'At the end of the street, turn left, and it's just a short stroll.'

After the bus left, Laila and Dagny looked around them.

'It's pretty here,' said Laila as she surveyed the cobbled pavement and the coloured wooden houses and shops; pastel shades of pink and lilac interspersed in between bold reds and greens. The first strings of Christmas lights had been hung from balconies overlooking the shop fronts.

They strolled along, their arms linked. Laila was pleased to see Dagny's face relax for the first time since she'd received the terrible news. Dagny gazed at the buildings with interest. It was a good idea to bring her. They stopped at a shop front. It was a haberdashery, selling sewing items, knitting wool, and small items of clothing.

'Let's look inside,' said Dagny.

A brass bell over the shop door clanged as they entered. The shop was small, fitted with rows of shelves packed with balls of wool neatly stacked in blocks of colour. Bright buttons like jewels lay in baskets on a countertop, and spools of thread and silky ribbons were displayed in a wood cabinet. Laila was surprised the shop was so well stocked.

From the back emerged a tall, elegant woman dressed in a hand-embroidered blouse and a slim, tailored skirt. It was obvious she was a seamstress and the shop owner. Laila thought of Hanna and how she would have loved this little shop of treasures.

'Good morning,' she said with a swift glance at the bulges straining under the girls' coats. 'How can I help you?'

'We are new to the village,' said Laila. 'Can we take a look around?' The woman nodded and withdrew behind the counter where she started to unpack a box of zips. Laila admired the wool selection and Dagny studied bolts of patterned cloth. Looking at the fine fluffy wool, Laila had the urge to knit something for the baby. Of course, not knowing if it would be a boy or girl, the wool would need to be neutral. The soft, pale-yellow of a baby chick caught her eye. She could knit a cardigan with matching booties. The image fostered a feeling of warmth inside her and she smiled.

Laila picked up the wool; it felt like down. She had a little money with her, all that was left from her savings. It occurred to her yet again how dependant she now was on Lebensborn. After a moment's hesitation, she took two balls of the wool over to the shopkeeper. As the woman took the money, she asked, 'Are you from the maternity home?'

When Laila replied yes, the shopkeeper pinched her lips and said, 'I thought so.'

Determined not to let the cool tone disturb her, Laila said, 'It's a beautiful house. Who owned it before Lebensborn?'

The woman's eyes darkened. 'What makes you think I should know?'

Laila kept her voice light. 'Oh, I just assumed you would've had this shop a while and thought the owners may have been a regular sight in the village.'

'I never met them. They kept themselves to themselves.' Then, addressing Dagny, who was holding a card of pearly buttons, she said, 'I see you have found something too.'

And that was the end of the conversation.

Back in the street, the two passed a queue outside the fishmonger, tired women with empty baskets hanging from their arms. A woman exited the shop and shook her head at the waiting customers. Her basket was still empty. The queue quickly dispersed, with groans and sighs.

'How can there be no fish?' one woman shouted. 'In Norway, of all places?'

'Those bastards send it all to their troops, that's why,' another replied.

Laila took Dagny's arm and lowered her voice. 'Did you notice how angry the shopkeeper looked when I asked about the Lebensborn home?'

'I think she looked more afraid than angry.'

'Hmmm, I think you may be right. Afraid of what?'

'Probably afraid of what everyone is afraid of. The Nazis.'

'That could be true. In Narvik, before I left, people were becoming suspicious of each other. There was gossip about neighbours, collaborators. Friends didn't trust each other any more.'

'Exactly. So, I suppose it's understandable that the haberdasher wouldn't divulge information to strangers.'

Laila thought for a moment. 'Her shop had good supplies, don't you think? Interesting. She must know the right people.'

They passed a small schoolhouse and approached another queue, this time outside a grocer's shop. Here the shoppers had more luck, leaving with carrots and potatoes.

'We're lucky to have the food at Lebensborn,' said Laila. 'But when I see these hungry people waiting in food queues, I feel grateful and guilty at the same time.'

'I wish I could feel grateful,' said Dagny, her voice catching. 'I feel guilty for not feeling grateful. All I feel is despair. All I see is an endless black tunnel. A world without Georg.'

Laila stopped and, facing Dagny, took a gloved hand. 'I feel for you, Dagny. My heart aches for you. Please know that you're not alone. I'm here for you.'

A tear rolled down Dagny's cold white cheek. She sniffed. 'There is one thing I'm grateful for, Laila. That's you.'

Laila smiled. 'Look, there's a café. Let me treat you to a warm drink.'

The friends peered through the crimson curtains at the window. It looked warm and inviting inside. Except for the fact that three German soldiers were sitting at a small round table, smoking, and playing cards.

'Change of plan.' Laila sighed. 'Let's walk down to the lake.'

Arm in arm, they picked up their pace to keep warm, and left the high street, their breaths small puffs of mist darting in front of them. The path took them past the old church and through conifers towards a lake that sparkled silver-blue in the midday sunshine. Frost-tipped spruces and bare silver birches were mirrored in the still water. Patches of ice had begun to form.

'It's so peaceful here,' said Dagny.

Laila took in the view, something sparking in her brain. A lake was a lake. Or was it? This one wasn't very wide, and on the opposite shore, the bank swerved into a distinct horseshoe shape. The trees close to the water were sparse enough to count...

'Dagny, don't you recognise this lake? It's the one in the painting at Lebensborn; on the ground floor near Matron Schwarz's office. In the painting, the lake is frozen, and people are ice skating. I remember studying the picture and counting the trees when... anyway, I'm sure of it.'

Dagny agreed. 'I wonder who painted it?'

'Perhaps a local artist,' Laila said thoughtfully.

They stood in silence for a while, absorbing the winter scene. Something else was going through Laila's head. She pictured the painting of the girl on the sleigh surrounded by trees, snowflakes on her tongue; the trees were painted in the same style as the trees in the lake painting. And the wisps of snowflakes... it was the same artist. Laila knew.

Dagny glanced at her watch. 'We need to head back. Einar will be at the post office in ten minutes.'

Laila wished she could stay longer, breathing in the space and beauty, turning over the many questions she had in her mind. Reluctantly, she agreed, and they hurried back to the village.

The bus was already waiting for them, and they boarded; Laila felt increasingly heavy and slow, and she had to use the handrail to haul herself up the three steps. On the front seat was an attractive woman dressed in a deep-brown, fur-collared coat with a matching hat, also trimmed with fur. She wore soft, leather, black gloves and had a gleaming, leather vanity case perched on her lap. She bid Laila and Dagny a good afternoon. She had the voice of an actress.

'Goodness. Who's that?' Laila whispered once the girls were seated and the bus had trundled off. 'She is the most elegant woman I've ever seen. Except for in the movies.'

'She must be the special guest the driver collected from the station,' said Dagny. 'Did you see her clothes? The fur, that bag?'

Laila chuckled. 'She almost makes Greta look dowdy.'

Dagny laughed. A sound that warmed Laila's heart.

Matron Schwarz, erect as a flagpole, was waiting as the bus pulled up in front of the house. The new guest was greeted with a firm handshake and a warm welcome. As Laila stepped off the bus, she saw Einar take a suitcase out of the luggage hold. A large suitcase. Much bigger than the recommended size the expectant mothers were supposed to bring. Laila nudged Dagny, who gaped.

They followed behind into the entrance hall. Matron ushered the new arrival towards her office and asked a passing maid to fetch tea and cake.

'Cake?' said Dagny, wide-eyed.

Laila thought of the food queues in the village. 'She must be an extremely important guest. I wonder who she is?'

19

Her name was Eva Dahl. She reminded Laila of Greta Garbo with her soft, blonde hair falling in waves to her shoulders. The women would all turn when Eva entered the room, admiring the grace with which she moved despite being highly pregnant.

Laila had never seen such exquisite clothes except in magazines and admired the skill of the dressmaker that could cut clothes to flatter Eva Dahl's pregnant figure.

Her arrival impacted everyone, not least Greta.

'I would like to dislike Eva, to be honest,' she said one evening as she and Laila prepared for bed. 'But she's so polite to everyone. I'm quite fascinated by her. Either she comes from a wealthy family, or she has a rich lover.'

'She must be important,' Laila agreed, slipping her nightdress over her head. 'She's the only one here who has her own room.'

'And have you seen how Matron fusses around her? Eva is being very evasive about herself, but I'm determined to find out more.'

Over the following days, Laila observed how Greta would flutter around Eva, rushing to sit next to her at mealtimes, showing

her around the house, and explaining the daily classes. Eva
continued to bestow gentle smiles on people she passed but still
she remained aloof. The less she said, the more people wanted to
know; Laila was as intrigued as everyone else.

One early afternoon, when daylight was fading, Laila was
sitting in the library in an armchair by the fire, her sketch pad
propped on her stomach. She missed the view from her bedroom
at home: the space, the ever-changing colours of the sea and sky,
her fjord.

Shaking herself from her reverie, she studied the festive
arrangements around her, looking for something to inspire her. On
a round, polished wood side table stood a ceramic vase with sprigs
of spruce; hand-carved Christmas decorations hung from the
branches. Laila started to sketch.

'How wonderful to be able to draw,' a languid voice said. Laila
looked up into Eva's green eyes.

'May I join you?'

'Of course,' she said, aware that others were watching their
exchange. Eva pulled up a chair and Laila felt honoured by the
attention. How silly.

'What do you like to draw best?' Eva smoothed down her hair
and tucked a wave behind one ear. Laila wondered how she herself
would look with a similar hairstyle instead of the one long plait
she always wore. Hanna had told her long ago to cut her hair.
Hanna would like Eva.

'I like to draw landscapes. I love the mountains and the sea.'

'Not much inspiration for you around here, then. Do you draw
people?'

'Sometimes. But not very well.'

'Would you draw me?' Eva tilted her head and smiled.

'Well, I don't know,' said Laila, surprised.

'Please. Just a quick sketch. Not now. Not here. But in my room, in private.' She looked at her in such a way, it was impossible to decline. Anyway, Laila was curious to see Eva's room.

Eva had a large room that must have once been a main bedroom; the double bed had a heavy brocade cover embroidered with green and gold thread, the same fabric as the curtains. A plump velvet armchair in forest green stood in the corner next to a brass reading lamp. Eva sat in the armchair and invited Laila to sit on the bed opposite.

'How best shall I position myself?' Eva asked.

'You should feel relaxed. Maybe legs slightly to the side?'

Eva swivelled sideways, placing her hands on her lap, and looked towards the window. She had dramatic features, sharp cheek bones, and a strong, straight nose, like a goddess.

'I hope you won't be disappointed,' she said, slightly over-whelmed by the task.

'Disappointment is relative, don't you think.' It was a statement not a question.

As Laila sketched, Eva fell silent, deep in thought. After a while, she stretched her back and stroked her stomach. 'Don't be shy in depicting the roundness of my belly. I want him to be able to see his unborn child.'

Laila paused, her pencil hovering above the paper. This was the perfect opportunity to ask who HE was. 'When is your baby due?'

'In two weeks. I could have come here earlier, but you know how hard it is to be separated from a beloved. When was the last time you saw the father of your child?'

The moment had passed for Laila to ask her question, and like always, Eva deflected the conversation away from herself.

'It's been several months since I've seen Josef. He's on the Russian front.'

'Does he know he is to be a father?'

'Yes, he's immensely proud. We are to be married when he is next on leave.' Laila continued to draw. 'I haven't heard from him for a while.'

'It must be hard for you, especially after your friend Dagny's loss.'

And then they talked about Dagny, the opportunity to learn about Eva now completely gone. When Laila announced she'd finished, Eva came and sat on the bed, appraising her work. 'It's wonderful. Captures the moment beautifully, so much more poetic than a photograph. Please draw me again another day. Thank you, Laila.'

That afternoon, Greta asked Laila where she had disappeared to. They had been assigned to light kitchen duties and were sitting at a table peeling potatoes. Laila plopped one into a bowl of water and reached into the sack for another.

'Just for a walk.'

'In this weather?'

'I needed the fresh air.' Laila did not like lying, not even to Greta, but Eva had asked her not to mention their meeting. Laila, flattered by the attention, had agreed to do further sketches; the idea lifted her spirits.

'I don't see why we have to work here like kitchen maids. All this community work is getting on my nerves. I can't wait to get out of this place.' Greta peeled off large chunks of potato with the peeler and threw the massacred spud into the water.

Laila was relieved at the change of subject.

* * *

The following afternoon, in the handicraft class, the women were informed they would be knitting warm clothes for the German soldiers fighting in Russia. A bitter winter had set in, and thick socks, gloves, sweaters, and scarves were urgently needed. The women exchanged anxious looks, envisaging the fathers of their children, frozen, hungry, facing the spectre of death. The irony was not lost on Laila; before loving Josef, each battle lost by the *Wehrmacht* had brought hope to her and her family. But now, as she drove her knitting needles furiously through the stiches, she prayed for his safety, trying to still the terror that grappled at her throat. Did she want the *Wehrmacht* to be successful in Russia? Yes, if it kept Josef alive. Did she want Hitler's power to continue unabated? No, of course not.

She felt a hand on her arm. It was Dagny. 'Are you all right, Laila? You're shaking.'

Laila placed her knitting on her lap and sighed. Lowering her voice, she said, 'My biggest fear is for Josef's safety, naturally. But there's something else. I don't know who I am any more, what I believe in, what's right or wrong. I've lost my compass.'

Dagny fixed her gaze on her. 'I know who you are, Laila. You are a strong, loyal friend, a mother who will love and show her child what's right and wrong, but also guide them through the grey areas. Life doesn't always fit into neat boxes.'

Laila looked at Dagny, filled with respect; this young woman whose world had been shattered had found the strength to give comfort. In that moment their bond became impregnable, and Laila knew they would always be friends.

Lowering her voice to a whisper, Laila said, 'Remember the extra child that appeared from nowhere?'

'The one who Lebensborn is looking after because his mother is ill?'

'Or so Matron says. I haven't seen him for days. I wonder where he is?'

'Maybe his mother has recovered, and he's been sent back home.'

'Maybe.' But Laila had a gut feeling that the tiny Gunther Schmidt had not been reunited with his mother.

After the class, Laila made her way to Eva's room. Eva was permitted to decline classes if she chose and had spent the morning reading in her room. Her face brightened on seeing Laila.

'I have an idea for a more artistic pose. I'll just prepare myself in the bathroom. Please, you take the armchair today.'

A few minutes later, Eva appeared from her ensuite bathroom clad in a floor length, turquoise, silk dressing gown tied at the waist with a large sash. She sat on the bed and loosened the sash, allowing the gown to fall open. Underneath, she was naked except for a pair of cream French knickers. Eva positioned the folds of her gown so that her full, blue veined breasts were partially covered, and her pale, taut belly was exposed. She leaned back on her bed, propped up by pillows.

'How does this look?' Eva said.

'Incredible.' Laila was overcome by Eva's confidence in her nakedness and the sensuality she exuded.

Eva placed a manicured hand on her stomach.

Laila sketched.

'Tell me about Josef,' said Eva. 'What sort of lover is he? Gentle or ferocious? Anything in-between is tedious, I always think.'

Laila stopped drawing, her cheeks flushing. No words came to her.

Eva's eyes sparkled with amusement. 'Ah, Laila, you are so young. How old are you?'

'Twenty,' said Laila, and in a flash of daring, added, 'and you?'

Eva gave a world-weary smile and turned away, presenting her profile as she spoke.

'I'm the oldest of six siblings,' she replied. 'We were poor and my father forced me to leave school to work in a shoe factory, although my teacher recommended me for higher education. She said I was blessed with beauty and intelligence, things of no interest to my father.'

Laila felt privileged that Eva was confiding in her. She wanted to know more but knew Eva only offered insights to her life when she chose to do so. Laila would be patient; maybe she would discover more at the next sitting.

However, the next few times they met, Eva was preoccupied and quiet, even sad, thought Laila, as she sketched Eva in various poses: reading a book, standing at the window, sitting at her dressing table, silver-plated hairbrush in hand.

The painting of the snowflake girl haunted Laila. When she got into bed at night and saw the poppy wallpaper, she imagined the room had belonged to the young girl; pictured her in bed counting the flowers. When Laila had a rare moment to herself, she would find herself in front of the painting, wondering. In the right-hand corner were the initials *L. K.*, the same as on the painting of the frozen lake. Could the artist be local? Laila would make some enquiries the next time she was allowed to the village. The weather deteriorated however, and the road to the village iced up. Matron forbade the mothers to make trips.

* * *

At breakfast one morning, Matron Schwarz addressed the women, clapping her hands in delight as she announced her exciting news: the home was to be honoured that evening by a visit from Herr Ernst Schneider; not only a high-ranking SS officer, but a personal friend of Herr Heinrich Himmler. The special guest would be holding a talk after the evening meal.

The grand entrance hall was prepared for the event; a lectern was positioned in front of rows of chairs, an enormous swastika flag was hung from the ceiling, and clutches of spruce and mistletoe bound in black ribbon were arrayed on the walls. The women filed in, and as customary, those pregnant sat on the left side and the nursing mothers on the right.

With bright pink spots on her cheeks, Matron Schwarz introduced Herr Ernst Schneider, her voice unusually high, thanking him several times before taking her seat. Laila was amused to see Matron so ruffled. Schneider was strikingly handsome, tall, broad-shouldered, and spoke with smooth confidence. He looked more regal than threatening, but the adornments on his Nazi uniform told a different story.

He started his speech by stating his admiration for the beautiful land of Norway and its people with their pure, Aryan blood, genes of strength and intelligence that the Führer so admired. Qualities that, combined with the German race, would dominate the world. The thousand-year Reich. He studied the faces of the women in front of him. 'And each one of you who sit before me has been selected to produce the ultimate gift, a child of the elite who will carry our vision into the future.'

Laila looked down into her lap and started to pull the skin around her thumb nail. Schneider went on to talk about how the new master race needed *Lebensraum*, living space to house the expanding population, and those peoples of inferior race were a danger that had to be dealt with, severely. Laila shuffled in her seat as his tone became more ominous. She tried to shut out words like *Untermenschen*, sub-human, filth of society; so many were the *Feind*, the enemy: Poles, Communists, Roma, homosexuals and of course the Jews. All to be driven out to make way for the selected – Laila stood up and mumbled excuses as she climbed over the legs of the women in her row and headed towards the downstairs cloakroom.

She splashed water over her face, gulping breaths as her heart hammered against her ribs. As she calmed, she patted her face dry with a towel and lay her hand on her round, hard belly. The reality stood before her as cold and hard as a glacier emerging from dissipating cloud. A reality that had lurked in the archives of her mind but was now open for public viewing. Her child would be born at the same moment that a life somewhere else would be eliminated, one deemed of no value. A person who had family, feelings, dreams, their life a gift to their loved ones. Murdered.

A life selected. A life extinguished.

And Laila was instrumental in this horrendous plan. How could an act of love be mutated into something so grotesque?

Matron gave Laila a sharp look as she returned to the hall and took a seat in the back row. At the end of the talk, Dr Albers and the rest of the German staff clapped loudly, scanning the room to encourage applause from the *guests* of the home. Most of the women obliged. Laila did not.

As the women filed out, Matron approached.

'Did you feel so unwell during the talk, Frau Olson, that you needed to leave?'

'I'm afraid so. I apologise.'

'Then I suggest a medical check-up first thing tomorrow morning. A thorough examination.' Her tone was that of punishment. 'What have you learned from Herr Schneider this evening?'

'I heard Herr Schneider say the Germans will be the master race and that other races are the enemy.'

'So, you have learned something valuable this evening.'

'Oh, yes. I've learned that you cannot believe everything you hear.'

Laila had gone too far. In her anger, she had disclosed her blatant opposition to the Nazi regime. Scared and elated in equal measure, she watched Matron's eyes narrow and her jaw clench.

'I will see you in the surgery at six-thirty tomorrow morning. Good night, Frau Olson.'

Matron turned on her heel and marched over to talk to Dr Albers.

Upstairs, Laila joined three others in the bathroom, washed her teeth and under her arms. After her conversation with Matron Schwarz, she had broken out in a sweat. When she returned to her bedroom to get undressed, Greta had still not returned from the meeting. Laila put on her nightdress which was beginning to feel too tight and folded her clothes away. She was just slipping beneath her eiderdown when Greta burst into the room and plopped herself down on her bed, causing the springs to creak.

'Have I got something to tell you. You'll never guess.'

Laila was too exhausted to play guessing games or even talk to Greta, but she summoned the strength to say, 'What news have you, then?'

Greta's eyes shone as she leaned forward. 'I hung around after the talk, hoping to speak to Eva, but she was too busy chatting to Matron, so to kill time, I went to the cloakroom. When I came out, Eva was then talking to Dr Albers. Imagine that! Dr Albers never talks to us girls.'

Laila wondered where this was leading. She just wanted to sleep. 'And then?'

'I stepped outside the front door for some fresh air. It was freezing but I was determined to stick it out a few minutes, thinking that I would finally catch Eva alone.'

The girl was obsessed with Eva, thought Laila, as the picture of Eva half-naked in her silk dressing gown popped into her head.

Greta took a deep breath, readying herself for the climax of her story.

'When I returned inside, the hall had emptied. Everyone had left except Matron, Eva, and our special guest of the evening, Herr Ernst Schneider. They had their backs to me, so they didn't see I was there. Matron walked ahead to her office with Eva and Herr

Schneider following. And just before Eva walked through Matron's door, she reached out and took Ernst Schneider's hand and placed it on her stomach. *He's the father of Eva's child. A top SS officer, a close friend of Himmler, and no doubt, Hitler himself!'*

Laila bolted upright. A liaison with Eva Dahl could either be extremely fortuitous or extremely dangerous.

* * *

At six-thirty the next morning, Laila entered the surgery for her examination. Matron Schwarz was already there and indicated that she get undressed behind the screen. She stripped off her clothes and put on the coarse, white robe that hung from a hook on the wall.

'The doctor will be along shortly. You can get up on the stool.'

Laila didn't mind Dr Brandt. He was a competent gynaecologist, polite, and gentle.

'Pop your feet in the stirrups. Let's get you ready.' Matron untied the robe and opened it in a brisk movement.

It was cold in the room so early in the morning. Had the stove in the corner been lit yet?

Matron switched the overhead lights on. Harsh, bright.

Laila waited. Cold, legs splayed, exposed.

Where was the doctor? Matron stood in the corner of the room watching Laila, her arms folded across her chest. Laila pulled at the edge of the robe in an attempt to cover herself. But the stiff fabric fell to the side.

'I'm feeling much better today, Matron,' she said. She hated how small her voice sounded.

There was no reply.

The sound of footsteps and the door opening. At last, Dr Brandt.

But it wasn't him. It was the doctor who had done all those measurements on her with his strange charts and instruments. The doctor with the soulless eyes. Dr Klinger.

Panic gripped her.

'Good morning, *Herr Doktor*. So good of you to come this early,' said Matron. 'Poor Frau Olson felt most unwell yesterday evening; she had to leave the fascinating talk given by Herr Ernst Schneider. I would suggest a full examination. It would be terrible if something went wrong just a few weeks before the birth.'

The doctor made a show of putting on his gloves and scooping out the lubricating gel from a large white tub. Laila tried to stop her thighs trembling as he placed his bony fingers between her legs. He poked and stretched. Her muscles clamped. It felt like he was ploughing his whole fist inside her, shoving and pushing. He took much longer than Dr Brandt ever did.

This was her punishment. Humiliation and degradation. And Matron looked on.

She felt the baby kicking against her stomach. Would the baby be harmed?

At last, he stood up and removed his gloves.

'Can you check the breasts please, *Herr Doktor*?' said Matron, her voice almost sweet.

He pulled the robe off Laila's shoulders and worked his hard fingers slowly across her full breasts, paying particular attention to her nipples.

His stagnant breath swamped her face.

Laila cringed and to her dismay, tears fell from her eyes and dripped down her face. The doctor tutted.

'My goodness. What a fuss. I hate to think what she'll be like at the birth. Probably a screamer.' He stood back and spoke to Matron. 'Everything seems to be in the best order. There will be ample milk.'

Laila started to remove her stiff legs from the stirrups. Matron held up her hand. 'Wait till the doctor says he has finished with you.'

A look passed between Matron and the doctor, and she had to endure a few more agonising moments before the doctor nodded, allowing her to close her legs and step down from the stool. Aching and sore, she moved behind the screen and buttoned up her dress. How she hated that woman. But she felt something else too. Fear.

When she came out, the doctor had left and as she made to leave the room, Matron put a hand on her arm and gave a strange smile.

'Between you and me, Dr Klinger now works in another department and that is for a reason. He was relieved of his gynae-cological duties after a report of inappropriate behaviour. If you get my meaning. Still, nice of him to help out today.'

As Laila hurried away, Matron called, 'Hopefully you won't experience any further episodes.'

Four days later, Eva Dahl asked Laila if she would come to her room after lunch. She said Laila didn't need to bring her sketch pad this time.

When she arrived, Eva handed her a small package wrapped in white tissue paper and tied with a red satin ribbon. 'It's a small thank you gift for your wonderful sketches. Please, sit down.' She gestured to the armchair and sat herself on the bed, smiling at Laila's delight at the gift.

Laila placed the parcel on her lap, pulled the ribbon, and parted the tissue paper. She gasped. A book covered in jade-green silk, embroidered with gold leaves. The blank paper inside was thick filigrane.

'You can use it to sketch, or as a journal,' said Eva. 'I thought you might like it.'

'It's beautiful,' said Laila, stroking her fingertips over the fabric.

'It's a Rubelli cloth, from Venice.'

'Thank you, Eva. It's the most exquisite thing I've ever seen.'

'I'm giving it to you now because my baby is due any day and I doubt there will be time for more sketches. He was here the other evening and I gave him your drawings. He was very impressed.'

Laila gave a questioning look.

'It's okay, Laila. Word has got out that the father, my lover, is Herr Ernst Schneider.'

Laila nodded. What a handsome pair they made. But how did a Norwegian factory girl become involved with an eminent Nazi?

As if reading Laila's mind, Eva said, 'No doubt you judge me.' Eva stood up and did a slow turn. 'What do you see, Laila?'

'I see you. Eva.'

'Yes, you see me, Eva, a person.' She spread her arms. 'But do you know what the Nazis see? What Ernst saw as I stitched shoes whilst he toured our factory? A tall, strong-boned, beautiful, blonde, Nordic woman. A breeder of genetically pure children. And I saw a powerful, handsome, rich man who would take me from my factory life into his bed. And into another life. I knew about his politics, but I made my choice anyway.'

'It's not for me to judge you, Eva. Only you yourself and God can do that.'

'Ah, God. But whose side is he on when we pray to him to keep our loved ones safe?'

Again, Eva expected no answer to her question. And Laila had no answer to give.

Just before Laila left, she took a deep breath and said, 'Do you know anything about this house? The family who lived here?'

Did she see Eva flinch? She paused before she answered. 'The house was donated, I believe. A gift for the Third Reich.'

'But where did the family go to live?'

Eva's voice turned cool. 'Why so much interest, Laila?'

'Just curious, that's all. It's such a lovely house.'

'And you think because of my connection to an eminent SS officer, you can use our friendship to gain information?' Her green eyes flashed.

This was not good. The sweet moments between them a few moments ago had turned sour.

'Of course not, Eva,' she said, trying to hide the shake in her voice. 'I apologise if I spoke out of turn.'

'I'm tired. I think you should leave.'

That evening, as Laila held the jade book in her hands, she thought about what she had told Eva: that she didn't judge her. It wasn't true. Laila was shocked that a Norwegian girl would choose a Nazi SS officer for her lover. Is that how people felt when they had learned about Josef? But that was different. He was not a Nazi. Though he was still the enemy. German. How would God judge her? How did she judge herself? She didn't know.

A few days later, Eva gave birth to a blond-haired, blue-eyed baby. A perfect child, Matron announced. There was to be a special naming ceremony instead of a traditional christening – new orders from Berlin. The news made Laila uneasy. And it wasn't just that. There were things going on in this home that were not right: secret and sinister, hidden behind a frozen wall of fear and silence. But she would search where the ice was thin. Peer through. And she would document everything in her new journal.

20

When the road to the village became passable again, Matron allowed Laila to make one last visit to the village before her baby was due.

'Where's your friend today?' asked Einar as he drove the bus through the iron gates.

'Dagny? She's resting. She's expecting her baby this week.'

'The father was killed, wasn't he? So tragic. Will she keep her child?'

'Oh, yes. She wants to keep him.'

Einar didn't comment, but she saw his sad eyes in the rear-view mirror. They drove the rest of the way in silence.

* * *

Peering through the café window, Laila saw only empty tables.

She entered and ordered a cup of *Ersatzkaffee*.

'There's no sawdust in my coffee,' said the shop owner, a woman in a floral apron. She puffed out her chest and turned from the stove, cup in hand. 'I make it myself from dandelion roots. Tastes far better than the chicory type.'

'Sounds good.' Laila took the steaming cup. She looked around her. 'It's cosy here. Very welcoming.'

The woman tucked in her double chin and gave a satisfied smile. She glanced down at the large bump beneath Laila's brown wool coat. 'I don't recognise you from round here. You must be from the home.'

'I am. I'm lucky to be there. I certainly wasn't expecting such luxurious surroundings. Who was the family who donated the house?'

The woman gave a sharp laugh. 'That's a good word for it. *Donated.*'

In that moment, Laila knew. Almost too scared to ask, she lowered her voice. 'Did you know the family?'

'Sorry, young lady. We're not supposed to talk to you mothers about the house.' She folded her hands across her chest. 'And since most of my customers are Germans, I'm keeping quiet.'

'Oh, I don't want to cause you any trouble.'

The woman nodded and stepped back from the counter, indicating that that was the end of the conversation.

Laila sat down and drank her coffee which was indeed better than anything she had drunk since the war started. She was getting nearer to the truth about the home. She thought about the paintings and decided to ask the shopkeeper one last question. Taking her cup back, she thanked her and complimented her on her dandelion root coffee.

'Do you happen to know a local artist? I'd like to get my portrait done. I was recommended one but I've forgotten the surname. Must be the hormones.' She gave her a smile.

The woman didn't return it.

'I think it began with K,' she continued.

'The only artist I know of round here is Lisbet Kristensen.'

'Yes, that's the name. Does she live near here?' She couldn't keep the eagerness out of her voice.

'Hers is the purple house near the church. Strange colour for a house.'

'Maybe not strange for an artist.'

After another sharp look Laila thanked her. And as she left, the door was held open by a man entering: a German in a long, grey coat with the SS insignia on his collar. He greeted her with a stiff nod. Laila's stomach turned. She felt as if it was written all over her face that she had been snooping around. She hurried outside. Would the café owner mention her asking questions?

The purple house was easy to find. Laila stood outside, doubt making her hesitate. Would her continued probing get her or others into trouble? And why weren't the villagers allowed to talk to the mothers? She didn't know what she was going to say to Lisbet Kristensen, as she lifted the iron doorknob. She almost wished no one would be home.

Lisbet wore her thick, grey hair in a braid around the top of her head that looked like a coiled fisherman's rope. She gestured for Laila to take a seat in the main living area which also served as an artist's studio. After Laila had introduced herself and said she was staying at Lebensborn, Lisbet looked at her warily.

'And how can I help you?'

Laila didn't know how best to start. So, she dived in, cringing at her own nervous prattle. 'I've been admiring the painting of the frozen lake in the hall at the home; it has the initials *L. K.*, which I hope are yours. I discovered another painting, tucked away, with the same initials – a small painting of a young girl on a sledge, catching snowflakes on her tongue. I keep wondering who she is and what's happened to her. I thought if I found the artist—'

'You've found her,' said Lisbet, sadness clouding her face. 'Do you not know whose home you live in? Whose home they have taken?'

Laila shook her head, dreading the words she knew she would hear.

'The young girl in the picture is Anne Solomon. I painted that picture when she was nine years old. I was a friend of her mother, Sarah. Her husband was often away on business, and I spent a lot of time with Sarah and her three daughters. Anne is the youngest.'

A pause. Laila waited, holding her breath.

'They took them all. Whilst Mr Solomon was away. He never returned.'

'Because they are Jewish,' whispered Laila. She felt the dandelion coffee rise in her throat. 'Do you know where they are?'

'Surely, you must know. The Nazis are sending them to death camps. We are not supposed to tell the mothers about the family. Not to distress them. Lebensborn likes to keep its secrets. But you are here in my home, and you asked. They were sent away to be murdered. Actually, it's a relief to say it out loud.'

A sob broke from Laila's mouth. For the Solomon family. For Anne. The snowflake girl had a name. Laila couldn't stop the tears.

Lisbet Kristensen sat quietly, watching her cry.

Freshly fallen snow creaked under Laila's boots as Einar helped her alight the bus. Dusk was falling; inside, lamps were being switched on in the main hall and blinds pulled down. Laila's mind was still whirling from her conversation with Lisbet Kristensen when Marit rushed up to greet her.

'Dagny's gone into labour! Matron took her to the delivery room.'

'When did it start?'

'About an hour ago. She was really distressed, Laila.'

'I'm going to ask Matron if I can see her. I know we're not allowed to accompany each other during the births, but Dagny has been through so much, maybe Matron would make an exception.'

Matron did not. Rules were rules.

Dagny's baby was born the next afternoon after fourteen hours in labour. It was a boy. Dagny named him Georg.

The following day, visitors were permitted for a duration of ten minutes. Dagny was alone in the small ward occupying one of the four beds, save for Matron who hovered in the background. Dagny sat propped up on pillows, her face ashen and vacant, cradling her newborn. Laila kissed her cheek and peeped at the sleeping baby, his tiny nose peeking out from a white crochet shawl.

'What long eyelashes he has,' she said, stroking his head which was not much bigger than her hand. 'He's beautiful, Dagny.' She sat next to the bed. 'How are you?'

'I didn't want him to be born. When it started, I didn't want him to come. Into a world without his father.'

Laila fought back tears. She didn't know what to say so she sat quietly watching flickers of movement on the sleeping child's face. When she left, Matron said, 'Such a wonderful baby boy. Perfect in every way. A true blessing.'

Laila couldn't help thinking that Matron was more excited over baby Georg than Dagny was.

* * *

Over the next few days, Laila's thoughts tumbled between concern over Dagny and horror over what she had learned about the Solomon family. Where once she saw beauty and comfort in her surroundings, she now saw only sadness. She chided herself for being so naïve; for not questioning the background of the home. Or had she, deep in her consciousness, harboured a suspicion?

Standing before the painting of Anne tasting snowflakes, Laila wondered why the Nazis had left the picture still hanging. Had it been an oversight? This part of the house was not frequented often. Or more likely, no one had noticed that the small painting of a forest contained one of the rightful occupants of the house. She reached out and touched the canvas. She felt the dust on her fingertip.

'I'll find out what happened to you,' she whispered.

Later, after she washed her hands, she could still feel the dust on her skin.

Laila started to sketch the snowflake girl from memory. Never satisfied, she would sneak to the painting to see what she hadn't quite captured and return to her room and sketch anew.

In the library one afternoon, Laila sat in a deep upholstered armchair, a cushion behind her back, her hands resting on her stomach, anticipating that flicker of movement. Nothing. As usual, their child was sleeping during the day, preparing itself for night-time play. Laila didn't mind the tiredness; it was a constant reminder of Josef, their love, and the result of that love.

She eased herself out of the chair and ambled over to the bookshelves. They were almost empty. What books had graced these mahogany shelves before the Jewish family had been driven from their own home? Perhaps leather-bound works from playwright Henrik Ibsen, classics from Dickens, maybe children's books: a collection of Norwegian fairy tales from Asbjørnsen and Moe like the treasured collection she had left behind.

Children. Three sisters.

Had they sat by their father's feet as he read aloud, sitting in the same armchair from which she had just risen?

Bitter bile filled her mouth. Where were those girls now?

Laila swept her fingers along the spines of the few books that remained, or had been added: *Faust* by Goethe, biographies of composers Beethoven and Wagner. One thick volume caught her eye. She pulled it out and read the title printed in red: *Mein Kampf*. The author's name was printed on a black band across the top of the dust jacket: Adolf Hitler. Her hands flew from the book as if she had been scalded. The book dropped with a thud to the floor.

She stared at the splayed pages.

What was she doing here, an imposter in another family's home? Taking refuge in a house that had been wrenched from its rightful owners? Shame swelled inside her. She had told herself that non-involvement and silent disgust at events taking place exonerated her in some way. That being in love with Josef and bearing their child was a capsule apart from everything else. But guilt sent out its tendrils and she saw her own compliance stark and hard. She was everything people said about her. A traitor. A collaborator. One of the women of shame her father had spoken about. She slumped into the armchair and leaned back, closing her eyes. She hated herself.

Over the following days, Dagny showed little sign of improvement. Matron said it was nothing to worry about, just a touch of the baby blues. Baby Georg was only brought to Dagny for feeding, then returned to the nursery.

Laila went to see her on the day she was to leave the ward and return to her room. Her nightdress lay folded at the end of the bed. Dagny was dressed and looking out of the window. When Laila said hello, she didn't turn round, but in a dull voice, said, 'I've signed the papers. For Georg to be adopted.'

'Oh, Dagny.'

'It's for the best.'

* * *

Laila watched Einar from the bedroom window as he climbed out of the bus, just as he did every day at this time to collect the post and take it to the village post office.

Laila had handed a letter for Josef to Matron that morning. She had no idea if he would receive it. It had been months since she had heard from him. All she knew was that his company was somewhere in Russia. Someone must know what's going on with the German troops, someone high up. She wondered whether Eva Dahl would be able to help. After all, her boyfriend was a top-ranking SS officer. Laila would speak to her at the next opportunity, although she had little contact with Eva now that she had given birth and was busy with her newborn.

Einar appeared with a sack containing the precious letters and stood at the bus door, waiting. A figure hurried out and boarded the bus.

She wore a crimson cloche hat and an oversized black coat.

Dagny?

Where was Dagny off to? Surely, she wasn't well enough to be going out. Laila was astonished that Matron would give permission for her to leave the house just a week after the birth.

Einar climbed aboard, started the engine, and the bus chugged away down the drive.

Laila waited inside the main entrance, her coat over her arm, peeping out every few moments, waiting for Einar to return with the new post delivery. After twenty minutes, she heard the sound of the engine. Checking over her shoulder, she slipped on her coat and stepped outside.

'You just took my friend, Dagny Larsson, to the village. I didn't know that Matron had allowed her to go. Did she have a permission slip?'

'She'd left it in her room, on the top floor. Didn't have the heart to make her go back up and get it.'

'I think that may have been a mistake. I don't believe she had permission.'

'She lied? Why?'

'I don't know. Take me to the village and I'll find her and bring her back.'

'And where is *your* permission slip?' He frowned.

'Listen. If Matron finds out Dagny has left the home on her own, there will be trouble. Let me get her back here before she's noticed as missing. Drive me to the village. Please.'

'I could lose my job,' he said, shaking his head.

'You may not have a job when Matron discovers what's happened. Please, I'm worried about Dagny.'

His eyes flashed concern. He glanced towards the entrance then back at the bus.

'Climb in quick and keep your head down. I'll hand over the post for Matron and be right back.'

Laila clambered aboard, panting by the third step, and crouched down behind the driver's seat. Moments later, Einar returned, and they set off for the village.

The bus pulled up outside the post office and she turned to Einar.

'You check the shops and ask if anyone has seen Dagny. I'll see if she's gone for a walk down by the lake.'

Einar looked troubled at the urgency in Laila's voice and grunted his agreement.

The weather had been milder the last few days, the mercury mounting above freezing, which was unusual for November. As Laila walked past the church and the purple house of Lisbet Kristensen, she heard the plop-plop of melting icicles that clung to branches.

She picked up her pace, breathing in short puffs, the baby heavy in her pelvis, squeezing on her bladder. Her feet skidded momentarily as she lumbered down the path, but she righted herself in time. That's the last thing she needed: to fall and break something.

Through the conifers, part of the lake came into view. It didn't shimmer today but lay a lifeless grey white under a sombre sky. She stepped out from the trees. The lake spread out bleak before her—

Her heart raced.

A figure standing out on the ice. Motionless.

A crimson hat. A black coat.

Dagny, no!

Laila hurtled down the path, stumbling over the strewn branches that had snapped off in the last storm. She called out as she ran, 'Dagny, Dagny!'

But her friend stood with her back to her and appeared not to hear.

Laila reached the water's edge. A layer of ice covered the lake, but it was thin in places and patches of water had gathered. She screamed out Dagny's name, hearing the panic in her voice. Dagny half-turned. Again, Laila screamed her name. Then Dagny circled round slowly. She was too far away for Laila to see her face clearly, but she seemed to be in a trance.

'Dagny, come back. It's not safe on the ice. Come to me. *Please.*'

Laila put a foot on the ice.

It held.

Twigs skittered in the wind across the ice.

She took another step. She could venture out to fetch Dagny. The ice groaned. She stood still. Noises in the ice were normal. Ice breathed and shifted. Stretched and retracted. But was it thick enough? What could she do?

Again, she called, waving her arms frantically.

Dagny stood, gazing in her direction. She didn't move.

Laila felt desperate.

A splitting, cracking sound.

Laila took two steps backwards.

What should she do? What should she do?

'Dagny, please come here. We can sort things out. Let me help you. But first, you must help me. By coming off the ice. Otherwise, I'll have to come and get you. And with my weight on the ice... think of my baby. *Please*.'

Dagny wasn't coming.

She would have to go out to her.

Laila stepped back onto the ice.

She looked at Dagny, her heart pleading.

Dagny took a step towards her. Then another.

Laila halted. Not daring to breath. *You can do it, Dagny.*

She watched as the small figure moved slowly, inching towards her. The crimson hat, the only pinprick of colour on a blank canvas.

Laila could hear the sound of the ice above the pulse in her ears. Creaking and moaning. Cracks had appeared. Dagny was closer now and Laila could see her face, colourless and still, looking in Laila's direction but not really seeing. An ethereal being gliding, lost and fragile.

Not far now.

'Nearly there, Dagny. You're doing well. Soon, I'll be able to hug you, you'll be safe, look, I can reach out to you.' She held out her mittened hands. They were shaking.

Another few steps.

It would be all right. She would get Dagny back on the bus, return to the home, and they would drink hot herbal tea in front of the fire in the sitting room. Maybe there would be some biscuits...

A sickening, wrenching noise.

A lightning bolt of cracks shot through the ice.

Dagny startled, eyes wide.

The ice split open, and she was sucked into the gaping hole.

She screamed.

Laila howled.

Dagny flailed in the water, her coat billowing out like a giant jelly fish.

Frantic, Laila looked around at the broken branches on the ground. She grabbed one. Too short. Another. Too thin.

Dagny's head disappeared beneath the water. The crimson hat bobbed on the surface. Laila snatched a branch and clasping tight at one end, she offered it out to Dagny who came up, spluttering and gulping.

'Grab the branch, Dagny! Grab and hold on!'

Dagny's arms spun like a windmill.

One arm reached out. Her hand clasped. Then the other arm. The other hand.

Dagny's sudden weight forced Laila to her knees. She leaned back on her haunches and pulled with all her might, feeding the branch through her hands as if climbing a rope, dragging Dagny through the water that had opened up before her.

Laila thought her heart would burst through her chest. Her lungs would explode. She could do this. She would pull and pull and pull. Get Dagny out.

Dagny, choking, hair plastered across her face, neared. She was in reach of the shore. Laila threw the branch aside and reached out, grabbing her wrists, leaning all her weight backwards. She managed to lift Dagny out of the water as far as her shoulders. But her wet clothes were weighing her down. Laila's arm muscles burned and trembled. She knew.

She would not be able to haul Dagny out of the freezing water.

Laila screamed into the frigid air.

She looked into Dagny's terrified eyes. They closed. Her head lolled to the side.

But still Laila held on. Dagny's hands had gone limp. They were slipping. Oh, God, no.

Crunching from behind. A grunt, and two thick arms above. Broad hands clenching Dagny's arms.

The bus driver, Einar. 'Let go, miss. I've got her.'

* * *

Huddled in an armchair, swathed in blankets, Laila was still shivering. She sat in the sitting room, cradling a mug of steaming chicken soup, and stared into the fire. Marit sat beside her.

'What was she doing out on the ice?' she asked her.

Laila shook her head. She wasn't sure herself.

Marit was quiet for a while. When she spoke again, her voice was hoarse.

'Do you think she meant to... you know, to end it all?'

Laila couldn't reply. It was too horrible to contemplate. She thought about the driver, Einar; how he'd carried Dagny into the bus, taken off his coat, and wrapped it around her. He'd shaken his head and mumbled, 'I can hardly bear to drive the young women back and forth to the home. My own daughter is now pregnant...' His voice tailed off as he rammed the bus into gear and sped off. Laila watched the trees fly past the windows as she enveloped the trembling Dagny in her arms.

* * *

After dinner that evening, Laila stopped Matron in the hallway and enquired after Dagny who was recovering in the sick room. Matron said only that Dagny was resting and would be kept overnight for observation. She denied Laila's request to see her.

Before breakfast the following day, Laila again spoke to Matron, who acted as if she was pestering her yet gave her an update: except for a temperature, Dagny was doing well. But in the evening, when Laila asked, the temperature had progressed to a fever. Again, Matron refused Laila's request to visit Dagny; she needed to rest.

That night, the sound of a motor engine and the slam of doors roused Laila from a restless sleep. She lifted the corner of the blind and saw headlights and two figures carrying a stretcher. An ambulance had arrived. Perhaps someone had gone into labour and there were complications. Unlikely. Women were not moved during the birth unless the mother or baby were seriously ill.

She shoved her swollen feet into slippers and pulled on her dressing gown, then hurried out the room to the top of the stairs.

Voices below. Matron. And some men.

Gripping the banister, she descended the stairs, stopping now and again to listen.

From the first floor, she looked down into the entrance hall; two men were carrying someone out on a stretcher. Dagny.

Matron, clad in a coat over her nightdress, followed outside. When she returned, Laila was waiting.

Matron was tight lipped. 'Frau Larsson has developed a high fever and I consider it best that she is cared for in hospital. Now, please return to bed. We'll know more in the morning.'

But the next morning, Matron was nowhere to be found. A nurse said she was in a meeting with Dr Albers. And no, the nurse had no news about Dagny.

Finally, Matron appeared at afternoon tea, accompanied by Dr Albers, who cleared his throat and asked for attention. Everyone looked up. Dr Albers addressing the mothers was rare.

'As some of you are aware, Frau Larsson fell into the lake yesterday morning. Due to the freezing temperatures, she developed a high fever and became very ill. We reacted swiftly and called an ambulance to take her to the nearest hospital. Unfortunately, she developed pneumonia and I regret to say, died this morning.'

Silence flooded the room.

Then gasps and choked sobs.

Laila studied Dr Albers. What he was saying was odd. Something not right. Something cruel. He shifted his feet, nodded at Matron, and left the room. Matron remained in front of the seated mothers.

'This of course, is tragic news. Tragic that Frau Larsson left the home unaccompanied and, most importantly, without permission, which led to her unfortunate accident.'

'You did this.' Laila was on her feet, her face on fire, her finger aimed at Matron. 'Instead of helping her with the trauma of losing the man she loved... instead of supporting her after the birth... instead of care and guidance, what did you do? You took her child.'

'Please calm down, Frau Olson. Either return to your seat or leave the room.'

Laila marched steadily towards her, her finger jabbing the air.

'You did this. You took her child. Forced her to sign papers. You're to blame for her death.' Her whole body shook.

'Nurse,' Matron yelled through the library door.

Laila swung round to face the mothers. 'Don't you see what's going on here? Things are going on behind the benevolent façade. And this house—'

Laila's arms were jerked behind her back, Matron on one side and a nurse on the other, as she was shoved from the room, shouting to be let go. They dragged her to the surgery where she was held down by three nurses.

Matron held up a syringe. A stab.

And then darkness.

21

DECEMBER 1942–JANUARY 1943

Each morning when the women lined up at the surgery to be weighed and have their blood pressure checked, it was dark outside. Only a few lights were dimly lit; to save electricity and to maintain the blackout protocol.

There was a rota system for the mothers to help the maids raise the blinds, when the thin, watery sun would appear around eleven o'clock. By three o'clock, the darkness would roll back in, and the blinds would be closed again, the dim lamps lit once more. A few candles were permitted to be lit, to promote Christmas cheer. Something hard to muster since Dagny's death, the mood sombre, the women subdued.

Marit was now Laila's constant companion, offering comfort where she could, and even Greta was supportive, her prickliness softened. After her outburst in the library and her forced removal, Laila had spent the night in the sick ward and had been visited early the next morning by Matron.

'Listen carefully, Frau Olson.' Her tone was pure venom. 'Your behaviour is unacceptable. Your insolence and ugly allegations, an outrage. In normal circumstances, you would be thrown out of the home. However, the child is due soon.'

Laila struggled to sit up, her head thick with medication. Matron's face was grim.

'This is what will happen. You will apologise to me in front of the other women and retract your accusations. You will say you took leave of your senses in a moment of grief. You will follow all the regulations without exception. You will refrain from negative comments about the home and the Third Reich. In fact, you will present yourself as the perfect example of German motherhood. Do I make myself clear?'

Laila felt herself submitting to the victor, a heavy weight of helplessness dragging her down a well of despair. She had no choice. Eight months pregnant, no friends or family to turn to, Josef thousands of kilometres away. Her strength was gone. She was broken.

'Yes. You have made yourself clear,' she said, her voice small.

Matron brought her face up close, her jaw set. 'If you fail to abide by any of these terms, I will throw you out of here. In the middle of winter, with no money and nowhere to go. Even if you are about to give birth.'

Laila knew she had meant it.

So, Laila had stood before the Motherhood class and humbled herself with an apology. She had watched a nurse climb inside a black car cradling Dagny's son and return hours later, her arms empty. She observed a new bus driver bring the post. Einar, who had carried Dagny, drenched and trembling from the lake, had been replaced and was no longer mentioned.

Withdrawing herself, Laila had concentrated on her journal, creating numerous sketches of a tiny figure on the frozen lake, drawings of Dagny sitting on a bench outside, her fringe poking out beneath her cloche hat. One day she would expose what really went on here. Dagny would not be forgotten. Her son would know how his mother loved him. Dagny deserved that.

Now, with Christmas approaching, Laila turned her thoughts to her soon to be born child, monitoring every movement, dreaming of how the boy or girl would look, imagining what it would feel like to cradle her baby at her breast. She was told at her regular check-ups that the baby was doing well.

Her favourite midwife was Herta. One day, with a hand on Laila's stomach, she sounded wistful as she said, 'You and the father have created a wonder. Your very own child.'

Laila was surprised. Till now she'd only heard that her baby was a gift for the Third Reich, for Hitler. Josef had hardly been mentioned.

About a week later, Laila was assigned to help Herta in the nursery. Laila folded the freshly washed nappies and Herta placed the glass feeding bottles in the cupboard. Not all mothers were able to produce milk, much to Matron's displeasure.

Herta seemed sad and distracted today. When one of the children started to cry, she swung around, her arm knocking a tray full of bottles onto the floor. The noise of the shattering glass brought Matron thundering into the room.

'Now I'm for it,' murmured Herta.

Laila stepped over the broken glass. 'I'm so very sorry, Matron. I suddenly felt faint and dropped the bottles.'

'For heaven's sake, girl. Go and lie down.' She waved a hand at Herta. 'Clear up this mess,' she said, already retreating from the room.

'Why did you say that?' asked Herta.

Laila gave a wry smile. 'I couldn't be in any more trouble than I am already.'

'Well, thank you. You might have just saved me my job. Or at the least an unpaid nightshift.'

Christmas Eve arrived. In Laila's childhood, Christmas Eve had been exciting. Always surrounded by family. Then, after the loss of Anton, Christmas was changed for ever. But they still had each other. Christmas in wartime had brought new challenges which the family tackled together. Always together. But this year, the festival bore no resemblance to what she had known. Without her family around her, she felt an aching hollowness.

There was no visit to church, of course; Laila smiled to herself at the thought of the horror on the villagers' faces if the rows of pews were to fill up with unmarried mothers; the shame of it. In a place of worship. Sacrilege.

However, Dr Albers allowed the women to sing hymns, even in Norwegian, in the sitting room. Then a small choir of the German staff led by Dr Albers's secretary sang '*Stille Nacht*', encouraging everyone to join in. At first Laila remained silent, but moved by the beauty of the singing, and spurred on by the thought of Josef on the front, she sang along. She sang the German carol for him. And prayed. *God, please keep them safe.*

Fräulein Hahn, Dr Albers's secretary, had a high, crystal voice. She was a slim woman who always wore black skirts and jackets, but she had a penchant for red accessories. Today she wore a bright-red, silk scarf tied at her neck. Laila noticed that Dr Albers had entered the room and stood to one side watching the proceedings. The singing seemed to please him, particularly that of Fräulein Hahn who he watched with a trace of a smile.

Laila remembered how surprised she had been recently when she found Dr Albers and Fräulein Hahn arguing in the hallway. Not like a disagreement between a boss and his secretary, but more one between two people who knew each other very well. In Dr Albers's office was the picture of a teenage boy, but no photographs of the boy's mother. This made Laila wonder.

The food was plentiful that Christmas Eve but Laila had little appetite, yearning to be seated around the meagre set table with her family. In her home.

* * *

A snow blizzard blew in the New Year and when after two days the wind died down, the home was enveloped in silent whiteness.

Greta became anxious when her baby was several days over-due. Matron had talked about inducing the baby, but Greta had no idea what that entailed. Laila and Greta had become closer in those few days, with Greta becoming less confrontational and confiding in Laila about her fears. Her mother had nearly died giving birth to her and she was terrified that the same could happen again.

Laila tried to reassure her.

'Plenty of women give birth safely,' she said. 'My mother had five children without complications. My baby sister, Inge, came in less than an hour. And before that, my brother, Olaf, in two hours.'

Laila had one week before her baby was due. She hoped her own experience would be like her mother's.

One morning, Greta reached for her dressing gown which was hanging on the back of the door, and gave a yelp before buckling forwards, clenching her stomach. Laila helped her back to her bed and lumbered down the corridor to find a nurse.

* * *

'How was it?' asked Laila. 'Honestly?'

'Well, at the risk of going against Matron's strict instructions, I'll tell you.' Greta sighed at her reflection and thumped the hand mirror down on the bed. 'It was damn awful.'

'I'm sorry,' said Laila sitting down next to her. 'What was awful? The pain? Matron? Or how long it took?'

'All of it. From beginning to end. Damn awful. You're supposed to feel great love and accomplishment when you hold the child. All I felt was relief it was over.'

Laila studied her face, looking for a sign that she didn't mean what she said. A maternal softening in her. There was none.

'And when I screamed, they stuffed something in my mouth to bite down on. Well, then I could hardly breathe, so I spat it out and screamed even louder. Did you hear me?'

'I think I may have,' said Laila thinking of the animal howls she'd heard. 'You don't need to be ashamed.'

'It's not shame I felt. Screaming was the best part. I enjoyed letting rip. Anyway, I have to stay and nurse the child for a few weeks, and then that's that.'

Laila fought back her distaste for Greta's callousness. She'd promised herself that she'd be less judgemental. But she couldn't help feeling sorry for the baby boy.

The following morning, everyone was to go outside for some fresh air and exercise in spite of the weather. The gardener had cleared a narrow path in the snow so that the women could walk in circles. Laila and the others collected their boots that were kept by the front door and sat on the low wooden bench to tie up their laces. Already bundled up in her coat, hat, and scarf, Laila struggled to lean over her large bump. She just couldn't do it. Sweat gathered across her forehead and her breath rasped in short gasps.

'Come on, Frau Olson.' Matron tutted. 'It will be dark by the time you get outside.'

Laila gritted her teeth. She managed to grasp the end of one lace but then it slipped through her fingers. She grunted with exasperation.

A jolt of pain seared through her body, from her pelvis to her breastbone. She gasped. Something popped inside her, and she felt a gush between her legs.

'I'm wet, Matron Schwarz.' She looked up into the woman's knowing eyes.

'Nurse.' Matron's voice dissected the air.

'I'm not due yet,' she murmured.

'The baby thinks otherwise,' said Matron. 'It's time. Let's get you to the delivery room.'

22

JANUARY 1943

The nightdress they had given her was rough against her skin. Hard and unforgiving, just like Matron Schwarz. She and a trainee midwife had shed Laila of her wet clothes, towelled her dry, and slipped the regulation gown over her head. The first spasms of pain had been brief. Unpleasant but bearable. Not as bad as she had expected. What she hadn't anticipated was the deep throb of back pain. Lying on her back she brought her knees to her chest and rocked herself gently on the narrow bed.

The room was warm, the stove in the corner lit. There were two doors; the closed one on the left had a sign: O. P. She prayed she wouldn't need to go in there. To her right, the door to the adjoining room was ajar, the voices of Matron and her assistant rising and falling. The day she had been waiting for with excitement and fear was here. She wished Josef knew that today he would become a father. If she concentrated on him hard enough, maybe her thoughts would be transported to him. Maybe he was chatting with his fellow soldiers as they drank coffee around a fire. Checking and cleaning rifles. Or riding in the back of a military truck. Or marching through snow and blizzards...

Matron was back, lifting Laila's nightdress, murmuring, 'Dilation... centimetres... a long way to go.'

Her hands pressing around Laila's belly. Matron listening with the wooden trumpet. Baby heartbeats. Per minute. Everything fine. A brass bell put on the table beside her, to call for attention.

Alone in the room. Another tightening deep within. A spasm of pain. Longer this time. A roll to the side, knees up, deep breaths.

What would her child look like? She couldn't imagine at all. A boy or a girl? She didn't care. Just healthy. A beautiful little being. Maybe a boy would be nice, a miniature Josef with deep, dark eyes. Or did newborns always have blue eyes? Like the babies in the nursery?

Dr Brandt appeared with Matron. His calm, kind voice was reassuring as he examined her, his gentle hands over her unborn child. He soon departed, followed by Matron, and she was alone again.

Not quite. The door was sill ajar to the adjacent room and she could hear a nurse rustling around behind the door.

Pain welled up, spiralling through her with a piercing intensity. Was that normal? Should she ring the bell? She cried out, perspiration running between her breasts. The young German midwife, Herta, appeared and sat beside her. Laila heard words like *blow*, *breathe*. She tried to follow the instructions. She was hot now; the room was too hot.

When the contraction eased, Herta told her to lie on her side and massaged her lower back. That felt good, comforting. She continued her massage, telling Laila how well she was doing.

Am I? she thought. She was not so sure; she felt more desperate with each contraction. The pain was getting worse. Surely it wouldn't be long now. Her mother had always birthed quickly.

But when Matron checked, she said, 'You'll be here for a while yet, Frau Olson,' and disappeared again.

Herta came and went, bringing water, then later tea. She rubbed her back and helped her try different positions and even got her to walk around the room.

To distract herself from the pain, Laila asked Herta why she'd come to Norway.

'I needed to see where my husband lost his life. I went to Narvik, where his ship, *the Heidkamp*, went down.'

'I'm from Narvik,' said Laila. She remembered the men's cries from the harbour as she and her family had fled their home. 'I'm so sorry.'

Laila studied Herta's face.

'When I learned of a job vacancy here, I applied,' said Herta, helping Laila back to the bed. 'We wanted a family.'

The next contraction came. She gripped Herta's hand, hearing her own grunts and cries which didn't sound like her at all. The pain in her body was continuous, either sharp and piercing with each contraction, or heavy and deep in the pauses between.

Daylight faded. Herta pulled down the blind and lit a small lamp by the bed.

She stayed by her side, words of encouragement, calm and steady.

On and on it went. Swells of pain, heat, and sweat.

Images of Josef flashed in her brain. His trousers rolled up to his knees, splashing around in the stream. The *hytte* in the soft evening light, with pops of colour sprouting from the grass-covered roof. Josef's lips on hers, on her skin, his hand stroking back her hair from her face, his rich voice whispering that he loved her.

Then Dr Brandt was there, at the *hytte*. Or was she back in the hospital room? She didn't know. She felt delirious. He asked her to lie on her back and bend her knees.

Dilation and centimetres. Not long now.

Her father looking at her in disbelief and anger; terrible words that came from his mouth. Mama, white and speechless, rigid on the sofa. Hanna's gasp. *You hypocrite.*

The pain had hardly finished before it came again. This time it was different, an overwhelming force. Matron was there, but her tone had changed. Excited. Something was happening. Laila must push. Now was the time. Her body knew, and it could do nothing else but push her child into the world.

Everyone was telling her what to do. She wished they would stop. If only the pain would stop. Why didn't they leave her alone? They should all go away.

Mama. She wanted her mama to be there to hold her hand, to wipe her forehead, like when she'd had measles as a child. Push, blow, breathe, push, blow, breathe – Matron's voice: the head, she could see the head. Push – stop. Don't push. Matron's urgent tone: something about the cord, stop pushing. What did it mean?

Her body was splitting, ripping apart. Heat, sweat, pain, she couldn't do this. It was over, she couldn't do this, it must stop. Somewhere, through the fog, she heard the words: Push. Now. Hard. Harder, again, again, again – a scream shattered the air.

Her scream.

Everything stilled. The pain, the voices, her trembling body. A silence hung for an eternity, just her heartbeat pounding in her ears.

A commotion between her legs. She looked down and saw the top of Matron's head, her white hat bobbing as her arms worked, pulling, lifting, cradling.

Where was her baby? Was it born? Was it still inside her? There was no sound. No yell of life.

Something was wrong.

'Give me my baby,' she croaked.

Silence.

Panic clawed at her heart.

Please. God.

A squeak of a cry.

Then stronger. Forceful, triumphant, alive.

'You have a baby girl, Frau Olson,' Matron said as she handed her the swaddled bundle.

* * *

The transition from expectant mother to nursing mother was a major one. Laila ate her meals at a different table, with women she'd had little contact with in recent weeks. She had a new daily itinerary with set times for breast feeding, nappy changing, and bathing. There were allotted times for mothers to play with their babies and to take them for a walk. But the greatest transition was from carrying an unseen presence beneath her skin to holding a tiny being against her breast.

Laila stared at her baby girl in wonderment: the plump hands, soft and white as pillows, miniature feet that fitted into her hand, and thick, dark eyelashes. Like Josef. She named her after her grandmother, Elise. After all, Grandma had lovingly created the *hytte* which had played an integral part in her and Josef's romance.

She retrieved the brown parcel Mama had given her from the top shelf of the wardrobe. For the baby. Alone in her room, she pulled open the paper and sighed. A small, soft toy: a hand-crocheted, black and white puffin with an orange beak and feet. It brought a lump to Laila's throat. There was something else in the parcel. A tiny, white, knitted one piece with ribbon ties at the side and matching baby mittens. If only Mama could see Elise wearing the clothes.

Laila tucked the toy puffin in Elise's cot but a day later it had been removed and sat on a shelf in the nursery next to a tin of baby powder.

The love she felt for her child was overwhelming in its intensity. As was the wrench when she was required to hand Elise back to the nurse each time the feeding session ended. Surely a baby should stay with its mother, she thought, as the children were whisked away by the nurses and deposited back into their clean white beds.

When Laila heard a baby cry, she fretted that it was Elise, but she soon learned to distinguish her child's voice from the others.

One morning, after she had fed Elise and handed her back to the nurse, she heard her crying in the nursery, next door. Laila went to the cot and bent down to pick her up.

'That's not a good idea, Frau Olson.' It was Matron. 'The child has been fed and changed. It lacks for nothing. Overindulgence makes a child soft.'

'But she's just a baby. She needs her mother's love.'

'Only to a point. Too much love smothers the child. Makes it weak.'

Elise's cries intensified as Laila hovered over her.

'You have succeeded in agitating her further. Please leave so she can calm down. You may help fold nappies in the linen room.'

Laila hesitated. She could see the menace in Matron's eyes though, so she forced herself to step away from the cot. Her baby's screams followed her down the hall.

During the allotted play hour, Laila sketched Elise, talking to her whilst she drew. 'Wait till your papa sees how beautiful you are. He'll be so proud.' She would send Josef the sketches with the official photograph taken after the birth.

At dinner, that evening, Laila told Eva Dahl that there had been no further news from Josef.

'Leave it to me. I'll ask Ernst – Herr Schneider – to find something out for you.'

Laila was grateful. Now that Elise was born, she was more desperate than ever to hear from Josef.

* * *

The dagger hovered over the baby's breast. Mothers gasped. The SS officer dressed in black, intoned in a strong, solemn voice, as if he were a priest.

We believe in God,
We believe in our mission to protect and further the pure blood
of the German race.
We believe the Führer is chosen by God.
We welcome you, Hartmut Dahl, to our brotherhood.
You will grow up in our protection and you will bring honour and
glory to your name and race.

The officer laid the dagger on the baby's chest. A proud father, Ernst Schneider, started to sing the SS anthem. Dr Albers, Matron Schwarz, and the rest of the German staff belted out the words.

This was the first *Namensgebung* held at this Lebensborn home. The intent for it to resemble a religious christening shocked Laila. But worse was the sight of this tiny baby laid out on an altar draped in the Nazi flag. How could Eva hand over her child's life into the hands of the SS?

Eva was then called forward and, standing in front of a bust of Adolph Hitler, she was presented with a certificate and a silver spoon.

A silver spoon for a child's soul.

That evening, whilst Greta ran her bath, Laila took out the jade silk journal and sketched the scene; a tiny baby on an altar, the dagger looming above. She wrote the date and the baby's name in the bottom right-hand corner and hid the book back amongst her pullovers.

Eva Dahl, Ernst Schneider, and their son left for Germany the next day. She and Ernst were to be married and baby Hartmut would then bear his father's name. Before she left, Eva promised Laila that she would investigate Josef's whereabouts.

Eva's departure left a gap at the home, and although she disagreed with Eva's choices, Laila found herself missing her.

23

The night Marit went into labour, a storm raged. Laila tossed in her bed, listening to the relentless wind fling iced rain against the window. She whispered Greta's name but there was no answer. That girl could sleep through anything. She sat up and hugged her knees, straining to hear sounds from the labour room. Was that Marit's cry? Perhaps it was the howl of the wind. *Please God let everything go well for Marit and her child.*

Laila swung out of bed and slid into her slippers. She felt the familiar drawing sensation in her milk-laden breasts. The need to hold Elise overcame her, and she tiptoed down the dark hall towards the nursery. A sallow night light shone through the open door. Perhaps Herta was on duty.

But the nurse on duty wasn't Herta. It was a sullen sister who was rigorous about regulations. Still, Laila stood in the doorway looking at the rows of cots. Some of the babies were restless because of the storm, letting out moans of complaint. One cried. The nurse adjusted the child's blanket and made a shushing sound. But she didn't pick the child up.

Laila stepped towards the cot where Elise always slept.

'Frau Olson, what are you doing here? Nursing isn't for another three hours.'

'I know. But I just wanted to see if Elise was frightened of the storm.'

'If every mother rushed in here every time it was a bit windy, it would be a right circus.'

As if in a trance, Laila crossed to Elise and looked down at her sleeping child. Love, pure and powerful, surged from the core of her being. As if sensing her mother's presence, Elise fluttered open her eyes.

'I must insist that you leave at once.' The sister's voice was shrill.

Laila did not react, but continued to gaze at her child, feeling her breasts tighten and warm drops of milk dampen her night-dress. She reached down into the cot.

Strong fingers gripped her arm. The sister hissed, 'Leave now or I'll fetch Matron.'

Laila wrenched herself free and stormed out of the nursery. Elise started to cry.

'See what you've done,' the sister called after her.

Back in her room, Laila made her decision. It was time for her and Elise to leave Lebensborn. As soon as possible.

* * *

The sight of Marit holding her baby son brought tears to Laila's eyes.

'Oh, Marit, I'm so happy for you.' She kissed her friend's pale cheek and sat beside the bed. 'Will you call him Albert? Like Bernd suggested in his last letter?'

'Maybe. For now. Look how strong he is.' Marit placed her little finger in his fist. The baby grunted with the effort of his grip.

'He's wonderful,' said Laila.

'He is wonderful. Special. But not perfect.' Concern crossed Marit's face and she lowered the blanket that covered him. Laila gasped, unable to hide her shock. The baby's right leg was withered below the knee, and his foot turned inwards, the toes bunched together like a claw. Marit wrapped her child back up and clutched him to her.

Laila placed a hand on Marit's arm. 'I'm sure something can be done to help him.'

Marit shook her head. 'Dr Albers examined him. He said he would never be able to walk.'

Laila was lost for words. She imagined how she would have felt if Elise had been been born like that. She could feel Marit's pain.

When she left a short while later, she found Matron Schwarz standing in the doorway, watching. She lowered her voice. 'Sadly, not every mother is blessed with a selected child. The purest specimen.'

Specimen? Laila gave Matron a hard look.

'Please come to my office after the nursing hour, Frau Olson. We need to talk.'

Laila nodded. She also had something to say to Matron Schwarz. She and Elise were leaving.

Half an hour later, Laila and Greta sat side by side, their babies nuzzling at their breasts. Laila held Elise's foot, cupping her heel in her palm, stroking each tiny, plump toe. She thought of Marit. Poor little Albert.

'I'm leaving at the end of the week,' said Greta as she lifted her son against her shoulder and patted his back. 'Adoptive parents have been found. A wealthy family in Germany. This little one will have a good life.'

'What about you, Greta?'

'Lebensborn have found me a job as a telephonist in Trondheim. Not my dream location, but I'm in touch with Eva Dahl. She'll try to find me something in Berlin.'

'You want to go to Germany?'

'Wake up, Laila. Germany is where the future is. And Berlin. What a city! The nightlife, the fashion, the excitement. How about you? Will you not take Elise to Josef's mother in Dresden? The war will be over soon, and you can start your life anew when Josef returns.'

'I've decided to leave here. I'm going to tell Matron this morning. But I'm not sure where to go. I don't know Josef's mother. Or Germany. I'd like to stay in Norway. It's my home. I thought if I show Mama and Papa their grandchild, they might relent.'

'A reconciliation? I'm sceptical, but I wish you luck.'

Matron's face was grim as Laila entered her office. She did not offer her a seat.

'I'll keep this brief, Frau Olson. I've heard about your behaviour last night in the nursery. This is yet another act of insubordination. Mothers are normally permitted to stay at Lebensborn for up to six weeks after the birth to give them time to sort out their domestic circumstances. However, in your case, I must ask that you leave at the weekend.'

'I'm perfectly happy with that arrangement, Matron. It was something I wanted to suggest myself.'

'You may leave your child here with us as a temporary measure should you feel unable to care for her adequately.' Children left behind at the home tended to disappear.

'I will definitely be taking Elise with me.'

'As you wish. Now, if you excuse me, I have work to do.'

24

The storm had subsided. Broken branches lay scattered around the grounds. The gardener had thrown sand on the pathways so that the mothers could walk their babies without fear of slipping over. Laila was deep in thought as she pushed Elise in her pram through the garden that Friday morning. What a relief to be leaving this place. This institution. She had only been here three months, but it felt an eternity. Her life had become regulated, moulded, controlled. Although excited to leave, she was also uncertain.

She would return to Narvik and try to reconcile with her family. Surely when they saw Elise, their own flesh and blood, they would welcome her. Love her. How could they not? Then, when Josef returned, perhaps Mama and Papa could accept him too. See what a good man he was. That would be hard for Papa. But maybe, maybe...

And then what? Where would Laila, Josef, and Elise make their home? Narvik or Dresden? Worlds apart. She couldn't think about that now. One step at a time.

After dinner, everyone gathered in the library to listen to a radio broadcast. Adolf Hitler praised the strength and bravery of the German soldiers in Russia. Their determination against the cold and the communist threat would bring victory to the Third Reich. Fresh food supplies and troops were on their way to Stalingrad.

Laila had no idea where in Russia Josef was. In his last letter, he'd said they were headed in that direction. But she hoped his company had been rerouted. Whispers and rumours were circulating around the home. The German staff spoke to each other in hushed voices, their faces grave. Everyone knew things were not going well in Russia, despite the upbeat propaganda reports.

Terrible images forced their way into Laila's mind, especially at night. Josef, half-frozen in a trench of ice and snow. Explosions and gun fire. Lifeless bodies strewn across the frozen ground.

No. Not Josef. God would not let that happen to him. It wasn't possible.

Laila took Elise for her final check-up before they were due to leave. At the first examination after her birth, measurements had been taken of her head circumference, arm, and leg length and the width of her pelvis. As in Laila's examination when she first arrived, baby Elise's nose, ear shape, and eye colour were documented. Today, however, the doctor just looked in her ears and mouth with a slim torch, checked her temperature, and listened to her chest with his stethoscope.

'Couldn't be healthier,' he announced.

Laila looked across the room. Marit was in the surgery with baby Albert, who was being examined by Dr Albers. He held a small bell and tinkled it on one side of the baby's head. The doctor frowned and repeated the procedure on the other side. Then he clicked his fingers in front of the baby's face.

'Is something wrong, Dr Albers?' asked Marit in a high, shaky voice.

He looked at her, his expression exasperated. 'Is there anything right with the child?'

Dr Albers gave the midwife a meaningful look. It was Herta. She nodded.

Marit scooped up her son and left the room in tears. Laila followed.

'Don't take any notice of him. He's a mean, bitter man. Once Bernd is back from duty in the Netherlands, you can both take Albert to a specialist doctor.'

'I don't know if Bernd will want a son with a deformed leg and a hearing problem. I don't even know if Bernd wants me.' Her tears dropped down onto Albert's face. He wrinkled his nose.

'What do you mean?' said Laila. 'Of course he wants you.'

'Does he? We hardly know each other. We had sex in the back of a truck. Twice. Hardly a great love match like you and Josef. No big romance or declarations of love. He said I was cute. That's it. The truth is, we don't love each other.' Marit's voice broke. 'Yes, he wrote he would do the honourable thing. He wanted a son. But one like Albert?'

Albert started to cry.

'Let's take the children back to the nursey and then go for a walk together. We'll try and sort this out.'

But as Laila and Marit walked around the garden, Laila realised this wasn't something that could be just sorted out. Marit had a disabled child that needed medical help. Her family wanted nothing to do with her. She had no money and no work. Her lover was a virtual stranger and Marit had no desire to go to Germany to live with Bernd's family who were also strangers. And anyway, there was no reason to believe they would take her and Albert into their home.

Marit's situation was dire. As Laila sank into her bath that evening, she knew how lucky she had been to fall in love with

Josef. A letter would arrive from him any day. Matron said field post was expected in the village. Hopefully it would arrive before she left on Sunday.

After her bath, Laila fed Elise and watched the nurse tuck her in for the night. It was half an hour before lights out. Laila decided to take a wander before bedtime. Despite her eagerness to leave, she was overcome with nostalgia for the house.

She descended the wide staircase, her grey felt slippers sinking into the red carpet. The polished wood of the banister glided under her palm. The glass chandelier that hung above the grand hall was turned off, as always, due to blackout regulations and electricity shortages. Laila had never seen it switched on. She imagined a time when it had shone prisms of light onto guests arriving below. Warm greetings and embraces within the Solomon family. Three excited young girls flitting about in taffeta dresses.

Downstairs, a maid was turning off lamps. Shadows from the grandfather clock and a high commode swept across the hallway. Laila passed the library, which was now in darkness, and wandered to the end of the hall. She pushed open the door that led to the spiral staircase. There were no lights on here, just the faintest glow from a hall light upstairs.

She stood before the painting, unable to make out the features. But she didn't need to. The snowflake girl was imprinted on her mind. Anne Solomon was imprinted on her mind. Laila would miss the painting, but she had her sketches of it. She made Anne a silent promise: she would find out what happened to her. Tell her story. How Lebensborn had wrenched her home from her. And maybe her life.

Laila placed a gentle finger on the painting. A flood of emotion and connection made her knees buckle. She sat down for a few moments on the stair.

Floorboards creaked in the hall above. Light footsteps. Laila sneaked up the spiral stairs and peeped down the hallway. The secretary, Fräulein Hahn, holding an armful of files, was unlocking a door. She left the keys in the lock and disappeared inside the room. Laila had passed this room several times after visiting the snowflake girl. No one seemed to know what was in there; the door was always locked. Now she could see the key in the lock was attached to a large brass ring that held several smaller keys. Fräulein Hahn stepped back out, the files now gone, and Laila withdrew from sight. She heard the click of the door and the bolt of the lock. The floor creaked and the footsteps receded.

Laila tiptoed behind and watched Fräulein Hahn descend the main staircase and return to her office. There she stood on the upper landing, looking down. The house had grown quiet. It must be nine o'clock. She should return to her room. But she remained on the landing watching.

Moments later, Fräulein Hahn left her office for the evening. She wore her black coat with the silver fox collar that she kept on a coat stand in her office. After locking the office door, she struggled with the clasp on her patent leather handbag for a few seconds before tutting and slipping the key into her coat pocket. She hurried to the front door, no doubt eager to get home. She lived in a rented room in the village and drove back and forth each day. She was halfway out the front door when someone called her name. Dr Albers stood in the open door of his office. Fräulein Hahn turned to face him.

'You should get off to bed before Matron catches you.' Herta came up behind Laila.

'I'm going now. I need to get some sleep before the two o'clock feed.'

The women smiled at each other, and Laila headed to her room.

* * *

The tiny hammer vibrated between the two alarm bells with such force that the small clock pulsated across the bedside table and fell to the floor. Laila groaned and leaned out of bed to retrieve it.

'I'm going to break that wretched thing,' Greta said as she yawned. 'Is it two o'clock already?'

'It feels like I've just fallen asleep,' said Laila, thumping the off button and placing the dented tin clock back beside her bed.

'I certainly won't miss the night feeds,' said Greta, yanking on her dressing gown.

But surely she will miss her child, thought Laila.

The two of them joined the other mothers in the nursery, who picked up their children, some of whom were already crying for food, and everyone settled down in the adjacent dimly lit room. Most of the mothers were groggy from lack of sleep so conversation was limited. Some dozed off sitting upright in chairs, their babies, sated, asleep at their breasts. The night nurse took the babies from their laps and sent the women back to their rooms.

Laila wondered what it would be like to feed Elise whilst lying in bed and to drift into sleep, mother and daughter together.

As usual, Laila was the last mother remaining. Elise was a slow drinker. Sucking seemed to tire her, and she liked to pause and doze. If Laila made a move, Elise would startle and would latch on again.

At three o'clock in the morning, she laid Elise back in her cot and said goodnight to Herta. Crossing the landing at the staircase, she looked down into the entrance hall. Everywhere was in darkness except an arc around a small table lamp covered with a cloth. Laila could just make out the coat rack by the entrance. A mass of dark shapes; thick winter coats, except something that reflected the faintest shimmer in the pallid light.

A silver fox collar.

She widened her eyes. It must be Fräulein Hahn's coat. Laila had seen her about to leave. But then Dr Albers had called her attention. Laila hadn't seen what happened next, but it appeared that Fräulein Hahn had changed her mind and stayed. And was still here in the middle of the night. With Dr Albers. Why?

Laila tried to imagine the thin, brittle man having sex with his young secretary, but she couldn't picture it.

Fräulein Hahn had slipped the office key into her coat pocket. Was it still there? Perhaps she could find some evidence of what was going on in this place before she left. This would be her last chance.

She tiptoed down the stairs holding her breath. If someone caught her, she could say she felt unwell and needed some fresh air. But that was nonsense. Everyone knew the front door was locked at night. Or she had left something in her coat that was important. But what was so urgent at this time of night? Or perhaps—

Before she knew it, she was standing in front of the silver fox coat.

She looked behind her. Everything was dark and still, just the tick tock of the grandfather clock and her pulse in her ears.

She slid her hand into one of the coat's pockets.

A lace-edged handkerchief. Nothing else.

Another peek over her shoulder. Then the other pocket. Cool metal.

The key in the palm of her hand, Laila tiptoed to Fräulein Hahn's office. The noise of the turning lock clang loud in the night. As she sneaked into the room and closed the door behind her, she knew she had crossed a dangerous line. If she was caught now, nothing could explain what she was doing here. She hardly knew herself.

The room was in total darkness. She felt her way forwards, remembering the rough layout of the room from the few times she had been here, to collect writing paper, pens, or stamps. Bumping up against the desk, she ran her hand along the surface till she touched the cord of the lamp. She hesitated. Far too risky to turn on a light. But she could see nothing.

Feeling her way around the desk, she banged her hip on the sharp edge. She ground her teeth till the pain eased. Hands straight out in front of her like a cartoon sleepwalker, she crept to where she knew the window was. She felt the stiff fabric of the blackout curtains brush her fingers. Running her hands across, she found the opening and parted the curtains. Just a crack. A sliver of moonlight fell into the room. She dared to part the curtains a fraction more. On this cold, clear night, the light from the stars and half-moon was enough for her to make out the shapes around her.

She worked fast, slid open the drawers, felt inside storage pots on top of the desk, ran her fingers along shelves, lifted piles of papers. There was no large bunch of keys on a brass ring. She tried a filing cabinet but that was locked. Were they in there? She couldn't possibly break into the cabinet.

She looked around the room, her eyes now accustomed to the darkness. On one side of the room was a row of bookshelves. She remembered the German and Norwegian dictionaries she'd seen there as well as a couple of atlases. But what had struck her most had been the copy of *Mein Kampf* positioned on the middle shelf. In the darkness she could only make out the outlines of the books, not the titles. She ran a hand over the spines of the books. One book jutted out from the others. She pulled it out and held it to the window. It was the book written by Hitler.

As she pushed the book back into its slot, she noticed that something was obstructing it from lining up with the other books.

She pulled it back out and reached into the space behind. Her fingers clasped around a small, leather-bound box.

She flipped open the lid and with a gasp at her success, she pulled out the bunch of keys on a brass ring. As she slipped the keys into her dressing gown pocket, she replaced the box at the back of the shelf and stood *Mein Kampf* in front.

Before leaving, she closed the curtains and waited by the door, listening. There was movement outside. Or was it upstairs? Floorboards creaked. What would they do to her if they caught her? She thought of how powerless she had been when that strange doctor had examined her. Whilst Matron had watched with her cruel smile. Laila knew they were capable of worse things.

She pressed her ear against the door. The sound of water. A toilet flushing. Then silence. Just one of the many expectant mothers' nightly bathroom visits. She prised open the door, checked the hall was empty, and padded down the hall to the spiral staircase.

This part of the house was in total darkness, and she had to feel her way, feet shuffling forwards, one hand on the wall, the other straight out in front of her. Her foot hit the bottom step of the staircase. Clasping the railing, she followed its spiral form upwards, wary how her slippers slid on the wooden steps. The railing ended and she took a step up into thin air. She had arrived at the first-floor landing.

There was no spot of light at the end of the hall from the nursery. The door was closed. Enveloped in blackness, she was disorientated. Straining her eyes, she saw a shape take form before her. Tall, broad, moving fast. Matron Schwarz. Still as a stone troll, Laila waited for the woman to be upon her. But there was no sound of footsteps. No boom of a voice. The shape dissolved and the blackness yawned. She was imagining things.

She sneaked on, running her hand along the wall. A door post and a door. Here was the first room on the right. It was the second door that Laila wanted, where she had seen the secretary enter with an armful of files. Her fingertips continued their search until she found the next door. She reached out, hands searching for the door handle and the lock. The tips of her fingers brushed over them carefully.

Now the keys. Cumbersome fingers and moist palms feeling for the largest key. Feel the shape of the lock. Feed the key in.

Why was her body so loud in the stillness? Her breath, her heart, the buzzing in her head.

The turn of the lock. Even louder.

But then she was inside; weak with relief, she leaned against the closed door, catching her breath. Again, she felt for the keyhole, and locked herself in the room. It was bizarre but she felt safer behind the locked door. But if she was discovered, what would she do? Perhaps they would force the door down. She could jump from the first-floor window. And break both her legs.

Focus, Laila, she told herself. *Do what you came to do.* With bold steps and arms outstretched she reached the window and parted the blackout curtains. Now she could make out the two filing cabinets. She tried the smaller keys on the brass ring. A cabinet opened and she pulled out the top drawer. Files and documents. She pulled out a document and held it up to the window. It was impossible to read in the dim light of the night sky.

She made a decision. She had come this far. In two days, she would be leaving Lebensborn for good. Now was the chance to find out what was going on within these walls. There was nothing for it. She must turn the light on and hope everyone would be fast asleep.

Her movements were swift, switching the table lamp on, closing the blackouts, and rolling the rug against the door to block any light from seeping out underneath. Adrenalin and purpose suppressed her fear. She would be careful to keep the files tidy and in the order they were stacked.

There were lists of the women who had been at the home. Norwegian names. The adjacent column held German male names. Obviously, their partners. But there were many gaps. In fact, only about half the women had a registered partner. The next column held the names of their children and date of birth. The final column indicated which children were given up for adoption. Names of adoptive parents did not appear on the list. Only the various adoption authorities, all with German addresses.

Laila opened the second cabinet. The documents in these files were different. There was a list that contained no details of a mother or a father. Only Norwegian children, some without surnames followed by *(m)* or *(f)*. A German name had also been allocated. Ages entered were often preceded by the word *circa*. The final entry listed adoptive agencies in Germany. Laila frowned. Who were the parents of these children?

She was just about to turn to the next document when a name on the list caught her eye. She gasped.

No, it can't be.

Tore X (m) circa 1 Jahr Holga 10/6/41
Lebensborn, Norway 20/6/41
Lebensborn, Hohehorst, Germany.

Memories sprang up: Gudrun lying in the earth, sobbing. The empty pram outside the house. Tore's teddy on the ground. Of course, there were other children with the same name. But children of the same age who'd gone missing at the same time? No. The Nazis had stolen him from his grandmother. Kidnapped him and brought him here to this very house before transferring him to a home in Germany. They had renamed him Holga. No doubt he was then adopted by a Nazi family. Another racially pure child to replace the dying German soldiers; to bolster a shrinking Aryan population.

She found something else. An entry for Gunther Schmidt: baby twelve. The child that had arrived without a mother and then just disappeared again. His real name was Nils and he'd been sent to Germany. Another stolen child.

Laila folded the list and slipped it into her dressing gown pocket. Rifling through the files with urgency, she took other lists that could be of significance. One that detailed where Dagny's son had been sent.

Another document in particular made her uneasy. A list of babies that had become ill at the home and had been sent to a special clinic in Bremen, Germany, where they had all died.

Cause of death: *Lungenentzündung*. Lung infection.

Tomorrow was Saturday. If she replaced the remaining files carefully and left the room how she'd found it, the documents she'd taken were unlikely to be missed. Not at the weekend. And on Sunday she would depart with Elise, taking the documents with her.

After closing the cabinets, rolling back the rug, and switching off the light, she listened at the door. All was quiet. Now she had to return the bunch of keys to the box in Fräulein Hahn's office and slip the office key back into the coat with the silver fox collar.

Perhaps Fräulein Hahn had already gone, leaving Dr Albers sleeping. It was unlikely she would invite gossip by staying till morning when the employees started the early shift. At some point she would notice the missing key.

Downstairs, the grandfather clock struck four. Laila knew that if she was caught now, her dressing gown pockets stuffed with stolen papers and a bunch of secret keys, she would suffer terrifying consequences. Perhaps the Gestapo. A firing squad.

She passed the painting of the frozen lake. And thought of Dagny.

Her hand shook as she opened the office door with the single key and slipped inside. Again, she felt her way to the blackout, allowed a sliver of light to lead her to the leather box where she returned the bunch of keys.

Back in the hall, she headed to the coat rack, straining her eyes, searching for the silver fox collar. She couldn't see it. My God, she couldn't see it. She had come this far. But the damn coat.

Cries from the nursery. A shuffle on the upstairs landing. The house creaked.

A streak of silver glinted. Laila fell on the coat, digging her hands into the silky fur with relief, and slid the small key in the same pocket where she had found it. Hiding in between the coats Laila waited until the noises from upstairs subsided before creeping back to her room.

Greta was snoring softly as she slipped the stolen papers between the pages of her jade journal, hidden between her pullovers.

25

It was Saturday. One last full day. One last, regimented, stifling day of luxurious imprisonment. Yes, she would miss the other mothers, the comradeship of all being in the same predicament; the knowing smiles they gave each other, the words of support and comfort. She would miss the good food and the beautiful house, the paintings of the lake and most of all of Anne Solomon tasting snowflakes. Laila had a mad impulse to pack the painting in her suitcase. But it was just a fantasy.

Marit didn't appear for breakfast.

Laila told the women at the table her plans. She would return to Narvik to try to reconcile with her family. Someone asked her what she would do if they wouldn't take her back. Laila shook her head. 'I'm still working on plan B.'

Greta explained that the driver would take her, Laila, and Elise to the station at one o'clock Sunday afternoon. Greta would travel part of the way with Laila. No one asked about Greta's child. They all knew.

'Has anyone seen Marit?' asked Laila.

No one had.

Laila sliced off the top of her boiled egg and gazed at the runny egg yolk. Her stomach churned. She thought about the stolen papers in her journal. Not an imaginative hiding place. But she couldn't think of anywhere else. Anyway, it was just till tomorrow lunch time and then she would be gone, taking with her the evidence of what was really going on behind the veneer of the Lebensborn homes.

'Are you going to stare that egg into ingestion?' asked Greta.

Laila laughed. 'I haven't much of an appetite this morning.'

'You should make the most of the food whilst you can. It'll be back to ration cards tomorrow.'

Something inside her shifted. She looked around the room; the tables laden with food that had impressed her so much when she'd first arrived three months ago. She didn't care about the food. It was tainted. Everything here was a façade. A lie. She couldn't wait to get out of here with Elise and see her family again. She missed them all: cheeky Olaf, little Inge who would probably be talking now, her parents, and even Hanna. And she missed Oda, who she'd let down in the worst possible way.

Laila gave her egg to Greta, took a few sips of coffee, and went to look for Marit. She found her in her room, sitting on her bed, her eyes red and swollen.

Laila sat down next to her and took her hand.

'What's the matter, Marit? What's happened?'

'When I went to the nursery this morning to feed Albert, he wasn't there. His cot was empty.' She choked back a sob and wiped her nose with the handkerchief clutched in her hand. 'The duty nurse told me he'd been taken ill in the night and was in the sick room. I ran there to see him. At first, they wouldn't let me in, and I had to wait outside for Matron Schwarz to arrive.'

'What did she say was wrong with him?' said Laila, trying not to show her alarm.

'That's the strange thing. Matron said he'd developed a high fever, but when they let me see him, he was in a deep sleep. Totally peaceful. Not at all red faced or restless. When I commented on that, Matron said the medication was helping.'

'What type of medication?'

'I don't know.' Marit started to twist the damp handkerchief in her hands.

'Come, let's go and see him together. Maybe he's awake now and feeling better.'

'He must be hungry,' she said, pressing her hands against her full breasts.

When Laila and Marit tried to enter the sick room, the nurse rushed to the door, blocking their way. 'No one is allowed in here without authorisation.'

'Surely a mother is entitled to see her child,' said Laila.

'Entitlements?' the nurse sneered. 'You need permission from either Matron Schwarz or Dr Albers. Now, let me get on with my work.' She shut the door in their faces.

Marit decided to speak to Dr Albers, thinking he was more approachable than Matron. Laila waited outside the office. When Marit emerged, her face was pallid and looked confused.

'They're sending him away. He's very ill.' Her voice was faint.

Laila put her hands on Marit's shoulders and gave her a fixed look.

'Where are they sending him? What's wrong with him?'

'To a specialist clinic. In Bremen, Germany. He can be properly cared for there.'

Bremen, Germany. That was the clinic where babies had been sent. All had died of a *Lungenentzündung*. Laila took a deep breath so as not to betray her fear.

'Are you allowed to see him?'

Marit shook her head.

'Try not to worry. We'll sort something out.' Even to Laila, her words sounded hollow.

Laila found Herta supervising the mother and baby play hour in the sitting room. She waited in the hall until the mothers came out with their babies and watched them climb the stairway to the nursery. When she went in, Herta was kneeling on the floor folding away the quilted playmats.

'Can I have a quick word?' she asked.

'Of course, if you help me tidy these away.'

Kneeling beside Herta, Laila folded a mat as she spoke about her concern for Marit's son. Herta had heard he had become unwell during the night but knew nothing about the proposed transfer to a clinic.

Laila thought about how to phrase her question. 'Does it often happen that babies are sent to this clinic in Bremen?'

Herta stopped folding and gave Laila a strange look. 'What do you know about the Bremen Clinic?'

'Nothing. Only that Marit was told that's where Albert is to be treated.'

'We have sent children with severe problems there a few times.' Herta frowned.

'What sort of problems do you mean? Disabilities, for example?'

'You're asking a lot of questions that don't concern you,' she snapped and stood up, tucking the playmats under her arm.

Damn. She had pushed too hard. 'Sorry, it's just I'm worried about Marit and I'm leaving tomorrow.'

Herta nodded and left the room, her expression troubled.

At midday, Laila fed Elise in the nursery and put her down for her afternoon nap with the other babies. Elise did not look sleepy in the least. Soon, Laila could decide her own routine for her child.

She went to her room and sat at the desk to write a letter to

Josef. She wrote how pleased she was to be leaving the next day and how she planned to introduce Elise to her family. And how she could hardly wait for him to see his beautiful daughter, who was so clever and advanced for her age. She drew a quick sketch at the bottom. And drew a heart around the initials J and L. Then as an afterthought, she added an E. They were a real family. She finished the letter with:

I cannot describe the pain of missing you. Only that the longing is made bearable by imagining that sweetest of moments when we are reunited. To be able to touch your face and see your smile. Please know how much I love you. Please know you are half of my heartbeat, half my soul, and the whole of my world. Come back safe, my darling. Come back soon.

Tears pricked her eyes as she popped the letter into an envelope. She would post it tomorrow at the station.

When Greta returned to the room, she pulled her suitcase out from under the bed and opened the wardrobe. 'Have you packed yet?' she said.

'I'll do it after dinner. It won't take long to pack the few things I have.'

Greta was unusually quiet as she sorted her own belongings. Laila thought she would be in a more euphoric mood.

'You must be looking forward to getting back to a normal life again,' Laila ventured.

'You bet. Working, meeting new people. Getting away from hormonal women and screaming babies.' Her voice was harsh.

Greta pulled out a tiny red pullover she had knitted for her baby in the craft group. 'I won't be needing this. I'll give it to Matron.'

Greta stared at the pullover that lay across her palms. Her

shoulders started to shake, and she made a loud gulping sound. She dropped her head, her hair flopping over her face.

'Greta, are you all right?'

Greta turned her back. 'I'm fine.'

Laila stood behind her and put a hand on her shoulder. 'You can talk to me. Maybe it will help.'

Greta whirled around, her eyes full of tears.

'Talk to you? Miss Perfect? I know what you think of me. That I'm a callous, self-centred tart who seduces married men and gives away her child without a second thought.'

Startled, Laila took a step back. 'That's not what I think.'

'Oh, really. Then what?'

'I think that's a role you play. I don't know why you do it, but you build walls.'

'You're wrong. This is the real me. A terrible, heartless mother that abandons her own child.' She flopped on the bed her anger spent.

Laila thought for a moment and then said, her voice gentle, 'When Dagny signed the papers agreeing to her son's adoption, she thought it was the best thing she could do for him. She saw no perspective for her future. No job, no family, no husband, no money. She felt she had nothing to offer her son. Did that make her a bad mother? Or a selfless one?'

'And look what happened to her.'

'She paid the ultimate price. But it shouldn't have been that way.'

'And what about you? You're taking Elise with you.'

'But I have Josef. I pray. And we'll be a family. All our situations are different. Maybe you are doing the right thing for your child.'

'To be raised by a Nazi family?'

'Oh, Greta. You know perfectly well that not all Germans are Nazis and are able to be caring, loving parents.'

Greta gave a wan smile. 'I'm not sure that you believe everything you're saying but thank you anyway.'

'We're all having to make the most difficult choices at the
moment. Let's not judge each other.' She held out her arms. Greta
stood up and they hugged each other.

'And by the way, I'm anything but perfect.' Laila laughed.

* * *

There was a rush of feet along the hallway accompanied by
excited voices. The post van was there. Laila, Greta, and Marit
were in the library talking about the proposed transfer of Albert.
Laila wished she could tell them what she'd learned from the
stolen papers, but she didn't want to endanger her friends. She
also didn't think it was helpful to scare Marit further with stories
of dying children.

Laila and Marit went to greet the postman in the entrance hall,
whilst Greta remained seated. She had no one to write to her. The
women crowded around the postman as if he were the Christmas
elf. Yes, he said he had field post, but as always it would be handed
to Matron Schwarz first. Everyone watched him carrying the jute
sack to Matron's office and then they dispersed. They would have
to wait for dinner time to receive their letters. Laila felt sick with
nerves.

There was one final task required of her before she left Lebensborn. An appraisal of her social and political orientation in the
form of an interview with Dr Albers. This was deemed necessary
for mothers intending to bring up their children themselves. If
they were to marry a German, then their suitability for the role of a
Third Reich housewife would also be assessed.

Sitting opposite Dr Albers, Laila thought of him on top of his
secretary the previous evening, the image of him puffing and

grunting at the forefront of her mind. He's just a man, she thought, and her fear dwindled. She fought to keep her expression neutral.

'So, Frau Olson. You are to leave us tomorrow and have decided to take your daughter with you. I understand you and Private Josef Schultz intend to marry at an appropriate opportunity. And I presume to make your home in Germany.'

'We haven't yet discussed where we want to live.'

Dr Albers gave her a sharp look. *Careful, Laila.*

'But more than likely, we will settle in Germany,' she added, thinking of her fjord outside her bedroom window.

He nodded and consulted the notes in her file. 'You declined the SS naming ceremony. May I ask why?'

Laila saw the raised dagger above Eva Dahl's baby. The SS men in black.

'I wanted to wait until the father could be present.' Lying to someone she detested was so easy.

He then went on to test what she had learned at the political orientation classes. She rattled out the stock answers he wanted to hear, her tone emotionless. It was surreal watching herself, a stranger, perform.

But when the conversation turned to selection politics and those of impure blood, she faltered. He asked her to name those who endangered the ideal master race and those who were the enemy.

'There are so many,' she said.

'Name a few,' he said, spreading his arms, attempting to appear reasonable.

A pause. The air was thick in the small office.

She had lived three months in Anne Solomon's home.

He waited.

'We were told, for example, Gypsies.'

He tipped his head to the side, waiting for more.

'And communists and homosexuals. Poles.' Her words felt bitter on her tongue.

'You have not mentioned the worst of all.'

Her snowflake girl. She would not betray her.

'I can't think of any others.'

'Really?'

'I apologise if I haven't paid attention in all the classes.'

'Do not play games with me, Frau Olson.' He snapped her file shut. 'You may leave now.'

Exhaling a deep breath, Laila left Dr Albers's office and went upstairs to pack her suitcase. She would leave out the clothes that she and Elise were to wear tomorrow. Elise would wear the things her mother had knitted. She hummed as she packed.

A knock at the half-open door.

'Come in.'

Herta popped her head round. 'Matron would like to see you in her office.'

Laila sighed. 'What does she want now?'

'She didn't say. Maybe she wants to say goodbye and wish you well.'

'I doubt that.'

Herta grinned.

Matron did not greet Laila as she entered the room but extended her arm towards the chair opposite her. Laila sat. A brass carriage clock with Roman numerals faced her on Matron's desk. It was five o'clock. This time tomorrow she would be home.

Matron shuffled some papers on her desk. Perhaps Dr Albers had spoken to her about her interview. But Matron did not mention anything that had occurred earlier that day. Instead, she picked up a white envelope. With Nazi insignia. She slid out the single sheet of paper and held it in front of her. It was a short letter. Just a few typed lines.

Matron looked up. Her eyes hard. Her jaw tight. Although her face was solemn, Laila thought she saw a flash of triumph in her eyes, but then it was gone.

Laila felt dizzy, breathless. She looked at the carriage clock, the clockface beginning to swim before her eyes. If only this moment would stop now. When everything was still okay. Before Matron spoke. She mustn't speak.

'Frau Olson, I am afraid I have bad news for you.'

No. She didn't want to hear it. She was standing on a precipice. Behind her was a life of hope, love, Josef. In front of her yawned an abyss of darkness and despair. She watched Matron, the image of her desk and the brass carriage clock receding, shrinking, and dimming. Laila's eyes glazed over. Josef was kissing her for the first time behind the boat house against an orange sky where the sun refused to set into the sea.

'Private Josef Schultz has fallen in action defending The Third Reich. He died bravely and with honour.'

Laila looked into the chasm, felt the force of its pull, and toppled into the blackness. She was lost.

Shadows and voices. Her eyes too weak to open. Her head too heavy to move. Images flashed. Matron saying something terrible. Laila plummeting. Matron and a nurse hoisting her to the sick room. Laila screaming: 'liars, liars.' A needle. Wonderful darkness.

She stirred, her mouth dry, her head thumping. She looked around her. Another woman was lying in the sick room hooked up to a drip. A nurse sat at a desk by the window making notes under the light of a table lamp. The blackout blind was closed.

There was the briefest moment between being asleep and awake when Laila's world was still all right. But within heartbeats, reality crashed in on her, squeezing the breath from her lungs.

Josef was gone.

Josef was gone; the letter announcing his death lay on the table next to her.

There was nothing left.

Misery rolled in like the sea, claiming her, dragging her into its cold depths...

But Elise.

'Where's my baby? I must feed her.' She heard the shrillness in her voice.

The nurse came over. 'Remain calm. I'll fetch Matron.'

'My baby, my baby, bring me my baby.' Laila repeated the words until Matron arrived and stood by her bedside.

'The child is being cared for. You may see her when you have calmed down.'

'I'm calm. I promise I'm calm. I must see her.'

'Soon,' said Matron and left.

The nurse brought a bowl of chicken soup on a tray. Laila looked at the pale flesh floating in the insipid liquid and gagged.

'Take it away. Tell Matron I'm calm now. Tell her.'

The nurse said nothing and removed the tray.

Time passed. Another nurse came on duty and removed the drip from the woman in the other bed.

Laila stared at the ceiling. She heard footsteps. Matron Schwarz and Dr Klinger with his soulless eyes stood at the end of her bed.

'How are you feeling now?' the doctor asked.

Laila remembered how she had been splayed out before him when he examined her. Punished her.

'Much better,' she said, climbing out of bed. 'I'd like to go to the nursery and feed my child now.'

Matron stepped in front of her. 'That is being taken care of. It may be better to keep some distance whilst you consider your new situation.'

'I don't understand.' She couldn't keep the panic out of her voice.

'You are now a single mother with no income or the support of your family.'

'That's not true. I'm taking Elise to my family tomorrow. We'll be reconciled.'

'I doubt you and the child will be accepted either in your family or your community. I strongly advise you to consider adoption.'

'No way,' said Laila, stepping closer to Matron Schwarz. 'You did this with Dagny. You drove her to her death.'

Matron turned to Dr Klinger. 'You see what I mean? Delusional. A tendency for paranoia.'

Laila flew herself at Matron, screaming, 'You heartless bitch,' shoving hard with both hands. Matron stumbled back, hit her head against the corner of the metal bed, and crumpled to the floor.

'Nurse,' shouted Dr Klinger, grabbing Laila by the arm, 'see to Matron.'

Then he swung his arm and struck Laila so hard across the face that she was flung backwards onto the bed. She heard a ringing in her ears and tasted blood in her mouth. She raised a hand to her burning face, but her arm was yanked down. The punch of a needle in her arm; the word *morphine*.

'Hysteria.' Dr Klinger's voice. 'The woman suffers from hysteria.'

'Absolutely, *Herr Doktor*.' Matron's voice, thick, breathless. 'Clearly unfit to raise a child.' Matron's face hovered over her, twisted with hate, blood trickling down the side of her face.

Laila was sucked into oblivion.

26

She was so cold. She thought she'd opened her eyes, but she could see nothing. She slept.

A clunk; a metal sound. She shivered from the cold. Again, Laila opened her eyes but saw nothing. The shuffle of footsteps. There was a click and brightness assaulted her. She squeezed her eyes shut. A voice said, 'Here, drink.' Something cold and hard pressed against her lips and drops of water trickled onto her tongue. It felt good. She opened her mouth wider, but then coughed and spluttered. The water was taken away.

The footsteps receded. A door shut. The metal clunk, clunk.

Tentatively, Laila opened her eyes, adjusting to the light from the lamp on the table next to her. Her head felt thick, and her vision swam. She waited a few moments, taking deep breaths and propped herself up on her elbows. She lay on a narrow steel bed in a small rectangular room. There was no window. The walls were grey painted brick. The floor was cement, no rug or carpet.

She was locked in the cellar.

The only other things in the room apart from the table and

lamp were a tin bucket in the corner of the room, and a roll of toilet paper that sat next to it.

She had been undressed and was now wearing a stiff white examination gown. A thin blanket covered her. The room was freezing.

As her head began to clear, she tried to assess her situation. It was dire. She had attacked Matron Schwarz, been refused access to Elise, and was now locked in the cellar. And Josef... she forced herself to say his name in her head. Dead. The man she loved. The only man she had ever or would ever love had been taken from her.

Why had God done this? Because she had betrayed her family and country?

But Josef had prayed to God too. To keep Laila and her family safe. Whose side was God on? Maybe she should pray and ask these questions. But what was the point? God was not here with her in this bunker, this coffin. She hugged her knees to her chest.

After a while, she padded over the floor, her woollen socks protecting her from the cold of the cement, hitched up the white gown, squatted over the tin bucket and relieved herself. She used one square of toilet paper. There wasn't much on the roll, and she didn't know how long she would be kept here. Her breasts ached with the undrunk milk; her yearning to hold Elise was a physical pain.

It was difficult to judge what time of day it was. She didn't know how long she had slept from the morphine shot. Maybe late Saturday evening. Perhaps it was already Sunday. No food or water had been left in the room, although she remembered a glass being held to her lips.

Sometime later, there were footsteps outside. The rattle of a key in the keyhole. The clunk of a turning lock. It turned twice.

Laila jumped up and faced the door. Herta appeared holding a tray. Behind her stood two nurses across the doorway. One held a syringe in her hand.

'What's going on?' she asked, hating the tremble in her voice.

'I've brought you potato soup and bread, and a jug of water,' said Herta. 'The small pink pill is to help you sleep.' Her voice was soft.

She set the tray on the table next to the bed.

'Herta, why am I here? I want to leave now. I want to see Elise. She needs to be fed. She'll be starving.'

Herta looked away and said nothing.

Laila took a step towards the door.

The two broad-shouldered nurses stepped aside, and Matron Schwarz strode in, filling the room with menace. She had a deep purple bruise on the side of her face, and a jagged cut above a puffy eye.

'There is no need to worry that the child is starving.' Matron's swollen face gave a half smile. 'Another mother with plentiful milk is feeding her.'

Revulsion twisted in Laila's gut. 'A stranger is breast feeding *my* child?'

'Sit down. I'll explain.' Matron indicated the bed. Her tone was light, almost playful.

'I don't want to sit. I want to know what's going on.'

'The situation is this: Dr Albers and Dr Klinger have signed an attestation that you are unwell—'

'There's nothing wrong with me.'

'—that the trauma of your recent loss has made you mentally unstable. You suffer from hysteria, and the signed attestation states you are unfit to be a mother. Elise is to be sent to Germany for adoption.'

'You can't do that.'

'We can and will, Frau Olson.'

'You're taking my child from me?'

'Correct. You will remain here till after Elise has been collected.'

Matron pulled herself up to her full height and squared her shoulders, her eyes glowing with power.

'Your conduct here over the last three months was only tolerated because you carried a child for the Reich. You were never of any importance. Just a woman of loose morals giving us what we wanted. The unfortunate death of one of our brave men and your consequent behaviour played right into our hands. What a foolish woman you are.'

Matron turned on her heel and swept out. Herta shot Laila a sad look and left with the two nurses. The steel door clanked shut. The key was turned twice. And Laila was left in her tomb of despair.

For a long while she stared into space, trying to process what Matron had said.

Then she ran at the door, slamming her fists against the steel, screaming and sobbing.

Her throat sore and her hands throbbing with pain, she went to the tray Herta had brought in. She swallowed the pink pill, lay on the bed, and waited to slip away.

* * *

It was so cold in the room that Laila could see her wisps of breath. Was it night or day? Sunday or Monday? Her legs were weak as she shuffled over to the bucket, trembling as she squatted. She wore no underwear under the coarse robe and her skin had puckered into goose bumps. She hurried back to bed, where she wrapped the light blanket around herself as tightly as possible and stared at a brown-yellow stain on the ceiling, letting the whirlwind of thoughts envelop her.

It had come to this. To nothing. She had nothing. She was nothing. Hollowed out. Dried out. Broken. She had wanted to protect and support her family, fill the space left by Anton. But instead, she'd alienated them and betrayed her country. She'd fallen in love. With the enemy. She'd made her choice. But Josef had been cruelly snatched from her. And the most precious gift he'd left her, she had managed to lose. She had failed in every aspect of her life.

The picture of Dagny standing alone in the middle of the frozen lake came to her mind. She understood her now. The draw of the ice-cold depths numbing the body of feeling, the mind of emotion.

She sat up and looked at the tray of food on the table. The bowl was made of plastic. So was the spoon. The cup was made of paper. The water jug, plastic. No glass or porcelain. Interesting.

Throwing the blanket aside, Laila started to jog around the small room. She must get warm. She swung her arms, punched the air, and did star jumps. Then, arm presses against the wall, push ups on the floor and leg squats. Afterwards, she ate the cold potato soup and stale bread.

She could smell her body odour so she poured some water into the cup, dipped a corner of her robe into it and then dabbed under her arms and between her legs. She emptied the dirty water from the cup into the tin bucket, refilled the cup with fresh water, swilled and gargled, and then spat out into the bucket. Feeling better, she sat on the bed and waited, listening for footsteps.

Her head had dropped sideways as she dozed when voices

echoed down the corridor outside. She sprang up, grabbed the tin bucket, and stood next to the door, flat against the wall. Her heart drummed in her chest. It was time to act. To summon all her courage and determination and fight back.

The key turned. Clunk. Clunk.

One of the broad-bodied nurses stepped into the room. Laila swung the bucket and its contents with all her might, hitting the nurse on the chin. Urine splattered into the woman's eyes, and she stumbled back against the person behind her, a kitchen maid holding a tray of food. The tray clattered to the floor and the maid ran off.

A second nurse came at Laila.

Arching her arm for full momentum, Laila prepared to throw the bucket a second time. It hit the nurse square in the face and she buckled, clutching her nose.

Laila bolted. Down the corridor, up the cellar steps, along the hall on the ground floor. It was daylight. Mothers were milling around. They stared opened mouth at the wild woman streaming past, her robe flapping open, exposing her bare back and bottom. At the main staircase, she hesitated. Upstairs was the nursery and her daughter. Ahead was the front entrance. Herta stood there, buttoning up her coat. She stared at Laila with horror.

Laila's adrenalin plummeted like a waterfall. She had no plan. She had fury and pain, and desperation. But she had no plan. And now it was too late.

She was surrounded. Dr Klinger, Matron, and an enraged nurse with a nosebleed.

They dragged her back to the cellar.

Laila waited for the needle, almost looking forward to the sweet oblivion. Dr Klinger and Matron watched Laila cowering in the corner of the room.

'You do realise that by attacking members of the Reich, you

have committed a crime.' Matron's face was rigid. 'Tomorrow, you will be transported to a correction facility.'

Two fresh nurses with strong arms arrived. Now Laila would get her shot. A sedative. Maybe morphine. Morphine would be good.

Matron whispered to Dr Klinger. He nodded and unbuckled his belt, slipping it from his trouser loops. He handed it to Matron, his fingers lingering on hers, and left. The two nurses pushed Laila face down on the bed.

Her gown was ripped from her body.

A nurse each side of the bed gripped her arms. Steel fingers bored into her flesh.

There was no welcome sedative.

There was a beating.

Matron grunted and cried out as she lashed the belt across Laila's naked buttocks and the backs of her thighs.

Again.

And again.

At some point, a nurse suggested perhaps that was enough.

Matron looped the belt round Laila's right wrist and tied it to the metal bar at the head of the bed. After snatching away the blanket, she moved the table lamp out of Laila's reach and snapped off the light. Laila remained motionless on her stomach, one arm wrenched above her head.

The three women left and locked the door.

It felt like hours that she lay there in the freezing darkness, whimpering from the pain. She had the urge to pee and held on for as long as she could. Then, not caring any more, she let go, feeling the warm urine trickle down the inside of her thighs. This was what the Nazis did: break you with humiliation.

But she knew they could do worse things.

Terror racked her body.

She had never felt so utterly alone.

* * *

The door clunked open. They were back. To beat her again? Or perhaps bundle her into a van. Maybe even shoot her right here. Footsteps. Nurse's sturdy shoes. A light flashed on.

'Frau Olson, I've brought you some food and something to dress your wounds with.' Herta's voice, sounding strange and stiff.

Laila swivelled her head around. Another nurse, arms crossed, stood across the doorway. Herta held out a mug, which had steam rising from it.

There was just enough slack in the leather belt that Laila was able to prop herself up on her elbows and take the warm mug in her free hand. She sipped the chicken broth and sighed as the warmth hit her stomach.

Herta had brought a tray with medical supplies. She waited till Laila had finished her soup, took the empty mug, and told her to lie flat. 'This will sting, I'm afraid. It's disinfectant.'

Sting was an understatement. It burned like hell. Next came a salve that Herta dabbed on her burning skin. 'I'll just put a light gauze on the worst parts, where the skin is split open.'

Herta picked up the white gown that had been hurled on the floor and covered Laila's shoulders with it. 'It's like ice in this room. I'll fetch some blankets.' Her tone was matter of fact. No sign of the compassion she had shown during Laila's labour.

'No blankets,' the nurse at the door said. 'Matron said no blankets.'

'The last thing Dr Albers would want is another mother dying of pneumonia. I'll tell Matron it was my idea.'

'As you wish.' The nurse yawned. 'Then let's be quick about it. My next shift starts in six hours, and I want to get some sleep.'

'You get off to bed. I can deal with it on my own. The woman is hardly a danger. She's strapped down.'

'I'm supposed to keep the key with me overnight.'

'How about I pop by your room with the key and put it on your bedside table when I'm finished?'

The nurse agreed and the two of them left.

Laila was alone again, but at least the light had been left on. Herta had been so cool and distant. Had she really thought that she could make friends with a Nazi midwife, whose job was to bring Hitler's chosen safely into the world?

Herta returned a short while later. She dropped a bundle of things on the floor, leaned over the bed, and untied the belt from Laila's wrist.

'Can you lie on your side facing me? Sitting will be too painful.' Herta's voice was softer now.

Laila turned on her side gingerly. Herta laid a warm blanket over her and crouched down next to the bed.

'We have to get you out of here tonight. They're planning to send you to a concentration camp. And a nurse is taking Elise to a Lebensborn home in Germany. Tomorrow.'

'I'm not leaving without my daughter.'

'I know. You'll take her with you.'

'How? And what about Marit? How's Albert?'

'They say he's too ill to stay here. But I don't think he's ill at all.' Herta's eyes welled up. 'They'll send him to the special clinic in Bremen.'

'That's where all the babies go that the Nazis consider inferior,' said Laila.

'It's a euthanasia institution. I realise that now,' said Herta, her voice breaking.

'Let Marit and Albert escape with me. Please help them. You

must. Otherwise, Albert will be murdered and who knows what will happen to Marit?'

The women fixed their eyes on each other. Laila reached out and placed the palm of her hand over Herta's heart. Herta returned the gesture. Moments passed as they felt each other's living rhythm.

'Okay. This is the plan,' Herta whispered.

27

The first thing Laila did was take the painkillers Herta had left for her. Then she unrolled the bundle of things she had brought: her ski trousers, a thick pullover, underwear, socks, boots, and a small torch. There was a washcloth wrapped around a baby's milk bottle filled with warm water. How thoughtful. Herta must have smelled the urine on her.

She soaked the cloth with the water and washed herself before getting dressed. It was a slow process. Even fragile movements caused her wounds to burn and throb. Once dressed, she tried the door. It was open. She closed it again. Herta had left it unlocked and returned the key to the nurse as she'd promised. She lay back on the bed on her stomach, this time facing the door.

Herta's fob watch lay in the palm of her hand. It was ten thirty in the evening. She would have to wait till midnight until it was safe to leave the cellar. She tried to doze but was too afraid that someone would come down to check on her and find the door unlocked and Laila fully dressed. It was unlikely though. She had been left tied to the bed and the next visit would probably not be until early morning. Still, she stared at the door like a dog waiting for its master to return.

A few minutes before midnight, Laila turned off the light, left her cell, and closed the door behind her. She hoped Matron would be the one to discover the empty room and she imagined her face contorted with anger.

Flicking on the torch, she followed the narrow corridor to the cellar steps. At the top she waited on the inside of the closed door, listening.

The grandfather clock struck midnight.

The door opened. Herta, dressed in a coat, stood in the dim light with a duffel bag over one shoulder and Laila's coat and scarf over her arm. She checked left and right before beckoning Laila to follow her, pointing at her torch. Laila turned it off and followed. Instead of heading for the main entrance, they made their way to the kitchen at the back of the house.

Fear pulsated through her. If they were caught now, the consequences would be horrific. Not just for her, but for Herta too, who was putting her life in danger. The kitchen was in total darkness. Herta switched on her torch that gave off a faint light; she had taped newspaper over the glass to dim the beam.

The large kitchen looked ominous in the torchlight: a glint of stainless steel, bulky shapes lurking in every corner, knives protruding from wooden blocks.

At the back door, Laila took her coat and scarf and pulled them on. In one pocket was her hat, in the other her gloves. Again, Laila was touched by the thoughtfulness. She threw the duffel bag over her back and looked at Herta expectantly.

'Soon,' Herta mouthed back. Footsteps shuffling through the kitchen. A baby's muffled gurgle. A circle of light danced towards them.

Marit appeared dressed in outdoor clothes, baby Albert swaddled in a wool sling across her chest, a duffel bag also on her back. And right behind her was Greta, in her pyjamas, cradling Elise.

Greta?

In her surprise, Laila broke her silence. 'I thought your train ticket was for yesterday?' she whispered.

'You didn't think I would leave you locked up in the cellar at the mercy of that cruel bitch, did you?'

'It was Greta that packed your duffel bag and helped with the children,' added Herta.

Laila's heart swelled with affection for her roommate. Her simple whispered 'thank you' was far too inadequate. Elise was already wrapped in a baby sling and Greta helped Laila to tie it around her.

'Let's go,' said Herta, producing the key for the back door.

'Goodbye and good luck,' Laila said to Greta, giving her a parting look. 'When do you leave here?'

'I changed my train ticket for tomorrow.'

She threw her arms around her friend, little Elise pressed between them.

'I found your journal and packed it in the duffel bag,' Greta murmured. 'The documents in there are crucial. Get them in the right hands.'

'We must go. Now,' hissed Herta.

Laila disentangled herself from Greta and wondered whether she would ever see her again. Thank God she had packed the documents.

Herta steered Laila and Marit around the back of the house, their torches switched off. The night was cold and clear with a light wind and no snow. The babies fell silent, soothed by the closeness of their mothers and the rocking motion as they walked.

The front gate was bolted shut each night, so Herta led them through the birch and fir trees to the back of the grounds and along the perimeter fence. The area here was overgrown; broken branches and frozen pinecones snapped beneath their boots as they hurried further away from the house. The trees became denser, and the women had to duck and clamber their way through. Laila gritted her teeth against the smarting pain of her wounds.

Herta stopped in front of the high wire fence. Clouds had drifted across the sky, and it was difficult to make out their surroundings. Marit reached out a mittened hand to Laila who gave her a reassuring squeeze.

They waited. They heard each other's breaths.

Herta put her hand on the fence. She shook her head and beckoned the others to follow. She ran her hand along the wire as they moved along the perimeter, as if looking for something.

She stopped again. The sky had grown even darker. Herta risked the shortest flicker of her torch along the fence before switching it off and moving on.

Laila tried to quell the panic that was bubbling up inside her. Would Herta be able to get them out? This was taking too long. How long before the babies were discovered missing?

Then Herta halted and shone her torch for another brief moment. 'Here, here, quick. You first, Marit. I'll bring up the rear.'

There was a hole in the fence.

Marit scrambled through first, clutching Albert close, whilst Herta held the wire apart, releasing Marit's coat when it caught. Laila went next.

A sturdy hand grabbed her arm and pulled her to her feet.

A broad-shouldered man stood before her.

They had been caught. It was over.

'Good to see you again, Frau Olson.'

She could just make out his face in the beam of Herta's torch. His beard had grown longer since she'd seen him last. That day he had fished Dagny out of the frozen lake and carried her back to the bus. Saved her from drowning and then had been fired by Lebensborn.

'Oh, Einar, it's so good to see you. What are you doing here?'

'Well, I met a very distressed young Herta yesterday afternoon in the village. Said you'd been chased through the house and dragged to the cellar, just as she was going out. So, I asked what I could do to help?'

He nodded at the hole in the fence. 'Not so difficult with a pair of wire cutters.'

Laila looked at the secluded forest around them. Einar and Herta had chosen a good spot.

'We're lucky the guard is patrolling the main gate, not the perimeter,' said Einar.

'What do we do now?' asked Marit.

'A bit of a foot march, I'm afraid. To my brother. He lives out in the wilds.' Einar waved his hand at the forest. 'But you'll be safe to take a rest there.'

Laila turned to Herta who was still on the other side of the fence.

'What will you do?'

'I'll get back to the home and slip into bed as if nothing's happened. I've got some kind of alibi worked out.'

'They won't believe you. Matron will know you let me out. You can't go back now. It's too dangerous.'

'They'll arrest you, Herta,' said Marit.

'Come with us, please. I hate to think what will happen to you,' Laila said, her tone urgent.

'I know what will happen to you, Herta,' said Einar. 'They'll send you to prison. Or put you in front of a firing squad. Come with us to my brother's. We'll sort something out.' He reached his arm through the hole in the wire and held out his hand.

'But I have nothing with me. And I'll be on the run,' Herta replied, her protestation weak.

'Better running with nothing than dead,' said Einar.

'You must come with us. Please come with us.' Laila was pleading now. 'We need each other. We need to stay together.'

Einar spread out his broad, gloved hand. 'Now, young lady.'

Herta placed her hand in his and in no time, she was through to the other side. The three women scrambled after Einar, following him deep into the forest.

On the journey, Laila asked Herta the question that had been puzzling her since they'd left. 'How did you get Elise and Albert out of the nursery without being noticed?'

Herta chuckled. 'Our night nurse is rather fond of a cup of cocoa when she's on duty. I kindly offered to make her one. Two sleeping powders and she was off with the fairies in ten minutes. Head flat on the desk. Greta and Marit came and helped with the children.'

'You're brilliant, Herta,' said Laila. And she meant it.

They walked for six hours, through the forest, across clearings, up and down hills. Einar followed the route of a seldom used country road but kept the group hidden in the trees that ran alongside it. Snow lay deep where the sun never reached, under the broad spruce branches.

Twice, the group stopped so the mothers could breast feed. Marit opened her duffel bag and handed out bread and sausage, and a thermos of acorn coffee. Laila admired how well prepared her friend was.

As they continued on trudging through snow on uneven ground, their legs weary, everyone fell quiet. Laila thought only of Josef. She couldn't imagine a life without him, all the plans they'd made. And he would never see his daughter. And his daughter would never know her father.

History was repeating itself. Josef never saw his father, who was killed in World War One. All that madness. All that pain. It was happening again. Did mankind learn nothing?

Hopelessness enveloped her. But then Elise stirred against her chest and a sense of purpose roused within. She would get their child to safety and a part of Josef would live on.

PART III

28

JANUARY 1943

There was no telephone in the single-storey house where Einar's brother lived with his wife. So, it was a complete surprise to him when, bleary eyed, he opened the door to see Einar standing on the doorstep with three women and two babies.

Einar said simply, 'Ulf, we need help.'

In no time, they were clustered around a wood-burning stove, drinking coffee. Ulf had the same hooded eyes as his brother and also sported a bushy beard, but he looked older, with deep lines across his forehead and a receding hairline. He'd thrown a long shapeless cardigan over his worn pyjamas when he'd come to the door.

His wife, Anja rustled up hot oatmeal for everyone and prepared a makeshift bed for the babies from sheepskins and pillows.

Einar explained the situation.

'What do you plan to do now?' asked Ulf.

Laila, Marit, and Herta looked at each other. There was silence as everyone considered the options.

Laila spoke first. 'I want to try and reconcile with my family in Narvik. I hope that showing my parents their grandchild will help.'

'But Narvik is the first place the Nazis will look for you,' said Ulf.

'That's true. But I have, or had, friends in the resistance who could help me find a safe house.'

'Why *had* friends?' Anja asked kindly.

Laila nodded towards Elise, where she was snuggled up beside Albert. 'My daughter has a German father. But I'm sure they will help. I have useful information.' She turned to Marit and Herta. 'My contacts could get both of you to the Swedish border.'

'We'll be refugees. What will I do in Sweden?' said Herta.

'You're a midwife. And a good one, as I know from personal experience,' Laila said. 'Babies will never stop being born. You'll always find work.'

'And me? And Albert?' said Marit, doubtfully.

'They'll help you in Sweden. And you'll be safe.'

'Will you go to Sweden too?' asked Anja.

Laila thought about it. In an ideal world, she would return home to her family and live there with Elise. But she was on the run now and would be arrested immediately once found. There might be no alternative other than to leave her country, her family, and home. The idea was daunting.

'It may be the only solution. But surely the war will be over soon. It's been nearly three years now. And when it's over, we can all go home.'

'First, you're all going to get some sleep,' Anja said, and Laila was grateful. She was overcome with exhaustion. 'We'll plan our next move when everyone has rested.' And with that, Anja slapped her hands on her thighs as if to conclude the conversation and started to organise places for people to sleep.

The discussion continued a few hours later after everyone had rested, washed, and eaten. Ideas were thrown back and forth as the group drank coffee around the kitchen table.

'Ideally, travelling at night is safer,' said Ulf, stroking his bead, 'but it's too cold for the babies.'

'The days are short, and we can use the hours around dusk and dawn,' said Einar. 'It's actually mild for January, only just below freezing.'

Einar fixed his gaze on Laila. 'Are you sure you want to go to Narvik? Patrols will be looking for you. Maybe you could head to Sweden from here. Although, to be honest, I wouldn't know the best way to get you there.'

'That's the point. My friend Finn has a group of Sami guides that regularly lead refugees over the border.'

Marit spoke up. 'We must be careful in Narvik. Perhaps, we can disguise ourselves somehow. But where will we stay until your friend can help us?'

'I know where,' said Laila.

Could she bear to stay in the *hytte* that breathed memories of Josef?

Ulf rose and fetched a map. He spread it out on the table.

'We're here,' he said, marking a cross with a pencil. He then drew a wavy line up north to Narvik.

'It looks a long way,' said Herta. She sounded dubious.

'Over four hundred kilometres at least,' said Ulf. 'Okay, let's face the facts. There's no way you can travel by train. Three women and two babies are far too visible. Plus, the Nazis patrol the trains, checking papers. We have no car. But with all the roadblocks, that would be too dangerous anyway.'

'I have a sinking feeling at what you're getting at,' said Laila. 'We have to walk.'

'Not entirely. I have a horse and wagon. I could take you much of the way, along lesser-known tracks. I know these trails from my hiking days and there are cabins where we can stop overnight. But there's a section that is heavily patrolled, and I won't be able to pass through the forest with the wagon. It's too dense. From there it'll be a brisk foot march.' Ulf turned his gaze to each of them.

There were slow nods around the table. 'I'll accompany you ladies to Narvik,' said Einar. He gave Laila a reassuring smile. She wanted to hug him.

They set off early afternoon, as the light was fading. The two brothers sat up front in the wagon while the women and the babies snuggled together in the back under the canvas roof, huddled in sheepskins, blankets, and cushions. Anja had filled their duffel bags with as much food as she could spare, and Ulf had loaded a sledge onto the cart that could be used to transport their supplies when they continued on foot. He packed a heap of straw to feed the horse which also provided the women with insulation from the cold.

The coming night promised to be clear, with enough light from a half moon and stars for Ulf's trusted horse to see the way. Ulf tied an oil lamp on the front of the wagon but would try not to use it if possible.

A sliver of moonlight shone through the gap of the canvas flaps at the back of the wagon and Laila could just make out the outline of Herta and Marit's faces. 'Thank you both for getting me out of the home,' she whispered. 'I owe you my life. I'm not sure I can ever repay you.'

'You have already,' said Marit. 'Without you, Albert would be on his way to the death clinic.'

'And without you, I would still be complicit in Lebensborn's evil programme,' said Herta. 'Wrenching children from their mothers and killing babies that don't fit the Nazi ideal.'

Laila held out her arms, and the three women shuffled in towards each other and held hands.

'Here's to us ladies,' Laila said. 'Friends for always.'

'Friends for always,' repeated Herta and Marit.

* * *

Laila was stiff and frozen when the wagon came to a halt. She had spent much of the journey lying on her side to avoid pressing against her wounded skin. They had whipped her like a horse. Or worse. You wouldn't whip a horse like that.

Einar's head appeared through the back flaps of the wagon. 'We're stopping for a few hours. Ulf has found us a *hytte*.'

The cabin was basic. Crates formed a narrow bed and a lone chair stood in the corner. There was only one other thing in the room. But it was the most important: a stove. Piled next to it was wood that had been axed into logs. The axe was propped up against the wall.

'Why are there empty, unlocked cabins scattered around Norway?' Herta asked.

Ulf dropped the duffel bags on the floor. 'Some are for hunters. Others are families' summer homes, and the ones near rivers are for the fishermen. Most are unlocked. There is an unwritten rule that travellers leave cabins clean and tidy and stocked with firewood.'

Laila and Marit carried the sheepskins and blankets from the wagon inside and prepared a makeshift bed on the floor. Ulf fed the horse and covered him in a heavy blanket whilst Einar lit the stove and Herta unpacked food for everyone.

The next job was to change the babies' nappies. At this point, the men decided to go out for a smoke. An old tin pot stood on top of the stove. Laila popped outside the front door and, grinning at the brothers, filled the pot with snow. Men could be brave and strong at times, but go near them with a smelly nappy, and they shudder and dive for cover. She heated the snow atop the stove and when it was lukewarm, she and Marit cleaned the babies' bottoms.

Herta had made sure they were well prepared, filling the duffel bag with nappies, cotton liners, safety pins, and wash cloths. After the babies were changed, Laila refilled the pot with snow and when the water was hot, she dropped in the soiled cloth nappies and scrubbed them clean with the bar of carbolic soap Herta had also packed. Marit hung the nappies to dry by the stove, and Laila buried the soiled nappy liners outside in the snow.

There was no toilet in the cabin, so everyone had to find a private spot amongst the trees to relieve themselves. Peeling down layers of clothes that then hung around your ankles whilst you squatted with a frozen bottom stuck in the air was not something that Laila would be sketching in her journal.

After the babies had been fed, everyone bedded down for the rest of the night, fully clothed with coats and blankets on top of them. The women and babies lay in the middle, pressed up against each other for warmth, whilst the men lay like bookends, their backs to the little group. At first, Laila felt awkward so close to Einar, but after a few moments she fell into a deep sleep.

Early next morning, Einar took the axe and went into the forest to chop wood for the next travellers who might need shelter for the night.

'It's damp,' he said as he stacked it next to the stove, but hopefully it'll be dry by the time it's needed.'

For breakfast, they heated up acorn coffee and ate bread with a slice of sausage. Then it was time to leave.

They carried the sheepskins and blankets back into the wagon and Ulf hoisted the duffel bags aboard.

'We'll have to leave the track for a while,' he said. 'There are more patrols round here. So, hold on tight. It'll be a bit bumpier through the woods.'

Ulf's words were an understatement. The women rolled around in the back, bumping into each other and colliding against the sides of the wagon as it tumbled over tree roots and rocks. Laila's wounds burned. The babies gurgled. Then they cried. They screamed. And then they slept.

* * *

Ulf stopped twice so they could stretch their legs and relieve themselves behind trees. It grew darker and colder. Laila wondered when they would arrive at the next cabin. She could hear snatches of the brothers' heated exchange from up front. It sounded like Einar was accusing Ulf of being lost, and Ulf was yelling about the damn map.

The women huddled together with the babies between them. Laila's toes were numb, and the tips of her fingers ached inside her woollen gloves. Marit was pressed up against her, shivering. Laila lifted her scarf up to her eyes. She was worried. Would they freeze to death out here if they couldn't find a cabin?

Hunger gnawed at her stomach. It had been agreed to unpack the food when they reached the next *hytte*. Elise was hungry too. It was cumbersome to free a breast under the weight of two pullovers, a coat, and a blanket.

An icy wind picked up and threw itself in gusts under the canvas. Laila's fingers stopped aching. She couldn't feel her hands at all now.

When the wagon shuddered to a stop, Ulf shouted that they'd arrived. Laila thanked God. Her body was so stiff, she could hardly crawl out of the wagon. She felt as if she was ninety years old.

This *hytte* was similar to the first one, only smaller and dirtier.

There were mouse droppings on the floor. The procedure was the same as the previous evening except that the women washed themselves too this time. Once a tin bucket of snow had been heated, the men went outside to smoke, and Laila suggested that the women open and loosen their clothes so they could wash themselves underneath. They dipped the washcloths in the water and wiped under their arms and across their breasts, and then undid their trousers to wash below.

When they removed their socks, all three could see that they had painful chilblains, which they dabbed gently with warm water. The men didn't feel the need to wash, saying tomorrow would do. Later, as Einar lay beside her, Laila thought that tomorrow was far too long to wait.

Falling asleep was harder that night. Laila listened to the sounds of the forest. So different to the sounds of her fjord. The trees agitated by the strong wind seemed to uproot themselves and shuffle about outside the cabin. Things scuffled outside snapping twigs. Foxes? Perhaps wolves? And something scuttled inside. A mouse? She longed to be back in her bedroom at home over-looking the fjord, listening to the sea. But she didn't know if that would ever be possible again. She fell asleep, finally, thinking of Josef paddling in the stream near Grandpa's *hytte* with his army trousers rolled up, his wet shirt clinging to his chest.

* * *

The journey the next day was more comfortable. Ulf chose a lane he deemed safe, and they made good progress, reaching the next *hytte* earlier than expected. But when they followed Ulf with his oil lamp inside, they stopped short and stared at the empty space next to the stove. No wood. Einar opened the stove door. None inside either. And no axe leaning against the wall.

'I have a small axe in the wagon, but it'll be hard work,' he said.

The women hauled the sheepskins, blankets, and duffel bags into the cabin and then sat around the oil lamp waiting. It was freezing.

'We need to keep moving to stay warm,' said Laila, and picking Elise up, she danced with her around the cabin, singing a folk song. The others joined in, spinning and swinging the babies through the air, making the little things squeal with delight.

Laila was dancing her way to the back wall when the tip of her boot caught on a raised floorboard. She stopped. She could see that the board was loose.

Cautiously, she put Elise down on a sheepskin and went to inspect the floor. Maybe some food had been stored underneath. Marit and Herta watched with intrigue as she kneeled down and prised the board away.

'There is something there,' she said, leaning forward into the space.

She pulled out a long object wrapped in oil cloth and laid it in front of her.

'Open it. Let's see what it is,' said Herta.

Laila unrolled the cloth. It was a rifle.

'A gun? Who would leave a gun here?' said Marit.

'It looks like a hunting rifle,' Laila replied. 'It's like the type my uncle owned before he had to hand it over to the Germans.'

When the men returned, their arms full of wood, the women were still staring at the firearm.

'Well, well, what have we got here?' said Einar.

He inspected the rifle whilst Ulf started to stack wood in the stove to try to get it going.

'Is it in working order?' asked Ulf.

'It's a hunting rifle. The sort we use for moose. Not sure about the bolt. I'd have to see what I could do.'

'Any ammo?'

'Three bullets,' said Einar as he checked the chamber. He searched the space under the floorboard for more but found nothing. 'That's all there is. But better than nothing.'

Despite Ulf's best efforts, the fire would not get going. The wood was too wet.

'We can't spend a night without heat,' said Ulf. 'There's a village nearby. I'll see if I can get firewood. And I need more straw for the horse. You'd better all stay here.'

As Ulf drove away in the wagon, the rest of them sat around the oil lamp, huddled into the sheepskins and blankets. To pass the time, Einar worked on repairing the rifle and they all talked about their lives.

Herta had met her husband at the hospital in Frankfurt. She was studying midwifery and he was a first-year medical student. He wanted to be a paediatrician.

Herta had only been married two months when the war started, and her husband was sent to die in the battle of Narvik. After he died, she took the job at Lebensborn, not aware of the real purpose of the home. She had become increasingly alarmed at events there and the final straw was witnessing Laila being dragged screaming towards the cellar.

Laila thought how alike their situations were. Enemies suffering the same fate. But she didn't think of Herta as an enemy. How ironic to think that just a short while ago she could not have envisaged having a German lover, or a close German friend.

Einar told them he and his wife would become first-time grandparents in March. This had made him really start to think about newborns and question what was going on at Lebensborn. It was what spurred him into helping the escape. He'd been hand-carving a cradle which he would finish as soon as he returned from Narvik. He grinned and rubbed his beard. 'Imagine that. Me, a grandfather. Only seems like yesterday that I was courting the lasses in the village.'

The clatter of wagon wheels. A horse's hooves. Ulf was back.

Einar strode outside and helped Ulf bring in the wood and straw. Ulf also proudly produced a large piece of cheese and some fresh bread. And oil for the lamp.

'Thank you, Ulf,' said Laila. 'You've done well.'

'Not me. It's all thanks to my father's pocket watch.'

Laila thought that sad.

That was the last night that all of them stayed together in a cabin. The next morning, Ulf spread out his map.

'We're getting closer to Narvik. The area is heavily patrolled.'

He drew crosses where he suspected road control points to be and highlighted where the forest was too dense for a horse and cart yet passable by foot. Laila studied the map. They would soon be in territory that was familiar to her. She estimated it would be a two-day walk, so they would have to find shelter for the night, a cabin or perhaps a barn. There were farmsteads in the area.

She could feel the tingle of adrenalin. Home was not far away.

Mid-morning, they all piled out of the wagon for the final time and Ulf unloaded the sledge. He bound the duffel bags, oil lamp, sheepskins, and blankets to the sledge with rope. Einar strapped the rifle to his shoulder.

It was time to say goodbye.

Ulf's eyes moistened. 'Take good care of these fine young ladies and the little ones. You're in charge of precious cargo.' He gave his brother a fierce hug and slapped him on the back.'

'Sure, I will. And I'll see you when you come to visit my new grandchild.'

Ulf hugged each woman in turn as they murmured their

thanks. Laila thought how insufficient their words were and tried to convey how grateful she was in the warmth of her embrace. When she pulled back and looked into his wrinkled grey eyes, she thought he understood.

The wagon trundled back the way they had come and Einar, pulling the sledge, led them deeper into the forest.

29

Laila unbuttoned her coat and lifted her two pullovers. Elise latched on greedily. In the last few days, Elise cried more frequently and continually sought her mother's breast. But then, when she fed, she took so long. This morning at the cabin, it had taken an hour before she was content.

Einar was getting restless to move on and kept glancing over at Laila.

'Come on, little one,' she whispered. 'You have to suck harder.'

But when she watched Elise's cheeks working, she realised that her baby was giving her best.

'More later, sweetheart. We must get going.'

She pulled her nipple free. Elise's face contorted and flashed red. She screamed. Bewildered, Laila squeezed her nipple. Nothing. She squeezed harder. One thin drop.

Her milk was drying up. Thinking about it, her breasts had felt less swollen the last few days. She had no milk for her baby. She was in the middle of nowhere and her baby was literally starving. Panic sucked her breath. Elise screamed.

Einar and Marit ran over.

'Try and soothe her,' said Einar, scanning the trees around them. We're not that far from the road.'

'I have no milk,' she cried, rocking her angry child.

'Give her to me,' said Marit, reaching out her arms. 'I have plenty of milk.'

Laila studied Marit, a mean, hard lump forming in her throat.

'I'll try again later,' Laila said, standing and bouncing Elise around. 'She'll fall asleep soon.'

They trudged on, Einar leading them deeper into the pine forest away from the road. Elise continued to scream, her cries becoming hysterical, her voice raw. Laila felt desperate.

Marit linked her arm in hers. 'Let me feed her. I have milk.'

'She won't feed from you.'

'She might. It's quite common for babies to have wet nurses.'

'I'm her mother.'

'Of course, you are. And taking milk from another woman doesn't change that.'

'It's not natural. It's not right.' Her voice was shrill.

Elise screamed.

'Let's try. Just once. Perhaps you'll produce milk for the next feed,' Marit coaxed.

Laila halted and kicked at the ground. Her shoulders slumped as she called out to Einar to stop.

Laila took the sleeping Albert from Marit and watched through a haze of tears as Marit lifted her clothes and held Elise to her breast. Laila's own child, her flesh and blood, had to be fed by a stranger. What a complete failure she was. What sort of mother was she?

Elise, after a moment of confusion and turning her head away from the proffered breast, soon changed her mind and took Marit's nipple into her mouth. At the sight, pain speared Laila's heart. She wanted to shriek and tear Elise from Marit's arms. Instead, she turned away and looked up at the grey, snow-laden sky.

Herta came up to her and placed an arm around her shoulders. 'Why are you so hard on yourself?'

Laila didn't reply. They waited in silence until they heard Marit's voice.

'She's asleep.'

Four hours later, the next feed was not so successful. Marit had enough milk for Albert but not for Elise. Laila punched at her breasts and pinched her nipples till they hurt.

No milk came. She cried out and dragged her nails across her breast in frustration, leaving deep bloody scratches.

'Stop it, Laila. Stop it now. This isn't helping,' said Herta. 'We need to put our heads together and come up with a plan. And quick. It's getting dark and starting to snow.'

* * *

Rusty hinges creaked as the farmhouse door opened and a tired old woman in a floral housecoat peered out. Her eyes widened at the sight of a girl covered in freshly fallen snow, a baby clutched to her chest.

'Please,' said Laila. 'I need help.'

Her story was simple. She was on the run from an abusive husband, on her way to take refuge with her aunt in Harstad. Her baby needed milk and they needed shelter for the night. Preferably in a barn, not in the main house. Just in case he came looking for her.

The farmer's wife had no powdered baby milk, but suggested goat's milk diluted with water. She brought out a churn from the cellar. 'Freshly milked this morning.' She rummaged around her kitchen cupboards and dug out two baby bottles. 'I have these for when my daughter visits with my grandson.'

Laila sat in an armchair by the stove and gave Elise the bottle. The child looked even more startled than her last feed with Marit. But after wrinkling her nose and pushing the teat back out with her tongue, hunger won over and she guzzled down the milk.

The farmer's wife kept looking out the window. 'My drunken bugger of a husband will be home soon. Let's get you settled down in the barn furthest from the house.' She filled two bottles of milk, wrapped some food in a tea towel, and fetched some blankets.

Two goats were sleeping in the corner of the barn, and the woman gestured to where a ladder led up to a hay loft.

'It's warmest up there,' she said. 'Packed with hay and straw.'

Once the woman had left, Laila opened the barn door, took a torch from her pocket, and flashed it three times in the direction of the forest. A risk, she knew.

A few moments later, Herta, Marit, and Einar appeared out of the darkness and Laila ushered them in. The goats bleated. Einar dragged the sledge to the far corner of the barn and heaped straw over it. Everyone settled down in the deep straw of the hay loft and the goats soon quietened.

Minutes later, a truck trundled across the yard. *That drunken bugger of a husband*, thought Laila.

* * *

Laila woke to a solid blackness. Disorientated, she reached into the pocket of her coat. She pulled out her torch and the fob watch she still had from Herta. It was five o'clock in the morning.

After Laila and Marit had fed the babies, everyone clambered down the ladder and Einar fetched the sledge. The goats started their rumpus.

'Let's get out of here,' said Einar and pushed open the barn door.

He blinked at the rifle aimed at his face.

'Step outside,' a voice growled. 'All of you. So I can see you. Or I'll blast his face off.'

One by one they came out and stood beneath the sallow light of an oil lamp which had been hung on a hook on the outside of the barn wall.

The farmer was heavyset, with a pockmarked face. He glowered at them.

'Well, I'll be damned. There's four of you. And with the stolen babies, by the looks of it.'

He gave a hard laugh and waved his rifle at them. Laila watched his finger on the trigger. She felt sick. They had come so far and now this. Her mind whirled with possibilities of escape. All useless with two tiny babies to protect.

'So, this is what's going to happen,' he drawled. 'You're all going back in the barn. This time I'll lock the bolt and you'll still be here when the Gestapo come. I'll take one of the babies as insurance against escape.'

He nudged the gun in Laila's direction.

'No!' she screamed, clutching Elise so tight that the child began to cry.

He pointed the gun at Laila's head.

'Hand the child over. Now.' He grinned. 'Nice reward coming my way.'

'The only thing that'll be coming your way is a bullet.' The farmer's wife stood behind him. Her body seemed small and frail compared with the gun she held. But there was nothing frail in her expression. Or her voice. 'Drop your gun and let them pass.'

The farmer stood stock still. Without turning to face her, he said, 'No way you'd shoot your own husband.'

'I would if he was a Nazi collaborator.'

No one spoke. No one moved.

Neither the farmer nor his wife wavered, still holding their guns aloft.

The goats bleated. The babies cried.

A bellow of a laugh and the farmer dropped his gun.

'That's why I married you, woman. For the fire in you.' He turned to face her.

With a steady hand, the gun still levelled at her husband, she said, 'Get going, all of you. I'll keep an eye on him till you're well on your way.'

They scuttled past and headed for the forest.

'Keep the torches low to the ground. And good luck,' the farmer's wife called after them.

* * *

Laila reckoned that if all went well, they could reach her grandfather's *hytte* that evening. They were now walking parallel to the main road into Narvik, but far back in the forest. This was perhaps the most dangerous stretch before they turned east towards the *hytte*.

The snow had stopped, but the way was icy. Laila watched the ground, trying to avoid half-submerged tree roots, slippery rocks, and boulders.

'Let's leave the sledge behind,' she said to Einar, seeing how he was struggling with it. 'It's not far now. We can carry the duffel bags.'

'And the babies, and the blankets, and the oil lamp?' he asked, puffing for breath.

'We can condense what's in the duffel bags. We've eaten most of the food. Let's see what we can leave behind.'

They pulled out the contents, repacked the bags, and put them on their backs. They were still quite heavy to carry, what with needing to hold the babies as well. And then there were the bulky blankets.

'We're not leaving blankets behind,' said Einar. 'We don't know for sure that we'll reach the *hytte* tonight. A blanket can save your life.'

Laila knew he was right. They piled everything back on the sledge and took turns dragging it through the trees.

Daylight came, but the forest was so thick that they continued to journey through the cold dark shadows of the pines. No one spoke. They all concentrated on putting one numb foot in front of another. Elise seemed to get heavier with each step and Laila's back began to ache. She watched Einar slow his pace ahead. He was tired. They all were.

The sledge hit against something and juddered to a halt. Einar let out an exasperated grunt and tugged at the rope. When it wouldn't free, he grasped the rope with both hands, leaned back and gave a powerful yank. The sledge leaped into the air and Einar stumbled backwards, caught his foot on a tree root and tumbled to the ground. Laila heard the snap of a branch. He screamed out.

Within seconds the women were by him, kneeling in the snow. It soon became clear the snap Laila heard wasn't a branch, but Einar's left ankle. He was in agony. Herta tried to remove his boot but that was too painful.

'What are we going to do?' said Marit.

'Let's clear the sledge and try to lift Einar onto it,' Laila suggested.

They took everything off the sledge and piled it on the ground.

Einar groaned and gritted his teeth as they tried to pull him up and yelled as he fell back in the snow. Herta kneeled next to him.

'We will have to lift you under your arms, and you can use your right leg and right arm to heave yourself onto the sledge.'

Laila and Marit unwrapped their babies from their chests and laid them on top of the heap of sheepskins and blankets. The women then hauled Einar onto the sledge, heaving and panting, their arms burning, whilst he cursed and cried out in pain.

'If your ankle is broken, we should stabilise it.' Herta looked around. 'Maybe some sticks—'

'I'm not taking this damn boot off.'

'We can leave the boot on.' Laila's mind was whirring.

'God, I'm such an idiot,' said Einar. 'I'm supposed to get you girls to safety and now I'm an invalid who can't walk. Go on without me. I can—'

'Out of the question,' said Laila.

How were they going to manage?

'We'll pull you on the sledge,' said Marit, but everyone could detect the doubt in her voice.

'Sure,' said Einar. 'You girls can travel through rough terrain with two babies, duffel bags, and an injured, heavy, old man on a sledge.' He sank his head into his hands.

They all fell silent as they considered the situation and what to do next. Laila doubted that with hauling Einar on the sledge, they would be able to reach her grandfather's *hytte* by nightfall. But the choice was clear. There was no choice. They would have to try.

Laila and Herta foraged around the area for slim branches. They used the rope that bound the supplies to the sledge to form a splint for Einar's leg. Once it was in place, he tested if he could take a step. It was impossible. Laila wished they had painkillers for him. They settled him on the sledge, stabilising his leg with the sheepskins and blankets. He carried one duffel bag and the rifle on his lap, and Herta slipped the other duffel bag over her shoulders. The babies were strapped back onto their mothers, and they set off.

Progress was slow and hard work. As Laila and Herta dragged the sledge through the trees, it bounced over the snow-covered undergrowth and Einar couldn't stop himself from letting out suppressed groans. The women were exhausted; their steps became slow and clumsy. Occasionally, one of them would stumble, righting themselves just in time. They were forced to take frequent breaks.

The territory soon became familiar to Laila. The forest was sparser, the fir trees' snowy canopy giving way to the bare, silver-frosted birches.

She halted and consulted her map. Then she handed Elise to Herta and told the group to stay where they were. She would creep forward in the direction of the road that ran beneath them.

Crouching down between rocks, she peered below her. About three hundred metres away was a roadblock. A group of soldiers were standing outside a patrol hut and two military trucks were parked on the side of the road.

Laila returned to the others. 'We need to move further back from the road to safely bypass the roadblock,' she told them. 'Once we're past, we can head for my grandfather's *hytte*.'

They continued on, making slow progress. In the clearings between the trees, where the sun had shone, the snow was thinner, and the sledge almost came to a stop in places. But it was the noise of the sledge grinding against the rocks and branches that worried Laila most.

Twilight fell and the temperature dropped. The babies began to whimper. Then Albert let out a howl that echoed in the still frozen air. Marit was quick to muffle his cries with his blanket, but he grew distressed and continued to wail. He had powerful lungs. Marit rocked him, whispered comforting words. She opened her coat and put him to her breast whilst she walked, which worked for a while.

Laila halted and put a finger to her lips. They all listened. Strained. Was there a snap of a branch? Perhaps the wind. A scuffling sound. Maybe a small animal. But Laila knew the sounds of the forest. Her chest tightened. They stood in a clearing about twenty metres from the next cluster of trees ahead of them.

'*Halt. Achtung. Keine Bewegung!*'

Three or four soldiers appeared from the trees behind them, rifles raised.

'Run!' said Einar, lifting the rifle from his lap.

'Not without you,' said Laila, clasping Elise to her chest.

Einar growled. 'Run. Now.' It was an order.

Then, roaring with pain, Einar swung himself round on the sledge and faced the oncoming Germans.

'Go!' cried Herta as she bolted for the trees. Marit sprinted after her. Laila threw a wild glance at Einar, snatched her duffel bag, and fled.

A shot rang out. Laila flew into the trees. Another shot. It pinged off a branch above her.

More shots. Einar had three bullets.

Einar.

Laila ran. She had long legs. One of the fastest runners in her class at school. But then, she hadn't been exhausted, hungry, and frozen. Then, she hadn't had a baby strapped to her chest.

The girls parted as they sped through the trees, but Laila could see them to her left and right.

The shooting stopped.

Einar.

An unfinished, hand-carved cradle.

Laila heard boots crunching behind them. How many Germans had made it past Einar?

A cry. A thump. Herta to her left had stumbled. But she was jumping back up.

Laila pumped her legs, her lungs bursting.

A shot. Close by.

Laila glanced over her shoulder.

Herta, flat on the ground, her arms spread in front of her. A splash of red on the white snow. Soldiers closing in on where she had fallen.

No! Laila let out a silent scream.

Terror twisted her stomach. Squeezed her heart. The daylight was all but gone. She could just make out Marit's duffel bag bobbing amongst the trees. In one last desperate surge of energy, she raced to join her. Marit was running along a ridge, jumping over fallen branches. Trees lined the ridge, but many had toppled from a storm, scattering broken conifer branches down the slope.

Marit stopped and stared at her in terror. Laila grabbed her hand and pulled her over the ridge. The slope was steep and icy; they dropped to their bottoms and slid down, bouncing over stones and pinecones, their padded ski trousers protecting them from serious injury. They tumbled down, clinging on to their children until a huge conifer blocked their path. On hands and knees, the girls scrambled under the fans of pine and curled up like two forest animals with their young. Night had fallen. They were swamped in blackness and the scent of pine.

Laila felt for Elise's fragile head. Had she been hurt? But her gurgles suggested she had found the tumbling around fun. And Albert's protests were mild for him. The babies fell asleep after all the excitement, huddled between the two mothers.

Men's voices and the trample of boots came from above. Laila and Marit lay still under their cloak of pine.

Still as stone trolls. Still as 'Silent Night'. Still as Josef.

And Einar and Herta? Perhaps they were still alive. Laila's heart said no.

She suppressed a sob as she lay facing Marit. She could feel her cold hectic breath fluttering against her face.

The sound of voices and footsteps faded. They waited a long time, listening. Laila knew they must break their cover before all four of them froze to death. The cold from the ground was seeping through her bones.

'They've gone,' she whispered. 'We must head to the *hytte* now.'

'And Herta? Is she, is she...?' Marit's voice was filled with despair.

'Yes, I think so. And Einar too.' Laila choked the words out.

'Oh, God. What shall we do?'

'I know where we are now. We'll scramble down to the bottom of this slope until we reach a stream. And then we'll follow that stream to my grandfather's *hytte*. We'll make it. For Einar and Herta.'

Keeping the beam of torchlight low on the ground, Laila led Marit down the slope, around and over the obstacles. A half-moon rose and the sky cleared to reveal a myriad of stars.

And then Laila saw the stream: a silver sash like the one Hanna had worn at her waist on her sixteenth birthday. The pang she felt at the memory spurred her on. She had to see her sister again.

They followed alongside the frozen stream, which lay still, pearlescent beneath the night sky. Neither of them spoke, each lost in a tumult of emotion at the loss of their friends.

About an hour later, they passed the waterfall where Laila had shown Josef the troll guard, the waterfall a row of iced spears poised over the frozen plunge pool.

'Nearly there,' she said.

Laila was weak with relief at the sight of the *hytte*.

They stepped up to the front door and Laila reached under the boulder, running her hand along the ground. The key wasn't there. She put her glove to her mouth and tore it off with her teeth. Again, she searched, her fingers prying the hard earth. Perhaps her father had removed it for the winter. It was possible...

Thankfully, she felt the metal beneath her fingertips.

30

NARVIK, JANUARY 1943

It was the most wonderful luxury. A stove full of wood, hot water to wash themselves from head to foot, cosy eiderdowns, and plump pillows.

'What a welcome refuge,' said Marit as she spread herself out on the bed with Albert tucked beside her. 'Thank you, Laila.'

'This place has been a haven for me many times,' she replied, searching the cupboards for food. She found tinned sardines, pickled cucumber, and a jar of blueberry jam. A feast.

For dessert, they spooned the jam straight from the jar.

Laila gave Elise the last drop of milk from the bottle the farmer's wife had given her.

'I must get milk, somehow.' She frowned.

'Elise is front of the queue tonight,' said Marit, patting her bosom. 'And no ration coupon required.'

'But you only have enough milk for Albert.'

'It'll be his first lesson in the gift of sharing. He's a plump little thing anyway.'

As promised, Marit fed Elise first. Laila fought to quash her complex emotions: inadequacy and jealousy mixed with grate-fulness.

That night, as Laila lay next to Marit and the children, she thought of the last time she had lain on this bed. With Josef. The pain was raw and relentless. She hugged Elise close to her and overcome by exhaustion, she allowed a heavy sleep to embrace her.

There was nothing for breakfast the next morning, just black *Ersatz* coffee which they drank whilst discussing their next move. Laila checked the time on Herta's fob watch, rubbing her thumb over the face as she did so. It was shocking how, in a twist of fate, an everyday object could become such a treasured possession. She had persuaded Herta to flee with them. It had been the wrong choice.

But if she hadn't, what would have happened? Would she have met the same end had she stayed?

Her kindness had saved Laila. Einar's too. She placed Herta's watch back in her pocket.

'The kindness of friends,' she mumbled. 'Why did they have to pay the ultimate price for their kindness?' Laila reached for her coffee, her eyes brimming.

'I'll always be grateful.' Marit sighed staring into her empty cup. 'I won't ever forget them.'

'I need to find Finn and persuade him to help us.'

'What if someone recognises you and tells the Nazis you're here?'

'It's lucky it's winter. Everyone is bundled up. If I borrow your clothes, no one will recognise me.'

When Laila left the *hytte*, she had Marit's green, knitted hat pulled low over her forehead, every strand of hair tucked out of sight, and the scarf wrapped up to her eyes.

Leaving Elise behind was difficult but she knew it made sense;

a woman on her own was far less conspicuous than with a baby. Marit agreed to stay in the cabin and take care of the children.

As she marched into town, her mind was a whirl. Should she go to Oda first? How would she react? Would Finn even talk to her?

Head tucked down, Laila made her way to the bookshop. At every moment, she expected to hear the shout, '*Halt!*' and see a gun pointed at her.

There were more soldiers patrolling the streets than she remembered. When they approached, she kept her head lowered as if wary of the icy pavement. An armoured tank trundled past, monstrous in the small street, the small shops cowering in its shadow. Having been shut away in Lebensborn for so long, she was dismayed to witness the reality in Narvik once more.

She was pleased it was snowing. Passers-by bent their heads from the wind and took no notice of her. At the corner of the book-shop, she peered through the glass. Oda stood behind the cash desk talking to two Germans.

Laila turned and went back up the street, halting at the bus stop, as if she were studying the timetable. She watched as two women entered the bookshop.

She waited. Crossed the street and looked in the window of the haberdashery opposite the bookshop. In the reflection she could see the Germans leaving. She waited some more, digging her hands deep in her pockets. She paced up and down. Went back and looked in the window of the haberdashery again. The two women left the bookshop.

Oda was now there on her own. Her stomach churned as she crossed the street and pushed open the door.

Oda stood on a step ladder, lining up books on the top shelf. She gave Laila a brief smile as she entered and then returned her gaze to the books. She hadn't recognised her.

Laila hesitated, not knowing where to begin.

Oda stepped back down off the ladder. 'Can I help you?'

Laila raised her head and watched as Oda's eyes widened. She despised her, she could tell.

'Hello, Oda.'

'My God. Laila, you're back.'

'Not officially. I know you must hate me, but it's so good to see you.' Her voice cracked as she spoke.

'I don't hate you. I've missed you.' And to Laila's amazement and joy, Oda threw her arms around her and hugged her fiercely.

'I mustn't be seen. Is there somewhere we can talk?'

Oda locked the shop door and hung up a *Closed for lunch* sign, despite it being ten in the morning. They went through the back of the shop and up to Oda's bedroom.

'My mama's in bed. She's not been well,' she whispered.

The two friends sat on Oda's bed like they had done since they were children; Oda cross legged and Laila with her legs tucked beneath her.

Laila told her story from the moment she'd discovered she was pregnant, her time at Lebensborn, to her escape with the papers. Oda listened without interrupting, sometimes flinching or gasping at the more shocking parts. When Laila finished, they sat a few moments in silence as Oda absorbed what she had heard. Her eyes were full of tears.

'I need help.' Laila's tone was an apology. 'From Finn. But I'm too scared to ask.'

'Leave Finn to me. But first I'm going to get you something to eat and drink.'

Around lunch time, Finn came back. Oda went upstairs to speak to him whilst Laila waited.

Sitting on Oda's bed, she looked at the familiar things around her. The birthday card she had painted for Oda's thirteenth birthday. The photo of them together in their national costume in its usual place. She wanted to cry.

Above she heard the sounds of pacing footsteps. Finn. His voice raised and angry. She wished she could hear what he was saying.

It went quiet. Light footsteps running down. Oda popped her head around the door.

'Come on up.'

She followed Oda up to Finn's attic room, where he was standing by the window, gazing out. She knew he wasn't looking at anything in particular. Avoiding having to meet her gaze.

'Hello, Finn. Thank you for seeing me.'

He waited a moment before he turned, as if the effort of looking at her was too much to bear. He was going to make this hard for her. She knew. When he finally faced her, he leaned back on the windowsill and folded his arms across his chest.

'You have a nerve to come begging for help,' he snarled.

'I understand if you don't want to help me, but my friend, Marit—'

'Yeah, Oda told me. She's running from the Nazis with a disabled baby. Is she fit? Can she make it to the Swedish border?'

Laila nodded.

'I'll organise a guide. For her.'

'I have some documents from Lebensborn—' Laila began.

'Oda told me that too. Show me.'

'I don't have them with me. I have to think about what's the best thing to do with them.'

'And you found out that the Nazis kidnapped Tore?'

She nodded.

'The bastards. We must tell Gudrun he's alive.'

'I'd like to tell her. Somehow.'

'How the hell do you think you'll manage that?' He gave a cynical laugh. 'Any other crazy ideas?'

'I want to see my family. Show my parents their grandchild.'

'Now I know you're out of your mind. Your family are ashamed of you. Your father has disowned you.'

'Finn, stop it,' said Oda. 'She's been through enough.'

Finn strode across the room and stood before the two of them, looking from one to the other, his arms rigid by his side.

'She's been through enough?' he yelled. 'And what have our friends in the resistance been through? Tortured by the Gestapo, sent to concentration camps, or executed in front of their families!'

Tears sprang to Laila's eyes. 'I'm so sorry for all of them; that they and their families had to endure such horrors. Let me at least try and help some innocent children find their families again. If I could get documents to Sweden...'

She realised in that moment that her dream of living again with her family was an absurd fantasy. She would be arrested and Elise sent to Germany for adoption. She must escape with Marit.

'Ha! So, these documents are your path to freedom? And I should help you get there?'

He spat as he raged. A drop of his saliva landed on her cheek. She didn't wipe it away. Instead, she put a hand on his arm.

'Please, Finn, I love you like a brother. After we lost Anton, you became my brother.'

Perhaps she saw a flicker of softness in his eyes. Calmer, he said, 'Why did you do it, Laila? Betray us with a Nazi?'

Laila fixed her eyes on him. 'He wasn't a Nazi. Just a young lad like you, with plans for his life when a mad dictator flung his country into war. His choice was fight or be shot. Fight or have his family sent to prison. But he remained a good man. He helped us where he could.'

'And now he's just another dead German slaughtered by the Russians.' Finn's hard tone faltered.

'Yes,' she said, a sob tightening her throat. 'Yes, yes, yes.'

He watched her cry for a few moments before cupping the back of her head and drawing it to his chest.

* * *

Oda packed a basket with what food she could spare and gave it to Laila to take back to the *hytte*.

'Now we have to see how we can get milk powder for little Elise without ration coupons,' she said. 'I might have an idea. Go wait in my room. I'll be as quick as possible.'

Twenty minutes later, she returned with a pack of baby formula, looking very pleased with herself.

'It's only a third full but it will keep you going for a while.'

'Where on earth did you get it?'

'Remember my cousin was pregnant last year? Well, her son is on solids now and there was formula left over. The family were thinking of using it in their coffee, but I persuaded them there was a little girl in greater need.'

Laila looked in awe at her clever, loyal, and resilient friend. Her best friend.

Aching with exhaustion, she threaded her way through the woods that lined the road. Her nerves jarred at the sound of falling pinecones and branches cracking under the weight of the snow. But she had come too far to be caught now.

Eventually she arrived. Snow was piled up at the door. She felt a wave of panic. What if...?

She banged on the door. Nothing. She banged again, harder.

A gruff voice called out, 'Go away. I told you, I don't need anything.'

'Gudrun, it's me, Laila.'

Slow, heavy footsteps. The door opened a crack and she saw Gudrun's face, peering out. She gasped and wrenched the door open, splintering icicles and sending a flutter of snow onto the doorstep.

'Laila, is it really you? Thank the Lord, you're alive! I've been hearing terrible rumours from those meddling women from the church. In fact, I thought it was one of them at my door.'

She spread open her arms and started to cry.

They sat together in two sagging armchairs in front of the wood-burning stove. For the second time that day, she talked about Josef and how he worked against the Nazi regime, and she told Gudrun about Lebensborn.

'...so you see, Tore is alive and we can track him through the German adoption authorities. We will find him, I promise.'

Gudrun shook her head in disbelief, fat tears slipping down her cheeks.

'I'm blessed to have you, Laila. Truly blessed.'

* * *

Back at the *hytte*, Laila and Marit ate, fed the children, and rested. Finn had said they should conserve their strength for the escape to Sweden.

But Laila burned to see her mother.

Maybe they *could* be a family again. Or maybe Laila was delusional. But she had to try. She'd go during the day, whilst Papa and Hanna were working – that would be best. Maybe Mama could help soften Papa's rage.

Avoiding the streets, she sneaked down alleyways and the narrow paths behind houses, bundled up in Marit's clothes, this time holding Elise wrapped to her chest.

The first thing Laila saw was the blackened rowan tree. Papa had not chopped it down. She stood a moment, succumbing to the bittersweet nostalgia. Then, after checking no one was around, she approached the front door. The adrenalin she had previously felt at the idea of being reunited with her family had flown, and doubt had taken its place.

She lifted the iron door knocker and gave a soft tap.

No movement from the other side of the door.

Two more taps. *Oh, come on Laila*, she told herself and rapped sharply three times.

'Yes, yes, I'm coming.' Her mother's voice.

The door opened and there stood Mama in her lilac housecoat, hair piled up in a lopsided bun. Her mouth flew open.

Laila murmured, 'Hello', then turned sideways to reveal Elise's sleeping face.

Mama's shocked expression softened and she ushered her daughter inside.

In the hallway Inge toddled towards them, pulling a wooden duck on wheels behind her. Laila recognised the toy. Papa had made it years ago for Hanna.

She pulled off her hat and smiled.

Inge hesitated a moment and said, 'Laila, play?'

Mama stroked her fingers against Elise's cheek. 'She's cold.'

She waited for Mama to invite them into the sitting room or to offer coffee in the kitchen. But she stood there, stroking Elise and shaking her head.

'Mama, I—'

'You must leave. Straight away. The Gestapo were here looking for you.'

Laila realised how ridiculous she'd been to think there would be some kind of fairy-tale ending.

'I would so like to see you all. Just once.' She looked around for Olaf but guessed he must be at school.

Mama gave a bitter laugh. 'Your father has disowned you. He would be furious if he found you here. Hanna too.'

The words gouged out Laila's last hope.

'And you, Mama? Have you disowned me?'

'Don't do this, Laila.'

Laila turned and opened the front door.

'Josef is dead,' Laila said, not looking at her mother.

'Then what was it all for?' Mama's voice was a wail of despair.

As Laila walked away from her home, something shut down inside her. And she welcomed the numbness.

31

They washed themselves, bathed the babies in the sink, and repacked their duffel bags. Laila took out her jade silk journal and checked the documents from Lebensborn before sliding it to the bottom of her bag. They were ready. Tomorrow, Finn would arrive with the Sami guide.

That evening, Elise started coughing. She coughed all night. Laila laid her in different positions using cushions to elevate her chest. But still she coughed. She walked in circles round the *hytte*, rubbing her back, fed her the milk formula, and put more wood on the fire.

In the morning, Elise's face was red and hot, and she refused her milk. Laila fetched a bucket of snow from outside, and when it began to melt, she cooled some cloths and laid them on Elise's forehead and around her legs. Her tiny body was on fire.

When Finn arrived with his friend Saba, the Sami guide, she had made her decision. She could not make the journey with a sick child. Marit would have to travel to Sweden alone.

'But what will you do?' said Marit, concern etched on her face. 'It's not safe for you to stay in Narvik.'

'I'll stay here at the *hytte* until Elise is better and make the journey then. We'll meet in Sweden.'

'No,' said Finn. 'It won't take long for the Gestapo to find out your grandfather has this place. They may know already. We have to move you. And Marit and Saba should set off immediately.' Finn's tone was urgent. He beckoned Marit to get going and picked up Laila's duffel bag. 'Get Elise wrapped up warm.'

'Where will we go?' she asked, alarmed at the speed at which everything was happening.

'Let's get away from here first. We'll think about it on the way.'

Laila and Marit clung to each other outside the *hytte*. Saying goodbye was hard; they had been through so much together. Planned so much together. 'Stay safe,' said Laila. 'See you over the border. Soon.'

'You take care.'

Saba patted Marit on the shoulder and started to march off. Finn was pulling at Laila's arm. The friends gave each other one last look and parted.

Nearing where the woods met the road, Finn and Laila heard the sound of a motor. Finn pointed in the opposite direction and, crouching low, they sneaked back into the woods and dropped down behind some boulders.

German commands. Stamping boots. Ice and snow crunching underfoot.

The SS made their way up to Grandpa's *hytte*.

'I know where we can hide,' whispered Laila.

* * *

Gudrun ushered them in, flapping her arms in excitement at the sight of Elise. She took the child and rocked her gently, lifting the swaddling from her tiny face. She let out a sigh.

'Oh, she's beautiful. How can anyone call her a child of shame? She is the future. A chance for a better world. She is a child of hope.'

Over the next two days, Elise's temperature returned to normal, and she started to feed again. Laila cleaned and tidied the house, which annoyed Gudrun. She sorted through her meagre food supplies and did her best to concoct meals. Finn brought his own rations to share with her too. He also shovelled the snow from the front of the house and chopped firewood.

* * *

On the second evening, Finn came to tell Laila that a storm was blowing in from Sweden. Marit would have reached the border, but Saba would probably sit out the storm in one of the mountain cabins.

'It'll be a few days before it's safe to travel,' he said. 'It's too dangerous to stay here with Gudrun. The SS will be searching for anyone who's had contact to you and your family in the past.'

'But where can I go?'

'I've found you somewhere. We should leave this evening.'

* * *

Laila lay on the narrow bed in the dark, listening to the waves crash on the rocks and the wind whip against the window. Elise lay sleeping, snuggled against her.

Finn had explained that Erik Salen was an experienced seaman who worked for an operation nicknamed 'The Shetland Bus' – a set-up between the British special forces and Norwegian fishermen, in which weapons, radios, and British spies were ferried from Shetland to the Norwegian coast. On the return journey across the North Sea, Erik would take refugees and escaped prisoners to safety in Shetland.

When she had arrived at Erik's house, Laila instantly took to him: a stocky man with a broken nose and a broad smile. His wife, Ragna, appeared to be wary of Laila and said little as she showed her to the tiny bedroom at the back of their house. Erik and Ragna had a two-year-old daughter, and at five months pregnant, Ragna had another baby on the way.

Laila assured her it would only be a few more days before she would depart for Sweden. There had been talk about her escaping on the Shetland Bus, but there was a storm over the North Sea, and anyway, Laila was adamant that she would meet Marit in Sweden. She had promised. And Sweden was only a train ride from Narvik. Once the war was over, she could come back easily.

The sound of the turbulent sea reminded Laila of her room at home, but she quashed the rising sentimentality. She must remain focused on her mission: to get the lists of the lost children to the authorities. And to get Elise safely over the border. To freedom.

Turning over onto her side and breathing in Elise's baby smell, she waited to fall asleep.

The next morning, Erik announced he was sailing down the coast to make a collection and would be back the following day.

'Look after yourselves and the children whilst I'm gone. Laila, you keep yourself hidden and don't go out. None of us wants any trouble.' He smiled at his wife. 'I have to keep my family safe.'

'Of course,' said Laila.

Ragna shot her a look. It was clear she didn't want Laila to be there. And Laila understood why. She could see herself through Ragna's eyes: a single mother who had slept with the very enemy her husband was risking his life to fight against. A lifetime ago, Laila would have felt the same. She tried to show her gratitude by helping clean the house and preparing meals. But by the evening, Ragna had still barely spoken to her.

Laila was keen to move on and hoped the weather would improve soon.

The next morning, whilst Laila washed up after breakfast, Ragna piled Erik's soiled fishing clothes into a basket and headed down to the wash cellar.

A moment later, there was a yelp followed by a thud.

'Ragna, are you all right?'

She found Ragna at the bottom of the cellar stairs.

'I've twisted my blasted knee,' she said, struggling to sit up.

'Grab my shoulders and I'll help you up.'

Laila hoisted her up and helped her up the stairs. After settling her on her bed, Laila went to the bathroom to make a cold compress for the injured knee.

A scream came from the bedroom.

She raced back to find Ragna ashen faced and clutching her stomach.

'I'm bleeding,' she cried. 'Get a doctor. The baby. Get a doctor.'

There was an old doctor Laila knew not far from the harbour. Could she trust him? She had to. Otherwise, Ragna could lose her baby.

Laila ran all the way. As she sped round a corner, she saw a familiar figure on the opposite side of the road. Sigrid, the housekeeper from Hotel Nordic. She bowed her head and buried her face into her scarf. Sigrid didn't recognise her, she was pleased to note. Though she wouldn't say anything, anyway. Sigrid hated the Germans.

When the doctor opened his front door, she could hardly speak. In great gulping breaths, she explained the situation and told him where Ragna lived. He fumbled around for his bag and paused briefly, not able to decide which coat to take, before finally setting off shakily on his bicycle. Laila started to follow him on foot, but a dizzy spell gripped her. Sitting on the low wall outside his house, she tried to slow her breathing and clear her head.

It was several minutes before she was able to stand again. She had to get back to Ragna. She groaned in frustration with herself. Where was her strength? This was no time to feel faint and frail. She steadied herself with one hand on the wall and waited for her head to stop spinning before she stumbled off. It started to rain.

Approaching the corner where she had seen the housekeeper, Laila paused. It would be better to take the quieter back streets where she had less chance of being seen. But that would take longer. She turned up the collar of her coat, tucked the stray hairs beneath her hat, and picked up her pace, taking the same route back.

The motor was loud in the wet air. She heard the swish of tyres on the damp road. A car pulled up alongside her.

'Get in the car, Fräulein Olson.' The wide, shiny face of Major Haas leaned out the car window.

She froze.

'I didn't believe you could be foolish enough to come back, so I came to see for myself.'

The car door flew open, and he jumped out, his arm reaching for her.

She bolted off down the road, a surge of energy fuelling her long legs. But he was faster than she expected, and she heard the click-click of his boots behind her. Ahead was the port where there would be soldiers on patrol who would stop her within seconds.

She turned down a side street, heading away from the harbour. He followed her; past warehouses and boarded-up shops. He shouted for her to stop, a breathless call. A shot rang out. Something clanged to her right.

The street ended at an unfinished building site. She crossed to the opposite side where a coastal path led out of town. She raced along it, the seagulls screeching, the wind flinging rain and salt against her face. Below to her left, the grey sea pummelled the rocks.

She dared to glance over her shoulder. He was close behind, surprisingly fast for his bulk. He levelled his pistol.

She didn't see the boulder in front of her.

She fell hard.

Her wrist twisted as she tried to break her fall and she lay sprawled on the icy mud.

His ragged breath came from behind her.

She got to her knees, but his strong arms grabbed her hips and spun her round to face him. Straddling her, he pinned down her arms, his huge face hovering above her, his fat purple lips inches from her face.

He laughed.

'My little, not-so-innocent Fräulein. I could hardly believe when I heard you'd been whoring around with one of our low-ranking soldiers. You were all so proper when I wanted you.'

'Let go, you pig,' she screamed.

A drop of sweat fell from his nose onto her cheek.

'The only place you're going is prison. But first we have unfinished business.'

He yanked her arms above her head and held her wrists in one huge hand, whilst he used his other to push up her coat and dress with the butt of his pistol. She screamed but the gulls and the wind screamed louder, and the sea thundered below.

Struggling with her woollen tights, he dropped the pistol and grabbed the elastic at the top in his fist.

There was a split second his hold on her wrists weakened, and she took advantage of it, twisting a hand free and clutching a rock from the ground. She struck him on the side of his head.

The stone was small and the gash slight, but he jolted back in surprise, just far enough for her to jab her knee into his groin. As he buckled, she squirmed free and jumped to her feet.

'You bitch.' He grabbed her ankle and yanked her down to her knees. As she tried to crawl away from him, she kicked her boot backwards into his face and managed to scramble free.

She sprinted forwards and halted.

There was nowhere to go. She was at the brink of the cliff, a pace away from the plummeting rockface.

Legs trembling, she turned to face him.

On his feet now, blood pouring from his nose, he let out a roar and lunged at her, his hands reaching for her throat.

Her knees crumpled and she dropped like a stone into a crouch. He lost his balance, his arms clasping at thin air as he catapulted over her towards the cliff's edge. She heard his scream. Or was it the cry of the terns or the whine of the wind?

She stood at the top of the cliff, her body buffeted by the wind, and looked down at the grey, surging sea. Then she turned her gaze to the mountains. The trolls were watching. And they were pleased.

* * *

Back at the house, she found Ragna propped up with pillows and looking better. The doctor snapped his bag closed.

'Everything will be fine. The bleeding has stopped. Just rest now.' He patted her hand. Turning to Laila he said, 'Is this your baby?'

He nodded to Elise, who Laila had left on the bed with Ragna. In the cot beside them, the two-year-old was rattling the bars, demanding to be let out.

'Please don't say anything,' she said, searching for a warmth in his eyes that wasn't there. He studied the two young women.

Ragna pleaded. 'It would put my family in terrible danger, doctor.'

The doctor nodded and without saying another word, left the room.

When Erik Salen returned that evening, he listened to Laila's account of events, pacing up and down the kitchen. 'It doesn't seem Major Haas reported that you'd been seen before he set off after you. Otherwise, the SS would've been here by now.'

'What about the hotel housekeeper?' asked Ragna. 'She obviously told Major Haas she'd seen Laila.' Ragna looked at her husband, anxiously.

'That might be a problem. She could raise the alarm when Haas doesn't turn up. We need to get you away, Laila.'

'I'll go to Sweden. Finn will find me a guide.'

Erik shook his head. 'There's a snowstorm over the mountains. I spoke to Finn earlier. The way is impassable.'

'She can't stay here. It's too dangerous,' said Ragna, her voice shrill.

'There is only one alternative,' said Erik.

* * *

The fishing boat rose and fell with the swell of the sea, the slow powerful rhythm of the engine pulsing through Laila's body. She sat on the bottom bunk as she gave Elise her bottle. Ragna had thrust a box of milk powder in Laila's hand as she left with a look of relief on her face.

Laila was stunned at the turn of events. Her plan had been to escape to Sweden and meet up with Marit. But now she was bound for Shetland, off the coast of Scotland, crossing the North Sea. The wind was rising, and a gale was forecast.

On the opposite bunk sat the *collection* that Erik had made yesterday. Two men: a British secret agent returning with vital information, and a Norwegian resistance worker fleeing the Nazis. The Norwegian smiled at Elise gulping down her milk.

'Don't worry,' he said to Laila. 'Erik Salen will get you both to safety. He's a good skipper, and this boat of his is a Hardanger cutter. A fine vessel.'

As the boat creaked, groaned, and battled through the waves, she prayed he was right. Crossing in winter seemed like madness, but Erik had explained the Shetland Bus operated under the cover of darkness and used the long winter nights to its advantage.

They sailed for five days and five nights. Both Laila and her companions were constantly seasick. The cabin smelled terrible. Only little Elise didn't suffer; the sway of the boat lulled her to sleep.

They entered the small harbour at dawn. The fog hung heavy on the water. Laila swung her duffel bag containing her precious jade green journal and the lists of children from Lebensborn on her back. Clutching Elise fiercely to her, she disembarked.

A young man in a British military uniform greeted her.

'Good morning. I'm Junior Officer James Williamson. Welcome to Scalloway. You're safe now, miss.'

32

SCALLOWAY, SHETLAND, 8 MAY 1945

They stood around the radio, too excited to sit down. Laila looked across at the couple who had given her a home, the couple who had made the last two years of her life bearable: crofters Mary and Ian. Their son, Patrick, stood close by her side whilst Elise toddled around talking to her rag doll.

It was three o'clock in the afternoon when the familiar deep tones of Winston Churchill's voice filled the cottage. After nearly six years, the war in Europe had come to an end. They let out a cheer and waved their hands above their heads. Ian grabbed Mary and spun her around, and Patrick scooped up Elise and threw her in the air. Tears, hugs, and laughter. An outpouring of emotion like no other.

That evening, everyone gathered in the village hall for a V. E. party. A band played and people danced with an energy that hadn't been felt for years.

After dancing for hours, Laila and Patrick stepped outside for a breath of air.

'It's hard to believe it's finally over,' said Laila, looking up at the night sky. Her English was fluent now. 'We've waited so long for this moment and now it doesn't seem real.'

'What does feel real is how you've become a part of our lives, Laila.'

She placed a hand on his arm. 'I'm so grateful for your family's kindness. The way your mother took me in, showered Elise with love. And your father has treated me like a daughter.'

'You've given us a lot in return. You helped Ma with her spinning and knitting. We made good money from knitwear during the war. But more than that; you're the daughter she never had.'

'You've been like family to me.'

Patrick paused and took a deep breath.

'Laila, I have something to ask you.'

Her stomach tightened. She didn't want him to say it.

He shuffled beside her before placing his hands on her shoulders and looking directly into her eyes.

'I know you don't love me. Not in that way. Your heart is still with Josef. But maybe, with time—'

'I'm sorry, Patrick. I can't.' She shook her head and looked down, unable to bear the pleading in his eyes. He dropped his hands from her shoulders.

'All I'm asking is for you to think about it. I have steady work at the boat engineering firm and can support a family. I'd be a good father to Elise. I love her as if she were my own child. We could build a life together.'

Could she love this man? They hadn't even kissed. Could she live the rest of her life in Shetland? Could she ever let go of Josef? Did she even want to?

'I need to travel to Norway and see my family. I've had no contact with them since I fled on Erik's boat. And I'll try to find out where Marit is. Hopefully her family know something.'

'I understand that, of course. Will you give me an answer before you sail?'

She paused. He was a kind, good man.

'Yes, I'll give you an answer before I sail.'

33

AUGUST 1945

Laila clutched the letter to her chest, shaking with emotion. She stood for a long time thinking about the house: the thick carpets, the sweeping staircase, the painting of the skaters on the frozen lake, the lilac poppy wallpaper in the bedroom, and the picture of the snowflake girl, Anne.

Mostly she thought about Anne. She placed the letter carefully in her packed suitcase.

A month after the end of the war, Laila had written a letter addressed to Anne Solomon and had sent it to the Solomon's house. After seeing the horrific newsreels of the prisoners that had been liberated by the allies, she held little hope that Anne was still alive. And even if she was, would she be back at her home? Yet two months later, a letter from Norway arrived. From Anne. She had survived. The only one from her family.

Anne did not go into any detail about her time in the concentration camp but was fascinated as well as outraged to hear about what had gone on in her home. Laila was relieved that Anne did not judge or blame her in any way. The two women vowed to keep in touch. Although the differences in their experiences could not

have been more extreme, they both felt there was now a bond
between them.

* * *

The sun shone as the ship pulled out of the harbour, past the ruins
of Scalloway castle. Laila held Elise on her hip as they waved to
Patrick and his parents who were watching on the dock as they
shrunk away to nothing.

Laila took Elise by the hand and with other refugees returning
home, they began to explore the ship. But her mind was elsewhere.
Two years ago, the day after she had arrived in Scalloway, she had
handed the Lebensborn lists to the colonel in charge of the Shetland military, who'd then sent them on to London. With the aid of
the lists and the Red Cross, the search for the missing children had
begun. And now, just last week, the miracle that Laila had been
praying for happened. A telegram from London arrived saying
Tore had been found. He was living with a German family in
Flensburg, in the north of Germany. She could hardly wait to tell
Gudrun the news.

Arriving in Narvik, she popped Elise in the pushchair that had
belonged to Patrick as a child, and pushed it along with one hand.
In the other, she carried the small suitcase that Mary had
given her.

The feeling of homecoming engulfed her. The sights and
smells. And the light. It was an early evening in August and the
summer white night hung waiting over the fjord. Memories of
Josef and the summer of 1941 flooded back and for a moment, she
had to stop and catch a breath. In a daze, she made her way
through the port packed with refugees from Finnmark, those who
had fled Hitler's scorched earth policy in the north and were now
homeless.

She approached her house, seeing the rowan tree first. It had leaves again, healthy and blossoming. Beneath the tree, Hanna kneeled on the grass tucking a blanket around a baby in a basket.

Elise pointed and called out, 'Baby!'

Hanna looked up in amazement.

* * *

Mama lifted Elise onto her knees. 'I'm so relieved both of you are safe. When I didn't hear from you, I thought something terrible had happened.'

'After the last time we saw each other, I didn't think you wanted to hear from me,' said Laila sheepishly. 'It took a lot of courage for me to come here.'

Mama took a deep breath. 'I regretted the way I spoke to you. The way I turned you away. And my own grandchild. It's been eating away at me ever since.'

Laila paused, unsure what to say. 'And now you have two grandchildren,' she said, looking at the baby in Hanna's arms. She turned to her sister. 'I'm sorry I wasn't here for the wedding.'

'It was a small celebration. Because of the war,' said Hanna. 'Just us and Karl's close family.' Her tone was neutral. Not aggressive but not warm either. 'What are your plans now?' she asked.

'I'm not entirely sure. Do you think Papa will allow me to stay here a few days? Or does he still hate me?' A lump formed in her throat.

'Hate is the wrong word,' said Mama. 'I'll speak to him.'

What was the right word for how Papa felt? She herself had felt outrage at the German girls before she fell in love with Josef. She had felt anger and betrayal. It was all so clear back then. Friend and enemy. Right and wrong. Black and white. But life wasn't like that. Life was nuanced and complex. Shaded like a sketch.

'You must be careful,' said Hanna. 'People are out for revenge. Gangs of men are attacking the so-called German girls, dragging them into alleyways and shaving their heads. Even the children are targeted. They call them "German brats". Don't let Elise out of your sight.'

Mama lifted Elise off her lap and stood up. 'I have something to show you, Laila. You can leave Elise here a moment.'

Hanna shot Mama a look.

They went up to Laila's old bedroom. It was just the same. Only the blackout blind was gone. Laila went to the window and looked out. The mountains, the sea, the conifers. Her fjord. Her home.

Mama crossed to the commode, flicked her hand at the layer of dust, and opened the top drawer. She withdrew a pile of letters and held them out.

'What are these?' Laila asked.

'Letters addressed to you. I didn't open them, but they came from Germany.'

Germany? Could they be from Josef's mother? Had she survived the dreadful bombing of Dresden? Or were they sent before the Allies' attack, so near the end of the war? The newsreels of the fire-bombed city had been horrific.

She took the letters. The envelopes were all different sizes and colours. Brown, white, and even pale lilac. But the writing was the same.

The room swayed.

Static whooshed in her ears as she collapsed on her bed.

'I'll leave you alone.' Mama left.

She looked at the postmark on the top letter.

Dresden, 7 July 1943

It was dated six months after she had fled on the Shetland Bus. With shaking hands, she opened the envelope.

My dearest, darling, Laila
I pray to God you and our child are well. I tried to contact you through Lebensborn and was informed you were on the run and a warrant was out for your arrest. I can only hope you found refuge and that somehow this letter will find you.
I fear you may think I was killed in action. When I turned up on my mother's doorstep after spending months in hospital, she collapsed in shock. In the terrible confusion in Russia, I unknow-ingly was pronounced dead, and my mother was informed accordingly. What a terrible error. How she suffered. And you, my darling? I can't bear to think what you went through.
Please, I beg you, let me know that you have received this letter. That you are safe. Each day not knowing if you are alive or not is torture. I love you more than ever and only the thought of being reunited with you and our baby kept me going through the dark days of my recovery.
My endless love, for now and always.
Your Josef

It couldn't be true. Josef was alive. Dare she hope to believe in what she had just read? It was his handwriting, his words.

He lived.

She tore open the next letter, dated three weeks later.

My darling, Laila
I have no further news from the authorities. You have disap-peared without a trace. I'm desperate to hear from you and can only hope you got my last letter. The post I know is dreadful. It's agony waiting to hear from you. I think about you and our baby

constantly. I don't even know if we have a boy or a girl. Lebens-
born will tell me nothing. Please God, be safe. My thoughts are
a continuous prayer. I long to be with you, to look into your
beautiful face, to hold you, kiss you. I ache with my love for you.
Please, please write that you are well. Even if you have decided
you don't want to be with me any more, I plead, let me know
you are safe.
All my love and prayers,
Your Josef

Tears streamed down her face, dropping on to his written words.

The next seven letters contained the same pleas. Begging and praying for her response. It clawed her heart to know he had waited in vain. And that all this time she had thought him dead.

The last letter was dated 15 March 1945. The address at the top was different.

Darling, Laila
I write this from my aunt's house in Ahrensburg, a small town
just outside Hamburg. We managed to escape the air raids on
Dresden with our lives. Everything we owned, our home, my
mother's studio, and her paintings, were destroyed in the huge
fireball that engulfed our once beautiful city. But we are the
lucky ones. So many lost their lives in the most terrible way.
I am beginning to doubt that you will ever receive these letters.
The fear that something has happened to you torments me. But
I will try to have faith that maybe one day I will find you safe and
well. I do not know what more I can do other than pray.
I will always love you,
Your Josef

She flew down the stairs into the hallway and snatched up the telephone.

'Even if I could find a telephone number for this address, it would be no use,' said the operator. 'The lines to Germany are down.'

'A telegram. I'll send a telegram.'

'There's no service. It's chaos, I'm afraid.'

She dropped the receiver into the cradle. She knew what she would do. But first she had to face Papa.

* * *

'Olaf, take Elise and Inge to play outside. I want to speak to your sister,' said Papa.

Olaf had not left Laila's side since he had come home. He looked very grown up as he took the two young girls' hands and led them to the front garden.

Laila and Hanna sat either side of Mama on the sofa. Papa went to sit in his armchair opposite, but decided to stand instead, his arms folded against his chest.

Laila spoke in a small voice.

'Papa, I know how you feel. I—'

'How could you possibly know how I feel? Were you here to see people's faces as they passed me by? Were you here to see how your mother's friends crept away whispering behind her back? How we lost respect because of your actions!'

'I... I'm sorry, I—'

'You have brought shame on the whole family. Where is the daughter I brought up to be honourable? To have integrity?'

'She's still here,' Laila murmured, choking back the tears. Shakily, she stood up to face him. 'She's still here. I'm here. But I've grown, suffered, and learned. I've been tormenting myself with the mistakes I've made. But now I realise they were choices, not mistakes. How could Elise be a mistake?'

She took a step closer, her voice stronger now.

'I'm truly sorry for the hurt I've caused. And the disappointment. So often I've asked myself: can falling in love be a betrayal? But my love for Josef has nothing to do with nationality and politics. It's just me and him.'

Papa shook his head. Mama came to her side and took her hand. 'It's time to forgive, Ivar,' she said softly.

Her father sank into his armchair, the fight gone from him. He looked exhausted and sad. Laila's heart ached for the relationship they had lost. But she had to look forward; she had a new family that needed her.

She suggested a walk after dinner, and Hanna agreed. They walked their familiar route to the large flat boulders where they sat in the evening sun. It was just over five years ago when they had spied Marion with a German soldier. Laila cringed inwardly remembering what she'd thought about the poor girl.

They sat for a while in silence. There was so much Laila wanted to say. But where to start? In the end she said simply, 'I missed you.'

'I missed you too,' said Hanna, her voice strained. 'What happened to you after you left for the home?'

Laila told her everything.

'My God, you've been through so much. Compared to me.'

'You too. You've married, had a baby...'

Hanna shrugged. 'A small life.'

'There was a time when that's all I wanted. To be here and settle down in Narvik. It's funny how things turn out.'

'I need to ask you something.' Hanna's voice was barely audible above the screech of the gulls.

'You can ask me anything.'

'You told Anton that night, didn't you?'

'Told him what? Which night?'

'The night he went missing. Midsummer's Eve. You saw me and Petra getting into the boat with the brothers, Mikal and Rolf. You knew they had a summer house on the island of Senja.'

Bewildered, Laila said, 'I don't know what you mean.'

'Don't lie to me,' Hanna started to shout. 'I saw you looking down from the cliff on your way to the bonfire on the beach. You told Anton that his little sister was off to party with the boys. I was only fourteen. You knew Anton didn't trust the brothers and would come after me.'

'I didn't see you. Really, I—'

Tears poured down Hanna's red, angry face. 'He came looking for us. We argued and I refused to go back with him. He rowed away without me. But he never made it home. You couldn't keep quiet. You with your holier than thou attitude. Your awful right-eousness. Ironic really.' Hanna's tone was acid. 'It's your fault that he is dead.'

Laila's head spun with confusion as she struggled for words.

'I didn't see you. I didn't tell Anton anything. I swear it's true.'

Suddenly, it all made sense: Hanna's anger towards her after their brother disappeared. Her sometimes-naked contempt. Even hate.

She grabbed Hanna's arm, but she pulled away.

'Hanna, look at me. I swear I didn't tell Anton where you were. I didn't know.' As she spoke, she knew it wasn't what Hanna wanted to hear. That if she couldn't blame Laila, then she would have to blame herself.

'Tell me what happened on Senja.' Laila's voice was a whisper.

Hanna was shaking her head, looking down, her tears drop-ping onto the warm stone.

Laila waited, dreading what might come.

Then her sister looked up, heaved a huge breath, and her words came tumbling out.

'Anton told me to go home with him at once. But Mikal got angry and told him to stay out of it. He said I was his girl. I was so proud to hear those words. I told Anton I was staying with Mikal. So stupid. I was so stupid. Anton tried to pull me towards the boat. Mikal punched him on the shoulder and a fight broke out. It was awful. They were really hitting each other hard. Anton was getting the better of Mikal; he had him on the ground. But then Mikal grabbed a rock and hit Anton on the side of his head—'

'My God,' Laila gasped.

'Anton was bleeding badly. He gave me the most terrible look. And then he stumbled back into the boat and rowed off. I watched him go. I got scared and called after him. I'd changed my mind, wanted to go home. But he was a long way out. I kept screaming. Finally, he turned round and shouted something. I couldn't hear him above the waves. Then, he... he stood up and waved an arm... and fell out the boat.

'I was frantic, waiting for him to surface. There was no sign of him. I rushed to Mikal's boat and he jumped in with me. We tried to find Anton. Mikal dived again and again. But the currents were strong out there and... and... Anton was gone.'

Laila stared at her sister in horror. 'Why didn't you tell anyone?'

'We were scared. Mikal was terrified he would be blamed. He begged me not to tell. He said it was better to let people think that Anton's drowning had nothing to do with us. I watched his boat drift away...'

'But all these years we didn't know what happened. And poor Mama was always hoping he might come back.'

Hanna choked back her sobs. 'I wanted to tell the truth, but it was never the right time. The longer I left it, the harder it became.

And all the while, I blamed you. It was easier than blaming myself. But it's all my fault, all of it.'

'It's no one's fault,' said Laila. She felt no anger towards her sister. A lifetime ago she would have been horrified and outraged. But now she just felt a deep sadness for Hanna, a young naïve girl in the most terrible of situations. What must she have been through? Laila of all people had no right to judge.

She reached for Hanna's hand, and this time Hanna took it.

'I shouldn't have gone with them.'

'You were young and wanted fun. You couldn't have possibly known what would happen.'

'Should we tell Mama and Papa?'

'What would be the point now? Just more pain. It's been seven years since we lost Anton. It's time to move on, Hanna. Accept what we can't change and look to the future.'

'Can you forgive me?'

'There is nothing to forgive. We're all just trying our best with what life throws at us. You're my sister. I love you.'

Hanna fell against Laila's chest, and they held each other close, crying softly.

34

HAMBURG, GERMANY, AUGUST 1945

The next afternoon, Laila and Elise took a ferry to Oslo. A few hours later, they boarded a ship for Hamburg. Sitting on a bench on deck, Laila watched the grey-white water churn in the wake of the ship and thought about her visit to Gudrun that morning.

Gudrun had collapsed into her chair, sobbing and laughing. Laila had kneeled before her and held her hands.

'I'm heading for Hamburg this afternoon, which is not so far from Flensburg. I'll go and visit him and sort out the quickest way possible to get him back to you.'

'Thank you, thank you. You kept your promise. You found him. I knew you would.'

Afterwards had come a tearful reunion with Oda at the book-shop. Sadly, their time together had been short as Laila flew around town getting everything sorted before the ferry's departure.

Now she watched the Norwegian coast reduce to a thin line on the horizon and then disappear. Home. Laila had left her home behind. Or perhaps her home was somewhere else now. With someone else. Thank goodness she had not agreed to marry Patrick before she left Scalloway.

How changed was she from the naïve, young woman who had woken that night to the sound of warships entering the fjord; she had learned to be forgiving to herself and others. Her purpose was no longer to be the replacement for Anton in the eyes of her family, to take up the gaping hole that he had left behind, a space that she could never fill. She could never do that. Others needed her now and her new purpose gave her strength and resilience.

They sailed up the River Elbe into the port of Hamburg. The city lay in ash and rubble. Crowds, mostly women, were shifting brick and stone with their bare hands, and the streets were full of British soldiers, tanks, and trucks. Laila stopped to ask a woman piling debris into a wheelbarrow for directions to the *Bahnhof*, from where she could take a train to the town of Ahrensburg.

Looking at the devastation around her, she was reminded of all the people lost in the war: Dagny, Herta, Einar, and so many others. But there were also those still there.

Like Josef.

As she pushed her way through the crowds in the vast main hall of the station, Laila heard a familiar voice. Someone calling her name. She turned.

Eva Dahl was barely recognisable. She wore no makeup around her tired eyes and her hair was dull and unwashed. She held the hand of her young son by her side. The women hugged and exchanged news.

'They've arrested Ernst,' Eva whispered, checking around her, 'as a suspected Nazi.'

Well, he is one, thought Laila, though she did not say this aloud.

'What will you do? Why are you in Hamburg?'

'I'm changing trains. I have to lie low for a while to avoid being taken in for questioning. Listen, Laila, you must say nothing about Lebensborn. Things could turn nasty.'

Once on the train, Laila and Elise left the destruction behind them and headed through the flat green countryside. Whilst Elise dozed beside her, Laila withdrew the jade silk journal from her bag. She had been in awe of Eva Dahl back then. But the desperate woman she had just seen at the station bore no resemblance to the elegant, mysterious Eva she had known at Lebensborn.

Engulfed in memories, she turned the pages of the journal. Sketches of Dagny with her son, another child Laila must find. Marit, now somewhere in Sweden. And Greta. Where was she? And Matron Schwarz. Laila's skin prickled.

She paused at a sketch; a dagger held high over a baby lying on a Nazi flag, the so-called christening of Eva's and her Nazi lover's son. This journal and the lists of the stolen children and the children sentenced to die all bore testament to what really went on behind the benevolent façade of Lebensborn.

One of the last pages was her sketch of the snowflake girl. Anne had survived, but not her family. The home they had been forced out of had been stolen from them. And used for the Nazis' sinister agenda.

You must say nothing about Lebensborn.

No, Eva. Everything must be said.

What happened at Lebensborn must be told. Anne had said in her letter that she wanted it that way.

Ahrensburg Schloss was a white, fairy-tale palace with four blue-green towers at its corners, surrounded by water. British soldiers directed refugees over the bridge that crossed the moat and into the castle. Laila took the address from her pocket and approached an elderly man who was watching the proceedings.

'Can you help me please? I'm looking for *Waldweg.*'

'Follow the path alongside the *Schloss* and it's the third street on the left.' He looked at Elise in her pushchair and the suitcase in Laila's hand.

'I hope you find him,' he said, tipping his hat.

'Thank you,' she said. 'I will.'

Number seven was a small red-brick house with a steep, pointed roof and a neat front garden. A cobbled pathway wound its way through the heavy blooms of lilac and pink hydrangeas. Laila stood opposite, her heart pummelling against her chest.

Suddenly the front door opened, and a shaggy black dog shot out.

'Wulf, get back here so I can put your lead on.'

That voice.

Wulf bounded to the nearest hydrangea and cocked his leg.

Josef stood in the doorway, dog lead in hand.

Laila didn't move.

He stepped out, his left leg stiff. 'Wulf, here boy.'

She watched as his expression froze. He looked at her in a mixture of bewilderment and wonder. She smiled and pushed Elise towards him.

Then Josef, half running, half limping, rushed towards her.

She ran into his arms.

'You're alive,' he said, burying his face in her hair.

'So are you.' She laughed and turned to pick up Elise, who was squealing in delight at the sight of Wulf.

'Meet your daughter.'

In that moment, she knew that Gudrun was right. Elise was the hope for the future. And Laila was her mother.

Finally, she felt the cloak of guilt slip from her shoulders. She was not a woman of shame. She was proud of who she was. A woman of hope.

AUTHOR'S NOTES

It is estimated that up to 12,000 children with a Norwegian mother and German father were born in Norway under the Lebensborn scheme set up by Heinrich Himmler to propagate the Aryan race. There were eleven homes in Norway, more than any country other than Germany.

The homes were shrouded in mystery and even the German population knew little about them. At that time, the subject of unwed mothers was taboo. After the war, many mothers were ashamed of their association with the Nazi-run homes and spoke little or not at all of their time there. Many of the children were not told about their place of birth or the identity of their parents.

In Norway, the children were targeted for revenge and abuse, often called German brats or children of shame. They were bullied at school, beaten by relations, and in some cases put in mental institutions and denied education. The children, innocent victims of war, were catapulted from being elite to being outcasts.

These persecuted Norwegians took the Norwegian government to the European Court of Justice in 2007 and were awarded damages for the suffering caused.

It's only in recent years that some of the children's and mothers' stories have come to light but much of what went on at Lebensborn remains a mystery.

ACKNOWLEDGMENTS

As a debut author I'd like to thank the people who helped me get started in my publishing journey. Firstly, a massive thank you to my amazing agent, Clare at the Liverpool Literary Agency who believed in me and my story from the outset and has guided me through the whole process. Thanks also go to my lovely editor, Emily and the wonderful team at Boldwood Books who have made me feel so welcome.

I am beyond grateful to my friends and family who have been invaluable in their support and encouragement. The biggest thank you must go to my husband, Sigi and daughter, Claire who I'm truly blessed to have in my life. I love you both.

Finally, my warmest thanks to you the reader for choosing this book. I hope you enjoyed the story.

MORE FROM HELEN PARUSEL

We hope you enjoyed reading *A Mother's War*. If you did, please leave a review.

If you'd like to gift a copy, this book is also available as an ebook, hardback, large print, digital audio download and audiobook CD.

Sign up to Helen Parusel's mailing list for news, competitions and updates on future books:

https://bit.ly/HelenParuselNews

ABOUT THE AUTHOR

Helen Parusel lives in Hamburg, Germany but was born and grew up in north London. Her favourite subject at school was English, and her head was always full of stories she'd read or made up. Although she considered studying English further, she started a career in the fashion industry. After she met her future husband on holiday, she then moved to his home country, Germany. When her daughter went to kindergarten, mothers asked Helen to teach their children English. She also taught a class of retired students. Their fascinating stories of the war years and her own love of historical fiction inspired her to write her first WW2 novel when empty nest syndrome loomed.

Helen is now working on her second book.

Follow Helen on social media:

 twitter.com/HelenParusel

Sixpence Stories

Introducing Sixpence Stories!

Discover page-turning
historical novels from your
favourite authors, meet new
friends and be transported
back in time.

Join our book club
Facebook group

https://bit.ly/SixpenceGroup

Sign up to our
newsletter

https://bit.ly/SixpenceNews

Boldwₒₒd

Boldwood Books is an award-winning fiction
publishing company seeking out the best
stories from around the world.

Find out more at www.boldwoodbooks.com

Join our reader community for brilliant books,
competitions and offers!

Follow us
@BoldwoodBooks
@BookandTonic

Sign up to our weekly
deals newsletter

https://bit.ly/BoldwoodBNewsletter

Made in the USA
Coppell, TX
30 September 2023

22235634R10193